———————————— ★ ————————————

"But why would my grandfather have changed his name?" said Emma, feeling as if she had been slapped across the face.

"To hide, perhaps," said Zuberan.

"Hide? Hide from whom? From what?"

"Obviously he had something to be frightened of. Do you know who killed him?"

Emma shook her head helplessly. She felt none of the relief or excitement she had expected after all the dead ends. Instead she felt terrified, as though she had already learned too much. It made no sense. She had come all this way precisely to find out about the *Kaito Spirit,* to tie it somehow to her grandfather's murder. Suddenly, however, she wanted to run away and not hear another word.

———————————— ★ ————————————

"Mathes has a real talent. He...creates interesting people and stitches them together with a wide-ranging and highly imaginative plot."
—*The Armchair Detective*

"Mathes makes good use of illusion—the kind Emma creates on stage..."
—*San Francisco Chronicle*

Also available from Worldwide Mystery by
CHARLES MATHES

THE GIRL WITH THE PHONY NAME

Charles Mathes

The Girl Who Remembered Snow

WORLDWIDE ®

TORONTO • NEW YORK • LONDON
AMSTERDAM • PARIS • SYDNEY • HAMBURG
STOCKHOLM • ATHENS • TOKYO • MILAN
MADRID • WARSAW • BUDAPEST • AUCKLAND

For my Arlene

THE GIRL WHO REMEMBERED SNOW

A Worldwide Mystery/December 1997

First published by St. Martin's Press, Incorporated.

ISBN 0-373-26257-4

The Girl Who Remembered Snow

ONE

EMMA PASSANT'S EARLIEST memory was of snow.

Someone had bundled her up like an important package. She had on so many layers of coats, sweaters, and scarves that she could barely move. Thick flurries, punctuated by the tall black skeletons of trees, swirled all around her. Great stone houses grew out of the mountains of snow on either side of the sidewalk. Beneath her feet was cold whiteness so deep she could barely lift her legs.

Emma wasn't frightened in the memory, however. Someone was holding her hand, guiding her. She knew it was someone who loved her, someone whom she loved. But who? She couldn't see the person's face. All her life she had been trying to remember who it had been.

Emma wanted to believe that it was one of her parents, but that was impossible. Her mother had died giving birth to her, nearly thirty years ago; her father had died in an auto accident a few months later—a suicide for grief, she had always believed. Nor had it been her grandfather, her mother's father, who had adopted and raised her.

Emma had asked Jacques Passant about the big snow many times over the years. She must have dreamed it, he had replied in his gentle voice, or perhaps seen it in a movie. Apart from a few freakish dustings, it never snowed in San Francisco. And she had never been out of the city as a child, he said.

But Emma knew her grandfather was wrong. She remembered. She remembered snow.

"Please don't bring it up again, Emma," Jacques Passant had finally declared in a rare outburst of impatience.

A balding dumpling of a man with rosy cheeks and a

twinkle in his eye, Jacques Passant was the kind of person who gave even panhandlers and politicians a sympathetic hearing. For him to turn away from his precious granddaughter in exasperation should have convinced Emma that she was mistaken, should have persuaded her that this was just another product of the overactive imagination that was constantly flooding her mind's eye with incredible images and lifelike fantasies.

But Emma knew what she knew. She remembered snow, and she said so, over and over. The white bedsheets she had pulled over her head as a child before crying herself to sleep had brought back the memory. So had the white rehearsal tights of the chorus of the San Francisco Civic Light Opera in which Emma had danced as a teenager, and the mound of white diplomas at her college graduation. But Jacques Passant had never believed her.

Now even he was gone.

Emma's grandfather had been murdered last week in a remote area of Golden Gate Park. The body might never have been identified had he not dined at Luigi's Restaurant on Fisherman's Wharf the previous June. The police had found a crumpled-up credit-card receipt for the meal in an inside pocket of his raincoat. The mugger who shot him had taken everything else.

Emma had had to go down to the city morgue to make the identification. She'd then spent a week answering questions from detectives and filling out paperwork, before they finally allowed her to claim the body and have it cremated.

Now only one obligation remained. That was why Emma was here on the Sausalito Ferry this windy mid-November morning.

San Francisco was sunny and bright for a change, after weeks of fog and rain. Emma had taken off her glasses to massage her tired eyes—the past few days had been very difficult. When she looked up, the waves in the choppy bay were just a blurred field of white. That was what had brought the memory of snow back again. For a moment he could actually see the cold and blustery street, feel the moving hand. But whose hand had it been? She couldn't see the person's face.

Emma returned the tortoiseshell eyeglass frames to the bridge of her nose, a nose so long and pointed that she feared it looked as if it had been sharpened in a pencil sharpener. The glorious panorama once again snapped into focus. The blue sky and sun-drenched harbor. The Golden Gate Bridge. The city's gleaming towers on the receding shore.

Emma stood at the stern of the ferry. In the black canvas knapsack at her feet was a small cardboard shoe box, neatly wrapped with brown paper and string. She had transferred Jacques Passant's ashes into the box last night. The only problem now was how to get it over the side without causing a fuss.

Emma had just come from the enclosed area of the boat below, where she had gone to make sure no one was near the back windows. She had assumed that all the passengers would have flocked to the bow or up to the top deck by now to gawk at Alcatraz—the notorious former prison was approaching on the port side—but to her dismay there were still five other people in the stern section of the ferry.

The plan had seemed so sensible last night. Now it looked impossibly risky. Emma was at the very end of the boat, next to the ensign—the ship's flag. There were two men and two women leaning on the Alcatraz-side railing a dozen feet ahead of her, talking together, laughing. Even if one of them didn't happen to glance back and catch her in the act, there was another passenger who might—a man standing on the starboard side dressed in a taupe-colored sport coat.

He must be freezing, Emma thought, crossing her arms in front of her, grateful for the down vest she had had the wits to bring along. The temperature was supposed to go up into the sixties today, but it was still early and it was always a lot colder on the water.

Emma looked down over the rear railing, warming her hands in the pockets of her blue jeans. The waves seemed miles away. There would probably be a noticeable splash when she dropped the box over the side. She could get arrested if someone happened to be looking in her direction when what remained of Jacques Passant hit the spray—there were strict laws against littering the bay, even with one's immediate family. That was why she had decided to use the shoe box, rather than just scatter the ashes where they would float for all to see.

Should she hold off for now and try again when the ferry made its return run from Sausalito? Or wait a few days, until one of the inevitable San Francisco fogs rolled in?

No, thought Emma. Better to get it over with now, before she had a chance to think about it too much. A promise was a promise. If she got caught, she would just say she was insane with grief. That sounded plausible, didn't it? What could they do to her? Make her walk the plank? Obligingly, a mental image of Captain Hook forcing her out above the waters on an ironing board flashed into her mind's eye.

The man in the taupe sport coat on the other side of the ferry glanced in Emma's direction, then quickly looked away. The two couples seemed to be wrapped up in conversation, but they could easily look around at any moment.

Captain Hook vanished and a crazy idea suddenly sprang into Emma's mind. Crazy ideas often sprang into Emma's mind, some of which worked out wonderfully. Like her recipe for apple pandowdy using Scotch whisky, and the dance scholarship she had won to Oakland College by persuading the coach of her high school's football team to write a recommendation for her. And then there were the crazy ideas that hadn't turned out so well—like that three-winged butterfly tattooed on her tush.

Was this a good crazy idea, Emma wondered, or just a

crazy crazy idea? There seemed only one way to find out. Leaving her knapsack on the deck by the railing, she walked directly up to the man in the sport coat.

"How do you feel about burial at sea?" Emma asked with as ingenuous a smile as she could manage.

The man looked around behind him, as if to see whether there was anyone else whom she could possibly be addressing. There obviously wasn't. He grinned sheepishly.

"I am still too young, I think," he said, "to be ready for such a drastic step."

His voice was deep and velvety. The French accent was noticeable and a surprise. Up close Emma could see that the man's sport jacket was elegant and obviously had been expensive. So was his patterned silk tie. He looked to be in his mid-forties, precisely the kind of older man who usually wouldn't give her a second glance.

"You're French," she said, running a hand over her straight brown hair, which she kept tied in a single thick braid that reached down nearly to her waist.

"I was born in France, yes," said the Frenchman. "But I live primarily in New York now."

"How do you stand it?" Emma exclaimed before she could stop herself. "All that dirt. All those nutcases."

"You have no nutcases in San Francisco?"

"Just lunatics," replied Emma, gazing meaningfully at her reflection in the glass of the door leading belowdecks.

There was that nose again. Emma hadn't really noticed just how long and pointed it was until she had given Jimmy Ryan his first kiss behind the Willis Avenue elementary school. Or, rather, had attempted to give him his first kiss. The poor boy had almost lost an eye because of that crazy idea.

"Perhaps you were not properly introduced to New York," the Frenchman said, apparently undaunted. "It can be very wonderful, provided that the right person shows it to you."

His own nose was straight and perfectly proportioned.

He also possessed a square jaw and soft-looking brown hair currently being attractively tousled by the brisk wind. He was quite tall, maybe six feet two, compared to Emma's five feet six. The sexy crinkle of smile lines around his blue eyes spoke of sophistication, breeding and experience. He was very, very handsome. Emma couldn't believe that the one time in her life she had gotten a man like this to talk to her, she was going to invite him to help her dispose of a body.

"You're a tourist?"

"No. Yes. In a way. I am here on business, but I wanted to see some of your famous San Francisco sights before I left."

"Alcatraz is coming up on the left," said Emma hopefully. "You should go up top. You'll get a better view."

It would make more sense just to get rid of him, she decided. Then she would only have the two couples to worry about. For the first time Emma noticed that they were all blond, the four of them. What was the proper grammatical term for such an assembly? she wondered. A peroxide of blonds?

"I rather like the view here," said the Frenchman, winking, and grinning at her.

Emma felt her cheeks grow rosy, but grinned back. It had to be a dream. A guy this good-looking had to be gay, didn't he? This was still San Francisco, wasn't it? Why was she dawdling? It was clear that he wasn't going anywhere, and as soon as they passed Alcatraz, other passengers were sure to drift back toward the rear of the boat.

"Actually, I need a favor," Emma said cautiously. "You don't seem like the kind of guy who would want to get a woman into trouble. Or am I wrong?"

"Depends upon what kind of trouble," he said, raising an eyebrow, the grin not leaving his rugged face.

"What would you say if I told you I had my grandfather in that bag over there?" said Emma, gesturing to her knapsack by the handrail.

"I would say that he must be a very small grandfather."

Emma didn't laugh. The man's beautiful smile instantly disappeared.

"Obviously I have not understood," he said soberly. "Sometimes when I am not sure of what to do, I try to make the joke. Your grandfather, he is dead, isn't he?"

"Yes," said Emma. "He died last week, and I had him cremated."

"I am truly sorry. Please forgive me."

He looked remarkably sincere. All that face and sensitivity to boot. How bad could the guy be? Emma took a deep breath and went for broke.

"Will you help me? I need to drop the box with my grandfather's ashes in it into the bay."

"Why?"

"A promise I made, years ago. It's not going to pollute or anything. The whole package is strictly biodegradable. Except, of course, for the brick."

"The brick?"

"I want to be sure he stays down."

"Ah," said the man, acknowledging the cold for the first time by pulling the lapels of his jacket together and shifting his weight from foot to foot. A stiff sea smell of salt and decay wafted up from the water.

"I'll tell them you were just an unwitting dupe if we get caught," Emma said hopefully, then shrank an inch as she heard how it came out. She had such a way with words.

"What is it you wish me to do?"

"You'll help me?"

"What man could resist helping a lovely lady to fulfill a promise?"

"All right," said Emma, taking a deep breath. "When I give the signal, you just throw your arms up in the air and shout 'I love San Francisco.' That's easy enough, isn't it?"

"I throw my arms in the air," he repeated carefully, "and I shout 'I love San Francisco.'"

"As loud as you can."

"As loud as I can. And why will I do this?"

"Those people on the other side will turn to see what's going on. When they do, I'll drop the box over the side. No one will see me, because they'll all be looking at you."

He smiled a skeptical smile and held his lapels of his sport coat a little more tightly together.

"And you are certain of this?"

"Absolutely. I have a great deal of experience."

"You bury many grandfathers at sea?"

"No, I work professionally as an illusionist."

"*Vraiment? An illusionniste?* You are a magician?"

"Well, I make a scantily clad assistant disappear, so I must be."

"How very charming!"

"Just watch me carefully," said Emma, anxious to get back to the matter at hand. "When I'm ready, I'll nod, then you'll shout...?"

"'I love San Francisco.' Very loud."

"And you'll throw your arms up in the air. You'll make it really big—like this great feeling for San Francisco has just come over you, and you have to share it with the entire world. Got it?"

"I will make it really big." He nodded, clearly amused by the whole situation.

Did he really understand? He looked suspiciously relaxed, considering the circumstances. Maybe he was too sophisticated to make a good distraction. Or too French.

"Pretend you're a cowboy," said Emma. "Pretend you're Jerry Lewis."

"Ah." He nodded.

"Afterward, I'll go belowdeck, and you'll come down and meet me there in a few minutes, okay?"

"Okay."

"Wait for my nod."

"Okay."

He was still grinning as Emma walked back over to her knapsack. She took out the shoe box and, concealing it with her body, got it up to the railing. Despite his small size, Jacques Passant had been very solid. Emma was surprised at how light the package in her hands was. Considering the brick.

This is it, she told herself. The moment had finally come. She supposed she should say something, but what was there left to say? "A promise is a promise," seemed hopelessly sentimental and melodramatic. "Good-bye forever, Pépé," sounded equally silly.

"I've got to be out of my mind," Emma whispered under her breath, casting an anxious eye toward the four blonds on the port side.

As a magician, she rehearsed even the simplest routines for weeks and still she was always a nervous wreck on stage. This performance she had to do perfectly the first time—plus worry about a stranger of unknown reliability. One of the women in the peroxide of blonds was now facing Emma, her interest in Alcatraz apparently waning. It was now or never. Emma turned her head to the Frenchman and nodded.

"I love!" he screamed, waving his arms wildly in the air. "San Francisco!"

Then he did a little dance.

The blonds at the rail spun around to see what the commotion was, their startled expressions quickly giving way to smiles. In that same instant Emma wordlessly let the box slip from her fingers, then walked briskly across the deck, between the Frenchman and the two couples, and made her way below.

She didn't breathe until she had parked her empty knapsack beneath one of the hardwood benches and sat down, her heart racing. In her overdeveloped imagination she could actually hear alarms going off and see crewmen come running to the windows and anxiously scrutinize the waves. None did. A few minutes later her accomplice descended into the cabin, wearing an admiring grin. A very handsome admiring grin.

"Thanks," said Emma, letting out a deep sigh as he sat down beside her. "Promise accomplished. I can't believe I actually did it. But you were great. Pépé would have loved it."

"Pépé?"

"That's what I called my grandfather. He raised me after my parents died. I'm Emma, by the way. Emma Passant."

"Henri-Pierre Caraignac," he said, shaking her hand. "Passant is a French name, yes? *Vous parlez le français?*"

"I understand the language a little from listening to my grandfather," she said, "but I don't really speak it. Pépé only spoke French when he was upset, which wasn't often. He was a very sweet man."

The Frenchman nodded soberly.

"You must have loved your grandfather very much, to do this thing for him."

Emma smiled.

"When I was seven years old, Pépé took me to Sausalito on the ferry for the first time," she said, staring at the approaching island, which was bathed in the morning's crystalline light. "We stood together at the side of the boat and looked at the water and the people and the city. Suddenly, from out of the blue, he began to cry. 'Why are you crying, Pépé?' I asked. I had never seen my grandfather cry before, and I was frightened."

"And what did he answer?"

Emma didn't say anything for a moment, fighting back tears of her own. She had cried enough when she had come back from the morgue last week, cried as if she would never stop. But Jacques Passant wouldn't have wanted to be remembered with tears, she knew.

"He said," said Emma after a moment, "that he had

tolen the most precious treasure of the sea and could
ever go back."

The Frenchman raised his eyebrows, but said nothing.

"My grandfather had been a sailor, you see," she con-
inued. "He'd traveled all over the world before settling
n San Francisco. When I asked him what treasure he had
tolen, he wouldn't answer. He just kept saying, over and
ver, 'I can never go back. I can never go back again.'
Yes, you can,' I told him. 'I promise you can.'"

"And so today," said Henri-Pierre, nodding his head,
'you made sure that he did."

"A promise is a promise," said Emma, suddenly feeling
omething deep inside of her finally relax. "And this was
ny last chance to keep it."

TWO

"I WEAR A MAN'S TOP HAT, white tie, and tails—with th
pants, mind you, not fishnet stockings," said Emma, dain
tily dunking her doughnut into black coffee as the fer
pulled away from the pier on its return trip to San Fran
cisco. "I'm billed simply as Emma."

Emma had assumed that Henri-Pierre Caraignac woul
get off once they reached Sausalito. He hadn't. It woul
hardly have been polite to refuse his invitation to breakfas
she told herself, after all the help he'd been. Or particular
rational, considering her recent dating history.

"But surely it is not just Emma?" said Henri-Pierr
sipping his own coffee, to which he had added both suga
and cream in unsettling quantities. "Surely it is the Amaz
ing Emma. Or Emma the Magnificent. Do not all magi
cians in America have something optimistic attached t
their names?"

"Not me," said Emma. "I'm insecure. I don't want t
press my luck." Coffee was practically her only vice, bu
this coffee was weaker than she liked it. And not hc
enough. The slatted bench on which they sat was as col
and hard as ice.

"You are insecure, and yet you walk out before an au
dience and make things disappear. *Merveilleux!* You mus
be very talented."

There were only a few other passengers in the cabi
with them, bored-looking men reading newspapers, wome
doing their nails—commuters, by the look of them. Hov
could anybody ever get tired of being out on the bay
Emma wondered.

"I don't know about talent," she said. "But I rent only e best illusions from the very best people."

"Illusions are for rent?"

"Sure. And they're not cheap, either. The good ones en't, anyway."

"But how can making someone to disappear be nted?"

"A nearsighted but darling girl magician with a long aid places her muscle-bound assistant, Sergio, into a ge," Emma explained. "She puts a drape around the ge and turns it around three times—it's on a little heeled stand. When she takes off the drape, Sergio is ne and in his place is a big, fat, ugly Saint Bernard. We ere watching all the time. The stand is obviously too thin conceal Sergio. How did the darling girl do it?"

"Magic?"

"Do you really think so?"

"I want to." Henri-Pierre smiled.

"Which is why I can charge five thousand dollars for a ght's work," said Emma with a sly expression, taking a dyllke nibble of her doughnut.

"How then does she make the muscle-bound assistant isappear?" said the Frenchman, leaning forward with an ager expression that Emma had seen too many times be- re.

"I'm sworn to secrecy."

"Please."

"Sorry. You'll just be disappointed. They're only tricks. 's much better to keep believing in magic."

"That may be so," said Henri-Pierre, "but I will keep n buying you more doughnuts and you will become very t unless you tell me."

"Well, let's put it this way," said Emma. "What's for nt is the cage and the stand."

"So your assistant is somehow concealed, even though appears that there is no room for him to be."

"That's why they're called illusions," she said. "T
art is making it look like it really could have happened.

Through the window Emma could see people on de
unbuttoning their coats. The temperature must alrea
have warmed considerably, though the wind was still bri
enough to keep the ensign dancing and make the caps
the waves as white as snow.

"It must be a very glamorous life," said Henri-Pier
with an innocent-looking smile.

Emma turned her attention away from the seascape
the window and did her best to smile back. "Glamorous
was hardly the word she would have used for spending h
Saturday nights trying to coax a big, smelly animal into
trick box. And besides Sergio, there was also the dog
worry about.

"It's more like endless rehearsals, drafty hotel room
and no money," she said simply.

"In New York we would say that five thousand dolla
for a night's work is not exactly chopped livers."

"That's just my gross. I'm lucky to get one booking
month. Five thousand dollars doesn't go very far when o
of it you have to rent illusions, lease rehearsal space, bu
costumes, pay your assistant and the stagehands, and tak
care of transportation, taxes, and insurance. Considerin
the price of hamburger, I think the dog makes more tha
I do."

Emma judiciously dunked the last bit of doughnut int
her cup and attempted to convey it into her mouth withou
incident. When she was finished, she nonchalantly cleane
up the coffee on her chin with her sleeve. Henri-Pierr
pretended not to notice. Angel Island loomed into view t
port. A bell buoy rang in the distance.

"I'm certain that you do very well," the Frenchma
said politely.

"What I do," said Emma, sighing, "is office temp wor
and waitressing on the side to make ends meet."

"But you are pursuing your dream."

"I wish that were true."

"But I don't understand," said Henri-Pierre. "You on't want to be the *illusionniste?*"

"Oh, I'm not complaining," said Emma. "It just isn't omething I've always dreamed about doing, if you know hat I mean. A few years ago I stumbled into a job as ssistant to the Great Martini—basically because I look ood in a bathing suit. One night the Great Martini got ogether with a cocktail shaker of little martinis, and I ded up doing the show alone. Somehow folks liked it. omebody offered me another booking. I was stuck."

"So what then do you really want to do, if not to make agic?"

"Actually I was going to be a dancer, but I screwed up y knee in my senior year of college, and that was the d of that. I don't know if I even had the talent to do it. ut I still would have liked to try."

"I am sorry," said Henri-Pierre, concern replacing the npish twinkle in his eye. "I would have loved to see you ance."

"Thanks. Anyway, being a magician's more fun than lling lingerie or driving an ambulance, believe me—I now. I even tried to be a model for a few days until I ll literally flat on my face. There aren't a lot of jobs for e choreographically kaput. What about you? What do ou do?"

"I am a dealer of antiques."

"Really? What kind? I love antiques. I have a wonderful astlake chair that I found at a thrift shop for only thirty ollars. It's probably a hundred years old."

"It sounds like you have a very good eye," said Henri-ierre without a trace of condescension. "I am interested period French furniture, Louis Quinze and Louis Seize ostly, but also certain European decorative pieces on oc-asion—porcelain, metalwork, some Fabergé—only the est quality, of course."

"Of course," said Emma. "Do you have a shop or something?"

"In New York I have a gallery, yes. And one in Paris. But much of my business is import/export. I buy in the States for clients in Europe and the Far East. I buy in Europe and the Far East for clients here. I do the major shows. Atlanta. Dallas. London twice a year. You know the life."

"Sure," said Emma. But she didn't.

An awkward silence fell between them, the first of many over the next thirty minutes as the ferry made its way back to San Francisco. Emma gave the Frenchman her recipe for apple pandowdy and tried to explain why she was still living with her grandfather at her age. ("Do you know how expensive apartments are in this town?")

For his part Henri-Pierre described how the season at Sotheby's was going ("Still slow, though Old Master drawings are on the upswing"); why he preferred the Dorcester in London to Claridge's (firmer mattresses); and what a schuss was, in case she ever found herself on new powder in Aspen—about as likely, it seemed to Emma, as her meeting a piece of chocolate she didn't like.

A long time before the boat pulled into its moorings at the Ferry Building at the foot of Market Street, it was painfully clear that the only thing they had in common—or were ever likely to have in common—was a brief episode of illegal dumping. Emma was genuinely sorry that they were from such different worlds. His sounded very nice, though obviously too rich for her blood. Perhaps it was just as well, she told herself—men who looked like Prince Charming were usually trouble anyway.

"Can I give you a lift back to your hotel?" she said just to be polite as they crossed the gangplank and headed toward the street.

Instead of gracefully declining the invitation, as she had expected him to do, Henri-Pierre flashed a toothpaste commercial smile.

"Thank you," he said, "that would be most conve-
ient."

Emma tried not to show her surprise.

"Are you sure you don't want to take a cable car? It's
ery scenic."

"I wouldn't want to impose, of course. If you don't
ally want to…"

"No, no, no. I'd be delighted."

They walked in silence the two blocks to the lot where
er five-year-old Nissan was parked—legal places were
mpossible to find on the waterfront as this hour, and
mma couldn't afford another parking ticket. Looking at
he discarded articles of clothing, fast-food containers, and
aperback books that littered her back seat, she felt even
ore self-conscious and out of her league.

"I'm staying at the Alhambra," said Henri-Pierre hap-
ily as he squeezed into the battered little car.

It figured. The Alhambra was one of the city's oldest
nd ritziest hotels. Jacques Passant, who had been famous
or his oblique turns of phrase, had called it "the hole on
Nob Hill down which fools throw money."

"How do you like it there?" Emma asked.

"Very nice," replied the Frenchman. "The mattresses,
hey are very firm."

Emma nodded. It was suddenly obvious what was on
Henri-Pierre's mind.

"I hope I can persuade you to join me for lunch," he
aid, confirming her suspicions. "It's nearly noon, and
here's a very nice restaurant in the hotel. That is, if you're
ot getting sick of me."

At least he proposed to feed her before the mattress
esson. Emma was embarrassed at how tempted she was.

"I'd love to have lunch with you," she said, narrowly
nissing a truck as she pulled out into traffic. "Only I'm
fraid I have a show in Phoenix tomorrow night with Ser-
io. I have to make a one-o'clock plane. I've got my lug-
age in the trunk."

"I see."

"I suppose I could try to take a later flight…"

"Please do not put yourself out on my account."

"It's just that we need some time to set up and rehears
before the show," Emma rattled on. "We haven't bee
able to get together since my grandfather died, and Se
gio's probably forgotten how to levitate already."

"No need to explain. You will be gone long?"

"Three days."

"Alas, I am long overdue to be back in New York a
ready, so I probably shouldn't stay and wait for yo
should I?"

Wait for her? Why on earth would he wait for her
Emma wondered. Did he really think she was the kind c
woman worth waiting three days in a strange city for, ju
so he could see her again?

"Probably not," she sighed.

"But perhaps I can see you the next time you are i
New York. Yes?"

"Yes, perhaps."

Like it would ever really happen, Emma said to hersel
unhappily, seeing her last chance with Henri-Pierre sli
away. She would look ridiculous anyway, having lunch a
the Alhambra in her jeans. And the food was probabl
overpriced and fattening.

"Do you get there often?" asked Henri-Pierre, inter
rupting her sour grapes.

"Where?"

"New York City."

"I was there exactly once, to do a convention. I staye
in a ratty hotel in Times Square. Somebody stole my fa
vorite wand."

"Well, next time when you come, you will stay at th
Plaza and have a wonderful time, I promise," said th
Frenchman. "It will be my pleasure to show you th
town."

Emma started to say something else, but finally man

aged to button her lip with an idiotic smile. She was making a total fool of herself. And why? Because a debonair older man had invited her to lunch. She was really going to have to do something about her self-esteem. Maybe she should clean up the car.

At least Henri-Pierre didn't try to break the silence with more conversation as Emma navigated up and down the city's steep streets to the Alhambra. Though he did smile at her periodically. And wink.

"I was serious about showing you New York," he said as she finally brought her car to a halt in front of the grand old hotel. "I do hope you will look me up."

"Sure," said Emma, knowing it would never happen, then went through the ritual exchange of addresses and phone numbers—his on a crisp white, elegantly engraved business card, hers scrawled on the back of a candy wrapper with a Bic pen.

"Thank you for breakfast," said Emma as he shut the car door. "And for helping me with my grandfather."

"Till we meet again," said Henri-Pierre. *"A bientôt."*

But she could see that he knew it would never happen, either.

"Another romance bites the dust." Emma sighed as she headed off to the airport.

In her rearview mirror, Henri-Pierre Caraignac stood in straight-backed perfection in front of the Alhambra, his sensuous lips turned up in a sad smile, his hand raised in a wave.

THREE

"WHERE'S MY OTHER CRATE?" asked Emma in a voice so calm it scared her. "There are only three. There should be four."

"This was all that came," said the assistant manager, casting a bored glance around the ballroom of the Phoenix Grand Marquis, where Emma would be performing the following night.

It was a large room, already filled with tables and chairs for tomorrow's party—a fiftieth-birthday bash for a big-deal local real estate developer. Like the three restaurants, two cocktail lounges, and everything else in the gigantic new hotel, the ballroom's walls were painted in colors that God might have chosen for a desert if He were an interior decorator.

The Phoenix Grand Marquis was hands-down the nicest place Emma had ever played, and her accommodations on the fourteenth floor were the cleanest. It was nearly seven o'clock in the evening, however, and Emma had already had more than her fair share of aggravation today. Her plane had been held on the runway an hour in San Francisco; she'd endured the flight down to Phoenix seated next to an elderly woman with a gas problem; and she had just spent half an hour trying to persuade a desk clerk that she wasn't supposed to pay for her and Sergio's rooms.

After the horror of last week, Emma just wanted to bury herself in her work. She was in no mood now for another argument, let alone a catastrophe. There was still too much else that needed to be done tonight.

"I'm sure that my other crate is around here somewhere," she said, smiling sweetly. "Won't you please do me a favor and just look around for it?"

"Not going to find anything," said the assistant manager with a shrug. He was a twenty-year-old with a bad haircut and the eyes of yesterday's flounder. The nameplate on the pocket of his cactus-colored blazer read:

THE PHOENIX GRAND MARQUIS'S OWN
HOWARD
PRIDE OF THE SOUTHWEST

"I don't think you understand," said Emma, still smiling. "I won't be able to do my show unless you locate that crate. Mr. and Mrs. Stallings will be very disappointed. So will their three hundred guests. So will a very nice lady whose Saint Bernard will be making his theatrical debut tomorrow night. So won't you please just look around a little for my other box? I'm sure it's in your shipping room or your package room or some other logical place, just waiting to be found. You'll do me that little favor, won't you, Howard?"

"Sure," said Howard, heading for the door. "But, like I told you before, we're not going to find anything."

Emma's frozen smile must have registered some degree of the panic she was feeling, for Sergio, who had been leaning against the back wall, sprang into action.

"You, man," he grunted. "Come."

Emma had almost forgotten her assistant. Wearily she plopped herself down on one of her crates and hoped for the best. If Sergio thought he could do something, let him try. Lord knew, he certainly *looked* effective enough, though Emma was painfully aware of his limitations.

Until he opened his mouth, Sergio was the stuff of a teenaged girl's dreams. He seemed to have sprung full-blown off the cover of a romance novel. Standing six feet five inches tall, he had the bearing of a king, shoulder-length blond hair, and perfectly proportioned muscles rippling across every inch of his body. He wore tight pants, tighter T-shirts, and a smile that seemed to say, "No self-esteem problem here." Even his eyelashes were perfect—long and lustrous. Emma had always suspected Sergio did special exercises to keep them in shape. Could you lift weights with your eyelashes?

Howard had almost reached the door. He stopped now and stared at the enormous figure emerging from the shadows.

"Yes?" gasped Howard with obvious respect. Clearly he was an eyelashes man.

Sergio thumped his enormous chest, which he depilated regularly lest he be confused with an ape, and motioned Howard over with a meaty hand. The assistant manager approached warily, the sneer he had been wearing replaced by a sickly smile. When he was a few feet away, Sergio roared, put an arm around the man's neck, and pulled him close enough to whisper in his ear.

Howard gave a squeak of surprise, then fell silent.

"Don't you hurt him, Sergio," Emma implored, rising to her feet.

"Sergio no hurt," shouted Sergio. "Sergio negotiate."

Emma held her breath. Basically, she trusted her assistant, despite his lack of subtlety. Besides, she was too far away to do anything. She could see the giant's lips move. Maybe he was reading.

After a few seconds, Sergio released his grip. The hapless assistant manager instantly flew out of the room as if jet-propelled. Sergio strutted his way through the tables to the elevated stage where Emma was standing in front of their three crates.

"What's the matter with you?" she demanded. "You want to get us arrested? You want to get us thrown out of the hotel?"

"Sergio no hurt. Sergio help. Emma mad at Sergio?"

His smile had disappeared, replaced by an expression like that of an anxious child.

"No." Emma sighed. "I'm not mad at you."

"Man find box now," said Sergio, his smile returning. "You see. Sergio fix."

Sergio claimed he was Dutch, but from his accent Emma suspected that her assistant had originally come from Russia or one of the old Soviet republics. From his insistence upon being paid in cash and his obviously phony last name (who could believe it was really Budweiser?), Emma judged he was in the country illegally. Not that she minded, however. In fact, she was thankful that there was no paper trail leading back to her. If immigration ever caught up with Sergio, Emma's failure to pay his social security taxes might wreck her chances of ever holding a cabinet position.

"What did you say to him, anyway?" Emma asked, not sure she really wanted to know the answer.

Sergio folded his arms in front of him and tossed his blond mane.

"I say, if he no find box, I give him keesssss of serpent's tongue."

"And what's that supposed to be?"

Sergio smiled dopily.

"I lick his ear and leave to imagination."

Emma stared at him for a few seconds, then burst into laughter. Sergio beamed.

"You big lug," she said, giving her huge assistant an affectionate punch in the arm, though not hard enough to bruise her knuckles the way she had the first time she had tried it. "Let's just hope he finds that crate, or we're sunk."

"If he don't," said Sergio, a suggestion of worry crossing his perfect brow for the first time, "I no really have to give keess, do I?"

"No, you just have to rehearse. Tomorrow, you're going to remember all your cues, aren't you?"

Sergio grinned, thumped his chest again, and studied his reflection admiringly in the polished metal tubing of a chair.

"Sergio no forget. Many womens will be impressed with his brain."

"All right," said Emma, knowing what they would be impressed with, trying to believe that everything would turn out okay, anyway. "Let's set up what we can before Mrs. Schneiderman gets here."

"Who?"

"The dog lady."

"Mrs. Schneiderman is dog?"

"Rudolpho is the dog. Mrs. Schneiderman is the owner."

For the trick-cage illusion to work properly, a large animal was required. Some magicians used tigers, but Emma was happy to settle for a big dog—preferably one smart enough not to bark prematurely and give the game away. Sergio would go into the cage; the dog would come out; the audience would marvel and be amazed at how the one animal turned into the other.

After working her way through sheepdogs, bloodhounds, and German shepherds, Emma had found that Saint Bernards produced the biggest oohs and ahs. It hadn't been practical to take Morris, their regular Saint Bernard, all the way to Phoenix for this booking, however. Fortunately the AKC had directed Emma to a local dog owner, Blossom Schneiderman, who had agreed to rent out her Saint Bernard, Rudolpho, for the gig several weeks ago—and at a much better price than Emma usually paid.

"When dog lady coming?" said Sergio.

"Actually, she's supposed to be here now," said Emma, glancing at her watch. "But it doesn't matter if she's a little late. The trick cage is in the crate that's missing."

"If cage missing, how we make Sergio disappear?"

"Maybe we'll just give him a condom and point him

oward the nearest waitress,'' Emma muttered under her breath as Sergio walked away admiring his triceps.

While her assistant unpacked their gear from the three crates, Emma walked each inch of the stage. She inspected the lights, the meager fly system, and the sight lines, trying to visualize how each illusion would work in the unfamiliar space.

At least the sound equipment seemed to be working. Emma set up her tape—mostly Mozart and a little Grieg—and spent the next hour running through the hundreds of carefully planned steps, gestures, and actions that constituted each illusion. Everything was choreographed down to the second. Only occasionally did Emma need to remind Sergio of the little details he was prone to forget—like the difference between right and left and how his feet interacted with one another.

At eight o'clock, the Phoenix Grand Marquis's own Howard and two porters appeared with the missing crate, which had been located in a basement storeroom. Mrs. Schneiderman and Rudolpho, however, still had not arrived.

Leaving Sergio alone with his reflection to unpack the trick cage, Emma went looking for a pay phone. She finally found one down the hall outside the Painted Desert cocktail lounge, which—judging from the droves of aftershave-soaked men and dolled-up women cruising in packs—seemed to be a local hotspot. It was time to find out what was keeping their Saint Bernard.

''It's Emma Passant, Mrs. Schneiderman,'' said Emma when she reached the woman. ''Why are you still there at home? You and Rudolpho are supposed to be at the hotel tonight to rehearse with me.''

''Oh, dear,'' replied the childlike voice. ''Didn't they give you my message? I left a message with the hotel operator this afternoon. They said you hadn't checked in yet, but they said that they'd give you a message. They promised.''

"I'm sorry, but I didn't get any message," said Emma, her palms suddenly breaking into a sweat, her heart plunging into her stomach. What now?

"Well, I called. I did. I really did."

"I'm sure you did, Mrs. Schneiderman," said Emma, resolving to steal a few towels from the Phoenix Grand Marquis to thank them for all their good work. "I hope there's not a problem. You can still do the show, can't you?"

"Oh, I can do it, yes..."

"Thank God."

"...it's Rudolpho who won't be able to make it."

"Please don't tell me that."

"Oh, but I have to. He can't do your show."

"Well, I'm afraid he has to, Mrs. Schneiderman," said Emma, raising her voice and putting a finger in her ear against the blare of music that came from the cocktail lounge each time someone opened the door. "We had an agreement. I paid you in advance. We're all depending on you."

"Well, I know that," said Mrs. Schneiderman, sounding at once guilty and defensive, "but Rudolpho has come down with something. He's as sick as a dog."

"I'm sure he'll be okay once he gets here. He's just nervous. It's just stage fright."

"But he's listless and his nose is warm."

"Oh, they're always like that," chuckled Emma, trying to sound doctorly. "Every dog I've ever worked with. You know what we say in the business? Warm nose, cold feet. Believe me, there's nothing to worry about. He just needs a little rehearsal to get his confidence up, that's all."

"But his eyes are all glassy."

"He'll be fine."

"His coat has lost its luster."

"No one will notice."

"He keeps throwing up, and he's had diarrhea all over the house. I nearly passed out from the smell."

"I think we may have a problem here," said Emma.

Emma spent the next five minutes trying to console the sniveling Mrs. Schneiderman, though she secretly hoped the woman would catch whatever it was that Rudolpho had. By the time she hung up, Emma had a pounding headache and the small consolation of Mrs. Schneiderman's promise to return the money Emma had paid her.

A girl in a party dress swept by into the cocktail lounge, releasing another burst of rock music. A porter dressed like a renegade from the French Foreign Legion rolled by with a rack of luggage.

Suddenly everything that Emma had been trying to forget from the past week crashed down on her: her grandfather's cold gray face at the morgue; the endless questions from the police; those horrible first few nights in the house alone, listening for Pépé's footsteps, knowing they would never come again.

It was too much. Emma sat down cross-legged on the floor beneath the pay phone, trying not to cry.

It was ironic, she thought. This was precisely one of those times she would have called him. When everything was going wrong on a job, her grandfather was the only one who could make everything seem better.

"Is not this the beautiful college graduate who makes men to disappear with her smile?" Pépé would have said when he got her anxious call. "But how could there be anything so grand as to bother her? What problem would not tremble in his shoes at such a pretty sight?"

Somehow it had always been all that Emma had needed, just to hear the pride in her grandfather's voice, to imagine the twinkle in his eye. She'd go back and fix the sound system or the lights or the equipment. She'd pretend she wasn't worried about the endless little details that made up this exhausting, thankless business.

But there was no one to call now.

What was she doing here? Emma asked herself, burying her head in her hands. What was the point? It was always like this. If it wasn't missing crates and no-show dogs, it was clients whose checks bounced and drunken hecklers. And for what? So she could go out onstage for an hour with her stomach in knots, bracing herself against the ten thousand things that could go wrong? What kind of life was that for a person? Where was the fun? Where was the magic?

"Why the long face, little lady?"

Emma lifted her eyes off the floor and found herself staring at a tooled-leather cowboy boot emblazoned with the name ED in gold letters. She thought that maybe if she kept very still it would walk away by itself. It didn't.

"You lost, honey? Is there something that Big Ed can do for you?"

Big Ed had squatted down now, and Emma found herself staring at a man in his indeterminate forties wearing a cowboy hat. She could instantly see why he was called Big Ed. He was built like a refrigerator, had several more chins than anyone could possibly use, and was flashing a smile as wide as all outdoors.

"Got a dog, Ed?" Emma asked weakly.

"Shucks, that all you need?"

"That's all. Just a dog. A big, smart dog."

"Hell, I got me the biggest, smartest dog in Phoenix. This dog is the biggest thing since Pepsi Cola. This dog is so smart, I can't let him fetch me my newspaper in the morning anymore."

Emma knew she shouldn't ask, but after ten seconds of silence she couldn't stand it.

"All right, I'll bite. Why can't you let him fetch your paper anymore?"

"'Cause when he reads it, he leaves it all dog-eared."

"That's very funny."

"Well, it does kind of give you pause. P-A-W-S? Get it?"

"I got it," said Emma, trying to smile.

"Then you got a real sense of humor, you know that,

ttle lady?'' said Big Ed, sitting down beside her. "I like at in a representative of the fairer sex. You don't mind I sit down here for a spell, and join you, do you? Now on't worry. I promise I won't sell you a Chevrolet.''

"This is something I should be worried about?''

"Hell, girl, you're looking at none other than Big Ed Garalachek, the top Chevy salesman in all of Phoenix. Big d's the Chevy King. But, like I say, I'm just sitting down ere 'cause I'm weary, though I must admit you get a retty nice view from this angle. Would you look at the egs on that little filly over yonder, yee-haw.''

"Yee-haw,'' agreed Emma.

"And who might I be having the pleasure of addressing, I can be so bold as to inquire?''

"Emma Passant,'' said Emma after a moment, too roud to give him a phony name, as all her instincts creamed for her to.

"Please to meet you, Emma Passant,'' said Big Ed, tiping his big hat. "Gorgeous name for a gorgeous gal. They all me Big Ed.''

"Well, it was nice meeting you, Ed, but...''

"Now I'm gonna tell you the truth, little lady, 'cause I ant us to be friends. Don't be fooled by this getup. I'm ot really a cowboy—I actually got a year of dental school nder my belt. It didn't work out, though. My hands was oo big to fit properly into people's mouths. See, I want s to start out on a honest basis. Honest Big Ed Garalachek, the Chevy King, that's what they call me. What bout you? You come here often?''

"This is my first time, actually, and now I really have o get back to—''

"How 'bout you letting me show you around then? I now this hotel like I know the trunk dimensions of a Caprice. It's a great place to meet people, to see and be een. C'mon. I'll show you all the sights. You seen the ool yet?''

"No, and it's really very kind of you to offer, Big E
but I think I'll have to pass."

Ed didn't answer right away. For the first time since h
had sat down, his big smile disappeared.

"What you really mean is you don't think you'd car
to have anything to do with a fat old Chevy salesman lik
me," he finally said, shaking his head.

"No, that's not it."

"Oh, don't worry, Emma honey, it ain't your faul
That's the way it always goes for Big Ed. Lucky at car
unlucky at love, like the saying goes. It's okay, though
Takes a lot to break a big ol' heart like mine. Guess I'
be seeing you around."

Big Ed started to struggle to his feet. Emma stoppe
him with a hand on his sleeve.

"You really have a dog, Ed?" she said. She knew tha
this crazy idea really was a crazy idea. But what choic
did she have?

"Sure do," said Ed, sitting back down, his smile re
turning, bigger than ever.

"And he's really smart?"

"Sure is."

"And he's really big?"

"Little lady, to me, Lionel is the single biggest thing i
this whole sweet mystery of life."

"Would you consider renting him?"

"Beg pardon?"

"Would you consider renting Lionel to a very nice an
highly responsible woman magician? I need a big smar
dog for a show I'm doing here tomorrow night."

Ed sat back and regarded Emma with a mixture of skep
ticism and awe.

"You funnin' me," he finally exclaimed. "You reall
a magician?"

"You really a Chevy salesman?"

"If that ain't the darnedest thing," cackled the Chevy
King, actually slapping his knee. "I knew there was some

ing special going on here when I sat down, I just knew
. And now I know what it is. It's magic! That's what it
. Pure unadulterated magic!''

"So what do you say, Ed?" said Emma, leaning for-
ard. "Would you rent me Lionel?"

"Well, that all depends," said Big Ed, massaging his
hins.

"Depends on what?"

"On what you're offering for Lionel's services."

"Well, the usual fee is a hundred dollars," said Emma.
'How does that sound?"

"Hell, I don't want your money," said Ed, rearing back
vith indignation. "I got all the money I need. Besides, I
on't like to take money from a lady. Unless she's buying
Chevrolet, of course.''

"I'm not going to buy a Chevrolet, Ed."

Ed smiled sheepishly.

"How 'bout your having a little drink with me, then?"

"I'll tell you what," said Emma. "If Lionel works out
kay, I'll have two drinks with you. After the show to-
norrow night. And I'll buy. What do you say?"

"I say you got yourself a deal, little lady," exclaimed
3ig Ed, grabbing her hand and pumping it.

"How soon can you have Lionel here?" asked Emma,
elieved. Maybe there really was some magic in the world.
Maybe things were going to work out after all.

"No time at all," said Big Ed with a big grin, reaching
nto the pocket of his coat. When he took out his hand, it
vas filled with a little brown Chihuahua. Before Emma
ould scream, cry or faint dead away, Lionel blinked sleep-
ly and licked the end of her long, pointed nose.

FOUR

THE SHOW THAT NIGHT was a smash.

Every trick worked perfectly. Emma got all her laughs and not a single proposition from a drunken guest. Sergio missed only two of his cues (a new record). Even Mil Stallings, the developer whose wife had thrown him the party and whom every speaker extolled as being the "toughest son of a bitch in the Southwest," had a good time. Apparently he didn't attach much significance to his wife's celebrating his birthday by hiring a woman who made men disappear.

True to her bargain, Emma met Big Ed Garalachek for a drink after the show in the cocktail lounge. Emma had fixed it so he could watch the show from the light booth.

"Didn't I tell you Lionel had talent?" Big Ed exclaimed, taking the little Chihuahua into his big hands and exchanging sloppy wet kisses with him. "You gonna be a star, you know that, boy? We gonna sell the Chevy franchise and take you to Hollywood!"

"Maybe you should give that some more thought, Ed," said Emma.

"What's to think about? You heard them cheering back there, didn't you?"

Emma had to admit that the Chihuahua had a lot of personality. The audience had screamed with laughter when Emma had pulled the drape from the trick cage to reveal Lionel where Sergio had been. The tiny dog had yapped happily, then jumped right through the bars of the cage into Emma's arms. The crowd had gone wild. A dozen people had appeared after the show asking for Lionel's paw print in their pieces of cake as a souvenir. Even

he two comatose stagehands, whom the union required
Emma to hire, had made a fuss over him.

Only Sergio had seemed unhappy, his dignity ruffled by
having to be transformed into a pint-sized Chihuahua instead of the usual manly Saint Bernard. He had quickly
found a peroxide of blonds to console himself with, however, at the party.

"You don't want that kind of life for Lionel, believe
me," said Emma as the waitress brought their margaritas.

"He's gonna be a star!"

"He's going to be stranded in the middle of Kansas
because somebody cancels a booking at the last minute
and refuses to pay. He's going to spend Christmas watching television in a Holiday Inn in Fort Worth."

For the next half hour Emma recounted horror story after horror story of just how unglamorous a life in show
business could be until Big Ed finally got the message.

"Well, I guess I don't want him fritterin' away his best
years if it ain't no fun like you say," said the Chevy King,
gently scratching Lionel's ear. It was clear that he adored
the little dog, who was presently taking a nap in the big
man's pocket.

"It's a life I wouldn't wish on a dog," said Emma. "As
you can tell."

"Then why'd you do it?"

"Very good question."

After another drink Emma found herself talking about
having wanted to be a dancer and what it had been like
for her growing up in San Francisco with only her grandfather. After the fourth margarita she promised to consider
a Chevy from Big Ed for her next car. After the fifth, he
declared he was going to name his first child after her,
provided he ever found the little lady of his dreams.

On Sunday morning Emma awoke with a headache the
size of one of those great Chevy trucks Big Ed had told
her all about. Somehow she managed to make her way
downstairs to one of the restaurants. The coffee wasn't as

hot or as strong as she liked it, but Emma figured that this wasn't the time to try to cut down. Judging from the condition of her head, she would probably die soon anyway.

"Hi, Emma," whispered a thunderous voice. "How you do?"

Emma struggled to pry her gaze off the piece of toast she had just buttered and which seemed to be throbbing. It was Sergio with one of the blondes from last night on his arm—a leggy girl of about twenty with a chest that rivaled his own and real-looking diamonds in her pierced ears. She was still wearing her dress from the night before—a seriously wrinkled designer original.

"I'm just great," Emma croaked. "How are you?"

"Sergio going to be married," he declared. The blonde smiled guiltily and looked at the floor.

"Don't lead the poor girl on, Sergio," said Emma, rolling her eyes. They seemed to make a clanking noise. Or was that the butter melting?

"No, is true."

Sergio's voice was strangely subdued and he wasn't wearing his usual morning-after smirk. In fact, he looked almost frightened. Emma suddenly realized that he might be telling the truth.

"That's great, Sergio," she whispered, not knowing what else to say. "Congratulations."

"This is Kiki," said Sergio proudly. "She can do hundred one-arm push-ups."

Kiki stepped forward and shook Emma's hand. She had a grip like a nutcracker.

"I work out a lot," said Kiki happily.

"Kiki think Sergio sensitive guy," said Sergio.

"I know it's kind of sudden," the girl went on, "but Sergie's what I've always dreamed about. And he really knows what he wants, don't you, Sergie?"

"Her father own big chain of supermarkets," said Sergio, his normal cocky expression returning. "Drives Jaguar. You okay, Emma? You look bad."

"No, I'm fine. I just had too much to drink last night nd I'm not used to it. I'm very happy for you both. Re-lly."

"Don't worry, I get you other big lug to replace Sergio. Iake calls. Not leave you up shitcreek."

"That's okay, Sergio," said Emma, turning her atten-on back to her throbbing piece of toast. "Maybe it's time or me to retire, anyway."

"You not be magician?"

"It wouldn't be the same without you."

"Ha, you kid Sergio," said the giant, laughing. "You lways be magician. You like when everything go wrong nd you go crazy. But you please to come visit us between hows sometimes. Kiki's father have big ranch. Sergio earn to ride horse, yippy kai yay. Time to pack up crates ow?"

"I think I'm going to need a few more minutes and bout eight more cups of coffee."

"You stay. Sergio no need help."

"That's very nice of you, Sergio," said Emma. The salt nd pepper shakers were beginning to throb now, too.

"Sergio nice guy," said Sergio. "Has great body and ood looks. Soon will be rich, too."

"Nice meeting you," said Kiki as Sergio moved away, esturing for her to follow. "And I really liked your show ast night. You shouldn't retire just because of Sergie and ne. You've really got talent. You could do this the rest of our life."

"That's what I'm afraid of," whispered Emma as the irl ran to catch up with her dreams.

WHEN EMMA FINALLY PULLED into the driveway of acques Passant's Potrero Hill house on Sunday afternoon, he sky was the color of plums, and bright fingers of light-ing laced through the heavy rain every few minutes.

She had felt strangely sad as she had given Sergio a inal kiss on the cheek at the hotel before getting into a

cab for the airport. It was hard to believe that she woul
probably never see the big ape again, never have to ad-li
a joke while he picked himself off the floor in the middl
of a performance, never hear his headboard pounding end
lessly against the wall in the next room after a show.

It was harder still to believe that she could really retir
from performing and find another way to make a living
Emma was certainly ready to try. Just the thought of step
ping out on another stage with a phony smile on her fac
and a brassiere full of colored handkerchiefs made he
sick.

Only what else could she do? She'd wither in an office
and she hated people telling her what to do. Charlemagn
Moussy, Jacques Passant's lawyer and oldest friend, ha
told Emma last week that there was some money in he
grandfather's estate. Maybe she could buy a little flowe
shop or something. But what did she know about runnin
a shop? What did she know about flowers, for that matter
other than how to make them pop out of her sleeve?

The flight up from Phoenix in the thunderstorm ha
been frightening. Emma was glad to be home.

Potrero Hill was a quiet neighborhood in San Fran
cisco's southern half, where working-class people sti
made their homes despite soaring real estate prices an
creeping gentrification. Emma's grandfather had bough
the house years ago, when things were cheap. The two
story shingled structure featured three bedrooms, a slive
of yard, and an attached one-car garage, where Jacque
Passant had parked the Plymouth he would never us
again.

Emma parked her own car in the drive as usual. The
she ran to the house through the pouring rain but wa
drenched before she managed to unlock the front door. The
telephone maliciously stopped ringing the moment she go
inside.

With the lights off and the storm roiling, the empty
house felt lonely and menacing. Emma dropped her suit-

:ase on the floor and went into the kitchen to check the answering machine. Nothing but hang-ups. A blast of thunder pealed outside in the storm. She reset the machine and went up to her room.

Occupying the back corner of the second floor and with windows on both sides, Emma's bedroom was normally he sunniest room in the house. Now rain beat on the windows and the dark fury of the storm made everything—the wicker dresser, the Eastlake chair, even the embroidered white duvet on her brass bed—look gray and lifeless.

The room was a mess, as usual. Emma automatically started to pick up a few of the paperback books that littered he floor by her bedside, then stopped. Jacques Passant wouldn't be poking his head in today, telling her to straighten up.

From every wall the eyes of children stared at her in the dim light. She had found the framed, hand-colored etchings in antique stores and thrift shops, though why she collected them she didn't really know. Both Emma's mother and grandmother had died in childbirth, so she wasn't particularly keen on the idea of motherhood.

Emma snapped on the light. The shadows disappeared, and the room suddenly became friendlier. She stripped off her wet clothes, wrapped herself in a white terry-cloth robe, and was drying her thick black hair with a towel when the phone rang again.

"I'm glad I finally caught up with you, Miz Passant," drawled a man when she answered. "I've been trying to reach you."

The raspy mellow voice belonged to Detective Benno Poteet of the San Francisco Police Department, who didn't sound nearly as short, fat, and bald over the telephone.

"I've been out of town," Emma said, bracing herself. "Why didn't you leave a message? I would have called you back."

"I hate them things. It's like you're having this stupid little conversation with yourself. You always rattle on like a idiot, and you know someone is going to hear the whole damnable thing. Hell, I don't even like the phone. I like to talk to folks face-to-face."

Detective Poteet had been the man who had broken the news to Emma about her grandfather, coming over to the house so he could tell her in person. He had been more than decent during all the trauma that followed—making runs to a diner so she wouldn't have to drink the police station's coffee, telling her all about his childhood in New Orleans—but Emma hadn't really wanted to hear his voice again. Had they found her grandfather's killer? Would there be a trial now, a filthy affair that would go on forever? Couldn't all the painful memories just be put to rest, as she had put Jacques Passant's ashes to rest in San Francisco Bay?

"So what can I do for you, Detective?" Emma asked in a very quiet, very tired voice.

"How long have you known Henri-Pierre Caraignac?" said Detective Poteet.

It was not a question Emma had expected, and it took her a moment to figure out who the policeman was talking about. The Frenchman. The man who had helped her on the ferry.

"I met him a few days ago," she finally stammered as thunder clattered in the skies above and lightning lit up her windows. "Why?"

"Mind telling me the circumstances of your meeting?"

"We struck up a conversation on the Sausalito Ferry."

"When exactly was this?"

"This past Friday morning."

"Did he seek you out, approach you first?"

"No, I went up to him."

"What did you talk about?"

"Nothing really," said Emma, getting a little nervous. She certainly wasn't going to mention dropping her grandfather's ashes in the bay to Poteet and get busted. Had there been a witness? Was the handsome and elegant

Henri-Pierre Caraignac a fink? What the hell was going on?

"You must have talked about something," drawled Poteet. "Did he ask you about your grandfather?"

"No."

"Your grandfather never came up in the conversation at all?"

"I may have mentioned something. He didn't bring it up, though. Like I said, we were strangers. Look, what's this all about?"

"And all you did on the ferry was talk? Nothing else?"

"He bought me some coffee and a doughnut. I drove him back to his hotel. Is that a crime? What's going on here, Detective? Why are you asking me all these questions about this guy? Is he in some kind of trouble?"

"He's dead. Murdered."

Emma nearly dropped the phone. She was so stunned that she couldn't talk for a few moments. When she finally tried, she found herself breathless, her eyes full of tears, her heart pounding.

"Are you all right, Miz Passant?"

"Yes," said Emma after a moment. "It's just the shock of it. Are you sure?"

"An acquaintance of his from a local auction house identified the body. Staff at the hotel knew him pretty well."

"But he was...I was just..."

Emma suddenly found herself crying uncontrollably. What was the matter with her? Poteet waited a long time before speaking again.

"I know this is hard for you, Miz Passant, coming on the heels of your grandfather's death and all," he said quietly. "It sort of builds up, is my experience. I've seen it before in folks in your situation. You think you're all grieved out, but your nerves are all raw and anything's likely to trigger stuff you didn't know was left in there. I've seen people go to pieces 'cause a can of beans falls off a shelf. This thing with Caraignac's bound to get to you, so unexpected and all.''

"I didn't know him, you know," said Emma, wiping her eyes, grateful for the time to pull herself together. "We just met, that was all there was to it. We were just passengers together on the same ferry.''

"I'm sure that's true.''

Why did he seem not to believe her? Emma wondered. How many people really fell apart at news of a stranger's death? For all his soft voice and good manners, Poteet was still a cop. But why should she feel guilty? She didn't have anything to do with this. She could see Henri-Pierre in her mind's eye, tall and smiling. The soft hair, the beautiful blue eyes. She could see him sweeping her into his arms and kissing the daylights out of her. Now he was cold and gray and dead in some shelf in the morgue. Just like Pépé had been.

"What happened?" Emma finally managed to whisper.

"The maid found Mr. Caraignac in his hotel room this morning. He'd been shot in the head at point-blank range.''

"Oh my God. Do you know who did it?''

"I'd very much like to find that out.''

"Was it a robbery?''

"Maybe a bungled robbery, yes. There was no money on the body or in the room, though Mr. Caraignac was known to be someone who carried considerable cash. He was wearing a mighty expensive watch, but a robber could conceivably have overlooked something like that in his haste to get out of there.''

"Why did you think to call me?" said Emma, suddenly frightened. How could the police have known that they had even met?

"We found your name and address written on a candy wrapper in his wallet.''

Of course. That's all there was to it. She still had Henri-Pierre's engraved business card in her own wallet. The *late* Henri-Pierre. It was still so hard to believe.

"We exchanged phone numbers," Emma explained, her voice still dazed and quiet. "He said he wanted to take me out if I ever got to New York. I'm sorry I can't be more help, Detective, but like I said, I didn't really know him."

"Like you said," agreed Poteet. "It is some wild coincidence, though, don't you think?"

"Coincidence? What coincidence?"

"Oh, didn't I say?"

"Say what?"

"We ain't recovered the weapon yet, but according to ballistics, Mr. Caraignac was killed by the same gun that killed your grandfather."

AT A QUARTER TO TWO in the morning, Emma finally gave up trying to fall asleep and turned on her bedside light. The storm was still blowing outside, but at least there was no more thunder and lightning now, only rain.

Emma put on her glasses and padded downstairs in her flannel pajamas and bare feet, wincing as she caught a glimpse of her reflection in the mirror in the hallway.

"Maybe I can get a job as a lumberjack," she muttered.

After fixing herself a cup of decaf—it would hardly do to have real coffee, though that was what she wanted— Emma fiddled with a crossword puzzle, watched a rerun of "The Mary Tyler Moore Show" on television, and tried to understand what could have happened to Henri-Pierre Caraignac.

How could have it been a coincidence, she asked herself over and over, both Jacques Passant and Henri-Pierre being killed with the same gun?

Detective Poteet had said that, as unlikely as it seemed, coincidence probably was the explanation. A mugger shoots a man in the park, then shoots another man in a botched robbery in a hotel a week later.

"Your perpetrator is in the business of robbin' and killin', after all," he had said. "Either that, or he was smart enough to throw the gun away after he used it on your grandfather. Then someone else found it and used it to kill Mr. Caraignac or sold it to the man who did.''

Emma still found it hard to believe, however.

She had spent another ten minutes with Poteet on the phone, trying to help him find some connection between the two victims, but other than their both being French, her grandfather and Henri-Pierre didn't seem to have anything in common.

To Emma's knowledge, Jacques Passant had never been to New York, and this was apparently Henri-Pierre's first trip to San Francisco. Jacques Passant was not someone who had any interest in antiques, and Henri-Pierre wouldn't seem likely to have needed the services of a carpenter—Emma's grandfather had retired from full-time work a few years before but still took odd jobs occasionally. The two men certainly hadn't moved in the same social or business circles. There was no evidence that they had ever met.

The policeman had promised to phone Emma if anything broke in either murder case, after extracting her pledge to call him if she should come across some connection between her grandfather and Henri-Pierre. But what connection could there be?

"This is getting me nowhere," Emma finally muttered aloud.

She turned off the television, left her mug in the sink—she could clean up in the morning—and headed upstairs.

She got back into bed, took off her glasses and closed her eyes. Nothing happened. Nothing like sleep, at any rate.

After fifteen minutes of struggling unsuccessfully to black out, Emma put her glasses on and went into her grandfather's room. Then she took the glasses back off, got into his big bed and pulled the covers up to her neck.

When she had been frightened in the night as a little girl, she would come in here, and her grandfather would et her into the bed with him. He had patted her hand and old her stories and sung her old French songs. She had not understood most of the words, but somehow they had always made her feel better, had made her feel safe. Or was it just the tone of his voice? She wished more than anything that she could hear that voice again.

"My poor Pépé," she said quietly.

The rain tapped gently on the windowpanes. The furniture cast strange shadows on the wall. The house creaked the way old houses do.

Emma suddenly sat bolt upright. She reached over and turned on the lamp next to the bed, put on her glasses, and held her hand over her eyes until they got used to the light again. When she finally took her hands away and looked around, she knew she was not mistaken. Something was different about the room.

Emma tried to figure out what it was. Her grandfather had been entirely set in his ways and had resisted even the slightest change. Emma practically had to hit him over the head just to get him to throw out his frayed and faded old shirts after she had bought him new ones. He certainly wouldn't have started redecorating after all these years—nothing had changed in this room since Emma was a little girl.

But something *had* changed now. What was it?

Not the little blue-and-white bedside lamp or his old-fashioned wind-up alarm clock. Not the rocking chair by the window where Jacques Passant would sit and listen to a little transistor radio he would hold in his lap.

Emma's grandfather's tastes were simple. Aside from a half dozen or so of the primitive carvings that he liked on top of the dresser, there were few decorations. The only picture on the wall was an old framed photograph of Emma's mother when she was a teenager, though there were photos of Emma on the bedside table and albums on the shelf below containing all the pictures he had taken of her growing up.

Emma looked at the dresser again. That was it.

She got out of bed and walked over to the dresser, where the heavy, dark wooden carvings stood guard—vague human shapes with deep eye sockets and elongated features. They ranged from eight inches to about two feet in height, and several of the squatting shapes had been carved with thick triangular blocks sticking out of their backs to counterbalance them. Between two of the largest figures there was a space where something else had been.

"The boat," said Emma, pleased to have figured it out.

A carved wooden model of a boat had always sat there on the dresser. When had her grandfather removed it? she wondered. And why?

It was funny, Emma thought as she got back into bed and turned off the light. She had seen that model boat a million times, but she could barely remember what it looked like.

The vague image of white sides, mahogany decks and an open back flashed through her mind. It may have been an old-fashioned cabin cruiser or something. A name had been painted on the stern in gold letters. She couldn't even remember that. What was the boat's name?

Emma was still trying to remember when she finally fell asleep.

FIVE

EMMA AWOKE WITH A START.

For a moment she didn't know where she was, but then the soft brown blur around her registered. Pépé's room.

Emma reached over and put on her glasses. Everything snapped back into focus. The sun was up and she could see the familiar things. Pépé's rocking chair. His old alarm clock, which now read eight o'clock. The portrait of her mother on the wall—so young, so defiant-looking. The dresser with the primitive carvings and the space where the model boat had always been.

The model boat!

Emma threw the covers off and stood up, looking around the room, remembering the horrible thought that had bubbled up in her unconscious mind and shocked her awake.

It made no sense that Pépé would have removed the boat. But what if it hadn't been Pépé? What if the model boat had been taken by someone else? Emma's grandfather's body had been found without his wallet. The murderer could have gotten the Passants' Potrero Hill address from the identification in that wallet. How difficult would it have been for him to pick one of the house's ancient locks?

Emma rushed to the dresser, opened the top drawer and anxiously ruffled through Jacques Passant's socks and undershirts for the few things of value he had kept in the house. Here were his gold cuff links. Here was the little leather box of silver quarters and dimes that he had plucked out of his pocket change over the years. In the toe of the red-and-green socks that he wore only on Christmas

Day was a crudely formed gold coin about the size of dime that her grandfather had always said he had won i a poker game.

Emma took a deep breath. Everything seemed to be i order, but how could she be sure? Why did it feel as someone had been here?

"I'm just imagining things," she muttered.

The horrible feeling she had awoken with didn't g away, however. If someone had been here, surely he woul have taken something besides an old model boat. Emm found herself rushing to her room and going through th drawers of her own dresser in mounting panic.

What little jewelry she owned—and which she rarel had occasion to wear—seemed undisturbed. The two hur dred and fifty dollars in cash she kept stashed in a ti candy box for emergencies was still there. Nothing wa missing as far as she could tell.

Emma looked around. The children in the etching seemed like strangers suddenly. The Eastlake chair looke old and tatty. What had Henri-Pierre Caraignac reall thought, Emma wondered, when she had bragged that was more than a hundred years old? He was an importar antique dealer. He had probably thought she was an idio

But Henri-Pierre Caraignac was dead.

Emma was suddenly digging into her dresser for jean and a turtleneck. She dressed in a flash, finishing up wit the fancy new running shoes for which she had shelled ou a hundred and ten dollars two weeks ago. She hadn't eve worn them yet. "The shoes that cost as much as feet," had been Pépé's outraged pronouncement upon learnin the price.

Why would Jacques Passant's murderer have come i and stolen an old model boat but nothing else? Emm asked herself again, tying her shoelaces. He wouldn't. made no sense. She was just being silly.

But the horrible feeling in her chest wasn't going away It was growing stronger, in fact. Someone *had* been there

Emma was sure of it now. A stranger's hands had gone through her things.

Emma pulled her two suitcases from the back of her closet and rummaged through her drawers for everything she was likely to need in the near future. When the two suitcases were full, she went into Jacques Passant's room and packed his ancient leather two-suiter with the overflow, taking a moment to remove only her grandfather's cuff links from the dresser drawer and the little gold coin from his Christmas socks. She parked both safely in her pocket alongside the money she had removed from her emergency candy box.

Emma sat on Pépé's suitcase and closed the latches, surprised at how little space her life fit into. She had left her magician's getup hanging in the closet. There were no bookings on the horizon, and white tie and tails wouldn't exactly fit in on the unemployment line—not that she qualified for unemployment, anyway. She could have somebody else retrieve her books and paintings later. She was not coming back.

At the front door, Emma turned and gave one final glance at the only home she had ever known. Then she walked out and locked the door behind her—for all the good it would do. Whoever had taken the lives of Jacques Passant and Henri-Pierre Caraignac had already also taken what he had wanted from the house.

"HELLO, ANYBODY HOME?" said Emma, poking her head through the glass reception window of the law offices of Charlemagne Moussy, Esquire. "It's me."

A tall, slender woman with lips the color of blood and nests of wrinkles around her eyes appeared from around the corner of the filing area. Her straight brown hair, cut in a pageboy, bounced. It was Charlemagne's secretary/receptionist/all-around gal Friday, the unfortunately named Jean Bean. Upon seeing Emma, she rushed to the window,

nearly dropping the stack of manila folders she was holding.

"Oh, Miss Passant!" exclaimed Jean in a voice as rapid
as the heartbeat of a hummingbird. "It's so nice to see
you, we were all so sorry to hear about your grandfather,
he was such a kind, sweet man, it's just terrible. How are
you holding up? Is everything all right? Do you need anything?"

"I'm fine, thanks," said Emma, relieved to be among
friends again. Her hands had been shaking for the entire
drive downtown to the old building on California Street
where Charlemagne had his office. It was a little after
nine a.m. now, and last night's rain had left San Francisco
cold and wet.

"You know, your grandfather was the first client I met
when I started working for Mr. Moussy," said Jean Bean
in a sympathetic voice, opening the inner door for Emma
and helping her off with her coat.

"Yes, you've told me that before."

"It must have been fifteen years ago," Jean rattled on,
"no, what am I saying? More like twenty. It was the same
year that Mother came down with colitis, which certainly
didn't make her any easier to live with, not that she's what
anyone would call easy now, mind you, but at least we
don't have to worry about the colitis anymore, thank God,
though of course there are a million other things wrong
with her, at least to hear her tell it, and she's probably now
lying about all of them. But I'm sure you're not interested
in my mother and Lord knows I'd just as soon forget about
the woman, if only I could! Coffee?"

"That would be great," said Emma. Jacques Passant
had always referred to Jean Bean as "she who speaks like
the machine gun." He had liked her, too.

"So you're all right?" said Jean, leading Emma to the
little kitchenette off the filing area. "There's nothing you
need, nothing we can do for you?"

"Actually, I was hoping I could see Charlemagne. Is he very busy this morning? I'll be happy to wait."

"No, no, no, no," said Jean, pouring coffee into a dainty porcelain cup with a gold rim and handing it to Emma on a matching saucer. "He doesn't have any appointments until eleven, and I'm sure he'll be delighted to see you. It will give him a perfect excuse to avoid catching up on his paperwork. He keeps promising me he'll do his paperwork, but somehow he never seems to get around to it. You take your coffee black, right?"

"Right," said Emma, though she was only able to take one sip before Jean was marshaling her down the hall toward Charlemagne's office. "Look, if he needs to do paperwork, I can come back later."

"Don't be silly, dear," said Jean, knocking once on the door and pushing it open. "You've been through so much. Look who's here, Mr. Moussy! It's Emma, Emma Passant."

The office they had entered was a high-ceiling space with wood-paneled walls and a worn Oriental rug. An old-fashioned sofa, upholstered in velvet hung with tassels, sat against one wall beneath an oil painting of a huge vase of flowers. A window overlooking San Francisco's financial district graced another wall, flanked by shelves full of books and knickknacks. Directly opposite the entrance door was a gigantic inlaid brass-mounted desk, its vast tooled-leather surface bare except for a silver letter opener, an appointment book, and a pink porcelain teacup full of tea. On the wall behind the desk was another large oil painting, this one of a woman playing a cello. Seated at the desk was Charlemagne Moussy.

Jacques Passant's attorney and oldest friend was a small man of enormous dignity and meticulous personal habits. He stood precisely five feet four, wore an impeccably tailored navy-blue suit with an almost imperceptible pinstripe, a dove-gray shirt, and a crimson bow tie. His lapel, as always, featured a fresh white carnation. As always, three peaks of white silk handkerchief protruded from the breast pocket of his suit.

Charlemagne's hair was still jet-black, though he had to be in his seventies. Emma wouldn't be surprised to learn that the little lawyer dyed it, but then she wouldn't be surprised to learn that he didn't. Despite his age, there was something outrageously vital about Charlemagne, from the tips of his tiny pink ears to the pointed toes of his Italian leather shoes.

"Emma, *ma chère*," said Charlemagne, rising to his feet. "What a delightful surprise for me. How very nice it is to have the pleasure of your visit."

Emma hadn't seen Charlemagne since that first terrible day at the police station, though she had spoken with him several times over the week that followed. Now she rushed to his open arms and let them embrace her, nearly spilling her coffee in the process.

"Oh, Charlemagne," she said, her eyes filling with tears.

"I'll leave you two alone," said Jean with a satisfied smile.

"Thank you, Miss Bean."

The secretary left, closing the door behind her.

Charlemagne led Emma over to the couch, a double-caned canapé with a few needlepoint throw pillows and a single cushion about as thick as a waffle. In an instant all that had been happening poured out—how she and Henri-Pierre Caraignac had met; how Detective Poteet had called with the shocking news of his murder, committed with the same gun that had killed Jacques Passant; how the model boat had disappeared from her grandfather's dresser, and why Emma was convinced that someone had been in the house.

Charlemagne listened attentively, reacting with a comforting mixture of amusement and solemn approval at the story of how Pépé's ashes had been deposited in San Francisco Bay, asking an occasional question to clarify just what it was that Emma had seem at the house. When she was finished, he clapped his hands on his thighs and nodded his head decisively.

"Ah, *oui*," he declared. "I see why it is that you were afraid. We must not take the chances with our peace of mind. You were right to leave the house, of course. You must not return until the locks, they are changed."

"I'm not going back at all," said Emma, taking a final sip of her coffee. It was lukewarm now, but strong enough for Emma's taste, meaning that it probably could be used to remove paint.

"But it is your home."

"Not anymore," said Emma, setting her empty cup down on the French provincial end table and shifting position on the couch. "Not without Pépé."

Charlemagne raised one of his eyebrows, thin black arcs so perfectly formed that Emma had always wondered if he plucked them into shape.

"I know you are upset, dear Emma," said the lawyer in a gentle voice. "But from what you tell me, it does not seem reasonable that someone was really there. You say nothing was missing."

"The model boat was missing."

"But Jacques, he may have done something with it. Do you know for certain that he did not take it himself?"

"No."

"And this invasive presence you seemed to feel, could it not have been just the sad events of the past weeks intruding into your mind?"

"Maybe I was imagining things," said Emma, shifting position on the couch again, unable to find a comfortable spot. "All I know is that I don't want to go back. Can we sell the house?"

"If you wish, yes," said Charlemagne quietly. "Such a house will bring much more than your grandfather paid for it, of course. The mortgage, she is paid up, and the real estate prices in San Francisco, they are absurd. I would

counsel you, however, to give this further consideration. It
is never wise to act hastily in the aftermath of a death. It
is *très difficile* for you to see clearly now, *n'est-ce pas?*
You can always sell the house later. Things may look very
differently to you a year from today.''

"I can't go back there," said Emma.

"Once it is sold, it is gone forever."

"I've made up my mind."

"If you have thought it through, then, very well," said
Charlemagne with a wave of his hand. "You would like
me to take care of this for you?"

"Please. You can put the furniture and everything in
storage until I figure out what to do."

"*Bien.* And where will you go?"

"I'll check into a hotel for now, I guess. Then maybe
get an apartment."

"Do you have money?"

"Some. Enough."

Living at home and waiting tables between magic jobs,
Emma had managed to put a few thousand dollars in her
savings account. Of course it wouldn't last very long if
she wanted to have her own place. She'd have to break
down and get a real job sooner or later. The thought made
her fairly sick.

"Maybe the estate can help you out with a loan."

"I'm sorry for being so rattled, Charlemagne. I obviously don't know whether I'm coming or going. Oh, I
almost forgot."

Emma reached into her pocket for Jacques Passant's
gold cuff links, which she handed to Charlemagne.

"I'm sure Pépé would want you to have these. You were
his best friend."

"*Merci beaucoup,*" said Charlemagne, staring at the
tiny gold articles in his open palm. "I am deeply moved."

"Would you mind if I left one of my suitcases here for
now?"

"No, not at all."

"Thanks," said Emma, still trying to find a comfortable position on the couch as Charlemagne deposited the cuff links into the pocket of his vest.

Her own jewelry in Jacques Passant's heavy leather two-suiter would be safer here, Emma knew, shifting position on the sofa, yet again. She probably wouldn't have much occasion to wear her party dresses in the near future. The last thing she needed now was to get ripped off in some hotel room.

Charlemagne, who had been watching Emma squirm around on the sofa, his ears growing pinker and pinker, now spoke.

"Are you having the problem?"

"No, I'm just uncomfortable."

"Do you perhaps wish to go to the little room?" said Charlemagne, looking at his shoes, then the wall, then his carnation.

"What little room?"

"'The little room where all must go,'" whispered the attorney, unable to meet her eye. "Is that not what poor Jacques called it?"

"The bathroom?"

"*Oui.*"

"I don't have to go to the bathroom, Charlemagne," said Emma, trying not to laugh at his embarrassed expression.

"You are sure? You have been wiggling."

"I've been wiggling because of your couch."

"And what is wrong with my couch?" said Charlemagne, glancing up indignantly.

"It's about as comfortable as a sack of potatoes. What am I sitting on? I think there's something in here."

Emma reached under the cushion of the sofa and pulled out what had been causing her discomfort—a bone about five inches long. It was dull gray in color, but otherwise exactly like the bones that dogs were always pictured burying in backyards. Except for the carving. The bone was entirely covered with crudely etched designs. Emma had heard of witch doctors before, but witch lawyers?

"So that is what happened to it," said Charlemagne, laughing, as he took the item from Emma's hands. "You will please to excuse me. Margaret, my granddaughter, came by with the baby last week, and this is what he does, the little thief."

Charlemagne deposited the bone on the end table, where it apparently belonged. Emma reached over immediately and retrieved it. The carved designs—stars and lines and faces—were striking, and strangely familiar.

"You said the estate could help me out with some money?" said Emma, trying to recall where she had seen such patterns before.

"Yes, that is true," said the lawyer, clearly happy to change the subject back to matters of business. "It is time for the reading the will."

"Oh, please, Charlemagne, not now."

"This is what you have said this to me before, Emma. But we cannot postpone this forever, *n'est-ce pas?* It is the law."

"I don't care about the details."

"There is money involved as well as details."

"I don't care about that either. Except maybe a little advance to keep me going. Can't you take care of everything?"

"It is not that simple," announced Charlemagne in his gravest legal voice. "It may take many months to sell the house, and the probate procedures must be handled, taxes and other obligations must be paid. As executor you must choose the attorney to help you do this, by the way."

"You mean you won't do it?"

"If you so wish, I will be honored. I did not wish to presume."

"I wouldn't have it any other way. Now what about an advance?"

"A small fee is available to you as executor, and I can

lend you whatever else you may need until funds are free in the estate.''

Emma shook her head.

''No, I don't like to borrow anything,'' she said, unable to pry her attention away from the carved bone. ''Just how small is this small executor's fee?''

What was it about the bone? Why was it so familiar?

''Two percent is customary.''

Emma glanced up.

''That won't go very far,'' she said, biting her lip, trying to imagine what the house could be worth. She had never even thought about it before.

''It is true,'' said Charlemagne sadly. ''The estate is worth maybe a million, so two percent of this would be only twenty thousand dollars.''

''Twenty thousand dollars! That can't be right,'' sputtered Emma.

''Two percent of a million dollars is not twenty thousand anymore? Mathematics have changed?''

''No. Pépé couldn't possibly have had a million dollars. That's crazy.''

''A million dollars is not so much money anymore these days,'' said the attorney, taking a sniff of his carnation. ''And most of it is tied up in the house. The income on the rest is not enough to live on—at least in this city of ours—considering present interest rates. Jacques had his social security and still took the odd jobs, you know.''

''But where did he get it, all that money?''

''Jacques did not *get* all that money, as you say,'' pronounced Charlemagne, shaking a perfectly manicured finger. ''It grew. Like the tree from the seed.''

''What do you mean, it grew?''

''Your grandfather had some capital when first we met so many years ago,'' said the lawyer, pursing his thin lips with obvious pride. ''A modest amount, from the sale of property he had owned. From this, the industrious Charlemagne Moussy helped him to make the down payment on the house you now wish to sell. The rest, we invested. I have the knack for such things, and the market, she did well. Your grandfather lived simply, letting the portfolio build up so that you could have a better life. The best way to make money is never to spend it, you know.''

"I'm stunned," said Emma. "I don't know what to say."

"Jacques loved you very much. Of this I am sure."

"Look at me," said Emma, digging into the pocket of her jeans for a piece of Kleenex and wiping her eyes, which were full of tears, yet again. "I'm a total mess. Maybe I can get a job as a fountain."

"It is understandable," said Charlemagne.

"What do you think happened, Charlemagne?" said Emma after a moment, collecting herself. "Why was Pépé killed?"

"It was a mugging. A random street crime."

"Yes, yes, that's what everybody said at first, but it makes no sense now."

"The senseless violence, it is the disease of our time."

"One isolated death, maybe. But how could it be a co-incidence—Henri-Pierre Caraignac being killed with the same gun?"

The lawyer stood, and walked to his desk, his hands clasped behind his back, his face inscrutable.

"This I do not know," he said finally. "I told the police last week everything I can think of, which is nothing. Nobody would have wished to harm dear, sweet Jacques, and I have never heard of this Caraignac person."

Emma looked down. She was still clutching the strange bone in her hand, clutching it so hard her knuckles were white. Now she forced herself to relax her grip.

"What is this thing, anyway?"

"It is a carved bone."

"Yes, I can see that."

"Probably not human, Jacques always assured me. He

gave it to me, you know. Many years ago. It was one of those primitive things he liked so well.''

Emma took a deep breath. That was it! She didn't know why she hadn't seen it before. The carved lines and figures were identical to the carving on the wooden figures in her grandfather's room.

"It was Jacques who first taught me that I should have little toys for the nervous clients to play with," Charlemagne continued, a sad smile passing over his face. ''Calm a man's hands and you calm his mind,' he used to say. He was very wise about such things. I miss him very much.''

Emma turned the bone over in her hand. The carving was not deep and had been worn smooth. The artifact felt old and strangely comfortable to hold, as if it had been specifically made for anxious hands.

"Where did my grandfather get it, do you think?"

"This, I do not know," said Charlemagne, wiping his eye, apparently still thinking of his friend. "One of my clients, he is a collector of primitive art—and greedy wives, I am sorry to say—told me he believed the bone to be Kaito."

"Kaito?"

"An Indian tribe, native to one of those islands in the Caribbean.''

Suddenly Emma remembered.

The name on the model boat that had disappeared from Pépé's dresser had been *Kaito Spirit*. And carved directly underneath had been other words.

"San Marcos," she whispered.

"Yes, that is it," said Charlemagne triumphantly.

"Is what?"

"The island where the Kaito live. It is somewhere near Puerto Rico and the Dominican Republic, is it not?"

SIX

The Alhambra sat on top of Nob Hill like the crown on the head of a king.

It was a huge yet strangely delicate stone structure which had risen, Phoenix-like, from the rubble of the 1906 earthquake just a few blocks from two of San Francisco's other grand hotels, the Fairmont and the Mark Hopkins.

Emma pulled her battered Nissan into the hemispherical driveway and stopped directly in front of the hotel's massive entryway. It had been only three days since she had dropped Henri-Pierre Caraignac off here, but it seemed more like a lifetime ago.

A doorman dressed in a uniform that would have earned nods of approval in Czarist Russia instantly swooped down on Emma's car, followed by two porters and a parking attendant. The team extracted Emma's luggage and departed with her vehicle with an efficiency she had thought reserved to car thieves. The doorman then ushered Emma up the steps and into the waiting clutches of another character dressed for operetta, who in turn guided her through the bustling lobby—a gigantic affair of plush furniture and palm trees, topped by a soaring skylight ceiling—and delivered her finally to the front desk. Presumably she would be reunited with her luggage at some other time; it was nowhere to be seen.

"May I have your credit card, please, Miss Passant?" sniffed the check-in clerk, barely looking up. He was a slender young man with long teeth and eyebrows that slanted upward at an ever steeper angle the closer they got to the middle of his face—as if they aspired to grow vertically, rather than in the usual horizontal fashion.

Emma dug into her wallet and handed over the appropriate piece of plastic, then turned her gaze back to the busy lobby as the clerk went about his business.

A few individuals sat reading newspapers or milling about in small groups, but most of the lobby's population seemed to be in motion. A continual stream of people rushed about in every direction: men dressed in dark suits and quiet ties, women with silk blouses and gold jewelry. Everyone seemed very serious and very well fixed. Even their hair looked expensive.

"And how long do you plan to be with us on this stay, Miss Passant?"

"Not long," said Emma, looking down at her blue jeans, feeling out of place, as she knew she would. "Maybe a few days."

The clerk continued tapping the keyboard of his computer terminal. He didn't seem to have noticed her outfit. In fact, he didn't seem to have seen her at all. No one had—not really. There was nothing so anonymous as a large hotel.

"That will be three hundred forty dollars per night for a single."

"Three hundred and forty dollars!"

"Not including tax. Sign here, please."

The price was outrageous, thought Emma as she signed the registration slip. The strange thing was that she could actually afford it.

Charlemagne hadn't let Emma leave his office until he had written her a check for twenty thousand dollars as an advance against her executor's fee and given it to Jean Bean to deposit in Emma's account. Emma would have more when probate was finished and they had sold the house, much more. She could order anything she wanted at dinner or from room service and not have to scrimp on gasoline and chocolate for the next month.

The only trouble was that Emma still couldn't understand how Pépé could have had so much money. How could she feel comfortable about spending even a nickel of it until she did?

And Charlemagne's insistence on reading Jacques Passant's entire will to her before she left the office had only made matters worse. In it her grandfather had actually referred to the Kaito Spirit as Emma's legacy, though his words had made no sense:

"...that she may take her place at the helm and turn the wheel on the legacy that I have kept hidden from her."

What legacy was Pépé talking about? The million dollars? What did that have to do with some boat that he had sailed on thirty years ago? And how was she supposed to take her place at its helm?

"A friend of mine was murdered here the other night," Emma said in a quiet voice, remembering why she had come to the Alhambra.

The desk clerk looked up, his eyebrows collapsing in astonishment. He certainly seemed to see Emma now.

"Beg pardon?"

"I said, a man was murdered here."

The most intolerable thing about her grandfather's death had been its senselessness. Henri-Pierre's death, however, had changed everything. Two apparent strangers shot with the same gun couldn't be coincidence, no matter what the police said. There was a single reason why both men had died, a connection between them; there had to be.

Emma couldn't believe Detective Poteet wasn't taking Henri-Pierre's death more seriously. Before getting off the phone with her he had even had the gall to suggest that their best hope was to wait for a tip from somebody to whom Henri-Pierre's murderer might have bragged. Just another random act of violence, he had said. But Emma knew Poteet was wrong. The Alhambra was the logical place to begin proving it.

"His name was Caraignac," Emma said aloud. "I understand he was shot on Saturday night."

"I'm certain that you're mistaken, Miss Passant. This is the Alhambra."

"No mistake, I promise you."

There had been no clues to Pépé's murder, but Henri-Pierre's was different. On the ferry the Frenchman had said he was overdue to be back in New York, so he must have stayed at the Alhambra awhile. He would have talked to people, perhaps had meetings in the lobby or the restaurants. This was where Emma had last seen Henri-Pierre, where he had died. Somewhere his path must have crossed Jacques Passant's. That intersection was the key to everything. Emma intended to find it.

She swallowed hard, steeling herself. She wanted to get the hardest part over first.

"I'd like to see the room where it happened, if I may."

"Perhaps you should speak with Mr. Anthony," said the distressed clerk, his eyebrows elevating again. "Please wait here a moment."

The young clerk hurried away to an office at the back, giving Emma a moment to catch her breath.

She couldn't believe she was actually doing this. She knew it was probably pointless wanting to see the room where Henri-Pierre had been killed, but as a magician Emma had learned never to assume anything. Illusions worked because of the audience's assumptions. People thought that Sergio disappeared into thin air because they assumed the base of the trick cage was too small to conceal him. They thought that Emma produced the playing cards they were thinking of by magic, because they assumed she couldn't have fifty-two different cards concealed in fifty-two different places on her person.

But they were wrong. She could. And she had.

The key here, Emma knew, was to make no assumptions. She had to see everything Henri-Pierre had seen, touch everything he had touched, and maybe, ultimately, she would understand why things had happened as they had.

After a moment the clerk returned with a well-groomed older man with iron-gray hair and half-glasses perched on the bridge of his nose. He stopped behind the desk directly in front of Emma and studied her as an owl might study a mechanical mouse.

"I'm Raymond Anthony, the manager," he finally said in a smooth baritone. "May I help you?"

"Yes. I'd like to see the room where Mr. Caraignac was killed Saturday night."

"I'm afraid that's not possible," said Mr. Anthony, picking an invisible piece of lint off the sleeve of his dark-blue suit.

"Someone was really murdered here?" gasped the clerk, his eyebrows fluttering with disbelief. "Why didn't anybody tell me?"

"Let's keep our voices down, shall we?" said Mr. Anthony between clenched teeth. A well-heeled middle-aged couple who were being checked in a few feet away apparently hadn't overheard.

"Why wasn't it on the news?" said the clerk in disbelief. "Why wasn't it in the papers?"

"It was," said Mr. Anthony, shooting an expression at the young man that seemed to say shut-up-or-I'll-kill-you-painfully-and-feed-your-body-to-my-cat. "Happily most of the media was too responsible to give it a lot of play. Why don't you take your break now, Jason?"

"But—"

"And don't repeat any of this. It's bad for morale. Do you understand?"

"Yes, sir," said Jason reluctantly, glancing back over his shoulder as he walked away.

"Now, Miss Passant," said Mr. Anthony, tapping the computer keyboard when Jason was out of earshot. "What's your interest in this? Why do you want to see that room?"

"Mr. Caraignac was a friend of mine. I want to understand what happened."

"We went over all this with the police. There's nothing to understand. It was an unfortunate incident, but no one on staff knows anything about it or about Mr. Caraignac."

"How long was he here?"

"Two weeks, I believe."

"He was here two weeks and nobody talked to him?"

"That's right."

"Surely there must be some way for me to see Henri-Pierre's room, Mr. Anthony," said Emma in her most earnest and innocent voice. "I know it sounds crazy, but it's very important to me. Please."

The gray-haired manager looked down at Emma's blue jeans, then punched a button on his computer.

"We don't show our rooms, Miss Passant, be it to the press, comparison shoppers, or merely the morbidly curious. It's against policy. I'm afraid the only way you can see that room is to rent it."

"What?"

"The staff is finishing the cleanup now, and it should be ready within the hour. You can have lunch at our restaurant while you wait."

Emma stared at the manager, whose thin lips had turned up slightly into the merest suggestion of a smile.

"But how can you be renting out the room already?" she asked. "I was told Mr. Caraignac's body was only found yesterday morning."

"That's true," said Mr. Anthony. "The police were here all day yesterday and into the evening. Happily our maintenance team is on the job twenty-four hours a day in order to keep things up to our high standards."

"But don't the police still need the room?"

"Not unless they wish to pay four hundred twenty-five dollars per night."

"Four hundred twenty-five! The clerk told me it was three forty."

"This is a more expensive room."

Emma didn't say anything for a moment, trying to think

it through. All it would cost was one night's rental, after all. She could afford it. She could see what she had come to see. She wouldn't actually have to stay there.

"Oh, by the way," said Mr. Anthony, glancing down at her jeans again, his smile growing almost imperceptibly wider—and crueler—"there's a minimum five-day rental on that particular room."

Emma stared at his smug, condescending expression only a moment longer. Whatever doubts she had had disappeared.

"I'll take it," she said, then turned on the heel of her tennis shoe and walked back across the lobby, leaving Mr. Anthony sputtering in astonishment at the desk.

She had the money, and it wasn't as if the room would be haunted or dripping with blood, Emma told herself. She had sawed too many people in half to be squeamish. The only thing to be afraid of in life was people like Mr. Anthony. Besides, it wasn't like she had anywhere else to go.

"One for lunch," said Emma, arriving at the arched doorway of the Le Petite Trianon, just off the lobby.

It was now a little after eleven-thirty. The hotel's main dining room had just opened and was entirely empty. Emma wasn't particularly hungry, but since she'd have to wait for the room anyway, she might as well check out the restaurant.

This must have been where Henri-Pierre would have taken her to lunch, had she been able to accept his offer last week. He could hardly have had the coffee shop in mind. Judging from the look of the place—strictly white tablecloths and crystal chandeliers—the Frenchman had been ready to put his money where his mouth was.

"If Madame will follow me, I will show her to her table."

The maître d', a stocky man with white hair, was dressed in a tuxedo. If he made any judgments about Emma because of her outfit, he didn't show them. They were probably used to the occasional rock star or schlubby software millionaire in a place like this, Emma thought as the man led her to a banquette.

"Bon appétit," said the maître d', handing her a menu the size of a kite. Judging by the nasal lilt of his French accent, Emma figured he had probably come from somewhere between Chicago and Indianapolis.

"What's your name?" she asked.

"Josef, madame."

"Pleased to meet you, Josef," said Emma, reaching up and shaking his hand in a move she had been practicing mentally for years but never had an occasion to use. "I'm Emma Passant. I'll be staying at the hotel for a few days."

"A pleasure to have you with us, Madame Passant," said Josef, smoothly transferring the ten-dollar bill Emma had just placed in his hand into his breast pocket without even glancing at the denomination.

"Did you know my friend, Monsieur Caraignac?"

Josef frowned.

"It's all right," said Emma in a quiet voice. "Mr. Anthony knows that I was a friend of Mr. Caraignac. He has already been kind enough to answer some of my questions."

It was only the truth, after all. She had told him Henri-Pierre was her friend, and he had answered *some* of her questions.

"The hotel has tried to keep it quiet, but it is very sad," said Josef, nodding. "Monsieur Caraignac took almost all of his meals with us."

"Did anyone ever join him?"

"No."

"No one?" asked Emma knowingly. "Not even a young lady or two?"

"No, Monsieur invariably ate alone. The police interviewed us all yesterday. There was not much to say. What does a guest tell a waiter? Or a maître d'? All I could say is that he was a very nice man who liked the fish."

Emma suddenly wondered whether ten dollars had been

enough to give Josef. How much had Henri-Pierre slipped into the man's hand every day to be considered "very nice"? How could she really hope to reconstruct Henri-Pierre's movements in this strange, unfamiliar world? There was a lot more to having money than having money.

"I think I'll try the fish today, too," Emma said quietly. "Would you please tell my waiter to bring me something that Mr. Caraignac would have liked?"

"Oui, madame. You shall have the poached salmon with a touch of dill, a salad of endive and garden greens, and a glass of Pouilly Fumé. It will be quite wonderful."

What it was, however, was quite bland. It was also quite thirty-eight dollars, not including tax and tip. The lukewarm coffee was an additional six bucks.

"DID YOU KNOW Mr. Caraignac?" asked Emma, parking five dollars in the hand of the porter who had just delivered her and her luggage to the room on the eighteenth floor where the handsome Frenchman had been murdered.

"Please?" said the porter with a big smile, putting the money into his pocket as Emma looked around the room with trepidation. He was a small man with a pasty complexion and thinning red hair.

"The gentleman who was staying in this room for the past two weeks."

"I no usual work this floor. Everybody got rotate."

"I see," said Emma with a sigh. "Do you think there's somebody downstairs who might remember him? Mr. Caraignac?"

"Capitán of the bells, he know everythin'."

"Captain of the bells? The bell captain?"

"Capitán of the bells." The porter nodded. "I help you more?"

"No, that will be fine," said Emma, wondering how much she would have to give the bell captain to get him to talk. At the rate she was going she'd be lucky to stretch her executor's fee and savings a month, let alone the year

harlemagne had said it would probably take to probate
e estate. Being an heiress was turning out to be an ex-
nsive business, and Emma still couldn't believe that
épé really had a million dollars to leave. Until she knew
here the money had come from, Emma had to assume
e'd have to pay everything back—an unsettling thought,
say the least. And the meter was still ticking.

The porter exited with a big smile after putting one of
er suitcases on the rack at the foot of the king-sized bed,
aving Emma alone for the first time since she had entered
e hotel. The L-shaped room was eerily silent. It was sud-
enly hard to think about unpacking. It was hard even to
emember to breathe.

Emma tried to shake off the feeling of dread, turning
er attention to the accommodations.

She had stayed in larger rooms—the one in Phoenix had
een twice this size—but never one so finished-looking.
he thick pile carpeting, the handsome furniture, the del-
ately striped wallpaper—all seemed more like what you
ould expect to find in some banker's Presidio Heights
ansion than in a hotel. Everything smelled freshly pol-
hed and new. The only thing Emma might have changed
ere the window draperies, which seemed too dark for the
st of the decoration.

The hotel had certainly done a good job getting the room
ack into action. It was hard to believe that someone had
een murdered here barely two days before. Emma took a
eep breath. This is what she had wanted, to see the room
here Henri-Pierre had spent his last days. Here she was.
Iow what?

Suddenly all the bravura Emma had manufactured for
Mr. Anthony disappeared, and the enormity of what had
appened here crashed down on her. A man had died in
his room. A kind man who had helped her on the ferry,
ho had laughed with her and made her laugh. Emma
esperately wanted him back. And she wanted her grand-
ather.

No, Emma told herself, forcing herself into a state of calm, just as she always had to do before she went out on stage. She had come here for a reason. There was nothing to be afraid of. It was just an empty room, and a nice one at that. At these prices it should be. And unless she wanted to give Mr. Anthony the pleasure of taking—Emma winced as she did the mental calculation—more than two thousand dollars of her money for nothing, she was going to be here for a while. Five days. She had better make the best of it.

There was a color television at the foot of the bed, a remote on the bedside table. Emma walked over and turned on the set. One of the premium cable movie stations flickered on after a moment. Who had last watched television here? Most likely it had been Henri-Pierre. Perhaps he had stayed up for a film one evening. It was lonely being by yourself in a hotel room. Emma knew that from personal experience.

Emma flipped off the television and closed her eyes. The memory she had been fighting poured into her mind.

She could almost actually see him. The impeccably tailored taupe sport coat. Black pants with a perfect crease and tasseled oxblood loafers with soles no thicker than a dime. His hair may have been windblown on the ferry, but it was expensively cut. His sideburns had been straight. Henri-Pierre obviously had been a fastidious man, and a fashion-conscious one.

The mental picture changed to one of Henri-Pierre lying gray and lifeless in a drawer in the morgue. Emma opened her eyes. The horrible image disappeared.

Shaken, she walked slowly around the room, opening drawers, studying the framed prints above the bed, trying to get some sense of what it must have been like for him. Henri-Pierre had stayed here for two weeks, the manager had said. At four hundred twenty-five dollars a night, he was clearly well-off, but Emma had already known that.

Had he been comfortable here? Had he known he was

n danger? Or had death taken him by surprise? Nothing bout the room seemed to tell her anything. For all its elegance it was as anonymous as any other hotel room.

Emma walked into the bathroom. There was a double marble sink with little bottles of expensive shampoo and conditioner in a basket along with small packets of soap—all wrapped in green paper with the hotel's logo. In a rack at the back of the tub were four thick white towels. There was a faint sweet odor in the air. The maid's perfume? Disinfectant?

Emma stared at the marble counter. This is where he would have put his toilet articles and his razor. Was he the type who lined everything up neatly in perfect order? Those well-groomed ones often were.

If she had come here that day for the mattress lesson, would he have gotten annoyed at the mess she usually made of the bathroom? Would he have expected her to fold up her clothes and use only one towel at a time and squeeze her toothpaste neatly from one end of the tube instead of from in the middle? Maybe it was better that she would never know.

Emma walked back into the room, closing the bathroom door behind her. The room had been combed by police and thoroughly cleaned by the hotel. What trace could be left of a murdered man?

The only place Emma hadn't yet checked was the closet opposite the entryway. She did so now. It was large and roomy. On a top shelf were extra pillows and blankets. Henri-Pierre must have brought a lot of clothes with him if he had stayed for two weeks, Emma thought idly. Such a man would probably have wanted to wear a different suit every day.

It was then that she noticed the floor.

She knelt down to be sure, but it was obvious even from a distance. The carpet in the closet did not exactly match the carpeting in the room. The color was slightly off. The pile was fractionally less deep. And outside the closet, the carpet had a different smell.

"Why, it's new," she said aloud. The carpet in the room had not merely been cleaned recently, it had been entirely replaced.

Emma looked around the room again and saw something else. The wallpaper of the outer wall, the wall that held the window looking out over the city, was slightly brighter than the wallpaper on the other walls.

She walked over and scrutinized the corner seam where the papers came together. There was no mistake. The wall with the window had recently been repapered. Why?

Emma fought down a sudden wave of nausea. The explanation was obvious. The wall had been repapered for the same reason that the carpet had been replaced: they had both been stained irreparably. With blood.

"He must have been standing by the window when it happened," said Emma, trying to reconstruct the scene in her mind.

The mirrored dresser took up the rest of the outer wall. If Henri-Pierre had been on the bed, blood couldn't possibly have splattered as far as the wall. It wouldn't have been necessary to repaper. Nor could he have been sitting anywhere else in the room for the same reason. Both the leather armchair and the backless seat by the little writing desk were too far away from the repapered wall.

"That's why the draperies seem out of place for the room," Emma whispered, shuddering. "They've been replaced, too."

Emma walked over and stood at the spot by the window where it must have happened and looked out. The view wasn't much. The street. A few buildings. Poteet had said Henri-Pierre had died between eight o'clock and nine, so it would have been dark outside. There would have been nothing to see.

Emma looked into the room. Directly in front of her,

en feet away, was the armchair. There was a floor lamp next to it—a place for reading.

"He wasn't standing by the window for the view," she said out loud. "So why was he here? To talk with someone seated in that armchair, maybe? If the murderer was sitting there, they must have been having a conversation. Henri-Pierre must have known him. The murderer in the chair, Henri-Pierre standing by the window."

Emma walked over to the armchair and acted out the picture in her mind.

"The seated man stands up and pulls out a gun. Henri-Pierre would have had nowhere to go. He would have been backed up against the wall. And then the killer would have come closer and closer and brought the gun right up to Henri-Pierre's head and…"

Emma stopped.

"I'm just guessing," she said.

There was nothing that really proved the murderer was sitting in the armchair, she knew.

"He might just as easily have barged into the room, gun drawn, and forced Henri-Pierre over to the window. But why force your victim to a window? A window is exposed. People look into windows and this one was in plain view to the street below. Why would a killer risk his act being seen?"

The problem was that people's actions didn't have to make sense. How could you figure out why someone did something when the person who did it probably didn't know himself?

That's why the police never solve crimes like this, thought Emma, walking over to the bed.

Maybe Poteet was right. Maybe this was just another random killing, just a crazed idiot with a gun who had killed Henri-Pierre. The same idiot who had killed her grandfather. The same gun.

Emma sank onto the bed, her mind filled with confusion and sorrow and memories of two murdered men. Her poor dear Pépé. A handsome stranger. The retired carpenter. The glitzy New York antique dealer. Where had their lives intersected? What had joined them in death?

Emma's lack of sleep was catching up with her. She had been up half the night last night, thinking about Henri-Pierre. Now she was lying on the very bed where he had slept the last two weeks of his life, and she could barely keep her eyes open.

"What's the connection?" she asked herself again. "There's got to be a connection."

Emma let out a deep, plaintive sigh. Had it been just an expensive mistake to come here? Was she just one of those fools Pépé had always made fun of, throwing her money down a bottomless hole?

As she began to drift slowly off to sleep, Emma realized that she had learned something. It was a small thing, something no one else in the world might have thought important, but somehow it made her feel a little better. At least she knew now that Henri-Pierre had been telling her the truth. The mattress *was* very firm.

SEVEN

OVER THE NEXT FEW DAYS Emma spoke with nearly a dozen members of the Alhambra staff, hoping to learn something about Henri-Pierre that might connect him to her grandfather.

Waiters at the restaurant and the coffee shop confirmed that Mr. Caraignac liked the fish. Porters agreed that he was a good tipper. The maid who had found him—a big Eastern European woman who spoke little English—blubbered hysterically when she figured out whom Emma was talking about but ultimately could tell her nothing. Twice, clerks scurried away from conversations after catching a glimpse of Raymond Anthony, the sadistic hotel manager, staring bullets at them.

Only the "captain of the bells," a florid gentleman with eyes of blue and breath of garlic, was able to say anything that even mildly surprised Emma: Henri-Pierre Caraignac had checked in with only one small suitcase.

"Are you sure?" Emma had asked.

"I got a memory like a elephant for these things," the bell captain had declared with pride. "Luggage is my life."

Why would Henri-Pierre have had only one suitcase? Emma asked herself. Surely someone so fastidious and fashion-conscious would have brought along more clothes for a two-week stay. Clearly Henri-Pierre had expected to be in San Francisco for no more than a few days. He had extended his stay for some reason. Why?

Emma didn't know, and by Wednesday she had about had it with the "good life." There was only so much rich food you could eat and HBO you could watch. Besides,

sleeping in the room where Henri-Pierre had been murdered wasn't exactly her idea of a good time. She had had
nightmares every time she went to sleep. A black depression took hold of her as more and more of her inquiries
failed to turn up any common ground between Jacques
Passant and Henri-Pierre Caraignac.

That night Emma watched TV until three o'clock in the
morning and polished off an entire box of gift-shop chocolates, including the ones with nuts which she normally
wouldn't touch. She awoke on Thursday at noon, consoled
only by the quart of fudge-ripple ice cream she had had
the foresight to procure for the day's big event—*Now Voy-
ager* was on the old movie station at midnight, followed
by *Mildred Pierce*.

At four o'clock in the afternoon there was a knock on
her door.

"You don't need to make up the room today," Emma
shouted from the bed. At least the morning maid had re-
spected the DO NOT DISTURB sign she had put out yesterday.

There was another knock, this one louder.

Emma turned off the television set with the remote. Who
was this? She was still in her pajamas and hadn't even
washed her face. Why bother? Where was she going to
go? What was she going to do? She had no home, no work,
and no one left to talk to at the hotel, though she was stuck
here for two more days.

Dragging a blanket around her shoulders to serve as the
robe she didn't have, Emma got out of bed and waddled
to the door, feeling as big a mess as the place looked.
Remnants of a room-service lunch littered the bed. Yesterday's clothes were strewn on the floor, punctuated by
an occasional towel.

"Who is it?" she shouted.

"Benno Poteet, Miz Passant," the familiar honey-toned
voice called back.

Emma opened the door. The short, fat, bald detective

grinned sheepishly. He wore a rumpled brown suit and an ill-fitting raincoat. In his hand he held a brown felt hat that looked as if it belonged in 1954.

"Hope I'm not disturbin' you," he drawled.

"They've got a house phone down there, you know," said Emma, too surprised to be properly embarrassed. "You could have called me."

"You know I hate them things, Miz Passant. I'm a person-to-person kind of individual. I'd like to talk with you if I may. Mind if I come in?"

"Yes, I do mind," said Emma. "I'm not dressed. I wasn't expecting company."

Poteet craned his neck to see the mess over her shoulder.

"I've been out jogging all morning," Emma lied, blocking his view with her blanketed body. "And working out at the gym, I was just about to do some aerobics."

"Well, according to regulations, we're not supposed to be alone with ladies anyhow," said Poteet with a sad smile, scratching an ear, which, like its mate, was half a size too big for his head. "'Course, I hate regulations. That's why I left my partner downstairs. I'd rather this wasn't part of the official record, if you know what I mean. But if you feel uncomfortable about us talkin' by ourselves, I won't take it personal. We can go down to the lobby."

"How did you know I was here?"

"Mr. Anthony, the manager, told us. He's a bit concerned 'bout you. Says you're frightenin' his staff."

"Is there some law against overtipping or something?" said Emma, her eyes rolling with outrage. "I can't believe that jerk called the cops on me. Don't you guys have more important things to do?"

"Come on, Miz Passant," said Poteet in a gentle voice. "I thought we was friends. Besides, you're all wrong about this. We didn't even know you was here. One of the gals in the cocktail lounge has been off since Saturday night. We came over to get a statement and had to see Mr. Anthony when we came in. He happened to mention that you'd taken a room, that's all.''

"Oh.''

Poteet started to say something else, but fell silent as a stout lady in a tweed suit came out of a room two doors down. She walked purposefully to the elevator, glaring at them all along the way.

"My, my, but we must present a pretty picture,'' said Poteet when the closing elevator doors finally made her disappear. "You in your little blanket and me with my hat in my hand, old enough to be your daddy. You see the way that old plate of soup was lookin' at us? She's probably gonna holler for the house detective the minute she gets downstairs. Can't I come in, Miz Passant?''

"Oh, all right,'' said Emma. "But wait until I put something on.''

When she opened the door again, Emma was dressed in a sweater over black tights and a turtleneck. In less than four minutes she had somehow managed to pick up all the clothes and underwear that had littered the floor and stuff them into the closet. The bed had been made as neatly as she could manage.

"They sure fixed the room up real nice,'' Poteet said as he entered, looking around. "The last time I was here it was quite the sight, believe you me. So how you been?''

"Fine,'' said Emma, hardly about to admit the sorry state she had settled into.

"Glad to hear it. So. Mind tellin' me what you're up to?''

"I don't know what you mean,'' said Emma, plopping down on the edge of the bed.

"Come on, Miz Passant,'' the policeman said, lowering himself into the armchair, obviously happy to be off his feet. "Let's not start plain' games with each other at this stage of our relationship. Why you stayin' here at the Alhambra? In this particular room?''

"Person's got to stay somewhere.''

"Person's got a house in Potrero Hill."

"Not anymore."

Emma briefly told the detective what had happened at the house. When she finished, Poteet was as polite—and pointed—as ever.

"Why didn't you call me?" he asked.

"I didn't think you would believe the murderer had really gotten in and stolen Pépé's model boat. Do you?"

"It's surely an awful thing that's happened here, Miz Passant," said Poteet sadly, "what with your grandpa and Mr. Caraignac and all. It's no wonder you're feelin' scared. This sort of stuff scares everybody. Half the time I got the shakes myself."

"See? I knew you wouldn't believe me."

"I didn't say that, I just think you just should have called."

"Would you have done anything?"

"That's not the point."

"You want my house keys?" said Emma. "You can still go over now and dust for fingerprints."

"Well, thank you, Miz Passant, that's very kind of you, but I don't believe it will be necessary."

"The killer's fingerprints might be all over everything."

"But we don't know that the killer was really there, now do we?"

"Not unless I'm telling the truth."

"All right, Miz Passant," chuckled Poteet, shaking his head. "You know we gotta have more than a maybe-missing model boat and the word of a scaredy-cat before we're gonna go off dustin'. The city got a lot of expenses just now since 1928. Dust ain't cheap, you know."

Emma wanted to be mad at him, but couldn't. He looked so rumpled and earnest and sweet. He looked like the puppy her grandfather had gotten her when she was eight. "The scourge of the bedroom slippers," Pépé had called

"Have you found out anything more about Henri-

Pierre?'' Emma asked, trying to change the subject to her advantage. "Like what he was doing in San Francisco?"

"You come over here to play detective, didn't you?" said Poteet, pointing a pudgy finger at her and grinning. "You wanna be a what-ya-call-it. A sleuth."

"Of course not."

"Come on, Miz Passant. You're asking everybody in the hotel questions about dead Mr. Caraignac, and now you want me to tell you everything I know. Reveal all the secrets of the official police investigation. That about right?"

Emma grinned back at him and nodded.

"So will you tell me?"

"Depends on what's in it for me."

"What do you want?"

"Got anything to eat?" said the detective, eyeing the untouched hard roll on her room-service tray. "The wife's got me on this crazy diet. Says it's for my own good, but I'm surely gonna perish of hunger. I told the boys on the squad that if I expire they can probably get her for homicide."

"You want that roll?" Emma said, gesturing hopefully at the apparent object of Poteet's affections.

"Only if you have no plans for it."

"None," Emma said, relieved. She could hardly afford to let him raid the refrigerator. She needed that fudge-ripple ice cream for herself. All of it. "Want some jelly?"

"More than life itself." Poteet sighed. "'Course, I don't want to put you to any trouble. I'll be happy to get it."

Before the detective could make it even to the prepare-to-stand-up position in the armchair, Emma had returned with the roll on a plate and the packets of jams, jellies, and marmalades which she had been hoarding to dunk chocolates into.

"Are you really going to tell me about Mr. Caraignac?" she said, sitting back down on the bed as Poteet began ecorating his prize with condiments. "Or were you just easing me?

"Never tease a lady if you hope to live a long and happy life," said Poteet. "That's a lesson I've learned over the ears from hard human experience. I'll tell you everything know, Miz Passant. Be glad to. You're not just another esky sleuth, you know. You're an official interested party. Besides, you're giving me this tasty little bribe."

Emma didn't say anything.

Poteet opened his mouth, took a big bite, and made one f those "Mmmm mmmm!" noises that Southerners were lways heard emitting on television commercials for sauages. He then demolished the rest of the roll and spent ome time licking his fingers.

"We've confirmed that Mr. Caraignac had an antique hop in New York City," the detective said when he was nrough, his face reverberating with satisfaction. "There's o reason to think he wasn't here on business like he told ou. There was an auction at Butterfield and Butterfield he night have come for, and some other sales 'round the area. Or he could have been buying privately. You see how this ll strengthens the possibility of robbery as motive for what happened, don't you?"

"He bought a few chairs and somebody killed him for hem?" said Emma.

"No, but he probably had a lot of cash with him in nticipation of a purchase," said Poteet. "Anyway, that's ne way we figure. Antiques is a cash business, you know. According to his bank records, Mr. Caraignac often withdrew and deposited sizable cash sums and obviously worred about it. He was licensed to carry a firearm in New York City."

"He carried a gun?"

"In New York, yes. There's no evidence that he brought with him to San Francisco, though. He would have been a a hellish load of trouble if they caught him at the airport with a weapon in his luggage. I don't think he would have been so foolish as to try."

"What did he come here to buy?"

"Unfortunately we haven't found anyone who can answer that question; Caraignac worked and lived alone. wasn't married. It probably doesn't matter anyhow. What's important is that he must have been havin' trouble consummating his purchase. His reservation at the hotel was originally for three days, but he stayed here two weeks. flashing cash money around the hotel like crazy."

So she had been right about Henri-Pierre's extending his stay, Emma realized.

"Unfortunately," Poteet went on, "at the same time that Mr. Caraignac was letting everyone know what a big tipper he was, the man who mugged your grandpa—or the punk who found the gun when the first guy threw it away—was out looking for somebody else with money. And what better place to find such a party than a fancy hotel?"

"You still think that Henri-Pierre's murder with the same gun that killed my grandfather was just a coincidence?"

"We haven't found any evidence to the contrary," said Poteet. "Somebody here might have even tipped the killer off, some waiter or clerk tired of seeing up close how the other half lives. In any event, the man surprises Caraignac in his room, holds a gun to his head and demands to know where the cash is. Caraignac tells him. The scum shoots him anyway and takes the money, which is why we didn't find any in his room. End of story. Now, give me one more minute to digest my little snack here, and I'll be lettin' you get back to your exercise program."

"Don't you want to know what I've found out?"

"Oh, I know you ain't found out nothin', Miz Passant. Nothin' we don't know, at any rate."

"He was standing by that window over there when he was killed," said Emma.

"Like I said, nothin' that we don't already know."

"He took all his meals alone. He checked in with only one suitcase."

"We know that, too. Luggage is the bell captain's life. Caraignac even went out and bought himself a whole load of new clothes while he was here. We found the receipts in his effects. Shirts, suits, ties—plus a suitcase to take everything home in."

"Maybe it was about a piece of furniture," said Emma.

"What was?"

"The murders. Pépé moved pieces of furniture occasionally. Maybe he had picked up an expensive antique. Somebody shot him for it, and dumped his body in the park. Then the killer tried to sell it to Henri-Pierre, who got suspicious and the man killed him, too."

"That's pretty good," said Poteet. "Anyone ever tell you you got a good imagination?"

"What's that got to do with anything?" said Emma. "My theory makes just as much sense as yours."

"Only we haven't got any reports of any missing antiques, and your grandpa's body showed no signs of being moved."

"Maybe the piece was already stolen, so the owner couldn't report its disappearance. Maybe the killer took my grandfather to the park and shot him there.

"You know for a fact that your grandpa was hired to move any antiques lately?"

"He didn't tell me much about his work."

"You have evidence that Mr. Caraignac attempted to buy stolen property?"

"No, but I think this is a lead you should take seriously."

"Ever study geometry, Miz Passant?" said Poteet with grunt, rising to his feet.

"A little, I guess," said Emma. "Why?"

"My daughter all's growed up now, two kids of her own, but I used to help her with her lessons. I always liked that geometry stuff best. If you got one point, you got a point. If you got two points, you can connect them and you got a line. If you got three points, you got a plane.''

"Well, obviously you must have some point here, too,'' said Emma. "I just don't see it.''

"The point is, Miz Passant,'' said Poteet, "that a human bein' ain't a point or a line or a plane. A human being is a complex, multidimensional organism, and what happens to him is the result of all manner of events and circumstances. That's why we professionals take weeks and months collecting evidence before we even think about what it all means. And when we do go connectin' points, we pay attention to geometry and look for straight lines to do it with, not go to hypothetical antique furnitureville and back. It just doesn't work that way, I'm afraid. Now we've had a pleasant chat today, Miz Passant, and you know I'm your friend. I'm tellin' you as a friend that you're wasting your time here, messin' around in this business. Why don't you just try to forget what happened and get on with your life?''

"I can't. My grandfather was killed. I've got to do something.''

"Your name Po-lice Department?'' said Poteet, staring stern-faced from the door.

"Am I breaking any law?''

"It ain't against the law to try to make yourself feel better, Miz Passant. I understand, believe me, I do. This is a senseless thing, these deaths, and you're just tryin' to make them fit into some pattern. Human bein's love patterns. That's why they always makin' 'em. Makin' patterns is what you call art. Finding patterns, on the other hand, is what you call science. That's what we do, but we ain't finding any patterns here.''

"Maybe you're not looking in the right places.''

"We're lookin' where we need to look,'' said Poteet. "And we know what we're doing. You don't.''

"I'm not breaking any law, you said so yourself.''

"God damn a duck, woman, what do I got to say to get through to you?" snapped Poteet, showing anger for the first time. "How you think you're gonna feel sometime down the road when something you've said or done this week gets the case against your grandpa's killer thrown out of court? Or worse, what are you gonna say if you have the bad luck actually to stumble on the person or persons responsible for this situation? We are dealing with killin's here, you understand what I'm saying?"

"I hear you," whispered Emma.

"Thank you, Miz Passant," said the portly detective, recovering his composure and bowing slightly. "It's not like I don't appreciate your concern. I do. But you're gonna have to leave the detectin' 'round here to us. At least you're gonna have some money from your grandfather to help get you through all this. Quite a bit of money, understand."

"How do you know about that?"

Poteet already had the door open, but he turned and smiled his sad smile.

"You really think we wouldn't look into your grandfather's finances, Miz Passant? It's not every carpenter who leaves an estate of a million dollars. Some of the boys even think it gives you a motive for murder yourself."

"I don't care about money," gasped Emma. "I adored my grandfather. I'd give anything in the world to have him back."

"I know that, Miz Passant. I also know you been under a lot of stress. Like I say, the best thing you can do is just put all this behind you. Take a vacation or something, get away. You hear?"

"You mean I'm actually allowed to leave town?"

"You can afford to now, can't you?"

"ONE MARGARITA, and here's the glass of water you wanted," said the cocktail waitress, bending down and giving Emma a peek of cleavage.

The girl's tan, flattened breasts were a good three inches apart and covered with goose bumps. Her naked legs were protected by only a black spiderweb of stockings. According to the brushed copper nameplate on her shoulder strap, her name was Sheila.

"Thanks," said Emma. She had worn similar outfits herself working in restaurants and bars over the years, which was why she refused to do so onstage. "Do you have some pretzels or something?"

"You don't like the crûdités?"

Emma eyed the raw broccoli and vegetable dip on the table. In the dim light of the cocktail lounge they looked about as appealing as broccoli and vegetable dip.

"I've been eating a lot of sophisticated food lately. I think I need something more basic."

"I'll see what I can do." Sheila grinned and hustled off to a table in the corner, where two men in suits were waving empty glasses.

Emma was still a little shaken from her conversation with Benno Poteet, but she was hardly going to let that stop her from talking to Sheila. Sheila was the cocktail waitress who had been off since last week, the one whom the detective had been talking about. Emma knew because she had already spoken to all the other waitresses. She wasn't ready to give up trying to learn what had really happened to Pépé and Henri-Pierre Caraignac just because the San Francisco Police Department had run out of ideas.

The tanned waitress with the goose-bumped chest returned in a few minutes with a black enamel bowl far too elegant for its contents.

"Will you settle for corn chips?" she asked in a husky voice.

"Even better," said Emma, taking the proffered bowl. "Did you talk to those cops this afternoon?"

"Yeah. How did you know?"

"I was Mr. Caraignac's...friend," said Emma truthully, hoping the waitress would leap to the wrong conclusion.

"You poor kid," said Sheila, her eyes growing wide. "Hey, I'm really sorry about what happened."

"Thanks."

"My sister just had a baby and I went up to Petaluma to be with her. I didn't hear until I got back today. I couldn't believe it. I went to the bathroom and I cried. I just cried. He was such a nice man, Mr. Caraignac. I'm really sorry."

"Were you able to tell the police anything that would help them?"

"Not really. Hey, now I get it. You're that girl's been asking about him, huh? Ray Anthony the manager has been trying to shut everybody up."

"I don't want to get you in trouble," said Emma. "But it would mean a lot to me if you would tell me about Mr. Caraignac. Anything you can remember. Please?"

"Don't worry, honey," said Sheila. "I don't give a shit about Ray Anthony. I'm not one of his little robots."

Sheila looked to her right and left. The lounge wasn't busy and there were no other waitress within earshot.

"Mr. Caraignac came in here practically every night," she said, sitting down on the edge of the chair next to Emma. "Always around eight o'clock. He would nurse a Pernod for a while, then leave. That's this funny French drink, Pernod. We hardly ever serve it, so I noticed him right away. Actually how could you not notice him with those eyes and that face? Hey, look, I didn't mean that. Maybe I'd better go. You must've enough on your mind without me making cracks."

"No, please," said Emma, touching Sheila's arm, preventing her from getting up. "I want to know. Was he ever with anyone?"

"No. Always by himself, like I told the cops."

Somehow Henri-Pierre's eating and drinking alone for

the whole of his two-week stay in San Francisco just didn't jibe with the way he had come on to Emma last Friday.

"There were never any girls with him?"

"Look, honey, I can see why you would be worried," said Sheila, blinking her mascaraed eyes earnestly. "The man was gorgeous. But like I said, he was always in here by himself. Not that they didn't try. Plenty of ladies went over to strike up conversations. One of the girls who works here even asked him straight out for a date. But he just wasn't interested, you know? A few of us figured he was gay, which would have been such a waste. Look, like I said, I'm really sorry about what happened. Your drink's on the house."

"Thanks. That's very nice of you. Did he ever say anything about what he was doing in San Francisco? I guess the police asked you that."

"Yeah, but I couldn't help them. You mean you didn't even know he was here?"

"We had had sort of a misunderstanding."

"Gee, that's tough, kid."

"Anything he said to you, I'd like to know."

"Sure, I got ya. But the only thing we ever talked about—beyond the usual 'hi, how are you, what'll it be tonight?' kind of stuff—was France. I always kinda wanted to go to France when I was kid, so I asked him a few times what it was like, and he would talk in that sexy accent he had about the way the light looks different in Paris and how food smells and tastes better and how everybody sits around in cafés, drinking espresso and watching the world go by. He was always real nice, real patient-like. Maybe he came here because he needed to get away, think things over, you know? I have to do that with my boyfriend sometimes. It's not like Mr. Caraignac was out having a good time or anything, believe me."

"What do you mean?"

"Oh, you could tell he had a lot on his mind, the way he just sat there, not talking with anyone. He just nursed

e one drink and looked sad. Yeah, it makes sense that
ou two had a fight. That last night... No, forget it. Never
ind.''

"Please, Sheila. It's very important to me.''

"I just don't want to hurt your feelings or anything.''

"You won't. I promise.''

"All right. Maybe you'll be okay with it, I don't know.
didn't mean anything. Anyways, this past Saturday was
e last time I worked and the night when he...you know.
o, like I told you, Mr. Caraignac usually came in around
ght, but that night it was closer to six. He ordered his
sual Pernod, but he didn't drink any. He just sat there.
ut he didn't look so miserable anymore. He looked like
e had come to terms with something, you know? When
gave him his check, he signed for it like always. Then
e kissed me on the cheek and gave me a hundred-dollar
ill, like he knew he wouldn't be seeing me again.''

"Did you tell this to the police?''

"In a kind of shorter version, yeah. They didn't seem
think it was very important. Hey, maybe he had decided
go back to you, huh?''

"Yes, maybe,'' said Emma and took a long drink of her
argarita.

Or maybe he knew he was going to be killed.

"Look, I gotta go,'' said Sheila, getting up. Her other
ustomers were waving their empty glasses again.

"Thanks for talking to me, Sheila,'' said Emma. "I re-
ly appreciate it.''

"Well, like I said, we're all real sorry. You need any-
ing else?''

Emma thought a moment before answering.

She thought about her grandfather and San Francisco,
e city she loved so much and which held such sadness
r her now. She thought about how little she had been
le to learn about Henri-Pierre Caraignac, what a dead
d the Alhambra had been. She thought about dancing
d about magic and about what she would do for the rest

of her life. She thought about snow and about a missing model boat and about what Detective Poteet had said.

"Yes," Emma said finally. "I do need something else. I need a vacation. And I know just where I'm going to go to get it."

EIGHT

MMA STEPPED from the sweltering heat of the ancient
rbo prop airplane into the balmy sunshine of San Marcos
ity and descended the metal steps to the pitted concrete
nway.

Her first impulse was to fall on her knees and kiss the
ound. She managed to resist, however. Somehow she got
e feeling that the two soldiers who stood at either side
f the steps, with the black barrels of their submachine
ans pointed at the deplaning passengers, might not un-
erstand.

Emma had been in the air for eight out of the last thir-
en hours, flying from San Francisco to Saint Louis, Saint
ouis to Miami, Miami to Puerto Rico, and finally, Puerto
Ico to San Marcos.

The last leg of the flight had been the killer. Emma had
own in old planes before, had survived turbulence,
reeching children and poor ventilation. Maybe it was the
mbination of all the conditions which can make a flight
bearable that had gotten to her now—or perhaps just the
certainty she was flying into.

In any event, Emma was now ready to concede that it
ad been a mistake not to fly to New York and spend the
ght, then take the only jet service to San Marcos, as the
avel agent had recommended. Emma smelled of second-
and cigarette smoke and first-hand perspiration from the
es of her loafers to the end of her braid. And it would
robably be days before her knuckles returned to their
riginal color from their present shade of ghastly white.

But at least she was here. In the Caribbean. On San
Marcos island.

Emma's stay at the Alhambra had settled nothing, simply raised more questions. Why had Henri-Pierre extended his stay in San Francisco? Had he been killed by someone he knew and talked to his murderer moments before it happened? What had he been so unhappy about?

No matter what Charlemagne Moussy and Detective Poteet believed, Emma knew she was not crazy. Somebody had really taken the model boat from Pépé's bedroom. Was the *Kaito Spirit* the connection between Jacques Passant and Henri-Pierre? Was it the reason they had both been killed?

Whatever the answers, San Marcos was the best place to look for them. Let Benno Poteet worry about what Henri-Pierre had been doing in San Francisco—the police had better resources than she to look into his affairs. Emma was going to find the *Kaito Spirit*. The real one. Pépé had said in his will that it was her legacy. Maybe she could even find someone who had known her grandfather when he was here.

At least that had been her plan yesterday, and yesterday it had seemed entirely reasonable. Now Emma was not so sure. "An island in the Caribbean" was something quaint and manageable when you were sitting in the cocktail lounge of a hotel in San Francisco.

Looking out her window on the plane, however, Emma had realized that there was nothing quaint or manageable about San Marcos. It was an entire country. It was mountains and farmlands and endless miles of coastline. It was sprawling cities and tiny nameless towns. Finding one small boat here would be like looking for a needle in the proverbial haystack—a haystack that was more than thirty years gone. What was she going to do? Stop people on the streets and ask if they remembered a little Frenchman with apple-dumpling cheeks?

Emma looked around the airport runway for some kind of sign directing passengers where to go, but there was none. The sky was an unfamiliar blue and the soldiers cast no shadows in the stark tropical sunshine.

Everyone seemed to be heading for a temporary-looking white structure attached to the brick terminal building. Emma followed, passing through an aluminum screen door into a large space with a concrete floor. The walls there were of corrugated metal painted a dirty yellow. Half a dozen soldiers with submachine guns slung over their shoulders stood at strategic locations around the room, their eyes dark with suspicion, their lips curled tight with power.

Emma's fellow passengers seemed to be waiting for something. She tried asking in English what was going on, but the people who didn't stare blankly at her just rattled long Spanish explanations that she couldn't understand. More soldiers arrived, all dressed in the same olive combat fatigues, and all armed to the teeth.

Ten minutes passed, then twenty. Emma chewed a fingernail, cleaned her glasses, and tried again to find someone who spoke English. Finally a middle-aged man in a powder-blue suit answered in a familiar accent.

"American?" he said.

"Yes," said Emma, relieved despite the man's annoyed voice and sour expression. "Do you know what's going on here?"

"Don't worry. We're just waiting for the luggage. This is customs."

"That's what I was hoping, but I was beginning to think it was the firing squad."

"No, they don't do that much anymore. Not since Peguero died."

"Peguero?"

"Rafael Peguero, the dictator. They shot him a few years back. Things have gone pretty much downhill ever since. Peguero knew how to keep the riffraff in line. Now's just catch-as-catch-can."

"I'm Emma Passant," said Emma, sensing the man was losing interest.

"Pleasure," he replied, craning his neck to see what, if any, progress was being made at what Emma now recognized as customs stations.

Men in black pants, white shirts, and ties had taken position behind caged-in tables. Passengers were forming disorderly lines. Just as on the plane, half the people in the room seemed to be chain-smoking cigarettes. Hadn't they heard down here that smoking was bad for one's health? Especially where there was jet fuel around? Maintenance people were even smoking out on the runways. The man in the powder-blue suit started to move away.

"Are you staying at the Casimente, by any chance?" said Emma, not wanting to lose her surly friend so quickly. Like all travelers in strange places, she was dependent upon the kindness of strangers. Maybe the man wasn't the most pleasant person she had ever met, but at least he seemed to know the territory.

"My company's got its own place," he said, taking a pack of Marlboros out of his shirt pocket and lighting up without offering her one. "That where you are? The Casimente?"

"Yes. The travel agent said it was the only good hotel in the city."

"Casimente's nice—if you like a place without a casino. Has its own purification system, which you need down here unless you plan to boil the water before you brush your teeth. You'll be fine."

The door to the runway opened and several rickety carts full of luggage were wheeled in. There was a mad dash of passengers in which Emma lost sight of her new friend but managed to retrieve her two suitcases. She was trying to figure out which line she was supposed to stand in when the American man returned, carrying one small bag.

"Hey, look, I don't want you to get the wrong idea," he said in a vaguely conciliatory tone, taking a deep drag of his cigarette and tapping a bit of ash onto the floor. "San Marcos actually isn't all that bad. The people are friendly and don't hate Americans as much as they do most places. The women are great. And things are cheap. You know about the money?"

"What about it?"

"The official exchange rate's bullshit, so there's a big black market in dollars. There'll be a bunch of locals when you get out, trying to buy your U.S. money. Don't change more than enough to get to your hotel. You'll get a better rate in the city. I have to go through the other line. Good luck."

"Thanks," said Emma weakly and watched her anonymous friend rush across the room to a station at the side that seemed to be reserved for business people. Disoriented, she tried to follow after a moment, but a thin man in khaki directed her back to the more crowded area.

The noisy room was beginning to feel unreal, dreamlike. Emma's nervousness gave way to a strange detachment. After another fifteen minutes she had reached the head of the customs line. In front of her one of the customs officers was inspecting the luggage of the passenger ahead of her, though "inspecting" was probably too kind a word for what the process looked like.

The passenger was a forty-something fellow with a bad complexion and an odd-looking white-on-white shirt that ended in a straight edge outside his pants. As he looked on with a worried expression, the inspector rummaged thoroughly through the contents of his badly packed suitcase, removing several toilet articles and some magazines. Then they ordered him to empty his pockets and began leafing through his wallet. When the passenger started to complain, a young soldier standing on the side—he couldn't have been more than twenty—snarled something in Spanish and threw the man's suitcase on the floor. Then he pocketed the wallet, shouting all the while at the man as he picked up his belongings. So much for the friendly people of San Marcos.

The passenger skulked away in silence under the angry eyes of the young soldier, who then turned to Emma and waved her to the table impatiently.

Emma's hand involuntary patted the pocket of her jeans where Pépé's little gold coin was cached along with two pieces of Kleenex and her car keys. She had brought the coin with her for luck, but for all she knew it might get her arrested now for smuggling.

Feeling like a sleepwalker, Emma stepped forward. She handed the inspector the declaration she had filled out on the plane and her passport. Then she opened her bags on the table as she had seen the others do and watched helplessly while the man pawed through her things like someone searching a kitchen drawer for a can opener. It all felt as if it were happening to someone else.

Finally it was over. No one had asked her to empty her pockets, though the inspector had removed the neat little soaps and bottles of lotions wrapped in green paper which she had taken from the Alhambra, plus all her paperback books. Perhaps historical novels and biographies of Irving Berlin were considered subversive in these parts.

One of the soldiers pushed the suitcases back at her and waved his hands impatiently. Emma closed her bags with as much dignity as she could manage as the inspector stamped her passport. Then she followed the other passengers through a door at the end of the long room.

Suddenly the picture changed. Instead of the claustrophobic, hostile space of the customs area, Emma now found herself in a spacious terminal teeming with people. The building reminded her of train stations from 1940s movies: old brick walls, yellow-green floors, departure and arrival boards with flights listed in plastic letters. Old-fashioned and vaguely threadbare, everything seemed clean, though the noise reflecting off the hard surfaces was deafening.

Instantly a dozen men descended upon her, jabbering in Spanish, grabbing at her suitcases. Luckily Emma was too surprised to scream. She quickly realized that her assailants were self-appointed porters, hoping to carry her bag for a tip. Breathing a sigh of relief, and carrying her own bags, she let herself be swept along by the flow of traffic, past several more armed soldiers and out the front doors of the terminal.

Suddenly the scene changed again. If there was any doubt she was in a foreign land, it vanished the moment Emma got through the door. She found herself facing a stand of palm trees on an impossibly crowded sidewalk surrounded by a crowd of men shouting at the top of their lungs. They seemed to have swooped down from nowhere, all of them waving thick wads of money and pocket calculators.

"*Dos diez!*"

"*Due quince! Dos quince!*"

"*Dos dieciocho! Dieciocho!*"

It took Emma a few moments to understand that the numbers were exchange rates—the number of pesos the men would give for a U.S. dollar.

The money changers were young for the most part and dark-complected. Many were dressed in white shirts like the one the passenger who had suffered ahead of her in customs had worn—with double-pointed collars and straight bottoms worn outside their pants. They shouted and waved their hands frenetically, but somehow didn't seem nearly as threatening as the soldiers inside had been.

"*Dos dieciocho!* Two eighteen!"

"Two two!"

"Best price! Best price for dollars!"

Most of the passengers were ignoring the money changers and trying to press their way to the curb, but a few had stopped to make deals, bargaining in Spanish. Emma was suddenly grateful to the surly American. If he hadn't warned her, she wouldn't have known what to make of this. The last thing on her mind when she had decided to come to San Marcos was the subject of foreign exchange.

Emma let herself be cornered by two money changers and put down one suitcase long enough to dig into the pocket of her blazer for her wallet. She had worn the jacket for its pockets and expected to have to buy some lighter clothes while she was here—her wardrobe was geared for the temperate climate of San Francisco. Now she wondered if it would be necessary. It was nearly noon, but the temperature was only in the mid-seventies, with little humidity. Plenty of people in the airport were dressed in slacks and cotton shirts, though almost all the women wore actual dresses, making Emma feel out of place in her blue jeans. Already she had gotten more than one disapproving stare.

The money changers hollered rates at her. Emma pulled a twenty-dollar bill from her wallet, then another. How much would it cost to get from the airport to her hotel in a cab? She settled on fifty dollars—better safe than sorry—and waited while the two men in front of her argued with one another in Spanish before apparently coming to some sort of pool arrangement to deal with her.

"*Dos veinticinco,*" one of them declared finally, shaking his thick roll of bills at her. "Two two-five."

"Two and a half," said Emma, having watched some other exchanges and seen how it was done. "Two five."

"We give you two three. No more."

"Two five."

"Two three."

"Two four-five."

The men looked at one another, shrugged and started to walk away.

"Okay, two three," said Emma.

In a moment Emma had a colorful stack of San Marcan pesos in her hand—a hundred and fifteen of them for her fifty dollars—and directions to the ramp where the taxis were parked.

Instead of familiar yellow cabs, the "taxis" she found

were all regular unmarked private cars, most of them of about the same vintage and condition as her own Nissan back home. A few drivers rushed over to solicit her business; the others stood around chatting with one another or simply leaned on their vehicles reading newspapers.

Emma chose a driver who was polishing the hood of a fairly clean, European-looking car. She didn't recognize the little vehicle's make but from its styling judged it to be at least fifteen years old—practically new compared to its neighbors.

"The Hotel Casimente," Emma said in answer to the man's lengthy Spanish greeting after she got in. He replied with another incomprehensible diatribe, shook her hand repeatedly, then started his engine, which purred like a cement mixer.

In a minute they were away from the airport and onto a modern four-lane highway. On one side of the road was an esplanade overlooking the ocean, which stretched out forever to meet the deep-blue sky. Tall, stately palm trees spaced fifteen feet apart framed the road on both sides as far as the eye could see. The bases of all the trees were painted white—perhaps to reflect oncoming headlights. Looking down the coast, Emma could see the jewel-like white buildings of a city gleaming in the distance.

"This is beautiful," said Emma, the unreal feeling she had had since getting off the plane beginning to lift. She was really here in San Marcos, where Jacques Passant must have been more than thirty years ago when he had sailed on the *Kaito Spirit*. She was following Pépé back in time.

"Peguero, he build the road," said the driver full of smiles, watching her in his rearview mirror instead of watching the road. "Take twenty years. Mucho dollars."

"Is it like this all the way to the city? With the palm trees?"

"Sí. Palm trees. And monuments."

Emma looked out her window in the direction of the

driver's gesticulations. A sandstone obelisk, surrounded by chained pillars and statues of dolphins, rose on the ocean side of the road, adding to the island's exotic strangeness.

"There are others like this? Monuments?"

"Many others. Many, many. Peguero, he build. Make good impression on foreigners."

"It certainly does," said Emma, the claustrophobia of the plane and customs fading against the clean beauty of the highway. The road was constructed so that nothing could be seen of the island and its people, save for picture-postcard views. There were no road signs and not a trace of litter.

As she looked more carefully, however, Emma could see that perhaps all was not as idyllic as the view suggested. There were many cracks in the concrete where clumps of grass had sprung up, as if the road had not been resurfaced in years. Military vehicles—jeeps and the kind of olive-colored trucks used to transport troops—were parked every few miles. There was strangely little traffic. What there was consisted mostly of elderly vehicles like the one she was in.

After twenty minutes Emma knew they must be close to the city, but still she could see nothing from the road except palm trees, monuments, and the beautiful blue sea. The highway was beginning to show even more signs of age here. Potholes and overgrown patches of grass were everywhere. Telephone wires began to be visible to landside, spoiling the perfection of the view.

The highway abruptly turned a corner and rose above its protecting embankment. Suddenly Emma was in the center of a bustling city. Squat, dilapidated buildings with colorful signs in Spanish rose on either side of the street, which had become narrow and crowded. Dogs barked. Horns blared. People were everywhere.

After the spacious highway, San Marcos City was a shock—a raggedy collection of buildings of every shape and size jumbled together without rhyme or reason. It was

if the downtowns of a dozen old rust-belt cities had
ddenly been crammed together and packed with a hun-
ed times more people than they had ever been designed
hold.

Now Emma understood. The highway had been just a
ctator's illusion for the outside world to remember when
ey thought of his country. This was the real San Marcos.
e garish facades and dirty windows of buildings
ueezed together like shoes in a crowded closet. The din
traffic and smell of livestock and rotting garbage. The
dewalks of the city were jammed with men and women,
oppers and hustlers, street children and beggars, though
ne of the faces seemed to have the anger and hopeless-
ss she was used to seeing in the downtowns of America.
Had Pépé walked these streets, known these people? Or
d he not been in this city at all, but somewhere else on
e island, miles away?

"How many people are there here?" Emma asked, lean-
g forward, speaking slowly.

"One and half million," said the driver proudly.

"That's the whole country, right?"

"San Marcos City one and half million. San Marcos,
ur million."

"Four million!" exclaimed Emma. The haystack was
en bigger than she had imagined.

"Almost as many people as Haiti," said the driver,
iling from ear to ear.

It took another ten minutes for the cab to get through
e bustling streets. At practically every traffic light ped-
ers descended upon the car, pushing handfuls of unfa-
liar-looking fruits through the window. The streets ech-
d with the noise of horns, merengues from blaring
dios, and the cries of vendors—*"Tengo plátanos!"* *"To-
ites!"* *"Cebollas!"* *"Lechuga!"*

Finally they came to a wealthier-looking residential
ea, with fewer people on the streets and large stucco
uses behind tall walls. Beyond this was a newer area of

town. There were fewer, more modern-looking structure here. The wide four-lane streets had center meridian planted with young palm trees only a few feet in heigh Almost immediately the driver pulled the car up to th gates of a large complex of modern brick buildings tha looked like apartments.

Even from the driveway, Emma could see that th sprawling structure was unlike anything she had seen i the rest of the city. Space suddenly wasn't at a premiun The hotel was surrounded by a large grassy area plante with shrubs and flowers. Everything inside the gates wa uncluttered and clean. It was almost as if the whole con plex had been plucked up and transplanted from som other country altogether.

The driver exchanged some words with one of th guards at the gate—a burly, dark-faced man in green pan and a sport shirt, who wore a holstered revolver on h belt. Another guard finally lifted the barrier.

Emma's driver steered slowly through the spaciou parking lot to the front door of the hotel, chattering happil in Spanish. As they got closer, Emma could see the hug clean, modern hotel. It looked something like a tropic version of the Grand Marquis in Phoenix, where she ha played her last magic show—all peach-colored with slan ing terra-cotta-tiled roofs and a jungle of professionall landscaped tropical foliage.

"Magnífico! Increible!" said the driver, stopping the ca at the door of the hotel and beaming with pride—as if h were somehow part of this San Marcos and not the Sa Marcos outside the gate. "Fifty pesos."

Emma had no idea whether the rate was fair or the ma was doubling his usual fare based on her destination. Sh was just glad to be here, and ready to hit the showers. Sh handed the man three twenty-peso notes, and waved awa the change with a smile—a smile which the driver returne several-fold as he drove away. A porter rushed out to tak

er luggage. Emma followed him through the double front
oors, which opened automatically.

She found herself in a cool, spacious lobby that rose to
peaked roof slatted with mahogany and punctuated with
azily spinning fans. Palm trees and other foliage were
laced strategically between the tall white columns that
upported the ceiling. Open archways led to covered court-
ards on either side, giving the effect of bringing the out-
oors in. The furniture was rattan, covered with rich, pat-
erned fabrics. The stucco walls were clean and pink. The
oor, where it was not thickly carpeted, was terra-cotta-
led.

"Welcome to the Casimente, Miss Passant," said the
esk clerk, taking an imprint of Emma's credit card and
ummoning a porter to take her to her two-hundred-fifty-
ollars-per-night room (so much for things in San Marcos
eing so cheap, as the American at the airport had said).

In a few minutes Emma was in her room, a simple space
vith rattan chairs, two double beds covered with light-
veight chintz spreads, and windows that overlooked land-
caped grounds and the limitless ocean. Apparently the
ecorator belonged to the Peguero school of design—noth-
ag of the dirty, noisy, bustling city was visible at all.

"There is an ice machine at the end of the hall," said
ae porter in perfect English, setting down her bags.
'Room service is available until eleven o'clock p.m."

"Thank you," said Emma, worried that she was begin-
ing to like luxury hotels. "Do you happen to know of
ny areas around here where pleasure boats might be
aoored?"

"Pleasure boats?" said the man, a slight fellow with a
ice smile. "I know that the *Queen of the Pacific* docks
t Puerta Lavaya. My cousin, he works for the cruise line."

"No, not like that. Cabin cruisers, I guess you would
all them."

"Cabin cruisers? What are, please?"

Emma tried to picture the model boat that had always

sat on Pépé's dresser, but it was just a blur in her mind.
A whitewashed hull. A wood cabin and deck. It had been
just an old-fashioned cabin cruiser. A pleasure boat. Or
had it been used for fishing? Or as a passenger ferry? Pépé
had rarely talked about the old days, just said he had been
a sailor, had been all over the world. That had been the
truth, hadn't it? The *Kaito Spirit* wasn't just some garbage
scow he had done the cooking on, was it?

"Never mind," said Emma. "It's not important."

"Will there be anything else?"

"No," said Emma, fumbling in her pocket for some
pesos. The man took them and exited, murmuring thanks.

"Do you happen to know where pleasure boats might
be moored?" Emma repeated in a mocking tone. "Potee
was right. I'm an idiot."

Emma sat down on the edge of the bed and stared out
the window at the ocean. Four million people. Who would
remember a boat that may—or may not—have been here
thirty years ago? Or her grandfather?

For a moment Emma couldn't even remember his face
herself. When his red cheeks and twinkling eyes and kind
smile finally winked into her mind, her eyes brimmed with
tears and she felt more alone than she ever had in her life.

NINE

AFTER A LONG, HOT SHOWER, Emma came downstairs dressed in clean white shorts and a light linen jacket over a cotton blouse. She felt a lot better, though she had to keep looking at her watch to understand what time it was. The long flight and time changes had left her confused, and now she regretted having napped so much on the plane. It would probably take days to get her internal clock back to normal.

One of Emma's mottoes had always been, "When in doubt, eat something," so she headed to the hotel's open-courtyard restaurant and ordered a fruit salad. Half the fruits were unrecognizable, but all were delicious. Around her the other guests conversed in English and French and German. The service was crisp and professional. Palm trees swayed in the breeze.

After lunch Emma wandered through the quiet lobby to the other side of the hotel, where dozens of hotel guests lay stretched out on deck chairs, absorbing sunshine and tropical drinks around one of the largest swimming pools Emma had ever seen in her life.

Though the ocean was just a few landscaped yards away from the pool area, there was no beach, nor any way to get down to the water. The pool was surrounded by a tall wall. Another, even taller and more solid-looking wall framed the edge of the hotel grounds, closing off any view of the city and preventing anyone from outside looking in. From what the happy swimmers splashing in the pool could see, there was no way to tell whether they were in San Marcos or Timbuktu. The deck chairs at poolside were all angled to give a view of the large, thatched-roof hut housing the bar.

Emma walked back to the lobby, amazed that people would come thousands of miles to sit by a walled-in swimming pool and drink fruit juice and vodka. That was certainly not for her—even if she were just here for pleasure, which she wasn't. She was here to find the *Kaito Spirit*. It was time to get started.

"I'd like to change two hundred dollars in traveler's checks for pesos," said Emma to the woman at the cashier's window at the desk. The pesos she had changed at the airport were running low and she'd need more. Emma planned to put everything she could on credit cards, but there were bound to be cash expenses.

"Please sign your checks," said the clerk, looking up from her paperwork. She was an attractive young girl with dark-blond hair and a deep tan. "Will twenties be all right?"

"Yes, that's fine," said Emma, signing the checks. The clerk counted out ten twenty-peso notes and went back to the forms she was filling out.

"That's only two hundred pesos," said Emma when it became clear that the transaction was over.

"Yes, that's correct," said the girl.

"But that's one dollar to one peso."

"Yes, the exchange rate is set by the government at one dollar to one peso."

"But you can get more than two to one from the money changers at the airport."

"That would be illegal," said the girl with a blank smile.

"My room is two hundred fifty dollars a night," said Emma, who was finding the subject of foreign exchange more interesting all of a sudden. "How much is it in pesos?"

"The same. Two hundred fifty pesos. The official exchange rate is set by the government at one to one."

Emma wasn't brilliant at math, but it didn't take a genius to see that it would make more sense for her to buy pesos from the money changers with her dollars and pay for everything in cash. Even if Pépé's million dollars turned out to be real, it was still no reason for her to start throwing money away.

"Can I take the money from those traveler's checks in dollars instead of pesos?"

The girl nodded and retrieved the pesos she had laid down on the table for Emma. Then she reached into another drawer and counted out greenbacks.

"I'll need to cash a check, too," said Emma, opening her checkbook, which she had brought downstairs with her along with her passport and traveler's checks, intending to put them all into the hotel safe. She certainly hadn't brought enough cash to pay for her entire stay.

"I'm sorry, but we don't cash personal checks," said the girl, the same blank expression on her face.

"Who does?"

The girl shrugged.

"Is there an American Express office in the city?" said Emma, remembering vaguely that her credit card gave her check-cashing privileges.

"I believe so."

"Can you give me directions?" This was like pulling teeth.

"You go out the front door, turn left and go the end of the block, then turn right, and it's on the left side of the road after the first traffic light."

Emma thanked the girl and walked out the front door. She crossed the hotel's long parking lot, nodded to the armed guards at the gate and found herself on the wide street.

Battered cars packed with San Marcans honked and sped by. The air felt strangely quiet and smelled of unfamiliar scents. A number of cars were parked down the street to her right. Next to them men milled about under trees, smoking cigarettes. When they saw her, they stopped talking and stared eagerly at her.

"Give you tour, lady?" shouted one. "Show you San Marcos?"

"Change money?" shouted another.

Emma shook her head and walked in the opposite direction, as the clerk had directed. Out of the oasis of the hotel and on the street, she was vulnerable, helpless, alone. Emma had felt that way many times before, however—every time she had walked out onstage in fact. It had never stopped her. It wouldn't now.

More battered cars crammed with passengers and painted with advertisements honked at her as they passed, slowing down, apparently looking to pick her up. Emma walked briskly to the corner, her chin down, her eyes straight ahead. Were tourists in this country in danger of being snatched off the streets?

Another quick glance at the cars and their passengers suggested not. The tired-looking men and dull-eyed women bore all the signs of commuters. The cars must be a kind of entrepreneurial bus service, Emma realized. She had seen no evidence of public transportation since she had arrived.

Feeling more and more like an ignorant foreigner—she was the only person on the streets in shorts—Emma crossed the street and turned right onto another four-laned road, then proceeded past low office buildings and walled properties to the next traffic light. As the clerk had promised, there, in front of a three-story brick structure, was a sign that said "American Express."

Emma went in and found herself in what looked like an airport waiting room: anonymous, fluorescent-lit, crowded. Uniformed armed guards were stationed at strategic points around the room. One long line of people leading to a pair of cashier's windows snaked through the room.

Emma took her place behind a short, prim young woman who was wearing a dowdy-looking white dress and a red ribbon in her dark-brown hair—the few women in slacks and shorts looked like tourists.

"Hi," said Emma automatically in response to the girl's shy smile.

"Hello," she replied in English and in a moment they were talking.

Celia Eschiverra, it turned out, had gone to college in New Jersey and returned to her native San Marcos to teach English at a local private school. She was a serious girl, exceedingly polite, and seemed surprised that Emma would show any interest in her. For her part Emma was so relieved to have someone to talk to that she was practically ecstatic.

"Yes, it is much better to pay for your hotel in pesos," Celia said when Emma brought up the subject of money. "Only the most naive or frightened tourists do not take advantage of the black market. Or those who are so rich they do not care. You cannot help but notice the money changers. They are everywhere with their loud, unattractive yelling. It is very embarrassing."

"But isn't it illegal?"

"Oh, yes. The authorities try to crack down occasionally, but it is not practical. There are just too many money changers and too much profit to be made."

"Why doesn't the government just set a more reasonable exchange rate? That would put them out of business, wouldn't it?"

Celia smiled.

"What the money changers take from the economy is merely a trickle. The government is playing a larger game. Pesos have even less value outside of San Marcos, you see. By setting the official exchange rate at one to one, the government can force big foreign companies to accept pesos for what they sell here; for what they buy, they must pay in dollars."

"I see," said Emma. Suddenly the whole situation began to make sense. "It's still a little frightening, having to deal with men on the street for your banking—especially if you have large sums to exchange."

"Oh, the street-corner money changers are not dangerous," said Celia. "They are out in the open. Most are just trying to earn some extra money for their families. But if you are nervous, you should go to the cambio."

"The cambio?"

"It is like a bank—they exchange money at posted rates, which are usually as good or better than you can get from the money changers on the street. The cambios are licensed and taxed by the government. There is one on the next block from here."

"But why didn't they tell me about this at the hotel?"

"I think perhaps the hotels do not mind to be paid in dollars instead of pesos, yes?"

Celia waited for another question with an eager, expectant smile. The line had moved too quickly. They were now practically at the cashier's windows.

"I'm going to be here in San Marcos for a little while," said Emma, "and I'd like to learn more about your country. May I take you to lunch? I'd love to ask you some more questions."

"I am very sorry," said Celia with obvious disappointment. "I am leaving tomorrow for the United States. I am taking a month-long class in educational science at my old college in New Jersey. That is why I am here today—I am arranging details of my tuition payment. Then I must spend the afternoon with paperwork at my school here."

"Well, I'm sure you'll have a good time in the States," said Emma, disappointed too.

They stood in silence for a moment. Then Emma spoke again.

"Look," she said, "I know you probably have a lot of packing to do, but maybe we could get together for dinner tonight. My treat."

"That is very kind of you. I would be honored, but I

would not wish you to go to any trouble or expense because of me.''

''No trouble—I'm glad to have someone to talk to. And I'm sure there's a restaurant at the hotel I'm staying at. Do you know the Casimente?''

''Oh, yes. The restaurant there is the best in San Marcos City, but it is very expensive. I could not accept such generosity.''

''Don't be silly. Do you know how much money you've just saved me? I'm the one who's in your debt.''

By the time they had concluded their business at the cashier's window, Emma had arranged to meet Celia in the hotel lobby at seven-thirty. She said good-bye and walked to the small brick building across the street where Celia had told her to go. The sign outside read CAMBIO.

Inside, two clerks dispensed money from behind barred windows under the watchful gaze of three boys who looked about fourteen years old. All cradled submachine guns in their arms.

The line here was short and consisted entirely of men who looked like money changers themselves and probably were. No wonder there were so many of them, thought Emma, realizing how easy it would be to make a profit off ignorant tourists.

It took only a few minutes for Emma to exchange the money she had cashed at American Express at a better rate than anything she could have gotten on the street. Paid in pesos, her hotel room would now cost less than ninety dollars per night.

Emma walked back to the hotel, feeling better for having made a friend and nervous for having so much cash in her pocket. She didn't relax until most of the cash was locked in the hotel safe, along with her passport, her checkbook and the rest of the traveler's checks.

It was now a little after three o'clock, still time to orient herself in San Marcos City. Emma got a map of the city from a rack by the door and brochures for the area's few tourist attractions, sat down in one of the rattan lobby arm-chairs, and began leafing through the pictures.

The largest and most impressive brochure was for Las Calvos, some kind of exclusive resort area in another part of the island. Rich people from all over the world apparently came here to play golf and tennis, stay in luxury bungalows and dance the nights away in tropically decorated discothèques. It all looked very expensive and very boring.

In San Marcos City there were an old Spanish fort, government buildings, and the botanical gardens to see. Several hotels featured their own casinos and nightclubs. Apparently a bus left the hotel twice a day and shuttled between tourist attractions. The afternoon bus had left half an hour ago and the next one wouldn't be until eleven o'clock tomorrow morning. Emma could buy a ticket now if she wanted to see the island from the safety of a crowd.

"Is there anything within walking distance of the hotel?" Emma asked a desk clerk, a small man with greased black hair.

"If you go out the door and turn right, there is the nicest part of town where there are many restaurants. In the other direction there is not much but offices."

"Except for the cambio and American Express."

"If you are interested in changing money," said the clerk, leaning forward and lowering his voice, "I have a cousin who can get you a better rate than the cambio."

"Maybe some other time," said Emma, feeling a little less green, a little more confident.

Outside at the hotel gates, Emma turned to the right and walked toward the group of money changers she had seen before. The hotel guards apparently made the men keep their distance from the hotel gate, but all bets were off where the property line ended. The money changers convened around her, chattering their rates, shaking fistfuls of pesos at her, tapping their calculators.

"*Dos cuarenta!* Two point four!"

"Tours of the city! Best tours of the city!"

"Better tours! Cheaper!"

Emma suddenly felt horribly vulnerable again, but she somehow manufactured a smile and shook her head. Most of the men seemed to take the rejection in good spirits, though a few stared after her with unsettling leers, laughing among themselves.

Emma kept walking briskly and didn't look back. She had done a lot of traveling alone and was used to the stares, the catcalls, the unwanted attentions. Long ago she had decided that she was never going to be a prisoner of fears, whether hers or anyone else's. Most situations that arose could be solved with the right attitude and some common sense. And, bum knee notwithstanding, she could still deliver one hell of a kick if she had to.

After a few blocks of large walled mansions with soldiers posted outside—embassies, perhaps, or the homes of high government officials—the street narrowed, and Emma found herself in a pleasant residential neighborhood.

The houses here were smaller and had the same baked-in-the-sun-for-too-long appearance that most of the buildings in the city seemed to have. The architecture was vaguely Spanish. Each house had a wall around it, just as the mansions up the street had had, but here the numerous trees, the parked cars, driveways and sidewalks made it seem rather like a nice old suburb of practically any city in America.

Emma came to a few restaurants, also walled, with colorful signs hung out front. Each had the same slightly seedy look, though according to the prices posted on the menus, none of them was cheap. All took every credit card known to man, Emma noticed ruefully. Tourists who charged their meals on a credit card would get the official exchange rate and thus pay more than twice what their meals would cost in pesos.

After a few more blocks the neighborhood changed abruptly again. The walled houses gave way to dilapidated

storefronts. The trees vanished. Crowds of people, poorly
dressed, jammed the narrow streets, traffic thickened and
slowed to a crawl. The area seemed even poorer than the
ones she had driven through on the way from the airport.
Apparently the nice part of town was not very big.

A group of young men standing on a corner against a
wall spray-painted with Spanish slogans spotted her and
called out, laughing, passing a brown bottle between them.

Obviously this was not where she belonged. Emma
turned around and headed back toward the hotel. In half
an hour she had covered only a few blocks. It was clear
that she'd never find out much about the island on foot.
What she needed was a guide and a driver, someone who
knew the island and spoke the language, someone who
could keep her from getting into trouble.

A dozen of potential candidates were still waiting like
a pack of wolves just outside the hotel property line when
she returned. They started shouting their pitches again as
they saw her coming.

"See the island. Take you everywhere."

"My car! My car!"

"Sell dollars? Two point four. Two point four."

Emma tried to look them over as she approached. Like
many men on this subtropical island, they all wore dark
pants. Most also sported enormous smiles and clean white
shirts, which somehow made them look even more menacing.

Emma's heart sank. How could she just get into some
stranger's car? These guys might be the salt of the earth
for all she knew, but any one of them could just as easily
drive her to a secluded spot and rape and/or kill her. But
how was she going to find what she had come here to find
from a tour bus?

Emma barely noticed the little hand slipping into her
own, but the next moment she was being pulled toward a
battered gray car at the curb by a black kid about ten years
old.

"You come with me, lady. My uncle got car, we give you greatest tour of the island. You see everything, come on."

The boy tugged at her hand insistently. At the curb, a small man with Caucasian features but the characteristic dark San Marcan complexion got out of the gray car—an ancient Ford—nodding happily and opening the back door.

Several of the other tour operators ran after Emma and the boy, complaining loudly in Spanish, but the boy shouted back in the same language what obviously were curses. A few men laughed in surprise at the boy's nerve, the others continued to shout. He hurled more curses and pulled Emma closer to the car.

"Don't pay no attention to those guys," the boy said to Emma with a look of contempt. "They are the dirt under your feet. Animals. They would cut your throat for five pesos. You cannot trust them."

"I can trust you?"

"Sure, I'm okay. My uncle got good car, we take care of you. Give you excellent tour."

The other men threw a few insults of their own and backed away, except for one gigantic hairy fellow, who strode right up to the boy and growled in low, threatening Spanish. The boy listened to him for a few seconds, then yawned and spit on the ground.

Well, not exactly spit. It was more like controlled stream of drool, which apparently was even more effective. The hairy brute bellowed like an enraged bull and looked as if he would have started swinging if two comrades hadn't restrained him.

The boy barely flinched. He said something else in guttural Spanish (which further enraged the man) and spit/drooled on the ground again. Then slowly, deliberately, he turned to Emma.

"You don't have to worry about him. He is not a man at all, he is a worm. He is full of shit. I tell him to crawl back into his hole. I'm Timoteo. You come with me, okay? What's your name?''

"Emma."

"Emma, that's a good name. You come with us, Emma. You come with Timoteo. We give you good tour of the island. You have fine day."

The hairy competitor shouted some final curses at the boy and let his friends usher him away. Timoteo pulled Emma toward the car again. The driver—the man the boy had said was his uncle—nodded happily and gestured to the back seat.

"Wait a second," said Emma, having second thoughts. And third. "How much is this little tour of yours going to cost?"

"Fifty dollars," said Timoteo.

"How about fifty pesos?"

Timoteo went over to his uncle and began chattering animatedly. The man finally shrugged.

"Okay," said Timoteo, returning. "He accepts."

Emma was still telling herself all the reasons why she would have to be crazy to go off with this boy as she let herself be pulled into the back seat. The time had come to make a decision. If she hoped to find the *Kaito Spirit* and her grandfather's killer, she would have to trust someone. Whom better than this boy? What other choice did she have?

"This my uncle, Changee Money," said Timoteo, breaking into a big smile as he shut the car door. "He change your money, that's why they call him that."

"Changee money?" said Uncle Changee Money, taking an immense wad of pesos from his pocket. His huge smile revealed teeth that looked as if they had been filed down—or perhaps they just came to sharp points naturally.

"You are very good-looking lady, Emma," said Timoteo with an innocent smile. "I am glad you come with us. No good-looking lady ever come with us before. They all afraid Changee Money kill them."

"What have I gotten myself into?" muttered Emma, as Changee Money started the car. With a sound like that of a dishwasher digesting a place setting of silverware, they screeched away from the curb.

TEN

WHAT SHE HAD GOTTEN herself into, Emma discovered to her great relief, was simply a tour of the island.

For the next two hours, Timoteo and Changee Money drove her through the crowded streets of San Marcos City, pointing out the local attractions: memorials to the late dictator, fountains and churches, natural rock formations, an enormous outdoor market complete with plantains piled to eye level and pens full of live turkeys.

Only once did they find themselves in an area obviously not on the standard tourist route, a street of what could only be called shacks, gray hulks of rotting timbers built directly on the dirt. Each shack was no more than ten feet square and was built only inches from its neighbor. Emma assumed they were some kind of deserted storage facilities until she saw a woman with a baby in her lap sitting in the doorway of one of them. As they passed, the woman looked up and made eye contact with Emma. There was no anger in her gaze, no hatred, no despair—which was somehow even more disturbing. There was nothing at all.

"People live here?" Emma exclaimed.

"They're nobody," sneered Timoteo. "Poor people. You don't want to see them. You wait. In a minute we're coming to great statue, twenty feet tall."

The boy was an endless source of chatter, laughter and charm. He regaled her with questionable information about the island's attractions (for some reason Emma doubted that the scenic highway along the coast was really two hundred years old) and boasted endlessly about his own talents.

"I am best of all the boys where I live," he declared as

ey drove past a group of ancient buildings that appar-
ntly had been built by the Spanish conquerors of the is-
nd in the seventeenth century. "Many girls chase after
e. I have gone to school and am always the smartest one
r I know all the answers."

"Why aren't you in school now?"

Apparently Timoteo didn't know the answer to that one.
"You like old buildings?" said the boy, looking out the
indow, changing the subject. "There are many old build-
gs in San Marcos, built by the Spanish, long time ago."

For his part, Changee Money—who spoke no English
all, but smiled endlessly with his sharpened teeth—
ered at Emma good-naturedly and offered through Tim-
teo to change all her dollars into pesos.

The sights and sounds and smells of San Marcos City
ere exciting and exotic at first: policemen in white pith
elmets, armed with automatics and truncheons; yellow
anners stretching across the narrow streets proclaiming
e wares of cafeterias and camera stores; food peddlers
d tropical flowers and throngs of people in colorful
othes.

Eventually, however, Emma grew weary of the endless
avelogue and depressed about her prospects of ever lo-
ating what she had come here to find, the *Kaito Spirit*.
he city was too big, too unfamiliar. And there was no
ason to assume that the boat her grandfather had once
wned had ever been anywhere near here. She'd have to
arch the entire island.

"Are there any marinas near the city?" she asked.

"Marinas?" said Timoteo, sticking his head back in the
indow with a quizzical expression. "What is marinas?"

"Places where boats are docked. I'm looking for
ats."

"Sure." The boy laughed. "We have lots of boats in
an Marcos. I have been all everywhere, so I know. I went
San Barnados, once—on the other side of the island,
ousands of miles away. There are many marinas there,

but we can't go there now. It is too far away. Changee
Money has to go home for dinner. He like to eat a lot. We
go back to your hotel now, okay?''

The boy let out a spurt of rapid-fire Spanish, which
Changee Money answered with a leer, a wink, and a few
grunts.

"Would your uncle let me hire his services for a few
days at a time?''

"Where you want to go? To see boats?''

"Yes.''

"Then you don't want him,'' said Timoteo, laughing,
not changing his tone of voice, though his eyes seemed to
narrow slightly. "His car's a piece of shit, won't get you
nowhere very far. My uncle will try to cheat you, too. He's
not so nice a guy like me. Hey, Changee Money, you don'
want to drive lady around a lot anymore tomorrow, do
you? You're the armpit of a smelly dog, aren't you?''

"Changee mon'?'' said Changee Money uncompre-
hending, looking back at Emma in the rearview mirror
with his usual leer.

"Forget it.'' Emma sighed. "I'll find somebody else.''

"Why not you go rent a car?'' exclaimed Timoteo.
"Then I come with you, show you everywhere you want
to go. All you need is a guide, and I'm your best guide
who has ever lived. You drive, I bet. Everybody in U.S.
drives. Everybody has big new car. You rent car, okay?''

"We'll see,'' said Emma, wondering why she hadn't
thought of it herself. Why wouldn't they have car rentals
on San Marcos? They had Coca-Cola, according to the
billboards that were everywhere. They had Kodak film.
They even had Indians who had had their own culture
before Columbus landed. Were any of them still left?

"Do you know the Kaito, Timoteo?''

"Sure. What's that?''

"They're an Indian tribe from the island. Do they still
live here?''

"Yeah, they got Indians in the country. They make stuff nd sell at market. You want to buy?"

"Maybe."

"We stop on way back to your hotel. Hey, Changee Money. Go to South Market. *Ve al Mercado del Sur.*"

Changee Money muttered something that sounded like complaint, but the boy persisted. Changee Money turned ne car down a series of side streets and in a few minutes ney came upon an open square full of outdoor vendors, nost of whom were packing up their wares. It was nearly x o'clock.

Changee Money waited in the car, smoking a cigarette, hile Emma and Timoteo got out. The boy led her by the and to a booth near the edge of the square. There, an ncredibly thin black man with graying temples, dressed in hite slacks and shirt, was beginning to collect wooden arvings from an outstretched blanket and pack them into ardboard boxes.

"Beautiful carvings," said Timoteo with an expansive weep of his hand. "Made by Indians. You buy many. This an give you good deal."

As Timoteo chattered in Spanish at the old man who istened without changing his tired expression, Emma bent ver and picked up one of the black wood carvings.

Like the carvings in Jacques Passant's bedroom, it was urprisingly heavy—almost as if it were made of cast iron nstead of wood. There, however, the resemblance ended. hese carvings were angular and crude compared with épé's rounded, graceful ones. The shapes of these were mpler, too—there were none of the counterbalanced quatting men, the long-jawed warriors or the stacked ces, just androgynous standing figures that all looked ike.

"Are these all he has?"

"A carving is a carving. What's wrong with them? They e beautiful. He give you good price."

"I'm looking for older pieces," said Emma, trying to

figure out how to explain the difference between tribal a
and cheap souvenirs. "These are just for tourists. I'm look
ing for more authentic things."

"Indians make these. They are very poor and stupid
They don't have houses, they live in the jungle. They don'
know anything. This man buys from them. They make al
these things. He give you deal."

"Tell him thanks, but this really isn't what I want."

Timoteo growled in Spanish at the man, who shrugge
and went back to packing up his wares. Emma walke
back to the car, followed by the disappointed boy. Obvi
ously he had planned to take a fat commission from an
transaction.

"Is there a car-rental place near the Casimente, do yo
know?" Emma asked after Changee Money had starte
the car and begun driving them back to the hotel.

"Around the block from the Casimente there is best ca
place in San Marcos," said Timoteo, brightening. "Yo
rent good car there, one that not break down like this piec
of shit. Timoteo take you everywhere. Show you all th
boats. You safe with me. I won't cheat you like Change
Money."

"Or split the fee with him," said Emma. "How muc
do you propose to charge me for your services, by th
way?"

"You pay me what you want. I don't care."

"Come on, Timoteo."

"I'm not like the rest of these guys, everything for dol
lars. I don't care about that. I do best job. You pay m
whatever you decide. It's okay. I trust you."

Timoteo stuck to this line until they got to the hotel
then he and Changee Money conversed in Spanish, bot
anxiously scrutinizing the crowd of money changers stil
waiting at the curb outside the gate.

The group was smaller now—no more than six men
Happily the big hairy fellow with whom Timoteo had ha

e argument before was gone. Changee Money brought
e car to a stop a few feet from the group.

"Fifty dollar," said Changee Money, turning in his seat
face Emma.

"Fifty peso," said Emma, reaching into her pocket and
unting out the bills. "As agreed."

Changee Money shrugged, leered, and took the cash,
ding it to the roll he kept in the front pocket of his shirt.
pparently he and the boy would settle later—if the boy
t anything at all.

"You meet me tomorrow at car-rental place," said Tim-
eo, getting out the car with her and speaking low so none
the men could hear. "You turn left when you get out
e hotel gate, then right. Car place is one block past
merican Express office, okay? We have a great day, see
erything there is. You buy many Indian carved statues."

"I'm still thinking about this," said Emma.

"It's okay," said Timoteo. "You can trust Timoteo.
hat time you want meet me?"

"Nine, nine-thirty, maybe," said Emma. "But I'm still
aking up my mind."

"Okay, nine-thirty," said Timoteo, getting back into
nangee Money's decrepit Ford. "Don't be late."

The group of money changers had already convened
ound Emma, waving their pocket calculators and wads
cash as Changee Money roared away. Timoteo waved
s hand at her from the window.

YES, THERE WAS corruption and cruelty under Peguero,"
id Celia, taking another tiny bite of her dinner—a sau-
ed sole amandine with wild rice. "But my father says
guero had vision for San Marcos. He also had the power
impose this vision. Now there is no vision, only constant
hting for power. Many people long for the old days."

The hotel restaurant reminded Emma of the most ex-
nsive place in a small town. Unlike the rest of the hotel,
nich was spacious, informal and airy, the Casimente's

dining room was a stuffy, pretentious place full of whit
linen tablecloths, tuxedoed waiters, and candelabra. It eve
appeared that someone wanted the tourists to believe tha
Michelangelo was still alive and decorating ceilings in th
Caribbean.

"The drive from the airport was very impressive," sai
Emma, trying to extract a final morsel of meat from he
duck à l'orange, also with wild rice. "But this afternoon
saw some shocking poverty in between monuments."

Emma felt pretty ridiculous, flying to the Caribbean t
eat a duck. She had had little choice, however. All th
entrées in the restaurant were old-fashioned American far
Most of the customers, in fact, were old-fashioned Amer
icans. If this really was the best restaurant in the city, Sa
Marcos was in deep culinary trouble.

"Yes, there is great poverty on San Marcos," said Celi
putting down her fork. "Many families live withou
plumbing and know nothing of personal hygiene. Not tha
things were so much better under Peguero, but at leas
Peguero tried to improve matters. Peguero gave every fam
ily a cow and a piece of land. The cow had to be milke
and the land had to be tilled. There were grave penaltie
for killing this cow, even if the crops had failed and th
people were starving. Now most people have no cow, n
land, nothing. Now little is certain and nothing is done
And there is still cruelty and corruption."

Emma took a sip of coffee—a rich dark brew that ha
been the best part of the meal so far, and the only thin
that didn't taste like something she could have gotten i
Indianapolis.

The island's politics were obviously complicated an
not a subject Emma wanted to delve deeply into. She wa
just a visitor here, one with very specific objectives. Sh
couldn't get the picture of the blank-eyed woman in th
doorway of the shack out of her mind, however.

"How do the people feel about Americans?" Emm
asked.

"Oh, they like them. On the whole we are just the opposite of people on many of the other islands. San Marcans do not resent the Americans. We admire you, almost too much, I think. It is like the people here have a cultural inferiority complex. Everything American is better than anything that is San Marcan. We watch American movies and listen to American music. I think we must find our own culture and learn to value it more."

"I'm sure you're right," said Emma.

They ate several more bites in silence.

"Do you think I'd be safe renting a car and driving around the island?" said Emma, changing the subject to the one that was really on her mind.

"Exploring a strange country is perhaps not something that a woman alone should do," said Celia with a concerned, surprised look. "The men are very chauvinistic here. It is not like New Jersey."

"Yes," said Emma. "I once played Atlantic City. The men are very enlightened in New Jersey. They threw money at the stage and barked like seals."

"Do you speak Spanish?" said Celia, apparently not understanding the sarcasm.

"No, but I'd be with someone who does."

Emma told her about the boy, Timoteo, the tour he had taken her on today and how she proposed to rent a car tomorrow. Celia listened in respectful silence and didn't speak until Emma had finished.

"I do not think this is such a good idea, perhaps, if I might say so, Emma. There are many children like this boy. Poor, uneducated, unwanted. It may be that he is not a problem, but there are many desperate people in this country. If there is trouble, what will you do? What if the car breaks down outside of the city? It is not like America here. There are not many gas stations."

"Yes, this isn't my favorite idea, but unfortunately I don't have a lot of other options."

"I have a cousin who might drive you," said Celia.

"But he works at a job during the week and you woul[d] have to wait until Saturday. And I do not know for sur[e] that he would be available. He sometimes must work o[n] the weekends, too, if they need him."

Emma nodded, knowing too well what it was like t[o] have to work weekends to make ends meet. It was Monda[y] now, however, and she was hardly going to sit around th[e] pool for four more days, waiting for a cousin who may o[r] may not be able to make it.

"Thanks," she said. "I'm pretty good about people, an[d] I think I'll be all right with Timoteo. What do you thin[k] I should pay him, by the way? He wouldn't quote me [a] price. I was thinking maybe fifty pesos for the day? That'[s] what I paid his uncle for the tour today."

"Oh, that is much too much. Even twenty pesos woul[d] be a fortune for a boy like this."

"I know I'll have to pay for the car, but if Timote[o] spends the whole day with me, figuring even three dollar[s] an hour..."

"That is why he tried to trick you by not telling yo[u] what would be fair. You automatically think what woul[d] be fair in America. But this is San Marcos. For a week o[f] work many men here earn less than a hundred pesos[.] Grown men. Give him ten pesos a day, that is all that i[s] required."

"Do you happen to know of any marinas near the city?" said Emma, changing the subject, uncomfortable at th[e] thought of exploiting the boy and that this quiet youn[g] lady would suggest doing so. "I'm trying to find a boa[t] that might have been here thirty years ago."

"Thirty years is a long time," said Celia. "I do n[o]t know anything about boats. Does this boy?"

"He says he does."

"Can you believe him?"

"No, probably not."

They spent the rest of the meal chatting about San Mar[-] cos, New Jersey, and what a nice restaurant it was. Emm[a]

couldn't bear to contradict Celia's breathless raves with a
critique of the dated menu, which seemed to have captured
America's sensibilities of the 1960s as perfectly as the am-
ber which Timoteo had shown her in the marketplace had
captured flies. And to prove the point, at least to herself,
Emma insisted that they have the flaming cherries jubilee
for dessert. Celia practically swooned.

After dinner Celia telephoned her parents to come and
pick her up, and Emma waited with her in the lobby until
they arrived. They were a quiet couple, who blushed when
they were introduced and were too shy or too intimidated
to get out of the car.

Celia thanked Emma again, and asked to exchange addresses so that they might stay in touch. Emma gave her
the address for Charlemagne's office, remembering suddenly that she no longer had a home, and waited by the
curb, waving as the car drove off. Then she walked slowly
back into the hotel, feeling more alone than ever.

It was not even ten o'clock. San Marcos time was four
hours ahead of San Francisco's. Though she hadn't gotten
much sleep on the plane, it still felt like only six o'clock
to her. With the excitement of being in a strange country
and the coffee she had had at dinner, Emma was wide
awake. Her mind whirled with images from the day, fears
about tomorrow, the dull ache in her chest for her grandfather that never went away.

There was a small cocktail lounge just off the lobby.
Emma wandered in and sat down at one of the little tables.
There were only a few other customers in the place—
sad-looking men at the bar, a few couples in the back.

A drink wasn't what she wanted, but a glass of hot milk
from room service sounded unutterably lonely. And totally
disgusting. Though Pépé had extolled milk as "the cow's
gift to children," Emma had hated the sight of it since she
was a little girl, to say nothing of the taste.

"What can I get you, señora?" the bartender called

across the room. He was a handsome man with curly black hair and a nice smile.

"Do you have something that will help me sleep?"

"Yes, I do," he said. After a moment he appeared at her table with a glass of hot milk.

"Do you know this stuff is full of cholesterol and saturated fat?" said Emma, wincing.

"I am sorry, señora," said the waiter, his proud smile turning to disappointment. "You looked like the wholesome type. Would you like some brandy instead?"

"No, thanks," sighed Emma. "This is fine."

The bartender's smile returned. He nodded and went back to his customers.

Emma stared at the white liquid in the glass. She wanted to be wholesome. She didn't want to be the kind of woman who came into a bar and slugged back brandies in order to sleep. She closed her eyes tightly and took a sip of the milk. It was awful.

On her way to the elevators afterward, Emma couldn't help but notice how quiet the lobby was, how peaceful. Still not ready to go to sleep, she took a detour and walked through the open courtyard. A couple was holding hands and kissing on a bench in a quiet corner.

The night seen from the landscaped yard behind the hotel was inky black and above her head a thousand stars twinkled with unfamiliar brightness. Sweet smells of palms and flowers pervaded the warm air and in the distance she could hear waves breaking on the rocky shore.

Emma walked along the hotel's outer fence and stopped at a place where she could see the ocean. On the horizon, above a grove of palm trees, a sliver of moon rose gently into the sky. All was calm. All was well. There was nothing to be afraid of tomorrow, she knew. Emma was basking in a feeling of overwhelming confidence and peace when she saw the movement out of the corner of her eye.

She nearly jumped when the man came into view—a stocky bruiser in a windbreaker and black jeans. The dark object he was holding in his hands was a pump-action shotgun.

Emma froze, her mouth dropping open in surprise. The man noticed her, smiled broadly with less than a full complement of teeth, and took one hand off the shotgun long enough to tip his baseball cap.

Emma nodded back, stunned. As the man walked past her, she could see the hotel's logo on the back of his jacket. He was not a thief or assassin, she realized, but merely one of the hotel guards, keeping the guests safe from the friendly people of San Marcos.

ELEVEN

"TURN RIGHT HERE, turn left at the first light," said Timoteo, fiddling with the air-conditioning controls and adjusting the passenger seat for the third time in as many minutes.

Emma pulled out of the car-rental agency's parking lot and into traffic. She hardly needed directions back to the Casimente. It was only a block—and three hundred pesos per day, twenty centavos per mile—away. Either the agency was wise to the ins and outs of currency exchange or it was just preposterously expensive to rent a car on San Marcos to begin with.

Timoteo didn't appear concerned about the pressure his suggestion to rent the little white Honda Civic was going to put on Emma's finances, however. If anything, he looked as if he had just been granted a dozen extra birthdays and been named Emperor of France. As they neared the hotel, the expression on his face changed from one of rank smugness to one of sheer bliss.

"Slow down, slow down," he commanded, jumping to his knees on the seat and rolling down his window.

Emma slowed the car. Directly ahead was the usual group of money changers and tour guides outside the gates of the Casimente. Timoteo leaned out the window, his smile growing even more enormous.

"Hey, Reginaldo!" he shouted. "Hey, Javier! Hola! Look at me!"

The boy then rattled off a rapid string of Spanish. Emma couldn't understand what he was saying, but from the disgusted looks and fist-shaking from the men at the curb she gathered that Timoteo was being less than gracious about his good fortune.

"What did you say to them?" she asked as the hotel fell out of sight behind them.

"Nothing," said the boy, grinning with satisfaction, not meeting her eye.

"Why did they get mad then?"

"I don't know. I just tell them hello."

"You're right," said Emma, braking the unfamiliar car as they came to a light. "It's none of my business."

"They're just a bunch of guys. They are nothing to me."

Timoteo's sneakers were cracked and dirty and at least two sizes too big for his feet. He wore tatty blue jeans rolled up at the bottoms and no socks. His old sport shirt, also too big, was unbuttoned because it had no buttons, revealing the boy's bony black chest.

"So where are we going to find these boats, Timoteo?" said Emma, glancing down at her own Gap chinos and the shoes that cost as much as feet.

"I show you," said Timoteo, his face at once earnest and defiant. "You get nowhere alone. Timoteo know all the places. We turn right at the light up here and stay on that road for a while. We go through the city, over to the other side. Over the big bridge. I take you."

They drove in silence to the ramshackle area Emma had hesitated to venture into yesterday on foot, then on through narrow streets crowded with noisy little cars and bicycles. Telephone wires stretched overhead. The gutters were filled with trash. The buildings were a crazy quilt of garish signs and peeling paint.

"I tell them they looked stupid," Timoteo mumbled after a few minutes.

"Who?"

"The mens who change money. I say I laugh because they are standing there with their thumbs up their asses, while I have a beautiful lady to drive me around. I tell them they look like donkeys. You are mad at me now?''

"Why would I be mad?" said Emma, trying to remember the last time someone had called her beautiful.

"We be friends," said Timoteo, his big smile returning. "I have lots of friends. My mother, she say I make friends with everybody."

"It's okay with her, right? Your driving around with me today?"

"Sure. She doesn't care. She's in U.S. In Hartford, Connecticut. She sent me this shirt from the guy she works for."

"What does your mother do in Hartford?" asked Emma.

"She's housekeeper for this man," said the boy, playing with the controls of his seat again. "She cleans and cooks for him. She's very good cook. He is very rich. She is making money so we can be together again."

"How long has she been away?"

"Long time. Three years, maybe. She's coming back soon. She sends me all kinds of things. She sent me these shoes. I live with my aunt. She have six kids. They all my friends. Everywhere I go, I have friends. The guys back at the hotel, they all my friends, too."

"I thought you said they were just guys," said Emma, "that they were nothing to you."

"They are jealous of me," sneered Timoteo. "Timoteo has the car and the lady to drive him, and they have nothing."

"Maybe they'd like you more if you didn't rub their noses in your success."

The minute the words were out of her mouth, Emma regretted them. Since when had she been elected Oprah? This boy's welfare wasn't her responsibility. He was just someone who could help her find what she had come here to find. His personal life was none of her business. She couldn't afford to get involved. She should just shut up and drive.

"They think they're so smart," said Timoteo angrily, 'but they're full of shit. They yell at me because I am small. They would cheat you if they could. They would kill you."

"That's why I came with you."

"How much you pay for those shoes?"

"None of your business."

"They are very beautiful. You give them to Timoteo, maybe?"

"Not a chance."

"Timoteo take you to find boats. We will have a good time. You will be happy lady, yes?"

"Your friends at the hotel—they did sort of look like donkeys, didn't they?" said Emma. The boy beamed.

"THESE ARE OIL TANKERS, Timoteo," exclaimed Emma, looking at the huge hulks moving in the brackish water. "The others are cargo boats. Freighters."

Emma didn't know why she should be surprised. The warehouses and deserted streets of the area should have been a dead giveaway as they approached, but Emma had just assumed Timoteo knew what he was talking about. She had asked him several times if they were going in the right direction, if he understood what she wanted. The boy had sounded so sure.

"These are magnificent boats," he said again now, defensively. "They are very big and come from the ocean. From across the world. Everybody like these boats."

"I'm looking for pleasure boats, Timoteo. Cabin cruisers. Like I told you. Small boats. Do you understand?"

"Sure."

But he didn't. The next pier he directed her to in a less-industrialized area of the city a few miles away held a small fleet of commercial fishing trawlers. Emma suddenly realized that the boy probably didn't know what a "pleasure" boat was. Why would he?

"Oh, you want little boats for fun," he said when she

tried to explain. "You got to say so. Why don't you say so?"

"I'm sorry," said Emma, swallowing her frustration, trying not to attack his pride. She was already a nervous wreck from competing for space on the city's narrow streets with drivers who seemed to come in only two varieties: suicidal and homicidal. The last thing she wanted was to try this again tomorrow with some thuggish money changer as her guide.

"I know this other place where there are little boats," said Timoteo. "That's what you want. I know."

"Where is it?"

"Outside the city. I show you. Keep on this road."

"How far?"

"Not far. You'll see."

They drove back through the center of town and out along the coast on Peguero's trophy highway. After twenty minutes they passed the airport and kept going. The highway in this direction quickly lost its meridian, its palm tree borders and two of its four lanes, until it was just an ordinary, not-very-well-maintained road along the oceanside.

There wasn't much traffic now that they were away from the city, and at first Emma didn't understand why the yellow car behind her was following so closely, honking its horn and flashing its headlights.

"You got to pull over," said Timoteo with a look of disgust.

"Why? What does he want?"

"It's the police. You were speeding."

"No, I wasn't. Was I? What's the speed limit?"

"Pull over," Timoteo said again. "You be quiet. I talk for you, okay?"

"Like I'm going to understand what they're saying anyway?"

She pulled over to the muddy side of the road. The police car—an old Volkswagen Rabbit—clattered to a stop behind her. On its side she could see the word POLICÍA in black paint, but other than that there was nothing to mark the car as an official vehicle. It was only slightly less battered than most of the cars she had seen on the road—even her rental had numerous dents and bruises, and the girl at the agency had seemed puzzled that Emma would even comment on them. Apparently no car in San Marcos went unbashed for long.

Two men in tan uniforms got out of the car behind her. One was tall and thin. The other was short and fat. Both wore sunglasses, mustaches and enormous revolvers.

"Buenos días, señora," said the tall one, smiling broadly, leaning down and tipping his hat. The short fat one smiled and tipped his hat, too. The words "banana republic" flashed into Emma's mind, and not for the first time today.

"Qué quiere?" barked Timoteo.

The tall policeman shrugged and launched into a lengthy speech in Spanish. Timoteo folded his arms in front of him and listened, his face a picture of pure contempt.

"What did he say?" asked Emma when the man had finished.

"He says you were speeding," answered Timoteo. "I told you so."

"I wasn't going faster than anyone else. How does he even know? I don't see any radar."

Timoteo said something to the policeman in Spanish. The man laughed and spoke again, pointing to his partner every so often.

"What did he say now?"

"Give me forty pesos," said Timoteo. "Don't let him see how much money you have."

"You're not going to try to bribe him, Timoteo."

"Give it to me now," said Timoteo, sounding serious. "They can take us to jail and beat us if they want."

The tall thin one who was doing the talking tipped his hat again politely to Emma. The short fat one wiped his sweaty face with a white handkerchief. In their ill-fitting uniforms they looked almost like clowns. Emma turned away momentarily, reached into her pocket, and took out four ten-peso notes and handed them to Timoteo.

Speaking in Spanish, Timoteo handed two of the notes to the tall policeman. The man's smile vanished and he shouted a flurry of words at Timoteo, none of which Emma could understand.

Timoteo growled back, his face curled into a sneer. For a moment Emma thought he was going to spit on the floor of the car, but instead he handed the other twenty pesos to the cop. The man snatched it, hissed a few final words which even Emma could recognize as obscenities, turned and marched back to his car, followed by his portly partner. In a moment the two policemen had started their engine and roared away.

When Emma turned on her ignition again, she found her hand was shaking. She had driven a mile before she was even able to speak.

"Don't you ever do that to me again, Timoteo," said Emma angrily.

"What?"

"What if he hadn't accepted bribes? What would have happened then?"

"Why he stop us if he didn't want money?"

Emma didn't answer.

"You should be happy," said Timoteo. "Why you mad? I take good care of you."

"I can take care of myself. It's no big deal to pay a speeding ticket."

"You pay everything these guys want, every time they stop you?" said Timoteo, laughing, baring startlingly white teeth. "You must be very rich lady. Or crazy."

"I'm just a visitor here, Timoteo. I don't want to get into trouble."

"Okay. Next time you see those guys, you give them the two hundred pesos they wanted. That's how much they

anted. Two hundred pesos! Give them all two hundred
sos. I don't care.''

"All right."

"I get you off cheap," Timoteo went on. "You couldn't
en talk to him. He was ignorant man. He did not even
eak English. What you do if he took you to station and
at you and take all your money? What you do then?''

What would she do? Emma asked herself. It was she
ho was the child here. She was as naive about this place
d how it worked as Timoteo would be if he were
unked down in the middle of the New York Stock
xchange.

"I'm sorry, Timoteo," she said. "You're right. You're
e guide."

"Okay," said the boy, staring at her with a strange ex-
ession.

"Okay. What now? Where are these boats? Where are
e going?"

"Not much further. You'll see."

After ten more minutes, Timoteo motioned for her to
t off the aging highway onto a road spur that led down
rough a stand of palms directly onto the beach. He had
parently forgotten the incident with the police altogether.
e looked eager and excited.

"What's here?" said Emma.

"This is where everybody comes. There are boats. Drive
wn there."

Emma steered the little white Honda where the boy dicted. In a moment they were on a patch of dirty gray
nd and gravel next to the ocean. A few whitewashed
wboats were stacked against a small shack. About twenty
ildren, some black, some white, none older than about
teen, were playing in the breaking waves and standing
the shore.

"What are we doing here?" asked Emma, as half a
zen of the children convened around the car.

"You want to swim?" said Timoteo, opening the c
door. "You give me your shoes now?"

"I want to find boats, Timoteo," said Emma, grabbi
his arm before he could get out. "You said you were goi
to take me to see boats."

Was it some kind of trap? she wondered. Had the b
tricked her, gotten her to this remote place so she wou
be at the mercy of some kind of gang? How could sl
have been foolish enough to trust him? How could sl
have been so naive?

"Here are boats," yelled Timoteo, pointing at the litt
rowboats. "We can take them out. Or we can swim. Y
can go in like that. Your clothes will dry quick. It's re
fun."

Around the car, the "gang" of children squealed wi
delight. Timoteo broke free from Emma's grasp and g
out of the car. He jumped onto the hood of the car a
began speaking to the group in Spanish. Emma opened h
door and got out, too. Laughing children convened arou
her, their eyes full of curiosity and wonder.

"I tell them you're this rich American who can b
anything she wants," bragged Timoteo with obvious prid
"They think you own this car and everything. They nev
see such a nice car. You want to go swim now?"

"No, I don't," said Emma, feeling more than a litt
foolish. "I want to find boats. Not ones like these. Bigg
boats."

"I show you big boats before, you not like. Here a
little boats, you not like. We go swim now. Okay?"

"Timoteo..."

"Just for a minute? Please?"

"Oh, all right," said Emma. "Go ahead."

Timoteo jumped down from the hood of the car and r
laughing down to the beach, followed by a dozen of t
kids. He stripped off his shirt, pulled off his blue jeans a
ran into the small, breaking waves in his white jocke
shorts.

Emma waited, surrounded by the rest of the children, who stood staring at her in awe.

Clearly no one else wanted this ugly piece of beach. That's how the poor children had taken it over as their own. Where else would they be welcome to swim and enjoy themselves? How often did Timoteo get here? Not often, judging from the look of him, splashing happily in the water and yelling his head off. For all his bravura and street smarts he was just a little boy. To him this place was paradise.

It was only eleven o'clock. There was still time to look for boats today. Figuring she may as well make the best of it, Emma boosted herself up on the hood of the car and smiled at the group of kids who stood around, staring at her.

"He say you very rich," said the tallest boy, stepping forward, shaking her hand. "He say you have many houses in United States. You buy me a house?"

"Me, too," said a bright-eyed, skinny little girl. "I want house, too."

In an instant all the children were chattering happily, mostly in Spanish, jumping up and down, laughing. By the time Timoteo came back to the car, Emma was laughing, too, and draped with a pair of six-year-olds.

"You go swim now, too?" Timoteo said happily.

"No, we've got things to do," said Emma, extricating herself from the giggling children. "What are you going to do about your clothes?"

"It's okay," said Timoteo. He picked up his blue jeans from the sand where he had left them in a heap and put them on over his wet underpants.

"They're still wet," said Emma, unable to stop herself. "They're going to soak right through your jeans."

"No, they won't. I always do this. It's okay."

Emma just shook her head.

"How far away is that fancy resort area?" she asked,

struggling to recall the name of the place in the hotel bro
chure. "Las Calvos, that's it, right?"

"An hour away, maybe," shrugged Timoteo.

"Have you ever been there?"

"Sure, many times," said the boy, leaning over an
spitting a slow stream of saliva onto the dirty sand.

"Is there a marina near there? Boats?"

"Yes, many boats. Las Calvos is very beautiful resor
Many rich people come there. You want I should tak
you?"

"Do you know the way?"

"Sure."

"You're certain you know the way?"

"My cousin live in Española," said Timoteo, gettin
into the car. "Right near Las Calvos. I go see him all th
time. Come on, let's go. I take you."

Emma opened her door and got in. The remaining chil
dren stepped back as she started the car, then ran behin
them, shouting and laughing, as Emma steered up th
sandy road and back onto the highway.

TWO HOURS LATER they were still in the middle of no
where and Emma was getting more than a little concerned

Timoteo kept on saying over and over that they wer
almost there, but it was obvious now he had little rea
knowledge of the island's geography. It had been nearl
an hour ago that they had passed Española, where the bo
claimed he had cousins. Emma had been expecting a city
but you couldn't even call Española a village. It was jus
a few rows of shacks at a crossroads in the baked-mu
countryside. No more than hovels, really—gray, unpainte
boards and corrugated sheet metal.

"Your cousin lives here?" Emma had asked, trying no
to show her dismay at the crushing poverty all aroun
them.

A woman dressed in rags walked slowly on the road
carrying an enormous bundle on her head. Against one o

e huts sat an old man with no shirt, flies hovering around
m. He apparently hadn't the strength or the motivation
shoo them away. Or perhaps he was merely dead.

"My cousins don't live here, like these pigs," Timoteo
d said breezily. "They live in the country, around here.
ey have a beautiful farm. I think they are away now. I
ink they have gone on a vacation."

Since then the road that they were traveling had gotten
rrower and more bumpy, if that was possible. The road-
le was overgrown with vegetation—not the straight
ately conifers she was used to from San Francisco, but
tle scrubby thick greenery, punctuated with palm trees,
angroves and ferns. There was no traffic, nor any evi-
nce that there had ever been people here, save the road
elf, and it clearly hadn't been maintained in years.

Emma was terrified they would get a flat tire or break
axle in one of the enormous potholes that seemed to
pear every few yards. Then what would she do? Emma
dn't thought to check the spare—not that she'd ever
anged a tire in her life. They hadn't seen a gas station
ice just outside of the city. There weren't even any elec-
cal or phone lines on the side of the road.

At least she knew where she stood, Emma thought to
rself. She was a foreign woman alone in the middle of
strange country with only a ten-year-old boy to help her,
d he was a confirmed liar. The thick wad of pesos she
d brought along in case of emergencies only made her
el more vulnerable. Celia had been right. This had been
ie supremely lousy idea.

"Do you have any idea where we are, Timoteo?" said
nma in exasperation.

"We're almost there," said Timoteo angrily—as if he
ere insulted that she could doubt his word, even though
had been wrong about everything up to now.

"That's what you keep saying."

"How come you not married?"

"Don't change the subject. Where are we?"

"Men no like you?"

"Men like me fine. And how do you know I'm n
married? I could have a dozen husbands back in the Stat
for all you know."

"If you had a husband, he would not let you dri
around like this without him. The man must be the bo:
The woman must do what he says."

"Oh, really? And why is that?"

"Because the man, he brings home the money," d
clared Timoteo. "The woman must make the house f
him."

"Well, I happen to bring home my own money."

"A woman cannot bring home as much as a man,
snorted Timoteo, folding his arms in front of him. "Wh
can you do?"

"I'm a magician."

"A woman cannot be a magician."

"A woman can be anything she wants. Including a m
gician."

"I don't believe you are a magician."

"I'm a magician."

"Ha, I laugh."

"I'm a magician. I'm a magician. What am I doing?
don't have to prove myself to you. You're just a little bo
I'm a magician. I do a big show. I've played all ov
America."

"If you are magician, why are you lost?"

"Because I've been listening to you!"

"Because you listen to Timoteo, you go where you wa
to be."

"Yes, and where is that?"

"Look!"

Emma looked to where the boy was pointing. For th
past fifty miles the only traffic they had seen had bee
comprised of ancient tractors and a few men herding cow
Now, far up ahead, a fire-engine red Dodge minivan w
heading toward them.

As Emma watched in amazement and relief, it turned onto a side road to their right. There were two signs when Emma came to the same spot. The first read, FOR TENNIS VILLAS A–H, TAKE ACCESS B. The other sign read ALTAR DEL SOL, with an arrow pointing in the direction the mini-van had come from.

"What's Altar del Sol?" asked Emma.

"It is another resort," said Timoteo, though from his expression, Emma couldn't tell whether he knew or was making it up.

"Is this Las Calvos?"

"I come here all the time," said Timoteo, glassy-eyed. Clearly he had no idea.

"I'm glad you knew the way," said Emma, not wanting to embarrass him further. She turned onto the side road, which was paved with a smooth asphalt. The smoothness of the ride after hours of driving on potholes was jolting.

Within a few yards trees and flowers began appearing—not the shaggy palms and scrubgrass they had been seeing, but Japanese maples and dogwoods, exotic camellias and frangipani. Soon the roadside was ablaze with every color of the rainbow and the air was fragrant with floral perfume.

Emma drove on for a mile or so and other signs of civilization began appearing: a crew of gardeners trimming trees at the side of the road; another fire-engine red mini-van with several couples dressed in tennis whites and carrying racquets; a pair of signs, one for the heliport, another for limousine parking; guard stations with sharp-eyed uniformed men wearing holstered automatics who looked at her car, smiled and waved them through.

Timoteo's eyes almost popped out of his head when they rounded a curve and found the rocky ocean coast stretching out before them, bounded by a seemingly endless golf course. Coral cliffs, huge white sandy spaces, stands of sugarcane, cashew, almond, orange and teak trees—all contributed to make the landscape breathtak-

ingly beautiful and exotic. It was more than like being in
a different country from the poor, ugly one through which
they had been driving for the past two hours; it was like
being on a different planet.

"I hope we can get something to eat here if we aren't
registered as guests," said Emma. "I'm starving. How
about you?"

For a change Timoteo didn't have anything to say. He
just sat on his knees, gaping out the window, as two beautiful young women galloped past on horseback, their long
blond hair dancing behind them in the breeze.

After a few minutes the road forked. Emma followed
the set of signs for the reception area, rather than the ones
pointing to the tennis village and beach. Soon they found
themselves in an area of thicker foliage and taller trees in
which several small buildings were set.

Emma pulled up the car into a small parking area in
front of the largest building, which had been invisible until
they were practically on top of it, camouflaged perfectly
by the trees. On the shaded walks between the buildings
several couples, tanned and prosperous-looking, strolled
by, looking as if they had just stepped out of advertisements for expensive summer fashions. The flashes of crimson in the trees were tropical birds. There were no clouds
in the perfectly blue sky.

Emma opened her door, got out and stretched her legs.
Timoteo had been running the car's air conditioner and
she was surprised by how hot the day had become.

"Come on," she said to the boy, who hadn't moved.
"Let's check it out."

Timoteo opened his door and followed Emma up the
path toward the large building with slumped shoulders and
his hands in the pockets of his jeans, which were rolled
up almost to the knees.

A boy not much older than Timoteo was walking down
the path toward them. He was wearing starched khaki
shorts and a matching shirt and was carrying a tray.

"Excuse me," said Emma as he approached.

"Yes, ma'am?"

The boy stopped and stood straight-backed, looking Timoteo over with a smug expression. According to his Las Calvos nameplate, his name was Hernando and he was a "China Steward." It took Emma a moment to figure out that a china steward must be someone who took care of plates. Hernando was a busboy.

"We've come up from San Marcos City for the day," he said. "Is there a place where we can get something to eat?"

"La Reserve, our largest dining room, is behind me in the main building, but it is not open for lunch," said the boy in a practiced tone. "There are seven other restaurants in Las Calvos. What type of cuisine are you interested in?"

"Nothing fancy."

"There are snack bars at the beach and the tennis village, but for these it is a fifteen-minute drive. Perhaps La Cocina Verde is for you. There you can get sandwiches and light entrées or the buffet. It is up ahead, past the pool."

Hernando indicated another path that led through a wall of flowers. Timoteo, who slouched and fidgeted but had not taken his eyes off the other boy, leaned over his shoulder and let loose a long, slow stream of spit.

"Timoteo, don't do that," said Emma. "Please."

She turned back to Hernando and thanked him, then put her hand on Timoteo's shoulder and steered him onto the path the china steward had indicated. The boy marched off, looking proud of himself.

"I'm not hungry, you go," said Timoteo as they rounded the corner of the pool, a huge arc of blue in a grassy glade.

A few tanned men and women frolicked in the water. Others sat sunning in deck chairs. Most of them seemed to be in their thirties and forties, though there were a few

young couples and some older people. Everyone had th
same prosperous air and bearing.

"Come on," said Emma. "You're a growing boy."

In another minute they came to a small building wit
open sides that blended perfectly into a surrounding gree
ery. Dark wood furniture, the tables set with white table
cloths and silver, filled the shady room inside. Appetizin
aromas filled the air, but all Emma could see was the bu
fet, which was set along one wall the length of the roon
On it were incredible piles of tropical fruits, chafing dishe
with hot entrées, bowls of shrimp two feet in diameter. A
chef stood by, ready to carve, in front of an array of ham
turkey, and roast beef.

A mustached man with a broad chest, wearing a colorf
shirt and tan pants, greeted them at the door.

"May I help you, señorita?" he said in a deep baritone
smiling broadly.

"Yes," said Emma, stunned by the beauty of Las Ca
vos after the past few hours of driving through the barre
poverty of the island. Probably less than a mile away fron
this groaning board, people were starving. "I'm not
guest, but I've driven up from the city and wonder if
might get something to eat."

"Of course," said the man. "Please follow me."

Then in a low voice he rattled off a string of Spanish a
Timoteo, his smile not wavering.

"I go wait in the car," said Timoteo and started t
leave.

Emma grabbed his arm.

"Aren't you hungry?"

"No," mumbled Timoteo, breaking away from he
grasp.

"The boy is not hungry, señorita," said the man wit
the mustache. "Please follow me to your table. You wi
have our buffet today, yes?"

Emma stood uncomprehendingly for a moment. The

she looked at Timoteo's frayed, buttonless shirt, his jeans and dirty sneakers, his defiant black face. She understood.

"Come on," said Emma, taking his hand in hers. "Let's go. I'm not hungry either."

Timoteo, a puzzled expression on his face, let her lead him back to the car.

"How come you didn't eat?" he said finally as they got back into the car.

"I decided to start a diet. I can stand to lose a few pounds."

"Americans are all crazy," snorted the boy.

"Let's see if we can find the marina," said Emma, still furious at the way the man at the buffet had treated Timoteo.

They drove back along the way they came, turning this time onto the road marked BEACH, VILLAS R–S. Fifteen minutes later they had passed the pristine, thinly populated beach, a dozen clay tennis courts, and a modern building that housed a restaurant and a discothèque. Nowhere was there a sign of any boats.

"You said there were boats here," said Emma. "Where are they?"

"I can't remember."

"What about that other resort? Altar del Sol? What's there?"

Timoteo shrugged.

"Okay, let's go see," said Emma.

They drove back the way they had come, back through the lovely landscaped vistas of Las Calvos, which now seemed strangely cold. When they reached the road on which they had been traveling before, they turned and followed the arrow on the sign that read ALTAR DEL SOL.

Ten minutes later the road began to rise. Emma didn't ask Timoteo any more questions, just followed the road, hoping that Altar del Sol would have a gas station. Their tank was half empty. Unless they found fuel somewhere, they'd never get back to San Marcos City.

Long before the canopy of trees thinned out, Emma had realized that they were on a mountain. Were they going the right way? Timoteo obviously didn't know. He was sitting on his knees, staring out the window, wide-eyed.

As they neared the peak, stone walls began to appear everywhere, then stone buildings—or what was left of them. Finally the narrow road ended at a plateau at the mountain's top in the ruins of an ancient city. Emma parked in a small parking area where there were several other cars. Far ahead on the side of one of the stone buildings she could see some Japanese people taking pictures of one another with fancy cameras.

Timoteo had gone off to the side, where there were several wooden signs with lengthy Spanish inscriptions, the kind Emma had seen before in national parks.

"People used to live here," Timoteo exclaimed as she caught up with him, looking up from the words he had been reading. "These are their houses. It was many hundreds of years ago and they are all dead now."

"Does it say if they left any gas stations behind?"

"This mountain is called Altar del Sol after their city," said Timoteo. "I have come here before many times."

"Sure you have." Emma sighed.

"Come on," yelled Timoteo, running ahead. "Let's go see!"

Timoteo dashed down the stone path along an ancient wall and was quickly out of sight. Emma followed, hands in her pockets, depressed and hungry.

When she caught up with the boy he was standing on top of the thick curving wall wearing an enormous grin. What could he possibly be so happy about? Emma wondered.

"Look," said Timoteo as if he had read her thoughts.

Emma looked down over the wall in the direction he was pointing. There, far below, as far as the eye could see, the ocean stretched out blue and beautiful, and at the base of the mountain the water was filled with hundreds of boats, white boats, like a forgotten yet familiar field of snow.

TWELVE

IT TOOK NEARLY FORTY minutes on the twisty ill-maintained road—including a stop for directions in Spanish from a man herding a flock of goats—for Emma and Timoteo to wend their way back down the mountain and find the small natural harbor where the boats were moored.

A chain-link fence eight feet tall surrounded the marina, but the gates were open and unattended. Emma drove in and parked in the small sandy area alongside the few other vehicles. A few men—boat owners by the look of their tans—were chatting in the parking lot and doing maintenance on the decks of their vessels. None of them seemed to pay her and Timoteo any mind.

Emma had now lost all the weight she wanted to and was ready for lunch. She was also seriously in the market for a bathroom, a problem Timoteo didn't have. Half an hour back he had told her to stop the car, then nonchalantly gotten out and done his business at the side of the road.

Timoteo didn't have to be coaxed out of the car this time, as he had had to be at Las Calvos. Before Emma could extricate herself from her seat belt, the boy had run out onto the nearest dock and was studying the snow-white boats moored all around. There were all kinds—everything from tiny single-masted sailboats to enormous cabin cruisers with teak decks and radar detectors half the size of Emma's rented car.

"See?" said Timoteo, his chin high with pride. "I told you I would take you to find boats."

"Like you ever heard of this place?" exclaimed Emma.

"Timoteo comes here often," declared the boy. "He

as many friends with big pleasure boats. All the time they take him for rides in the ocean.''

Emma shook her head. Her little companion was incorrigible. Before she could stop him he had run off into the maze of docks. Emma was too tired to follow at comparable speed. In a moment Timoteo was out of sight behind the forest of bobbing white vessels.

It was nearly ten minutes before she caught up with him again. When she did, the boy was sitting in a canvas-back chair on the deck of one of the smaller boats. He was wearing somebody's blue-and-red Cleveland Indians baseball cap and looked uncharacteristically nervous. The source of his concern was instantly evident.

The man was seated beside Timoteo—a stocky brute about five feet ten with a totally shaved head and graying eyebrows bushy enough for a community of small creatures to make their home in. He wore green Bermuda shorts and a grubby white T-shirt that did nothing to conceal his enormous belly. In one hand he held a baseball bat at its center, which he slowly thumped against the palm of his other hand. It was clear from the expression in the bald man's tiny brown eyes, presently fixed on Timoteo, that he was even more annoyed than Emma was.

"See?" shouted Timoteo indignantly as he saw Emma approach. "I told you. I told you!"

"Shut up," ordered the man, his voice somewhere between a bullfrog's and a collie's. He glanced over at Emma, not taking his eyes off the boy for more than a split second. "How'd you two get in here?"

Emma tried to smile. When in trouble, smile, her grandfather had always counseled. A smile, Pépé had declared, was the "irresistible flower of the face."

"The gate was open," Emma said. "We just drove in."

"What about Julio?" barked the man with the shaved head. The flower of his particular face was Venus flytrap.

"Who's Julio?"

"He's supposed to be the guard, the lazy bum. I ought break his head."

"There weren't any signs," said Emma. "Nobody said anything. If we're trespassing, I assure you it wasn't intentional."

"Kid claims he works for you," said the man. "Say he's your assistant. That right?"

"I'm afraid so," said Emma evenly.

The man broke into a yellow-toothed smile.

"I was admiring his hat. We don't get many Cleveland Indian fans down here. Barry Castleman's the only one know. He's got his boat moored over in B-twenty-three right near where I found your little friend here. In fact he's got the exact same hat. I've seen him wear it about million times."

"What an interesting coincidence," said Emma, glaring at Timoteo. "I'm sure Timoteo would love to talk to this Mr. Castleman. He's a great Cleveland fan, too. Aren' you, Timoteo?"

"Yeah," mumbled the boy.

"Thing is, Castleman's out playing golf today," the bald man went on in his distinctive growl. "But maybe we could just go over and wait for him. I'm sure he wouldn't mind. Barry's such a hospitable guy, he's alway forgetting to lock his boat."

"I don't think that will be necessary, Mr…?"

"Garr. Sid Garr. I run this marina."

"Pleased to meet you, Mr. Garr. I'm Emma Passant."

"Yeah. Your assistant here tells me you're a famou magician."

"Oh, he did, did he?"

"Yeah. He says this is yours."

Still holding the baseball bat in one hand, Sid reached down and picked up a chrome-plated Art Deco ice bucket

"Part of the act, huh?" he chortled. "Funny—Barry Castleman's got one just like this, too."

Emma didn't say anything. She was too angry to speak

"I think maybe it's time for me to call the policía."

"The ice bucket is mine," said Emma after a moment, seeing the panic in Timoteo's eyes. "You're right. It's part of my act."

"Yeah?" said Garr. "Then you won't mind showing me. I ain't been getting much entertainment since Madonna walked out and left me for a younger guy. Come aboard."

Timoteo tried to rise from his chair on the boat, but the big man pushed him back.

"I didn't do nothing," he muttered, hanging his head.

Emma ignored him and stepped carefully from the dock onto the boat. There were witnesses all around. It wasn't as if Sid Garr could whack her over the head with his baseball bat and toss her into the water. Could he?

"May I?" Emma said, reaching out her hand when the boat stopped rocking.

"Sure," said Sid, handing her the ice bucket. "This I gotta see."

Emma took off the bucket's top, turned it over and placed it upside down on Timoteo's head.

"Hold on to this," she said to the boy. "Use both hands."

"Why?"

"Just do it."

Timoteo warily raised his hands and placed them on either side of the ice bucket. Garr watched in unconcealed amusement.

"Are you holding it tightly?" Emma asked Timoteo.

"Yeah," said the boy.

"Are you ready?"

"Yeah."

Emma gave the bucket a sharp whap with her open hand.

"Hey!" yelped Timoteo, looking up with surprise.

"Don't let that fall off your head," ordered Emma.

"But you—"

"Now, open your mouth and say 'aaah.'"

Timoteo looked at her with a puzzled expression.

"You want me to leave you here with Mr. Garr?"

"Aaaah," said Timoteo.

Emma put three knuckles of her fist into the boy's mouth and whapped the ice bucket on his head again with her other hand, even harder this time. When she pulled her fist out of the boy's mouth it was full of pesos—a colorful pile of notes in every denomination.

"Hey! How you do that?" cried Timoteo with new respect, turning the bucket over and scrutinizing it for remainders. "Do it again! Make more money appear from my mouth!"

Emma had practiced the art of palming for years during down moments in restaurant jobs, experimenting with everything from meager tips to toasted bagels. She had never found much use for the skill in her act, however. Making Sweet'n Low appear from thin air in a Greek joint was pure magic. Onstage it just seemed like a trick.

"I wonder if I could persuade you to keep this, Mr. Garr," said Emma, handing the stack of pesos to the bald man. She wouldn't have used nearly as much money had she had a chance to count it off properly from the wad in her pocket.

"You trying to buy me off?"

"Not at all. Why don't you just think of it as kind of a souvenir?"

"A souvenir," said Garr, taking the bills. "I like that. That's real creative. Hey, you're okay, honey."

"And maybe you could give these to that Mr. Castleman," said Emma, snatching the ice bucket from Timoteo and handing it over to Garr, together with the stolen baseball cap. "It sounds like he might appreciate them."

"I'll do that," said Garr, storing both items in his armpit and putting down his baseball bat so he could put his "souvenir" in his pocket.

"How you do that? How you do that?" said Timoteo. "Teach me. Teach me."

"You just be quiet for a minute or I'll turn you into a toad."

Timoteo shut up.

"I appreciate your consideration in this, Mr. Garr."

"No sweat," said Garr amicably. "I appreciate yours."

"Actually, if you're in charge here, then you're the man I came to see."

"Yeah?"

"Yes. I'm looking for a boat."

"Well, we got plenty of 'em. What kind of boat you want?"

"Well, it's sort of a long story… Is it possible for me to use your bathroom first?"

"Sure, it's possible. I just don't know if you'd want to, that's all."

"I'd want to, believe me."

"Thing is, it ain't exactly the most elegant facility in the world," said Sid, a blush racing up his fat face, over his bushy cyebrows and across the vast expanse of his naked head. "Now that Madonna's moved out, I mean. She kinda cleaned it more oftener than I did, if you catch my drift."

Emma closed her eyes in pain at the thought of it, but didn't say anything.

"In the bow," said Sid. "Down the stairs. Don't step on the cat. I already stepped on him once today. He don't like it."

"Thank you," said Emma.

"Okay, I meet you at the car," said Timoteo, rising from his chair. Garr caught him by the arm.

"You stay here with me."

Garr and Timoteo were still sitting in awkward silence when she returned from the facilities a few moments later, only slightly worse for wear.

"So what boat you want to know about?" grunted Garr,

looking almost happy to see her. He clearly had no id
of what to do with a ten-year-old.

"It might not be here now, but it was somewhere
San Marcos about thirty years ago."

"Thirty years ago? You must be kidding. Thirty yea
ago I was a candy-ass kid learning boiler maintenan
from the U.S. Navy."

"Aren't there records you can check that go back th
far?"

"Sorry. Marina's only fourteen years old."

"Well, maybe it was still around when the mari
opened," said Emma hopefully. "Boats live a long tin
don't they?"

"Sometimes. If they're maintained okay. What's t
name of this tub?"

"The *Kaito Spirit.*"

"Never heard of it. It's not here now, that's for sure.

"Can you check your records? It's very important
me. I've come all the way from San Francisco to find it

"San Francisco, huh?" said Garr, his thick lips curli
into the wicked yellow semblance of a smile. "Nice tow
I knew a broad once in San Francisco...well, never min
But she was okay."

"Can you check?"

"Yeah, I guess. Come on. Keep an eye on light-finger
Louie there."

"Timoteo. My name is Timoteo."

Garr struggled to his feet and led the way onto the do
and back toward the gate where they had come in. Sever
men in shorts, boat owners from the look of them, nodd
to Garr as they walked through the marina. The bald m
acknowledged them with grunts. Emma walked direct
behind Timoteo, with her hand on his shoulder, though t
boy showed no apparent inclination to escape.

Eventually they came to a small wooden shack alo
the outer fence, a few hundred yards past the parking l
The shack had no windows and was painted white. T

adlock which was supposed to secure the door was open
and hung uselessly from the side of the latch.

Garr, his bushy eyebrows colliding angrily in the center
of his face, yanked the door open. Out fell a man who
Emma could only assume was Julio, judging by the guilty
expression on his face as he hit the ground and woke up.
He had been sleeping upright on a chair. The shack wasn't
large enough to contain much more than Julio, his rifle,
and a few stacks of books.

"Julio, goddammit," shouted Garr, kicking angrily at
the man's shoes. "If I catch you sleeping one more time,
I'm going to throw you in the ocean, you understand? You
gotta do your job, man. Go back there and guard the gate,
goddammit. What if there had been trouble? Jesus H.
Christ!"

Julio scrambled to pick up his rifle, then fled in the
direction of the front gate.

"Is there a lot of trouble here?" asked Emma.

"Nothing major, just kids looking for what they can get,
mostly. We pay the cops pretty good, and the San Marcans
are really pretty honest, just miserable poor. When the rev
olution comes, though, look out. Bad business, believe you
me. You get the kind of poverty they got here, you're just
asking for trouble. So let's see what we got here."

Garr entered the shack, rummaged around in the stacks
of books, and came out with two ledgers and the
straight-backed, armless chair on which Julio had been
sleeping.

"What was the name again?"

"The *Kaito Spirit*."

"Whose was it?"

"My grandfather's. Jacques Passant."

"Navy man?" asked Garr hopefully.

"No, I don't think so. He was French."

"Too bad," said Garr, disappointed. "Don't get many
Navy men down here. Just guys who learned their sailing
out of a bank account."

He placed the chair on the dusty ground in front of the shack, sat down, and leafed through the books for a few minutes.

"No *Kaito Spirit,*" said Garr finally, closing the volume. "Sorry."

"Well, it was a longshot." Emma sighed. "It would have been too easy to find it on my first stop, I suppose. There must be dozens of marinas on the island."

"What makes you think that?"

"I don't know. The ocean. A lot of people down here must have boats. Don't they?"

"This ain't exactly yacht-club territory, honey. Most of the locals don't got two sticks to rub together. The only reason you see all these boats is Las Calvos. People sail the Caribbean and stop here to play golf. Las Calvos is supposed to be one of the top courses in the hemisphere."

"You can't mean that this is the only marina on San Marcos?"

"It's the only one on this side of the island," grunted Garr. "There's another big one in Puerto Lavera, up north where you find the good beaches, but that's about it. The kind of folks who can afford these kind of craft don't have reason to go anywhere else on San Marcos but here and Puerto Lavera. Unless they've got their own estates. There are some of those. They got private docks. Nothing else in the whole country but dirt and poor people."

Emma was silent a moment, trying to think.

"Was the marina in Puerto Lavera in existence thirty years ago?" she asked finally.

"Sure. It's the been around since the twenties."

"How far of a drive is it?"

"Two or three hours, through the interior," said Garr, scratching the graying beard stubble on his face. "You can't drive there, though. Not from here."

"Why not?"

"Roads are for shit, and there's no gas. Bandits, too. Leftist guerrillas. Whatever you want to call them. You

tta take a plane from San Marcos City. But get yourself
room first, that's my advice. You're in the middle of
urist season, and it gets pretty crowded up there. Most
the decent places are sold out months in advance. A
ddy of mine went up last week and had to share a room
th eight cock-a-roaches and a rat.''

"Thanks for the tip," said Emma, discouraged. "Is
ere a place to get gas near here? And maybe something
eat?"

"Yeah, Las Calvos."

"Anywhere else?"

"What's wrong with Las Calvos? I woulda thought
u'd love it there."

"Well, you thought wrong."

Garr looked her over as if seeing her for the first time.

"There are gas stations in Benitra, that's up the coast a
ays."

"That's it?"

"Well, it's against regs, but I suppose I could sell you
tank for a hundred and fifty pesos."

"A hundred fifty pesos! Isn't that pretty expensive after
e nice souvenir I gave you, Mr. Garr? I only need about
lf a tank."

"Half a tank, whole tank, the risk's the same to me, and
at's what you're paying for. Now for twenty pesos more,
l be glad to throw in a couple of salami sandwiches..."

"I'll take them."

"...only I ate them for lunch."

"I guess I'll just take the gas then."

Garr grinned broadly, walked Emma back to her car and
d her pull around to the first dock, where an old-
shioned pump was concealed. It took a few minutes to
l her tank. Timoteo had gotten into the car and Emma
d handed over the extortionate payment before Garr
oke again.

"I just remembered," he said, leaning in on the door.
There used to be a marina in Migelina. You might poke

around there, see if they got any old records, before y
schlep all the way up to Puerto Lavera.''

"Where's Migelina?'' said Emma.

"South of the city. An hour's drive, maybe.''

"But the marina isn't there anymore?''

"No, not for twenty years, but there are still son
old-timers around who might remember this *Kaito Spi*
you're looking for. There's some rich folks with their ov
docks down there, too, from the old days. Migelina us
to be a resort town, pretty fancy—the Las Calvos of
day, until it got clobbered in Hurricane Jane. They st
talk about that one. Wrecked the whole south of the i
land.''

Emma thanked Sid Garr—though for what, she wasr
sure, the interlude had cost her a small fortune—and dro
out of the marina's sandy parking lot to the gate, whe
Timoteo had to get out of the car to open it. Emma didr
want to bother Julio, who was sitting against the fence fa
asleep, his rifle on his lap.

Timoteo was uncharacteristically quiet, and Emn
didn't speak until they were several miles away from tl
marina, back on the road they had taken up from San Ma
cos City.

"That was pretty stupid, Timoteo,'' she said finally.

"What?'' grunted the boy, crossing his arms in front
his chest defensively.

"Stealing those things.''

"I didn't steal nothing. A man gave them to me.''

"What man?''

"I don't know. A man.''

"Lying about it is worse.''

"I'm not lying. Why you call me a liar?''

Emma stamped on the brake. There was no one behir
her—there was no traffic in sight. The car skidded to
halt on the pitted concrete road. She leaned across the se
and opened Timoteo's door.

"Get out.''

Timoteo looked up at her, startled.

"Why you want me to get out?"

"I don't like thieves. Get out."

"I'm not a thief. I'm your guide. You can't find your way back to San Marcos City without Timoteo."

"I'll take my chances."

"You are joking," he said, laughing nervously. "You make joke on Timoteo."

"Get out, Timoteo. I'm bigger than you are and I'm as strong as a hickory stick. I'll throw you out physically if I have to."

Staring at her, the boy slid over and got out of the car. Emma leaned over and shut the door.

"You don't know nothing," Timoteo said, leaning in the open window. "You are ignorant lady. How you are going to talk to people without me? What if the police stop you again? What are you going to say? It is many miles back to San Marcos City."

"I thought you were my friend, Timoteo."

"I am your friend."

"No, you're not. I can trust my friends. My friends don't steal. My friends don't lie to me."

"Okay. I not lie to you or steal anymore."

"How am I supposed to believe you?"

"Because I'm telling the truth."

"You said you were telling the truth before, but you were lying."

"I'm telling the truth now."

"How do I know that? All I have is your word."

"My word is good. You believe me."

"Well, sorry. I don't. That's what happens to liars. People stop believing them, even when they aren't lying. How can I ever know if you're telling me the truth?"

"I'm telling the truth!" shouted Timoteo, his voice shrill with anger, frustration, and perhaps a little fear, Emma couldn't tell. "I'm telling the truth! I'm not lying! I'm telling the truth!"

"Okay," she said quietly.

"Can I get in?"

"Yes."

Timoteo opened the door and jumped onto the seat.

"We are friends?"

"I'm your friend," said Emma. "Are you mine?"

"Timoteo is your friend. He will not lie anymore to you. You are having your period, right?"

"What?" exclaimed Emma. It was not a question she expected from a ten-year-old boy.

"My aunt sometimes gets crazy like you, when she says she is having her period."

"I'm not having my period," said Emma, restarting the engine.

The boy nodded soberly.

"Then I think maybe you are hungry. I know I am. And that is the truth."

"WHAT EXACTLY DOES THE sign say?" asked Emma forty minutes later, outside a place she wouldn't have stopped at on her own in a million years.

It was no wonder she hadn't noticed it on the drive up—it looked like the kind of abandoned, boarded-up joints you passed on stretches of road that had lost all their traffic to interstates and McDonald's. No interstates had ever stolen business from "Comedero," however. And there were no McDonald's in sight.

"It says they have good food, come on," said Timoteo, getting out of the car and leading the way to a screen door at the side of the building.

They entered and found themselves in a dark little room with five Formica tables. Two chubby women with stringy black hair were sitting on stools at one end of the single small room. Next to them was a four-burner white stove and an old green refrigerator, neither very clean.

"*Qué tiene de comer?*" said Timoteo in the direction

f the women, walking to a table in the back and sitting
down without ceremony.

"Sopa de carne y habichuelas," giggled the taller of
the two, brushing away a stray hair from her face. Or was
it a fly?

"They have bean soup with meat today," said Timoteo,
leaning back in his chair as if he owned the place.

"What kind of meat?" asked Emma, sitting down
cross from him, feeling very American and very squea-
nish.

Timoteo shouted the question to the women in Spanish.
A conversation ensured that lasted several minutes, with
both of the women chattering happily at once for most of
the time and Timoteo putting in his two cents occasionally.
Finally everybody fell silent.

"It is meat," said Timoteo to Emma, nodding posi-
ively. "Okay?"

"What else do they have?"

The tuna-fish salad didn't seem like a good bet in a
place where they kept the mayonnaise in an open dish in
the cupboard. Neither did a dish that Timoteo could translate only as "peanut-butter corn." Emma settled for two
lusty bags of Cheeze Doodles and a bottle of Coke after
ascertaining that the packaging was intact.

Timoteo had the bean soup with meat, which he seemed
to enjoy. Emma finished a whole bag of Cheeze Doodles
without commenting on the boy's table manners. He apparently had adopted for use on his spoon the grip Sid
Garr had employed on his baseball bat.

"How is it?" she asked finally.

"Good," said Timoteo, his mouth full.

"What are those?" Emma asked, indicating the plate of
yellow things one of the women had brought out and
which Timoteo ate with his fingers between spoonfuls of
soup.

"Fried plantains. You want some?"

"No, thanks. It would be easier to eat if you sat up straight."

The boy was hovering an inch over the dish on his elbows while he shoveled the food into his face.

"Mmmphgaagh."

"And don't talk with your mouth full."

"Why not?"

"Because it's not polite."

Timoteo looked at her, confused. Then he sat up a little straighter and grinned, remembering only too late to close his mouth.

"We are going to Migelina tomorrow?" he asked.

"I don't know. Have you ever been there?"

"Sure. I go there all the time."

Emma didn't say anything.

"No, maybe that was another place I go." Timoteo caught himself. Then he brightened. "But there is only one road south from the city. It will be easy to find. I have taken that road to El Morro and to Guachupita. We will get on it, and we can find Migelina easy. I can take you tomorrow. What time should I come?"

"I have to think about this, Timoteo," said Emma.

"Maybe tomorrow you let me wear your tennis shoes? They will fit me."

"No."

The boy slurped his soup happily and stuffed the remaining plantains into his mouth.

Emma spent the rest of the long trip back to San Marco City—two and a half more hours—trying to decide what to do next: head up to Puerto Lavera or try to find Migelina? The odds of finding the *Kaito Spirit* in either place seemed slim.

It was nearly seven o'clock before she pulled up to the gates of the hotel and dropped Timoteo off, telling him to meet her in front of the hotel tomorrow.

"You will not be sorry," said Timoteo, smiling hi

broad bright smile, his big brown eyes dancing. "We are friends. We will have fine time. Just like today."

Emma watched him run off into the waning light, wondering how he could possibly be so happy. What kind of place was he going home to tonight? Did he really live with an aunt and Changee Money? Or was he going home to a cardboard box in the street somewhere? Did he know where his next meal was coming from?

As she drove into the hotel parking lot, Emma caught a glimpse of herself in the rearview mirror—a bright young woman with a nice hotel room, and an inheritance on the way. Timoteo had looked as if he were on top of the world. She looked as if she had its entire weight on her shoulders.

THIRTEEN

"ASK HIM IF HE REMEMBERS the marina," said Emma wearily, looking around for a shady place to sit down—or at least get out of the sun. There wasn't any.

It was the next morning, and Emma had found Migelina with surprisingly little trouble. There was only one main road south from San Marcos City, as Timoteo had said, and it had led directly to the old resort town Sid Garr had told them about, the place where a marina had disappeared twenty years ago in a hurricane.

The problem was that, except for its location on a sheltered inlet, Migelina looked like all the other poor villages they had driven through the day before, only larger. The buildings were of crudely painted wood and corrugated steel. The decaying streets were more mud than concrete. If Migelina had been the Las Calvos of its day, then it was a good advertisement for hurricane insurance. Not a trace of anything but poverty remained.

"He say he remember the marina," said Timoteo, who had been chattering in Spanish to a man without shoes whose broad smile revealed numerous missing teeth.

"Does he remember the *Kaito Spirit?*" said Emma.

They had talked with dozens of people, it seemed, since parking the car and getting out to walk the narrow streets of Migelina. Most had not even known that there had once been a marina there. Emma was not sure they were in the right place until they found an elderly man who walked them down to the water and showed them what was left of the rock pilings where the piers had once stood. But he had not heard of the *Kaito Spirit*. No one had.

The man without shoes spoke again.

"He say he knows a man who talks about the *Kaito Spirit*," translated Timoteo, turning to Emma.

"Where is this man?" asked Emma, perking up.

"He say he will tell for ten pesos," said Timoteo, staring at the shoeless man contemptuously and spitting a long stream onto the dusty ground. "He is lying."

Emma dug into the pocket of her jeans and produced a ten-peso note, which she held out. Timoteo grabbed it before the man could.

"Why do you give him money? He is lying. He is a miserable lying dog."

"Give it to him, Timoteo," said Emma. "We might as well check out his story. We don't have any other leads."

Timoteo reluctantly held out the note, which the man took with much bowing, scraping and smiling. Then he spoke animatedly in Spanish for several minutes to Timoteo, who listened with his arms folded in front of his chest, his face skeptical. Finally the man finished and walked off, turning back every few feet to nod and smile.

"So?" said Emma, when the man had turned the corner and disappeared out of sight. Timoteo spat in the dust again, then spoke.

"He say there is an old man who lives on Calle de las Flores on the other end of town, who used to work on the boat, the *Kaito Spirit*. He say this man lives in a big yellow house next to an almond tree. He is called Eduardo and he is big and fat and well-known to everybody on the street because he gives candy to all the children."

"All right, let's go find him."

Emma led the way back to the car. It took fifteen more minutes to find Calle de las Flores, a narrow dead-end street on the far side of town. There were some potted plants in front of one of the rickety-looking wooden buildings, but no almond or any other kind of trees. None of the houses was yellow.

"I told you he was lying," said Timoteo, snickering.

"Ask her," said Emma, pointing to a sad-looking black woman sitting in front of one of the buildings.

Timoteo walked over and spoke to her. The woman shrugged and eventually replied in a low, slow voice. Timoteo nodded and returned to Emma's side.

"She say there is no almond tree, no yellow house, no man named Eduardo, no big and fat men living here at all. And nobody gives candy to the children. I told you."

"You told me."

"What we do now? Go swimming?"

"Ask her if she remembers the marina," said Emma, indicating the woman again.

Timoteo made a face, but walked back to the woman. They spoke again, longer this time.

"She say there are men at the market who used to work at the marina," said the boy when he returned. "They sell all kinds of things now. She say she knows the man who sells tires and he is very nice. His name is Fimo. You want to go there?"

"She's talking about the market near where we came into town?"

"Yeah, I think."

Emma looked over to the woman, smiled and waved. The woman nodded and smiled a sad smile.

They drove back through Migelina to the hilly street where Emma had first seen the market. It occupied a large open-sided building—no more than a roof on wooden supports, really—where people were selling merchandise of every kind. Inside, the dirt floor was covered with straw. The air was ripe with smells of pigs and chickens.

A thin black man with grizzled hair was sitting in one of the first stalls by the door, atop a pile of worn automobile tires. He wore no shirt, revealing a sinewy chest and protruding ribs. A tiny gold cross hung on a chain around his neck.

Timoteo addressed him in Spanish, but after a moment the man waved his hand and smiled brightly at Emma.

"It's okay. I speak English very good."

"Are you Fimo?"

"Fimo, sí. You want buy tires from me?"

"Not exactly…"

"It's okay, I have many other things," said Fimo, bounding down from his perch and digging through the cardboard boxes at the foot of his pile of tires.

"Please don't go to any trouble."

"I sell to you cheap," declared Fimo, triumphantly holding up a toaster and a plastic umbrella covered with pink polka dots.

"Thank you," said Emma. "They're very nice, but I'm just trying to find out some information about a boat that used to be at the marina. We were told you used to work there."

"Sí," said Fimo with a big smile. "I was crew for many fine boats. I very good sailor, like very much."

"Did you ever hear of the *Kaito Spirit?*"

"Don't think so…*Kaito Spirit.* It was long time ago. Before the big hurricane wreck everything, and all the rich peoples go away, never coming back. What you gonna do?"

Fimo smiled broadly.

"Do you know anyone else who worked at the marina who might know the *Kaito Spirit?*"

"We go ask. Come."

Fimo tossed the toaster and plastic umbrella unceremoniously onto his pile of tires, then led the way from stall to stall, greeting people with the same broad smile. He stopped occasionally to speak in Spanish—conversations that Emma could not understand, but which all included the words *Kaito Spirit,* and which all ended with head shaking or shrugs.

"Sorry, but cannot find your boat for you," said Fimo finally, throwing his hands in the air, his big smile unperturbed. "The marina was very big. Many boats. All gone now. What else can Fimo do for you?"

"Thanks anyway," said Emma with a sigh. "This whole idea is hopeless. I must be nuts."

"You want to buy some fruit?" said Timoteo, who had wandered over to a stall across the way from where Emma and Fimo were standing and was looking at a pile of peaches.

"I know," declared Fimo, holding up his finger suddenly. "Maybe you go talk to Señor Zuberan. Maybe he can help you."

"Señor Zuberan?"

"Sí. It was Señor Zuberan who own the marina. He is a great man, very rich. He take care of many people."

"Where do I find this Señor Zuberan?" asked Emma.

"You must drive to the south and then follow the road to his property. Señor Zuberan own much land. My cousin used to work there in the kitchen and he say that Señor Zuberan's house is as big as the stadium in Benitra."

"We buy these?" said Timoteo, holding up a handful of peaches.

"Yes, let's buy those," said Emma happily, digging into her pocket for money. If this Señor Zuberan had owned the marina, he was more likely to remember the *Kaito Spirit* than anyone they had yet talked to—provided, of course, that the boat had been here.

Emma owed Fimo a debt of gratitude. After giving some change to Timoteo for the peaches, she peeled off a twenty-peso note and held it out to the happy tire man.

"You no buy anything," said Fimo, shaking his head.

"You've helped me, Fimo," said Emma. "I'd like to give you something in return."

"Fimo help everybody. No take money unless fair and square. You want to buy something, yes?"

Without waiting for an answer, Fimo dived into his pile of tires and surfaced with a big smile, a flowerpot, and an original-cast LP of *Oklahoma!*

Emma smiled back. So far the polka-dot plastic umbrella looked like the best bet. She apparently had to take some-

ing for the sake of his pride, but didn't need a toaster
nd sure as hell wasn't going to buy any tires.

"You have wood carvings from Indians?" said Timo-
:o, coming over chewing a peach, his mouth full. "She
>oks to buy carvings."

"Ah," said Fimo happily and dug back into his pile of
res. What he held up after a moment next to his smiling
lack face sent a chill down Emma's spine.

It was about nine inches high—a kneeling figure with
encil-thin legs, high forehead and huge eye sockets. The
'ood from which it was carved was dark brown, almost
lack, and obviously heavy. Emma recognized the style at
nce. She had seen others so similar that they might have
een made by the same hand. They had stood in solemn
>rmation for as long as she could remember in the exact
ame place they must be standing now: in the house on
otrero Hill, on the top of Pépé's dresser, around the
10del of the *Kaito Spirit*.

MMA FOLLOWED Fimo's directions, heading south from
ligelina for twenty minutes, then taking the poorly
1arked road to the Zuberan estate. Immediately the
:rubby vegetation that had bordered the main road was
:placed by tall trees and masses of flowers.

A ten-foot-high wall surrounded the estate. Made of
rown and gray stones mortared together and covered with
10ss and lichens, the wall looked as organic as the veg-
tation, almost as if it had grown out of the earth. On top
f the wall, jagged pieces of broken glass embedded in the
:ment glistened in the sun.

It was an ugly way to keep people out, Emma thought
ncomfortably, realizing suddenly that Señor Zuberan
1ight not be as eager to see her as she was to see him.

But see him she had to.

The wood figurine that Emma had bought from Fimo
ad clinched it. It was Kaito. Fimo had declared that what
'as left of the tribe lived in the forests near here; Migelina

was where they had always sold their handiwork. The fig
urine tipped the odds that her grandfather had indeed sailed
on the *Kaito Spirit* from this harbor. Zuberan was the only
person Emma knew who might be able to say for sure.
She had come too far to go away now without talking to
him.

"How are you doing over there?" Emma asked, glanc
ing at Timoteo, who was slouched in the passenger seat
with his feet on the dashboard and his eyes closed.

"I'm okay," grunted the boy.

"Didn't get enough sleep last night?"

"Yeah."

Where had he been? Emma wondered. What had he
been doing? She tried not to think about it. It was none of
her business.

"Would you like me to take you back to Migelina?"

"Why?" said Timoteo, not opening his eyes.

"You could sit on the beach and take a nap or some
thing while I see this Mr. Zuberan. I don't know how much
fun this is going to be for you."

"I don't need any nap."

"You're sure?"

"I am your guide. I stay with you."

Emma drove for several more minutes along the forbid
ding wall of the vast estate, wondering again what she was
doing there.

"Did you ever do something that didn't make any log
ical sense," Emma asked, "But you just had a feeling that
you should, that it was important?"

"I guess." Timoteo yawned, stretching in his seat.

"Is it healthy to do something like that, do you think?
Or is it some kind of compulsive behavior?"

"Huh?"

"I'm asking if you think I'm crazy."

Timoteo opened his big brown eyes at her and grinned.

"Yeah. You pretty crazy."

"Thanks a lot!"

The stone barrier had curved inward. Emma turned into the drive and brought the car to a halt in front of a pair of enormous iron gates. Next to the gates was a stone gatehouse from which three men in khaki uniforms stared coldly out at her.

Emma waited, uncertain what to do. For nearly a minute nothing happened. Then the door of the gatehouse swung open. One of the men came out and slowly approached the car. He was tall and thin, with the catlike bearing of a professional soldier. His eyes were concealed behind dark sunglasses. In one hand he held a clipboard. In a black leather holster on his belt was the biggest gun Emma had ever seen in her life.

The guard came directly to her window, bent down and scrutinized Emma and the boy. Then he spoke in crisp, authoritative Spanish.

"He wants to know who we are and what we want," said Timoteo, staring back defiantly at the man.

"Interpret for me," said Emma, her mouth suddenly dry. "My name is Emma Passant. I've come from the United States. I'm looking for information about a boat that I believe may have been at the marina in Migelina that Mr. Zuberan used to own. I'd like to talk to him about it."

Timoteo had been translating as Emma had gone along. The guard listened silently, his face opaque, his eyes invisible behind his sunglasses. Now he checked his clipboard and spoke again.

"He say your name is not on his list," said Timoteo when the man stopped talking. "He say we have no business with Señor Zuberan and must go away."

"I only want to ask a few questions," stammered Emma.

Timoteo translated. The guard shook his head.

"It will only take a few minutes of Señor Zuberan's time. Say please."

The man shook his head again.

Emma fought down a moment of panic. She smiled h
sweetest smile and did her best to bat her eyes from behir
her glasses. Emma knew she wasn't great with men, b
figured it was worth a shot. The guard's reaction did notl
ing to improve her self-esteem. He unsnapped the leath
thong of his holster and put his hand on the butt of h
revolver.

"He is a pig," sneered Timoteo. "He will not reall
shoot you. Only a coward would shoot a woman."

"How much money does he want just to call Señd
Zuberan and ask?" said Emma in desperation. "Tell hir
I'll give him a hundred pesos. Two hundred."

Timoteo shot her a smug, I-told-you-so smile and bega
to speak, but the guard cut him short with a few curt wore
in Spanish.

"What did he say?" asked Emma, feeling her be
chance to learn about the *Kaito Spirit* slipping away.

"He say the guards of Señor Zuberan are not for sale.

"Apologize to him."

"Why should we apologize?" said Timoteo. "We di
nothing."

"Don't argue. Tell him I'm very sorry if I've offende
him. Tell him I must talk with Señor Zuberan. It's e:
tremely important."

Timoteo made a face, then began to translate. The gua
spoke angrily before the boy could finish.

"He say we are on private property," said Timote
"He say we must go away right now."

"It's not private property across the road, is it?" Emm
said, suddenly angry herself.

She started the car and backed out of the drive, parkir
beneath a group of palm trees across from the gates of tl
Zuberan estate. The guard stood for a few moments watcl
ing her, then returned to the gatehouse.

"We go swimming now?" asked Timoteo hopefully.

"No," said Emma, glancing at her watch; it was a litt
before noon. "You hungry yet?"

"I guess," said the boy, shrugging his shoulders as if he could take food or leave it.

"Come on. We'll have a picnic."

"Picnic?"

"You'll see."

Emma reached into the back seat for the two white boxes the hotel kitchen had made up at her request. After yesterday's lunch experience, Emma had decided to come prepared. She and Timoteo got out of the car and sat down between the flowers at the foot of the largest palm.

Emma had had fruit and cereal for breakfast a few hours before and wasn't very hungry, but for the next fifteen minutes she ate her chicken sandwich, drank her lemonade, and pretended to be having a great time.

Timoteo didn't have to pretend. He happily wolfed down his food, chattering with his mouth full about how he had picnics all the time. He was still hungry after he had finished his sandwich and all the fruit in the boxes, so Emma let him eat her piece of cake as well as his own.

In the gatehouse across the road the unreadable faces of guards filled the windows. Fighting down the impulse to hurl a rock at them, Emma picked some flowers and made a garland, which she set like a crown on Timoteo's head. She thought the boy might brush it away as not macho enough, but instead he seemed delighted. The guards, however, turned to one another in evident dismay. At last she was getting somewhere! Emma took Timoteo's hands in hers and began dancing around the palm tree, determined not to lose the initiative. Veins began to bulge visibly out of the guards' necks.

Within a minute one of them emerged from the gatehouse and crossed the road. This man was older and smaller than the guard who had spoken to them before. He had the sleek build of an athlete and wore the same enormous revolver on his hip as the man who had tried to send them away. Timoteo seemed disappointed that Emma stopped their dance to talk to him.

"I am Capitán Ortiz," said the guard in English, re
moving his sunglasses. His voice was curt and profes
sional. His small brown eyes were cold, his face stern
"You cannot stay here, Señorita."

"Are we standing on Señor Zuberan's property now
Capitán Ortiz?" said Emma cheerfully, demonstrating he
sweetest smile again.

"No, but you still cannot stay here."

"We're just having a picnic. Are we breaking some
law?"

"You cannot dance across from our gate."

"Why not?"

"Because it is not allowed."

"But why?"

"Because it is not...appropriate."

"Come on, Capitán Ortiz." Emma laughed. "It's in
nocence itself. Are you afraid that people won't take you
guns seriously if you allow women and children to have
picnics within your field of vision?"

"We are not afraid," said Capitán Ortiz, squaring hi
shoulders. "It is just not allowed, that is all. You must g
away."

"You seem like a reasonable man, señor," said Emma
"I've come a very long way. Won't you just call Seño
Zuberan and ask if he'll see me? If he says no, then we'
leave. That's fair, isn't it?"

The capitán glanced over his shoulder. Across the roa
in the gatehouse the two other guards were staring back
their expressions unreadable behind their sunglasses.

"It is pointless," said Capitán Ortiz, shaking his head
"Señor Zuberan sees no one without an appointment."

"Then you'll lose nothing by calling, will you? He'
just say no."

Ortiz stared at the garland of flowers in Timoteo's hai
and frowned.

"When he says no, you will go away?"

"We'll go away," said Emma, figuring to use tears only as a last resort.

The guard captain stared at her another moment, then took a walkie-talkie from his back pocket.

"Tell him I'm looking for information about a boat that may have been in the marina here thirty years ago," said Emma. "Tell him it's extremely important."

Capitán Ortiz frowned, then nodded.

"Your name?"

"Emma Passant."

He took out a walkie-talkie and spoke into it in Spanish. A curt voice answered through a fog of electronic static. A brief conversation ensued. After a pause, another voice came on. Ortiz spoke into the walkie-talkie again. After the response, he looked up and spoke to Emma.

"What boat is it that you wish to know about?"

"It was called the *Kaito Spirit*," said Emma.

Ortiz repeated the name into his walkie-talkie. After a long, silent moment, the voice on the other end spoke again. The guard captain stared at the walkie-talkie, then at Emma. Then he spoke a few more words in Spanish and clicked off the device.

"Señor Zuberan has graciously agreed to receive you," he announced stiffly. "Wait here."

Ortiz walked back across the road and conferred briefly with his colleagues, who turned to stare at Emma periodically. As he returned to Emma's side of the road, the other guards began opening the huge iron gates.

"I will accompany you to the house," said Ortiz, holding the car door for Emma. "You will stay on the road as I direct."

"Thank you," said Emma, getting in, wondering herself why Zuberan had suddenly agreed to see her. What was she getting herself—and Timoteo—into?

Unconcerned, the boy ran around the car and let himself in on the passenger side. Their escort took his place in the back seat, staring pointedly at the offending floral crown

on Timoteo's head and clearing his throat until Emma re
moved it and deposited it on the dashboard. In anothe
moment they were through the open gates and into th
estate.

Emma drove as the guard directed, along a winding roa
flanked with an astonishing array of vegetation. The tree
here seemed to have found their places naturally. The flow
ers, which bloomed on every side, might have evolved i
their beds—so perfectly did their colors and shapes com
plement one another.

Twice the road crossed streams that ran through th
property, and several times Timoteo pointed in open
mouthed astonishment at the peacocks in full finery stroll
ing at the sides of the road. Emma also caught sight c
several more guards patrolling the property. Each wa
dressed in the same uniform as the men at the gate, thoug
these guards carried submachine guns in addition to th
gigantic revolvers on their hips.

It took a full ten minutes for them to reach the house
For all Emma knew, Fimo's cousin might have been righ
about it being as large as a stadium. The Spanish-styl
hacienda was nestled in a sea of trees and vines and flow
ers, and there was no way to tell how far its adobe wall
extended or how many courtyards they enclosed.

"Quite a spread you've got here," she said, pulling th
car up as instructed in front of a massive wooden-and-iro
entryway framed with palm trees and tropical flowers.

"Wait here," said Capitán Ortiz. He got out of the bac
seat, walked to the door and pulled a chain by its side.

Emma flashed Timoteo a grin, but the boy did not re
spond. He looked distinctly unhappy, out of his elemen
intimidated, frightened. Again she regretted bringing hir
here, but it was too late to turn back now.

After a moment the door of the house was opened by
small white-haired man in black pants, a white waiter'
jacket and a thin bow tie. The man spoke a few words i

Spanish to the guard captain, who nodded and then returned to the car.

"Abraham will bring you to Señor Zuberan," said Ortiz, opening Emma's door.

"Thank you for your help, Capitán Ortiz," said Emma, getting out.

Ortiz touched his hat with the tip of his fingers, then stood by the car at parade rest as Emma and Timoteo made their way to the door. They stepped inside into a large cool room with a high ceiling.

It took Emma's eyes a moment to adjust to the dimmer light. The first thing she noticed was the shields and suits of armor lining the walls. The second was the two hulking, apelike characters in dark-blue suits standing in the center of the room. They had no weapons in open view, but their armpits bulged unnaturally. One growled several sentences in sibilant Spanish.

"He say they are Señor Zuberan's bodyguards," said Timoteo, obviously impressed. "He say they will give their lives for him."

"I'm pleased to meet them, too," murmured Emma. "Señor Zuberan certainly has a lot of guards. I wonder why?"

"All rich people on San Marcos have mens to guard them," snorted Timoteo, but Emma could easily see the frightened little boy behind the bravura.

The white-haired man whom Capitán Ortiz had called Abraham gestured with his hand for Emma and Timoteo to follow him. They did so, through an archway into a series of cool rooms and corridors. The men in the blue suits brought up the rear, looking ready to die at any necessary moment.

The floors here were terra-cotta tile or slate, though most were covered with beautiful Oriental carpets: room-sized medallion serapes; hunting and garden rugs; elegant Persian runners with fantastic floral arabesques and muted, perfectly matched colors. Furniture of dark, rich wood gave an austere but solid warmth to long corridors hung with tapestries and oil paintings. Every bit of space seemed to harbor some antique or work of art. Huge silver candlesticks and Hispano-Moresque plates sat on wooden tables braced with iron. Marble statues stood in quiet corners on stone bases. Emma counted five grandfather clocks, most of them with heavy ormolu mountings and intricate dials.

No wonder Señor Zuberan had the kind of security he did, she thought, relaxing a bit. This kind of wealth in a country as poor as San Marcos was bound to attract attention. One look at Timoteo confirmed this: his eyes were wide with amazement; he looked like Ali Baba in the cave of the forty thieves.

Abraham—who Emma decided was some kind of ancient houseboy—led them through a door into an open colonnade that framed a courtyard with a central fountain of white marble. From here they entered another, more modern wing of the house, where the floors were carpeted wall-to-wall and the furniture was overstuffed and comfortable-looking.

After passing through several plush rooms, also packed to bursting with objects of art, they came to what Emma realized must be a ballroom—a huge open space with parquet floors, ornate moldings, and French doors. Three enormous rock-crystal chandeliers hung from the ceiling, providing light. The entire room was painted a luminescent white, and for an instant Emma had the unsettling illusion that she was surrounded by vast banks of snow.

Their escort opened a pair of the French doors.

Emma found herself at the top of a short flight of steps leading down to a grassy lawn that extended a few hundred feet and ended at a short wall. From where she stood, Emma could see the sheer drop-off beyond the wall and could imagine waves breaking on a rocky shore far below.

In the center of the lawn was a round table, sheltered by an umbrella and surrounded by four white iron chairs.

Seated at the table was a slight man with close-cropped salt-and-pepper hair. Behind him the vast blue panorama of the Caribbean stretched out to infinity.

Emma descended the stairs. The man sensed her presence after only an instant. He put down his newspaper and rose from his chair as they approached.

"Miss...Passant, is it?" he said in a soft voice with barely a trace of an accent when Emma stopped a few feet from him. "Welcome to my home. I am Bernal Zuberan."

"Thank you for seeing me, Señor Zuberan."

"It is I who must thank you, my dear. We don't get many unexpected visitors out here. Certainly none as charming as yourself."

His skin was fair. His eyes were pale gray and set in a web of faint wrinkles. He had a kind smile and seemed genuinely pleased to see her. Emma estimated him to be in his early fifties.

"And who is your friend?" he said, grinning at Timoteo.

"My name is Timoteo," answered the boy, wide-eyed. "I am the best guide in San Marcos."

"I am very pleased to make your acquaintance, Timoteo."

Zuberan smiled benignly and extended his hand. Timoteo reached out and shook it, tentatively at first, then as if it were the handle of a pump.

"Don't break the man's arm, Timoteo," said Emma.

"It's all right," said Zuberan, laughing, as he finally managed to extricate himself. "Boys are naturally enthusiastic. We will be having lunch in a short while. Perhaps you will join me?"

"Thanks, but we've already eaten."

"Do you have ice cream?" asked Timoteo in an eager voice.

"Timoteo!"

"Of course we have ice cream." Zuberan laughed again. "Abraham, why don't you take Timoteo to the

kitchen and see that he gets all the ice cream he wants. I
it is all right with Miss Passant, of course."

All eyes turned to Emma.

"You don't want to make yourself sick," she said, un
comfortable at the thought of being parted from the boy.

"You cannot get sick from ice cream," said Timote
knowingly. "I eat ice cream all the time and do not ge
sick."

"Well, if it's what you want..."

"Are you certain we can't get you anything, Miss Pas
sant?" said Zuberan. "Some coffee, perhaps?"

Emma hesitated. She was drinking entirely too muc
coffee. She should really cut down.

"Yes, please," said Emma, wondering why she was al
ways faced with the one temptation she was unable t
resist. "If it's not too much trouble..."

"No trouble at all. Two coffees for us, Abraham, whe
Timoteo is settled. Let him play with Esteban's Nintendo
if he likes."

"Sí, señor," said the white-haired houseboy. Then h
turned and headed back to the house. Timoteo ran afte
him, not glancing back.

"Esteban is my son," said Zuberan after a momen
"He is about Timoteo's age, but is not often here anymor
to enjoy his things. He lives mostly with his mother now
In Switzerland."

Emma nodded, barely listening. She stared at Timoteo'
small departing figure, wondering if he would make him
self ill, despite his protests. She suddenly felt very muc
alone.

"Won't you sit down?" said Zuberan. He indicated th
chair with the best view of the vast blueness of the ocean
then nodded to the two Neanderthals, who retreated to a
alcove by the side of the house, out of earshot.

"You have a lot of men to guard you, señor," sai
Emma, taking her seat as Zuberan held the chair.

"Yes, unfortunately the political situation here is ver

unsettled at present," her host replied, sitting down across from her at the table. "In other countries only gangsters and politicians need this kind of protection. On San Marcos, however, anyone with money and property must think about his own safety—the authorities are no help at all; part of the problem, in fact. As you see, I have done well and have much to protect."

"I didn't realize that owning marinas could be so lucrative."

"It isn't, I assure you," Zuberan replied with a gentle laugh. "That is why I have not owned a marina for many years. I am in financial services now."

"I'm sorry. I didn't mean to pry."

"No, no. It would be unnatural if you were not curious. Money is a fascinating thing. No matter how much we have, we all seem to want more. I have been a very lucky man. Is that seat comfortable for you?"

"Yes, it's fine, thanks," said Emma. Her iron chair had a thick seat cushion and was surprisingly comfortable.

"So, tell me, my dear," said Zuberan, studying her face carefully, almost like a boxer sizing up an opponent. "You have been in San Marcos long?"

"No, only a few days."

"And you are staying at the Casimente?"

"Yes. How did you know?"

"Just a guess. Many Americans stay at the Casimente. Do you like it there?"

"Yes, it's very nice."

Zuberan nodded.

"Obviously you are a resourceful young woman. You have been in San Marcos for only a brief time and yet you have found your way down here to this remote place. As I said, we don't get many tourists in Migelina these days."

"I'm not a tourist. I'm looking for information. It's very important to me. It may be the key to two murders."

"Indeed?" said Zuberan, raising an eyebrow. "Who was murdered?"

"My grandfather and another man," said Emma. "[
think their deaths might be somehow tied to a boat th
was once in your marina."

"The *Kaito Spirit*," said Zuberan slowly.

"Do you remember it?"

"Yes, I remember the *Kaito Spirit*."

"You do?" asked Emma, almost afraid to believe h
ears.

"Yes, but frankly, Miss Passant, I do not see what po
sible connection there could be between the *Kaito Spir*
and these murders of which you speak. This boat was d
stroyed twenty years ago in the hurricane. You must hav
been just a little girl."

"My grandfather used to own the *Kaito Spirit*," sai
Emma, almost bursting with excitement.

"I'm afraid that is impossible."

"What do you mean? Why is it impossible?"

"It was I who owned the *Kaito Spirit*."

"Then my grandfather must have owned it before yo
did," stammered Emma.

"When was this? What was his name?"

"His name was Jacques Passant. And it was more tha
thirty years ago. I don't know exactly. Sometime before
was born."

"No," Zuberan declared. "It cannot be."

"It's true. I promise you my grandfather owned th
Kaito Spirit, Señor Zuberan. A model of it disappeare
from his dresser in his room after he was killed. In h
will, he said that the *Kaito Spirit* was my legacy."

Zuberan's face had gone pale. When he spoke again, h
voice quavered.

"What did he look like, this Jacques Passant?"

"He was short and a bit round," said Emma, suddenl
feeling frightened herself, though she could think of r
reason why. "With high cheekbones and sandy hair. H
was French and spoke English with an accent. He had

eculiar manner of speech, I don't know exactly how to
lescribe it..."

"Someone who might call a boat he owned 'the hole in
he water into which I pour money'?"

"Yes, that's exactly like something my grandfather
vould have said. You *did* know him!"

"Yes," said Zuberan in a voice so small it was almost
naudible. "I knew him. But not by the name of Jacques
'assant."

"What do you mean? That was his name!"

"Maybe at some later date it was. But the little French-
nan who owned the *Kaito Spirit* and who spoke in the
eculiar manner that you describe was not called Jacques
'assant when he lived here in Migelina. His name was
:tienne Lalou."

FOURTEEN

"BUT WHY WOULD my grandfather have changed h
name?" said Emma, feeling as if she had been slappe
across the face.

"To hide, perhaps," said Zuberan.

"Hide? Hide from whom? From what?"

"Obviously he had something to be frightened of. D
you know who killed him?"

Emma shook her head helplessly. She felt none of th
relief or excitement she had expected after all the dea
ends. Instead she felt terrified, as though she had alread
learned too much. It made no sense. She had come all th
way precisely to find out about the *Kaito Spirit*, to tie
somehow to her grandfather's murder. Suddenly, howeve
she wanted to run away and not hear another word.

"Why, you must be Marie's daughter," said Zubera
his face lighting up with surprise.

"You knew my mother, too?"

"Of course. Now I see the resemblance. But she wa
just a little girl then. It was so long ago. Tell me how sh
is. Did she grow up tall and lovely like you? It is impo
sible for me to think of her as an adult."

"I'm sorry, Señor Zuberan. I'm afraid my mother die
when I was born."

"No!" shouted Zuberan, banging the table with the fl
of his palm, his smile collapsing. "Don't tell me this!"

Emma froze at the violence of his outburst, not knowi
what to do. The men at the side of the house suddenly ha
guns in their hands. They began moving toward the tabl
but had taken only a few steps when Zuberan recovere
his composure and waved them back to their places.

"Forgive me, my dear," her host whispered. "It is horrible to hear this sad news all at once. Somehow, I always thought I would see them again. Etienne. Marie. Both dead."

Zuberan put his hands to his temple and lowered his head. Emma waited in uncertainty and anticipation until he finally looked up again, his expression seemingly calm, his face unreadable.

"I know my reaction must seem very odd to you, Emma," he said in a hoarse voice.

"I..."

"No, please. I know I am a stranger to you. It is you who have suffered the loss. Your grandfather. Your mother. But I assure you, my dear, we share a common bond. The man I knew as Etienne Lalou was like a father to me. Everything I have today I owe to him. Whoever killed him must be brought to justice."

"That's why I've come here," said Emma, searching for words, still shaken by the bodyguards' armed response. "The police think it was just a random killing."

"But you don't."

"No."

"What can I do to help?" Zuberan said, his face suddenly hard, his gray eyes blazing.

"You can tell me about the *Kaito Spirit*."

"Of course. But where to start? I sailed on the *Kaito Spirit* with Etienne—with your grandfather—for almost ten years."

Emma blinked her eyes. The *Kaito Spirit* had been the little model on Pépé's dresser to her. Suddenly it was no longer that symbol, but the real thing. Real people had sailed on her across a sea of time as well as water. Whatever secrets the boat concealed would be four-dimensional, too. Asking for information about the *Kaito Spirit* was like asking about the Supreme Court or about Chicago—the answer would depend on what point in time you wanted to know about. Where along the *Kaito Spirit*'s time-line

did the strand of destiny that had led to Jacques Passant
murder cross? Where had this all begun?

"My grandfather once told me that he had stolen th
most precious treasure of the sea and could never g
back," said Emma, remembering the day on the San Fran
cisco Bay so many years ago. "Do you know what h
could have meant?"

Zuberan bit his lip. An odd expression crossed his fac

"I may," he said after a moment. "Did you say tha
the model of the *Kaito Spirit* had been stolen?"

"I can't be sure," said Emma, "but I think so."

"The other man who was murdered—who was he?"

"I didn't know him, really. His name was Caraigna
He was a New York antique dealer."

"An antique dealer...that would fit." Zuberan nodde
"Yes, I may know what this is about, Emma. I may kno
why Etienne was killed."

"What is it? What happened?"

Zuberan stared out across the ocean and didn't speak fc
a long time.

"It is a long story," he said finally. "One I have neve
told anyone. It started on the *Kaito Spirit,* many years ag
before you were born. Apparently it has not yet ended."

"I want to know everything," said Emma. "Please te
me everything."

"I will," said Zuberan, reaching across the table an
gently patting her hand. "We are all bound togethe
Emma, like a family—you, me, Etienne, Marie...the *Kai
Spirit* binds us all."

"Was it some kind of yacht?"

"*Dios,* no." Zuberan laughed, the gentleness havin
fully returning to his face, his voice. "The *Kaito Spir
was a working boat. An old wreck, really. She must hav
been twenty years old already the first time I saw her, b
even then I loved her. We took tourists out for sightseein
and fishing excursions."

"You sailed from the harbor here?"

"Those were the days when Migelina was an important place," said Zuberan, sitting back in his chair. A faraway smile crossed his lips, as if he were reviewing a pleasant memory. "It is impossible to see it now, but thirty years ago this area was one of the most lovely resorts in the Caribbean. People from all over the world came to Migelina. The best people. Etienne took me aboard when I was not much older than your friend Timoteo. He taught me everything. My family had nothing. My father was dead. My mother took in wash in Migelina. Because of Etienne we were able to eat. I worked hard for my wages, of course, but I received more than just money. Etienne taught me to read, taught me to think. He was a wonderful man."

"Yes, I know," whispered Emma.

"The incident that this may all go back to," said Zuberan, "happened after I had grown from a boy into a man. Some tourists came to us and rented out the *Kaito Spirit* and our services for two full weeks. You have to understand how unusual this was. There were many boats for hire in Migelina. Often we went for weeks without even a day charter. Our work was mostly two-hour sight-seeing trips up and down the coast. These tourists, however, were very rich. Etienne asked them for a preposterous amount of money for the *Kaito Spirit*, ready to be bargained down, but the man just opened his wallet and paid the full amount in advance."

Zuberan stopped speaking and smiled.

"What is it?" asked Emma.

"These people—I do not remember their names, of course, it was so long ago—but all these years I have remembered them as being so rich. Now I realize that it was we who were so poor. The two-week charter Etienne received for the *Kaito Spirit* probably would not have paid for a single night in their hotel, and yet to us it was a king's ransom. As I said before, Emma, money is a fascinating thing. Even now with all that I own, I still cannot imagine being as rich as those tourists who could charter the *Kaito Spirit* for two full weeks.''

Zuberan fell silent and stared out over the ocean. Emma didn't speak. Finally he resumed his story.

''Some days our tourists did not even use the *Kaito Spirit,* taking the time to go inland and see the sights. We had been paid nevertheless and were ready on call. We took them fishing for tuna and marlin. We sailed up the coast for picnics in secret inlets and coves. We arranged for diving gear and waited while they explored coral reefs and underwater caves. Do you dive, my dear?''

''No,'' said Emma.

''You really should try it sometime. Of course, skin diving wasn't the popular sport thirty years ago that it is now. I was just learning to dive then myself, though today there are few things that I enjoy more. It is a wondrous, quiet world down below the waters. A world full of beauty and color and life. A world that no man can ever really know. I love it. It was down there in that quiet, magical world that we found the dragon.''

''The dragon?'' said Emma.

''That is what I have always called it,'' said Zuberan, ''though I am not sure if a dragon is what it really was. Perhaps there is some other name for the creature. Some name out of science books or mythology. I do not know. All I know is that it was unearthly and ferocious and beautiful. And it was made of gold.''

''I'm sorry, Señor Zuberan. I think you've lost me. You found some kind of sea monster?''

''No, it is I who must apologize. I am telling the story very badly. It is just that the dragon is a living thing to me. It still appears to me in my dreams, these many years later—its eyes bulging, its flesh scaly, the sharpened fins that ridge its spine cutting the water like a sword. But of course it was not a real creature that we found in the sand. It was an artifact.''

''An artifact?''

"An ornament. A fantastic dragonlike creature more than three inches long, crafted of rich gold and suspended from a long golden chain. The workmanship of it was wondrous. Each link of the chain was a work of art. Each scale of the dragon was separate and distinct. The creature was hollow, and if you opened its jaws and blew through it, it made a shrill sound—like a whistle."

"But what was it?"

"This I do not know. I know where it came from, however. It was Spanish treasure. Gold from the conquistadors."

"You're kidding."

"No, I assure you, my dear, I am not kidding. They were all over these islands. Their galleons set out from here back to Madrid with holds filled with the stolen wealth of the Incas. Many such treasure ships were sunk in hurricanes and tropical storms. Millions of dollars' worth of gold and silver bullion have been recovered over the years."

Emma couldn't speak. She was breathing shallowly and could feel her heart beating like a bird's. Sunken treasure! Found by the *Kaito Spirit*. This had to be it. This had to have something to do with why her grandfather had been killed.

"It was Marie, your mother, who actually found the dragon," said Zuberan, interrupting Emma's racing thoughts. "She was just a girl then, a pretty little thing, maybe fourteen years old. Etienne would sometimes take her out with us when the clients weren't the usual crude boors and didn't mind. One of the tourists on this trip took a shine to Marie and showed her how to use the scuba gear. Etienne wasn't happy about it, but he finally let her go down. When she surfaced from her first dive, she was holding the dragon in her little fist. She had seen it sparkle in the sand. Gold is incorruptible, Emma. Eternal. The dragon and its thick, intricate chain—it must have been four feet long—had lain there on the ocean floor for hundreds of years, but both were in perfect condition, as though they had been made yesterday.''

"She must have been very excited," said Emma.

"Of course she was. She was dancing all over the deck, laughing, shrieking the way young girls do. I can still see her in my mind's eye. I was certain the tourists would claim the dragon for themselves, since they had chartered the boat and paid for the diving equipment, but to my surprise they did not. They couldn't have been nicer, more gracious. They congratulated Marie, telling her how well she had done. They were so rich, they didn't care. Even though they must have understood its value, it was still just a trinket to them. Just a trinket."

"What happened? Did you sell it?"

"Etienne certainly would have liked to," said Zuberan, "and that, of course, was the problem. The authorities would have confiscated the dragon the instant they learned about it. There are still strict government laws about recovery of sunken treasure, but in those days Peguero was the government, and Peguero was more interested in lining his pockets than in preservation of historical artifacts. The only way for Etienne to sell the dragon was to get it out of San Marcos, but this was risky. The police were keeping a close eye on us."

"The police?" said Emma, surprised. "Why?"

"Because we had been arrested a few months before this."

"Arrested?"

"Yes, arrested," said Zuberan, his lips curled into a frown. "The charge was gunrunning. I have told you, my dear, that I revered Etienne like a father. I had always believed him to be a fine man, honest and upstanding. It therefore came as a terrible shock to me when the police boarded the *Kaito Spirit* and dragged us away in handcuffs, fingerprinted us like common criminals, threw us into jail. It turned out that—unbeknownst to me—Etienne had been engaged in all manner of criminal activities to supplement his income from the boat.''

Emma sat stunned, unable to speak. Zuberan glanced at the house, then continued.

''Smuggling guns was an extremely serious offense in those days, but somehow Etienne managed to find the right official to bribe. We were in jail for only a few weeks. My mother came and stayed with Marie the whole time. Things were strained between Etienne and me from then on, however. I felt humiliated, betrayed. I was a young man, just starting out. I was grateful that Etienne had taken me out of the gutter, but now, thanks to him, I would have a criminal record for the rest of my life. That is why I have never talked about this to anyone. I was ashamed. I am still ashamed.''

Emma started to speak, but fell silent as the white-haired houseboy appeared from the house carrying a silver tray with her coffee. The man walked briskly to the table, placed elegant blue-and-white porcelain cups in front of them, and from a silver pot with a looping ivory handle poured coffee that smelled as if it had been brewed for a god.

''Thank you,'' whispered Emma as the servant finished his task and retreated back to the house.

Up to this point Zuberan's story had been excitement itself. It was wonderful to imagine that Etienne Lalou, the mysterious Frenchman who had owned the *Kaito Spirit*, was really her dear grandfather, Jacques Passant, and that he had found some kind of sunken treasure. Now, however, Emma felt sick. If Zuberan was telling the truth, it meant that her sweet little Pépé had been a criminal when he was young.

Not that smuggling was such a terrible crime, Emma rationalized—especially if you were very poor and living in a place like Peguero's San Marcos. Emma was certain that Pépé must have had very good reasons to do what he did.

Suddenly many things began to make sense—for in stance, why Jacques Passant would never tell Emma about his past. She had always believed her grandfather was sim ply a private person. Apparently he had also had something to hide. Perhaps, like Señor Zuberan, he was ashamed, too

"For several months Etienne kept the dragon hidden in a false compartment in the bow of the *Kaito Spirit*," said Zuberan, resuming his story. "It was pleasant, dreaming of how we would be able to buy a bigger boat with all the money Etienne would get from selling his treasure one day—more pleasant than thinking how we would actually get it off the island without being cheated or killed in the process. With the dragon sailing with us in its hiding place our lives on the *Kaito Spirit* had not really changed, but somehow we felt richer, more optimistic. The tensions that had grown between us after the arrest began to fade. Then Marie got sick."

"What happened?" said Emma, her hand moving in voluntarily to her throat.

"I do not know," said Zuberan. "She left the island and went to stay with an aunt in New York. It was not supposed to be serious, but Etienne soon came to me, dis traught. He said Marie had taken a turn for the worse. She was now very ill and needed an operation. Etienne had to find the cash to pay for her treatment. His only hope was to smuggle the dragon out of the country, but how? The answer was suddenly obvious—the model of the *Kaito Spirit* I had just completed."

"The model? You built it?"

"It took me over a year to carve the pieces and assemble them," said Zuberan. "I had learned the art of model-building from an old Portuguese seaman at the marina. I had built many models, but the *Kaito Spirit* was my mas terpiece. I had planned to keep what little savings I had in its secret compartment."

"Secret compartment?"

"Yes, if you put your finger through the window and

urned the tiny steering wheel, the cabin would slide back,
evealing a hollowed-out interior.''

"'That she may take her place at the helm and turn the
wheel on the legacy that I have kept hidden from her....'''

"I beg your pardon?" said Zuberan.

"That's what my grandfather said in his will about the
model of the *Kaito Spirit*," said Emma.

"Then it all fits," said Zuberan with a deep sigh. "In-
ide the model of the *Kaito Spirit*, wrapped in rags so it
vould not knock around, we placed the golden dragon.
Etienne planned to sell it in New York to pay for Marie's
operation. The authorities were alert to the possibility of
Etienne smuggling in contraband, but they saw no danger
n a sentimental sailor taking with him a model of his boat.

"When Etienne left, he asked me to take care of the
eal *Kaito Spirit*. He said he would return in a month or
wo, but that was the last time I ever saw him. As I prom-
sed, I took care of the *Kaito Spirit*. I eventually parlayed
t into a whole marina full of boats, into everything I have
oday. Years later, after I had become a rich man, I hired
he best investigators to find him, but Etienne had left no
race. There was no aunt in New York that we could find,
o record of Marie's operation, no word about the sale of
a priceless gold dragon."

Emma took a sip of her coffee. It was lukewarm now.
And bitter.

"At least that part of the mystery is finally solved,"
Zuberan said softly. "Etienne must have kept it. He must
ave still had it when he was killed."

"What are you talking about?"

"The dragon. Marie must have recovered without need-
ng the operation, which is why there was no record of it.
And since Marie never needed the operation, Etienne
wouldn't have had to sell the dragon."

"You mean, all these years this thing was there on his
dresser in the model of the *Kaito Spirit?*" gasped Emma.

"Until your antique dealer killed him for it," answer Zuberan, staring out over the ocean.

"No," said Emma. "That can't be. Mr. Caraign didn't even know my grandfather. He was just a strang I met on a ferry."

"You are sure?"

Emma started to speak, then stopped. She wasn't su of anything anymore. Was it mere coincidence th Henri-Pierre had been on the Sausalito ferry that day? (had he been following her? How could she be sure th Henri-Pierre hadn't taken the model? It had been t model, not the real *Kaito Spirit,* that had been her lega all along. And if Henri-Pierre had taken the model, perha he had also...

"If Henri-Pierre killed my grandfather," Emma sai her voice cracking, "then who killed him? And why?"

"Why is very clear," said Zuberan soberly. "With i long chain, the dragon weighed nearly a pound. A poun of solid gold would be motivation for many men to ki but its value as an historical artifact was incalculab greater—a fortune, for all I know. Perhaps the antiqu dealer shopped it around for the best price. Perhaps som one to whom he tried to sell it wanted the dragon witho having to pay for it. Perhaps he had a greedy partner."

"I don't believe it," Emma said softly. "None of th makes any sense. If what you say is true, then wh couldn't my grandfather ever return to San Marcos? H hadn't stolen anything. The dragon belonged to him."

"Yes," said Zuberan. "This thought has occurred to m as well. It may be that your grandfather was afraid Peg ero's agents had gotten wind of his secret. They were ver greedy men. They still are."

"What do you mean? Wasn't Peguero assassinate years ago?"

"Yes, but he had been in power for many years. Th men who worked for him and their sons live in wealth exile all over the world. They still scheme how they can return to power here and squeeze the country dry again.''

"Are you saying that one of them might be involved in this?''

"Anything is possible, but one thing is unmistakable: if you find the dragon, you will find the killer.''

"It's hopeless then,'' said Emma. "It could be anywhere in the world by now.''

"Perhaps not,'' said Zuberan. "One cannot sell something so unique just anywhere. If the murderer has any degree of sophistication, he will know that the dragon can realize its full value only in a very esoteric and rarefied marketplace.''

"Like where?'' asked Emma. "Where would you sell such a thing?''

"I would go where Jacques went. Where your antique dealer had come from and no doubt expected to return. Where the world's elite congregate to spend their money, and where the world's most unusual treasures change hands at the world's great auction houses. I would go to New York City.''

"I ATE ICE CREAM. I watched VCR and played Nintendo!'' declared Timoteo, his eyes bright, his white teeth flashing in a carefree smile. Another of the blue-suited men, looking distinctly worn out, had just brought him from the house.

"I'm glad you had a good time,'' said Emma, leaning over from her seat behind the steering wheel and opening the car door.

"Are you sure you won't stay for dinner?'' asked Zuberan from the curb. "I have very nice rooms. I can put you both up for the night. For as long as you wish. I would like very much to get to know you better, Emma.''

"Thank you, Señor Zuberan, but we really have to be getting back. There are things I must do.''

"Please call me Bernal. We are friends, yes?''

"Yes...Bernal."

"You are going on to New York then?"

Emma nodded.

"I am having grave reservations about this now, my dear," said Zuberan, looking uncomfortable. "I regret now suggesting it to you. The idea of your pursuing a trail that might lead to a killer makes me very uncomfortable."

"Don't worry about me," said Emma, smiling and tousling Timoteo's hair. "If things get tough, I can always send for my bodyguard here."

When Timoteo made a face and pulled away, she playfully grabbed his nose and gave it a yank. A little gold coin the size of a dime seemed to materialize out of it and dropped into her hand.

"How you do that?" exclaimed Timoteo. "Teach me, teach me."

"May I see that?" said Zuberan. Emma handed him the coin. He stared at it, his face unreadable.

"Where did you get this?"

"Pépé said he won it in a poker game. Why?"

"Just before he left, I persuaded Etienne to return to the spot where we had come upon the dragon, though how he found it again I do not know. He was the sailor, I was just his helper. I thought maybe we might discover something else—a whole wreck, perhaps. I made one dive and came up with a single coin. A gold two-escudo piece. Like this one. Etienne said we didn't have time to make a proper search, but he made a map and said we would come back when he returned with Marie to San Marcos. He told me to keep the gold coin we had found. Before he left I gave it back to him to help pay for Marie's operation. He tried to refuse, of course, but I insisted he take it. I never saw him again. He never returned."

Zuberan tried to hand the coin back to Emma, but she shook her head.

"You keep it, Bernal," she said. "I think Pépé would want you to have it back."

Zuberan did not speak for a moment.

"Please stay in touch and let me know how you are doing," he said finally. "I have powerful friends in New York. I may be able to help you again."

"That's very kind of you."

"I am not being simply polite, Emma. I have a personal interest in this matter. In Etienne. In you, now."

Emma bit her lip and nodded, then turned to Timoteo.

"Don't you have something to say to Señor Zuberan?" she asked.

The boy's face lit up.

"Will you hire me to be one of your guards and carry a big gun?"

"Maybe when you grow up." Zuberan laughed. "Come and see me in a few years."

"I can do it now," said Timoteo eagerly. "I am very strong and very smart."

"That I can see."

"If you were really smart, you would know enough to thank the man," muttered Emma.

"Thank you, señor!" shouted Timoteo with a big smile. "I will be back soon."

"You come back soon, too, Emma," said Zuberan quietly, leaning down toward the window. "You are always welcome here."

"Thanks. For everything."

"I believe there are no accidents, Emma. I believe that fate brings people together, brings them what they need. That is why it brought you here to me. It is what brought me to you. Promise me you will be careful. And don't put too much trust in the police. They are all bunglers and fools."

"I promise," Emma said softly. "Good-bye, Bernal."

"Adiós, Emma Passant."

He placed his hands behind his back as she drove away. Emma watched him in the rearview mirror as she headed down the road toward the gate. He never moved. The concerned expression on his face never changed.

"So tell me what else you did in there," Emma said to Timoteo as they rounded a corner and the house fell out of sight.

"They've got all kinds of electric stuff. You can watch TV and play with computer things and everything. It's real fun."

"Did you eat anything besides ice cream?"

"Cookies. They had cookies, too. I ate some cookies. And cake. I made friends with all the mens. They showed me their guns and everything."

"Marvelous."

"I will go to work for Señor Zuberan very soon, I think. He is very important man. Very rich. Many people want to steal from him because he has so much money. How did he get so rich?"

"He's in financial services."

"What is financial services?"

Emma realized that she had no idea.

"Do me a favor, Timoteo," she said. "Don't be a guard when you grow up. Be a doctor."

"Maybe I will be a magician. Like you."

"That's very flattering," said Emma, glancing over at him and returning his big grin. "But study medicine, too. Have something to fall back on. Just in case."

The guards at the gate were waiting for them and waved them through. Emma didn't talk much on the drive back to San Marcos City, though Timoteo chattered on about Nintendo and ice cream and money. She felt as if she had lost her innocence.

Only now did all she had learned begin to sink in. Her dear sweet grandfather running guns, smuggling gold artifacts, pursued by assassins. It was all so unbelievable.

But it made a strange kind of sense, too. If Marie—Emma's mother—was ill and had needed an operation hen Pépé would have done anything, Emma knew. He would have had no choice.

And what of Henri-Pierre? Could he actually have been nvolved in this? Just thinking about such a possibility made her want to cry.

Back in San Marcos City, Emma returned the car to the agency and paid the exorbitant two-day rental fee in cash. Timoteo followed silently at her side as she walked back o the Casimente.

They stopped at the gate to the hotel parking lot. It was a little after three o'clock. The other "tour guides" were n heated discussion down at the end of the block and didn't seem to notice them. The battered cars and trucks that constituted afternoon traffic whizzed by.

"Well, I guess this is it," said Emma, looking at Timoteo, suddenly realizing that she would never see him again.

"You go back to States now?" said Timoteo, shuffling from one foot to the other, trying to smile.

"I'm not sure what I'm going to do. So. How much do I owe you for our two days together?"

Timoteo shrugged.

"You pay what you want."

Emma reached into her pocket and counted out bills, remembering what Celia had told her, that twenty pesos would be enough for the boy.

"Here's three hundred pesos. How's that?"

The boy stared at the money in her hand, but didn't move. Emma took his hand and pressed the bills into it.

"Thank you, Timoteo," said Emma when the boy didn't speak. "I couldn't have done it without you. You were a wonderful guide. And a good friend. I like you very much."

Timoteo grinned.

"You give me tennis shoes now?"

"You really know how to wreck a tender moment, don't you?"

"Please?" he said. "You can buy more in States. Yo[u]
rich."

"Forget it!" exclaimed Emma.

"Why not?"

"Come on, Timoteo. Can't you see they wouldn't f[it]
you?"

"Yes, they would. They fit perfect. I will wear them a[ll]
the time. I will always think of you."

"I'll tell you what," said Emma in exasperation. "Yo[u]
can have either the tennis shoes or the money. Yo[u]
choose."

The boy's mischievous smile vanished. He stared at th[e]
bills in his hands, then looked up.

"I don't want to charge you at all," he said sheepishly[.]
"I'd work for you for free."

Emma swallowed hard and nodded, staring at his brave[,]
cunning face, wondering what chance Timoteo really ha[d]
in life. How many boys from these streets escaped th[e]
poverty, beat the odds like Bernal Zuberan had? Could h[e]
even grow up to be a security guard, let alone a doctor[?]
The worst thing of all, Emma knew, was that there wa[s]
nothing that she could do to help him. His fate woul[d]
depend upon himself.

"I guess I have to take the money," said Timoteo. "[I]
guess I need it more, okay?"

The next moment her arms were around him somehow[,]
and he was hugging her back. They held the embrace fo[r]
several seconds, then Emma turned and walked into th[e]
hotel parking lot. When she glanced over her shoulder[,]
Timoteo was standing there, biting his lip, watching her.

Emma stopped. She walked back to him and pulled of[f]
one of the "shoes that cost as much as feet," then th[e]
other.

"No..." began Timoteo.

Emma put her finger on his lips, handed him the shoes[,]
then hobbled quickly across the hot pavement of the park[-]
ing lot to the hotel in her bare feet without looking back[.]

FIFTEEN

EMMA WAS WAITING for the elevator in the Casimente's lobby, her mind so filled with images of boats and dragons and Timoteo that she didn't recognize her name at first.

"Emma Passant!" repeated the deep, familiar voice. "Well, saddle me with a standard-transmission Pontiac!"

Emma looked up and found herself staring at a refrigerator-sized figure in tooled-leather boots and a cowboy hat.

"Big Ed Garalachek!" he said, reaching out and pumping her hand. "Remember me, little lady? Big Ed? The Chevy King?"

"How can I forget?" said Emma, finally breaking free from his sweaty grip. He looked just as ridiculous as she remembered him—and even bigger, probably because she was in her bare feet this time.

"Well, ain't this the damnedest coincidence," boomed Ed, "our running into each other like this, way the hell down here in the middle of nowhere! Ain't this some cockamamie place? Usually people try to buy my hat. Here they been trying to buy my money! So what brings you to these parts anyhow? You doing your magic show for some banana baron or something?"

"Just a vacation," stammered Emma. "What about you?"

"Business, of course. I got me a fellow here wants to sell a classic 'Vette convertible."

"'Vette?"

"Corvette to you. That's your Chevy sports car, the way they used to make them. Two hundred eighty-three horsepower, V-eight engine, Ramjet fuel injection...oh, heav-

enly goodness, what an automobile! You know I also se
your one-of-a-kind and your hard-to-get collector's veh
cles, don't you? If this fella here's tellin' me the truth, h
could very well have the sweetest memory of 1957 left i
the whole Western Hemisphere.''

His eyes sparkled. Beads of sweat glistened on his fore
head. Emma tried to smile, though her stomach was sud
denly doing somersaults.

''Pretty far to travel to buy a car, isn't it, Ed?''

''Hell, honey,'' laughed Ed, ''I've bought cars in Saud
Arabia, Moscow, the Philippines... Your really rich for
eigners, see, your big-shot businessmen, your kings an
dictators and the like, they've done a lot of shopping i
the good ole U.S. of A. over the years, and what better fo
a well-off foreigner to buy than automobiles? They go t
Detroit and get theirselves some fancy car, bring it bac
to their palace or their dacha or whatever, drive it aroun
a few times to impress the peons, and then it's on to th
next toy. The car gets stashed away somewhere and for
gotten about until somebody finally finds it and decides t
turn it back into cash money. That's where I come in.
advertise for old Chevys all over the world. You got
classic Chevy, you call Big Ed. 'Call Big Ed, the Chevy
King. He'll go to outer space for the right vehicle'—that'
what my ads say. You see any UFOs, Emma honey, yo
let me know. I'd love to get my hands on what them E.T
boys picked up over the years.''

''How's Lionel?'' asked Emma, looking around Ed':
pockets for signs of the Chihuahua.

''He's my best friend. You remember everything, don'
you? Except your shoes, maybe.''

''I was just...''

''Oh, Lionel's fine.'' Ed laughed. ''He's fine. Only th
crazy customs people down here wouldn't let me brin
him. Like he's gonna contaminate the local breedin' stock
or something. Can you imagine? I got him holed up with
my sister back in Phoenix. Lionel's the only one in the

whole family who likes her cooking. But then, of course, he likes dog biscuits, too; there ain't no accounting for taste. Hey, ain't this crazy, our running into each other like this? The odds must be a million to one."

"Yes. It's pretty unbelievable."

"Must be fate, that's what I say. Must be destiny. I hope you're gonna let me buy you a drink or something?"

"Sure," said Emma. "Just let me go upstairs and freshen up. I'll meet you in the bar, okay?"

"Great! See you soon."

Emma smiled and escaped into the waiting elevator. The instant the doors closed, her expression changed from frozen politeness to the dismay she had been feeling. She lifted her glasses onto the top of her head, cupped her hands over her long, pointed nose, and took a deep breath. What was going on? What was Big Ed Garalachek doing in San Marcos?

The elevator doors opened on the third floor. Emma got out and darted down the hall, almost breaking into a run. Once inside her room she bolted the door and put on the chain, then dropped into the armchair, and found herself shaking.

It was ridiculous, Emma told herself. Big Ed was just a giant overstuffed teddy bear. How could she be afraid of him? Maybe it was the residual effects of Bernal Zuberan's story that had made her paranoid, the thought of treasure maps and name-changing and murder.

The irony of it was that Zuberan had just been speaking about fate, and what he had said had made sense. Could it really be fate that had brought Ed Garalachek to San Marcos? It was fate that had put Big Ed at the Phoenix Grand Marquis so she could use his dog in her act, wasn't it? Surely the Chevy salesman couldn't be connected to the murders of Jacques Passant and Henri-Pierre Caraignac. Or could he?

Emma had been staring at the room without seeing. Suddenly everything came into focus. She had unpacked only

one of her two suitcases when she checked in, but ha
gotten a belt out of the other suitcase that morning an
had left it open when she went out. Now it was close
Emma rushed over, opened the suitcase, rummage
through the packed clothing, feeling invaded and frigh
ened and helpless. Even though nothing seemed to b
missing, someone had been here. Someone had closed th
suitcase. Who?

"The same person who made the bed," Emma finall
said aloud, feeling like a fool: the maid had already com
and gone today.

Emma collapsed onto the bed and forced her mind bac
to the weekend she had been in Phoenix and had met Bi
Ed. Henri-Pierre had been killed the Saturday night sh
had performed. Big Ed had been with her that night, ha
watched the show from the light booth, so he couldn'
possibly have killed the Frenchman in San Francisco, eigl
hundred miles away. If Emma was right about the sam
man having killed Jacques Passant, then Big Ed was in th
clear.

So what did he want? Was he stalking her? Was h
some obsessed crazy? Or could he really just be here t
buy a Chevrolet, as he claimed? Could it be that incredibl
of a coincidence?

There was only one way to find out.

"DR. JOSÉ JACINTO GAUTREAU-GODOY," said Big Ed. "
got the picture here somewhere."

Ed patted down his pockets, eventually producing
color snapshot, which he passed to Emma. She ha
changed from her shorts to white slacks, put on some shoe
and some lipstick, and was sitting across from the Chev
King in a back booth of the downstairs bar.

Emma glanced at the photograph of a man in dar
glasses sitting in the driver's seat of a red-and-white sport
car, while Ed continued searching his pockets. He ha

taken off his cowboy hat. The wave in his light-brown hair made him look like a little boy. A very big little boy.

"Here it is," said Big Ed triumphantly, holding up a crumpled blue aerogram with four canceled San Marcan stamps, which he passed to Emma. The letter was addressed to him at Buena Vista Motors on Alameda Boulevard in Phoenix and postmarked October 25—more than a month ago. Before Pépé had been murdered. Before she had ever heard of Henri-Pierre Caraignac.

"'Dear Señor Big Ed,'" read Emma aloud. "'I have seen your classified advertisement in the *International Herald Tribune* and wish to know if you are interested in buying a 1957 Chevrolet Corvette, which has been in my family for many years and which is in perfect condition. You may telephone me at the above number for further information. Truly yours, Dr. José Jacinto Gautreau-Godoy.'"

"He's a psychiatrist, can you believe it?" chortled Ed. "Never occurred to me they had psychiatrists down here, but it makes sense when you think about it. You can go nuts anywhere, I guess. José and me been dickering all this time about the car there in the letter, and I finally had to come down and see this baby for myself. Apparently it originally belonged to the son of Peguero—he was the dictator here for a while, until they shot him. You know that big modern highway that goes from the airport into town?"

"Yes?"

"Well, it's supposed to be this great public works/public relations project, but the way I hear the story, Peguero really built the road so his spoiled kid could have a place to race his cars. Finally killed himself in one."

"Somehow that makes sense," said Emma, leaning back and making room for the bartender, who deposited their drinks on the table.

Ed, who had ordered a margarita, stared at the glass of mango juice Emma had ordered.

"I thought you were a margarita gal," he said finally his nose crinkled up in distaste. "I hate it when a fun ga reforms."

"I hate it when I wake up and my head explodes," said Emma. She was damned if she was going to let her guard down this time.

Emma had been racking her brain trying to remember exactly what she had told Ed the night they had spent drinking together in Phoenix. She knew she had talked about Pépé and about growing up in San Francisco. Beyond that, all she could remember was Lionel's wet tongue on her cheek and the taste of salt in her mouth. And her exploding head the next day.

"So, when did you get in?" she asked.

"Just this morning," said Ed. "I already took the bus tour of the city—that's where I was coming back from when I ran into you. How about you? You been here long?"

"A few days."

"Then you must be an expert by now. What's there to do down here, now that I've seen the botanical garden and all the monuments?"

"There are casinos, I understand."

"No, ma'am. Never gamble. 'Eddie,' my mamma used to say—that's what she called me, Eddie—'Eddie,' she'd say, 'don't be a sucker. Put your money on a sure thing. Put your money on a Chevrolet.' She worked with Daddy at the lot, you know. Big Muriel, they call her."

"What do they call him?"

"Nick."

"Just plain Nick?"

"Sometimes they call him Shorty. He's not big like the rest of us."

"I didn't realize it was a family business."

"Yes, ma'am. Two generations of Garalacheks. I'd like to make a go for three, but it kinda depends on my finding that little lady of my dreams. I'm still looking, though. I'm still looking.''

"I'm sure you'll find her."

"So what else is there to do down here? What you been doing?"

"Just sight-seeing."

"What? You rent a car or something and drive around?"

Emma stared at Big Ed, searching for some sign of cunning in his broad, ingenuous, dopey face. If he had ulterior motives, they didn't show.

"How did you know I rented a car?" she said finally.

"How else you gonna sightsee?" he asked, looking genuinely confused.

"I did rent a car."

"So where'd you go?"

"Around the city. Up to Las Calvos."

"Las Calvos? What's that?"

"Big resort to the north."

"That where you were today?"

"Yes," lied Emma. "You'd probably like it up there if you play golf."

"No, ma'am. I can't see myself whacking little balls around. I may look like an idiot in this getup, but I'd look even stupider dressed the way them folks do. Besides, I'm about as coordinated as a back seat full of monkeys. I'd probably kill someone."

"They've got some nice restaurants at Las Calvos, too."

"Now that sounds interesting. Up north, you say? Anything to the south?"

"I haven't been down that way yet."

"No?"

"No."

"So you meet any interesting people while you been down here?"

"Why are you so interested in where I've been going and who I've been meeting, Ed?"

"What do you mean?"

"Why are you really down here?"

"I told you, Emma honey. I'm gonna buy me that 'Vette from the shrink, provided it's all it's cracked up to be. You seen the letter. Hey, what's the matter with you? Don't you believe me? What do you think I'm doing? Following you around or something?"

"The thought has occurred to me."

"You mean... You think that I... Jesus, Emma. I thought we was friends. You think I'm some kind of kook? Is that what you think?"

"I'm sorry if I've hurt your feelings, Ed. But you must admit that this is pretty strange, our both being here on San Marcos in the same hotel like this."

"Synchronicity," declared Big Ed, leaning forward and fixing her with his big earnest puppy-dog eyes.

"I beg your pardon?"

"Synchronicity. It's like fate, see? Only more scientific. You know how sometimes you're thinking about somebody and the phone rings and it's that very person? Or you hear some funny word in a conversation and for the rest of the day you keep running into it?"

"Yes?"

"Well, that's synchronicity. Happens all the time. Happens to everybody. And that's what we got here, our running into each other like this again so soon. At least that's what I think. But if you think I'm some kind of masher, hell, I'm out of here."

The big salesman rose to his feet and reached for his hat. He looked like an abandoned cocker spaniel. An abandoned cocker spaniel the size of the refrigerator. Emma couldn't stand it. She leaned across the table and grabbed his sleeve.

"Sit down, Ed," she said.

"I'm not staying if you think I'm some kind of wacko."

"I'm sorry. I'm sure you're not a wacko. I've been under a lot of stress lately."

Ed settled back into his chair.

"It's okay, I guess. You still upset about your grandfather, aren't you?"

Emma nodded. She had mentioned Pépé's recent death to Ed the night they had spent drinking together in Phoenix, but not the circumstances.

"Sorry," she mumbled.

"It's okay, honey," said Ed. "You're right to be careful. Pretty girl like you. Big ole ugly Chevy salesman you barely know. And this is a little weird, our meeting down here like this. Tell you what…"

Ed reached into his back pocket and took out a fat wallet. He extracted a business card and passed it to Emma.

"…if you're feeling nervous, you call Mamma at the lot. Now she might not be the most impartial person in the world, but she's honest as an apple. Honest Big Muriel, they call her. She might try to sell you a Chevy, but she ain't gonna lie to you about me."

"It's all right, Ed," said Emma, uncomfortable. "I'm sure you're telling the truth."

"No, no, no," said Ed. "If you have any doubts, you call Big Muriel. She knows all about the psychiatrist, she'll set you straight. Now you put that card in your pocket, you hear?"

Emma slid his business card in the pocket of her blouse.

"Look," said Ed, making as serious a face as Emma had ever seen him manage. "This obviously isn't a good time for us to get caught up. How 'bout you having dinner with me tonight?"

"Thanks, but I'm kind of tired."

"I'm really not trying to press my attentions on you, Emma honey, I swear to God. I'm just a long way from home, and it's nice to find a friend."

"Look, Ed…"

"You're a long way from home, too, you know. Maybe you could use a friend, too. So how 'bout lunch tomorrow? I'm not seeing Dr. José until three o'clock. What do you say?"

"I don't know," said Emma.

"Dinner tomorrow, then. Please, Emma honey? You don't want to ruin my self-confidence, do you? How am I ever going to find that little lady of my dreams if I have to go through life knowing that you think I'm some kind of nut?"

"All right." Emma laughed, shaking her head. "I'll have dinner with you."

"Great," said Ed. "Why don't you meet me in the hotel restaurant at seven? The food's pretty good here, they tell me."

"Fine," said Emma. "Maybe I'll go upstairs now, if you don't mind. I am a little tired."

"Sure. Tomorrow night, remember."

"I'll remember."

Big Ed was on his feet before Emma was, holding her chair, waving away the pesos she offered to pay for her drink.

Back in her room Emma sat down on the bed and reached into her pocket. Ed's business card was baby-blue with the Chevy logo in black superimposed over the image of a car in white. The address and phone number for Buena Vista Motors was in Phoenix. Ed had given her a card just like it when they had met the first time. She had left that one back at the house in San Francisco. The house she would never see again.

Emma picked up the telephone, glanced at the instruction card for phoning the United States, and began dialing the number for Buena Vista Motors. Then she hung up.

If Ed had given her a card with a phone number and encouraged her to call, there surely would be someone who would answer, someone who would say that she had reached Buena Vista Motors. Calling would tell Emma nothing: certainly Big Ed's mother—or someone claiming to be—would give him a good reference.

Emma picked up the phone again and dialed international information for Phoenix.

"Do you have a listing for Buena Vista Motors in Phoenix?" she asked.

After a moment, a electronic voice responded with the phone number, which matched the number printed on Big Ed's business card.

Emma hung up the phone, walked to the window and looked out at the ocean. All her life she had looked out over an ocean, but the Pacific off San Francisco was usually cold and choppy and austere. Here the part of the Atlantic that cradled the Caribbean islands seemed warm, calm, benevolent. Her grandfather's ashes rested in the ocean back home. A golden dragon had emerged from the placid waters here, waters that could also rear up in a hurricane and destroy everything in their path.

There really was such a thing as coincidence, Emma knew. There were such things as synchronicity and fate as well. If Big Ed wasn't who and what he said he was, then he had gone to a great deal of trouble. The letter. The photograph. The directory listing for Buena Vista Motors. And who could make up a name like Dr. José Jacinto Gautreau-Godoy? Ed's explanation was all very reasonable.

Only Emma didn't believe it.

Emma dialed international information again and got phone numbers for five other Chevrolet dealers in Phoenix. No one at the first four numbers was familiar with Buena Vista Motors or any Garalacheks, big or otherwise. At the fifth number she reached Marv Hopperman.

"I'm not one of those car dealers who needs all kinds of gimmicks, Miss Passant," he said in a smooth drawl. "I don't have to tell folks I'm Mighty Marv or Honest Marvin or Marv-who's-going-to-come-to-your-house-and-barbecue-a-steer. No, ma'am. I've just been in the business of selling good cars to good people since 1969, and I will tell you for a fact that this Garalachek fella is pulling your leg. I'm the biggest Chevy dealer in Phoenix and I know

all the others, I promise you. I never heard of this Bue
Vista Motors. Where is it supposed to be located?''

"At 15983 Alameda Boulevard," said Emma weak
looking at Big Ed's business card.

"Well, there you have it. The fifteen-thousand block
Alameda is right around the corner from here. Vince C
paletti is the only car dealer anywhere near there—se
Ford Lincoln Mercury—and he's half a mile up the ro;
Now what kind of vehicle are you interested in, Miss P;
sant? Maybe I can help you out.''

Emma freed herself from the sales pitch and hung
the phone. The next instant she was digging through dra
ers, frantically throwing clothes into her suitcase. May
there was some good explanation for there being no Bue
Vista Motors in Phoenix, for Ed Garalachek turning up
San Marcos. Emma had no intention of sticking around
find out what it was, however. She had to get out of the
Now.

It was only after Emma had packed that she stopped, ;
on her knees, forced herself to breathe slowly and list
to her head, not her racing heart.

The most important thing was to remain calm, she tc
herself. Whatever was going on, whatever Big Ed was
to, panic would only hurt her chances of escaping. Emi
didn't know if Ed would still be downstairs, but seeing h
come through the lobby with a pair of suitcases was a su
tipoff that she was wise to him.

Emma went through the closet and removed the bla
gabardine jacket she had hung up to unwrinkle. She stuff
a clean bra and a pair of panties into the pockets, th
went into the bathroom and put her toothbrush and toile
ries into her big leather purse. Then she scribbled a nc
on hotel stationery requesting that the hotel send her su
cases to Charlemagne Moussy's office in San Francisco
her expense. The hotel had taken an imprint of her cre
card when she had checked in, so Emma doubted th
would mind her leaving without formally checking o

he room would cost nearly three times as much if she
aid on her card rather than in cash, but there was no point
worrying about that now.

After taking a final look through her suitcases to ascer-
in that she hadn't forgotten anything she couldn't live
ithout, Emma put the room key, the note, and twenty
esos for the maid on the bedstand. Then she put the purse
ver her shoulder, tossed the gabardine jacket over her
m, and went downstairs, directly to the front desk.

"I have something in the hotel safe that I'd like to get,"
ie said quietly to the clerk, who took her behind the
ounter. Emma opened her box, put her passport, check-
ook, and money into her purse, and emerged from behind
e desk to find herself face-to-face with Big Ed.

"We meet again," said Ed, smiling from ear to ear. "I
ought you was tired."

"I was," said Emma, returning the smile, though inside
e was screaming. "Sometimes, though, I get so tired that
ily one thing can relax me."

"Oh? What's that?"

"Shopping."

"Hey, if you need some company…"

"Thanks, Ed, but there are some things that a girl must
ay alone, if you know what I mean. And they're not
hevrolets."

"Sure, sure" said Ed, turning lobster-red. "Of course.
an I get you a cab?"

Emma followed his glance to the battered cars with taxi-
ompany emblems that were parked outside the glass en-
ance doors of the hotel. Would it be possible to trace
here they had dropped passengers?

"Thanks, but I think I'll walk."

She started for the doors. Ed sprang in front of her and
ened them for her.

"What you need a jacket for? It's hotter than hell out
ere."

"I plan ahead," she said. "I get carried away when I

shop sometimes. I might be gone awhile, and it gets c—
here in the evenings. Thanks, Ed. See you tomorr—
night.''

"Seven o'clock, right? The restaurant here.''

"Right.''

She left him standing at the door and walked bris—
through the parking lot and out the gates. Only wh—
Emma was on the sidewalk by the street did she gla—
back. There was no sign of the big Chevy salesman—
whatever he really was.

At the end of the hotel property was the usual group
tour guides and money changers, all of whom started y—
ing at once as she approached. Neither Timoteo or Ch—
gee Money was anywhere in the crowd. Emma selec—
the quietest and shortest man, the one who looked le—
likely to cut her throat.

"Do you speak English?'' she asked, getting into —
man's battered old Chevrolet, trying not to think of —
synchronicity of it.

"Sí, sí,'' he said eagerly. "Where you want go? T—
of city? Old fort? Central market?''

"Take me to the airport,'' Emma whispered, think—
of a little Frenchman with rosy cheeks who had smugg—
a golden dragon away from these islands thirty years a—
and had maybe died because of it.

The car lurched into traffic. Emma sat back, closed —
eyes. The picture of another Frenchman suddenly filled —
mind—a tall, handsome man with a sad smile whom s—
had known for only a few hours. She had made a prom—
to him, not so long ago. It was time to keep it.

SIXTEEN

ROOM SERVICE," declared the metallic voice on the other d of the line.

"Room three-oh-five," Emma said, sleepily. "Continental breakfast. Lots of coffee. Hot. Strong. Thanks."

Emma rubbed her eyes and concluded her yawn. Light eamed into the small, cozy room from three narrow winws. The bed on which she lay was large, the mattress m. The walls were as fancy as the French-style furniture, aswirl with moldings and brass fittings, but then this om had been built in a gilded age when artisans had orked for pennies and ruthless men had raised monuents to wealth, unencumbered by income taxes or conience.

This was the Plaza Hotel in New York City. Emma had omised Henri-Pierre Caraignac that she would stay at the aza the next time she came to New York, and now she d kept her word. Henri-Pierre, however, wouldn't be owing her around the city as he had offered.

After fleeing Big Ed at the Casimente yesterday, Emma d managed to get a seat on a late-afternoon flight to New ork. It was after eight o'clock by the time she had cleared stoms at Kennedy and walked outside into the frigid ght air.

"What are you, a Eskimo?" the taxi dispatcher had ked, gaping at Emma's tropical attire. "Doncha know got December here?"

"I like to freeze."

"What about luggage? You got luggage?"

"I travel light."

"So where you want to go?"

"Shopping."

"Finally she's makin' sense."

"I don't suppose you know any place in the city tha open late?"

"What, are you kidding?" said the dispatcher, openi the door to a cab for her. "This is New York City, a there's only seventeen shopping days left until Christm Take the lady to Bloomie's, Mac."

By the time she had arrived at the Plaza last nig Emma was the proud owner of a new winter coat, slac blouses, sweaters, and underwear. And a suitcase to ca them in. It had been strangely therapeutic to leave all I clothes in San Marcos. There would be plenty of time worry about how much everything had cost when I credit-card bills came in. With everything new, she I new herself, almost reborn.

Emma rolled out of the comfortable bed and picked the room-service menu on the night table for the first tin The breakfast she had just ordered cost as much as a r taurant dinner in most cities. Emma tried not to think it as she went off into the old-fashioned marble bathroo to brush her teeth. This was New York City, after all. she was going to start worrying about prices while she w here, she'd soon be diving out the window.

By the time Emma had performed her ablutions a dressed, her breakfast had arrived. She let the waiter se up on the room's small table, signed the check and ga him a generous cash tip on his way out. Then she pou herself a cup of coffee and tried to start her brain.

It was a little after nine—still too early to call Ben Poteet in San Francisco, where the time was three ho earlier. Emma had arrived too late last night to call as we She wouldn't be able to relax until she had told the dete tive about Big Ed. What Poteet would be able to do fr three thousand miles away was another matter.

The real problem was the dragon, Emma reminded h self, taking a sip of coffee, which was hot and strong. S

ad planned to fly back home through New York anyway
avoid another nightmare plane trip, but now she might
ctually be able to do something useful while she was
ere.

What Bernal Zuberan said had made sense: New York
as a logical place to sell a unique item like the dragon,
selling it was indeed the killer's objective. Of course
ere were probably a dozen other places in the world that
ould do just as well. London. Tokyo. Even Spain or
outh America. Wouldn't a collector of Spanish heritage
e the one most interested in such an artifact?

But this is where Pépé had come and where big auction
ouses were located, Emma told herself, trying to be op-
mistic. The killer would have every reason to believe that
o one else knew that the dragon even existed, let alone
at it had been stolen. Why shouldn't he just put it up for
uction?

Forty minutes later Emma was downstairs at the desk,
undled up in her new red coat and a sweater against the
venty-five degree, dazzlingly bright morning.

"How do I get to Sotheby's and Christie's?" she asked
e clerk behind the counter—a short, middle-aged woman
ith thick glasses and an impish smile.

"Sotheby's is up on Seventy-second and York, but
hristie's is right down the block," said the woman in a
eerful voice. "I go over there on my lunch hour some-
mes."

"What's it like?" Emma asked, feeling distinctly intim-
ated, wondering if she should call first for an appoint-
ent. This was not like her little antique stores and thrift
ops in San Francisco. This was the big time.

"Oh, I love the auction houses," said the desk clerk,
blivious to Emma's discomfort. "They're much better
an museums: you can touch everything. I always check
t the drawers of expensive furniture. You'd think some-
e would clean things like that out, but they don't al-
ays."

"Found anything interesting?"

"Candy—mostly sour balls, which says something
think. Combs, every last one of them full of hair, whi
says something else. Once I found a shopping list. 'He
ring, vanilla ice cream, Ajax cleanser.' This from a dress
that belonged to that big newspaper heiress. I think th
poisoned her."

"Could be."

The clerk nodded, her impish expression turning smu

"Another time I found twenty-seven cents in a desk th
was estimated to bring sixty thousand dollars. I walked c
with it. The twenty-seven cents, not the desk."

"Good for you," said Emma. She had expected Ne
Yorkers to be unfriendly and glum, but so far this trip th
were talkative and nice, though maybe all a little loopy

The woman cackled with unconcealed glee, then to
out a map and circled where each auction house was.

"Is Sotheby's too far away to walk?" asked Emn
studying the orderly grid of streets, trying to get her be
ings.

"Not really, but you might want to take a cab if you
not used to it. We New Yorkers walk everywhere. Bea
tiful day. I like your hat. You look very French."

Emma touched the navy blue beret she had gotten ye
terday at Bloomie's.

"*Merci*," said Emma. "I am French."

"*Il n'y a pas de quoi*," replied the clerk. "I'm fro
Pittsburgh."

"I thought you said you were a New Yorker."

"All real New Yorkers are from out of town," pr
nounced the clerk knowingly.

Emma thanked the woman again and walked throu
the opulent lobby of the grand old hotel, down a red carp
and onto Fifty-ninth Street. Across the street, half a doz
horse-drawn carriages were lined up in front of Cent
Park, ready to take her for a ride—literally, it seemed, fro
the rates printed on their placards.

By the time Emma had made her way to t̶ Fifth Avenue through the teeming throngs of p̶ three panhandlers had shaken plastic cups in her fac̶ spare change. Emma's supply was exhausted by the tim̶ a fourth man, less steady on his feet, but with a happier expression on his face, had inquired if she could spare a hundred dollars.

She walked across Fifty-ninth Street, as the clerk had instructed, past Madison to Park Avenue. Christie's was right there at the corner. Somehow it was not at all what Emma had expected. Except for the two-story glass lobby and pictures of multimillion-dollar sale items in a discreet window case, it looked like all the other large, stone-faced apartment buildings lining the avenue.

A smiling doorman in a fancy navy-blue uniform was stationed outside. He tipped his hat and held the door. Emma entered and followed a thin man with a heart-shaped scar on his cheek up a short brushed-brass spiraling staircase. The man looked vaguely familiar, but Emma couldn't place him for a moment. Then she remembered. She had seen him at Bloomingdale's last night and had wondered what he was doing in the lingerie department. Perhaps he lived in the neighborhood—Bloomie's was only a block away from there.

At the top of the stairs Emma found herself in a small space with a low ceiling. There was a small gallery to the right, a much larger one to the left. A long corridor and another staircase apparently led to other galleries. In the center of the room was an island where three nicely dressed women stood behind a counter amid a slew of glossy catalogs.

"Excuse me," said Emma, approaching one of them, a short blonde with a pearl necklace. "I'd like to speak with someone about an antique gold...ornament...and chain."

"Your name, please?"

"Emma Passant."

"Please have a seat, Miss Passant," said the woman,

‛king up a telephone. "Someone will be with you
lortly."

There was a small area with couches across from the
counter. Unbuttoning her coat, Emma walked over but
didn't sit down. Instead she checked out a glass-topped
display case full of small silver objects—porringers, beak-
ers, spoons. After a few more minutes she wandered over
to the entrance of the larger gallery and looked over cases
full of silver teapots, trays, and tableware. According to
the labels she could own a tankard made by Paul Revere,
if she was willing to shell out seventy-five to eighty-five
thousand dollars for the privilege.

"Miss Passant?" spoke a soft female voice.

Emma turned and found herself facing a woman about
her own age, dressed in a tasteful gray suit.

"I'm Jill Boxer. You have a piece of jewelry you wish
to sell?"

"No, not exactly."

"Oh, I'm sorry. That's what I had understood. How can
I help you?"

"I'm not sure," said Emma. "I've come about a gold
artifact which may have been stolen from my family."

"Artifact?"

"It's a gold dragon. Well, it's shaped like a dragon. Or
something like that. It's about three inches long and is on
a long link chain. Together they weigh nearly a pound. I
believe they originated with the Spanish conquistadors."

"It sounds interesting, but I'm not sure that this sort of
thing would fall into my department," said Ms. Boxer,
smiling politely. "You say the piece was stolen?"

"I think so. I believe somebody may try to sell it. That's
why I'm here. Has anyone tried to consign something like
this?"

"Not that I'm aware."

"Well, as I said, there's a chance they might."

Ms. Boxer nodded, her professional smile showing no
trace of impatience or condescension, though Emma felt

increasingly foolish. She wished she had checked her coat; she was beginning to perspire.

"I'll be happy to keep my eyes open for your property and alert our legal department," said Ms. Boxer after a pause, "but again I'm not sure this would fall into a jewelry sale. Do you have a picture?"

"No," said Emma. "But it's very distinctive. If you blow through it, it makes a sound like a whistle."

"I see."

"Do you have any idea of what such an item might be worth?"

"No, not really. If it's gold, however, it will certainly have value. I'm trying to think where I could direct you. Your piece might fall into *objets de virtu*. And we do occasionally run sales of sunken treasure, though these are unusual affairs that involve several specialties. Your best bet would probably be to speak with our silver department. Unfortunately, things are a bit frantic for them right now, what with their big sale tomorrow. You might call and make an appointment to see someone in a few days."

"I'll do that, thanks," said Emma. There was no reason for her to feel embarrassed that she could think of, but she did nevertheless.

Ms. Boxer remained courtesy itself, not allowing Emma to escape until Emma had taken a business card and given her her room number at the Plaza and Charlemagne Moussy's address in San Francisco.

Finally Emma was down the stairs and out the door, so relieved that she barely acknowledged the doorman's offer to get her a cab and advice to have a nice day. She was five blocks away before she had cooled down enough to button her coat against the icy air.

It was no sin to feel intimidated, Emma told herself. New York had been designed to intimidate people. The towering buildings, the fast-paced manners, the glitz and razzamatazz had been cultivated and refined over centuries specifically to separate people from their money in the

most efficient manner. Though San Francisco was a sophisticated town, Emma was just another rube here. Everybody was, until he or she learned the territory.

The thought centered her, but Emma wasn't ready to
tackle another auction house right away. She took out the
map she had gotten at the Plaza and stood studying it for
a minute, until a dazed-looking young woman wandered
up and asked her if she had a dollar. No wonder people
walked so fast, Emma realized, taking off in the opposite
direction. Once you stopped, you became a target.

In a moment Emma found herself on Madison Avenue.
Sotheby's, she knew, was on Seventy-second Street, over
by the East River, several avenues away. It could wait.
There was something else she wanted to do first.

Without slowing down, Emma dug into her wallet and
found the business card Henri-Pierre Caraignac had given
her outside the Alhambra. It seemed like years ago now.
H. P. CARAIGNAC, ANTIQUAIRES, read the card, specifying
an address at Eighty-first Street and Madison.

Emma was presently in the low sixties. Madison was
full of yellow cabs heading uptown, but the city blocks
were short and it was a beautiful day, albeit cold. She
walked up the sparkling, seductive street, past boutiques
and jewelers, art galleries and restaurants. The streets went
by quickly. Each window vied for her attention with daz-
zling merchandise in appealing arrangements. By the time
she turned onto Eighty-first Street and had come to the
address on the card, Emma had seen two actors she recognized from movies and counted twenty-five mink coats
worn by an assortment of men, women and children.

H. P. Caraignac, Antiquaires, occupied a tiny, quiet
storefront in a brownstone just off Madison, next to a small
clothing boutique. The name appeared in small gold letters
on the door and again on a small green canvas awning that
looked well-established, rather than old. A metal gate
stretched across the window in which two chairs were dis-
played discreetly, their spotty gilding penetrated with

worm holes, their pink silk upholstery looking more antique than practical.

It was the kind of store Emma would ordinarily have walked right past without even seeing. She pressed her face close to the barred gate to see better through the glass. Inside, the shallow space was packed tightly with bureauplats, armories, and clocks. According to the hand-lettered sign in the window, the hours of H. P. Caraignac were Tuesday through Saturday, 11 a.m. to 5 p.m. It looked as if the owner might be arriving any minute. Emma knew he wouldn't.

She swallowed hard, wishing with all her might that Henri-Pierre had been simply someone who had happened to be on the ferry with her that day, not someone involved with Pépé's murder.

The walk to Sotheby's took less than fifteen minutes.

This auction house, too, looked nothing like what Emma had envisioned. It occupied a gray, almost industrial-looking box, except for the bands of windows that ribboned the front. At least the structure was large—it took up the entire block front.

Another uniformed doorman—this one in charcoal gray—held the door. This time Emma checked her coat and hat with a courteous attendant at the cloakroom directly inside the door. At the top of a short flight of granite stairs was a plush reception area, much like the one at Christie's, though larger. The ceilings here were high, and vast galleries stretched off to either side. Behind a spacious catalog counter stood a young man and three young women, all of whom might have been hired for the quality of their appearance and wardrobes.

"I'd like to speak with someone about an antique Spanish gold artifact," said Emma, feeling less nervous, knowing what to expect now that she'd done this once before.

"A piece of jewelry?" asked the young man, after taking her name.

"No. More of an *objet de virtu*. A collector's item. Sunken treasure."

The young man didn't bat an eye. Apparently people came here with sunken treasure on a regular basis. He conferred with one of the women, then picked up a telephone. A short conversation ensued.

"You can see Mr. Pilkington on the third floor," he said finally to Emma, putting down the phone. "Go down the stairs and around to the left for the elevators."

Emma thanked him and followed his directions, going back to the front entrance and walking down a short hall to the single elevator. When she arrived on the third floor she found a quiet waiting area that had none of the drama of the salerooms downstairs. In fact, it looked just like any office. Like the area downstairs, the ceilings here were high. The walls were painted white.

Emma gave her name and took a seat as directed on a comfortable leather couch in front of a row of windows. The well-dressed woman next to her rested a hand on a framed painting she had turned to the couch so the image couldn't be seen. A fellow in a heavy winter coat that he should have checked was seated on the other side. He had some kind of heavy metal casket-shaped box in his lap.

Several minutes passed. Then a tall, stout man appeared from a hallway. He had thick glasses in transparent frames and wore a slightly rumpled blue business suit. Not only was he the heaviest person Emma had seen at either auction house, he was also the oldest—well into his sixties, Emma estimated by his cotton-white hair.

"Ms. Passant?" inquired the man of the general vicinity in a breathy, but resonant bass voice. He had a vaguely upper-class British accent and a second chin, considerably bigger and softer-looking than the first. It seemed to have replaced his entire neck.

"I'm Emma Passant," said Emma, rising. "You're Mr. Pilkington?"

"N. C. Pilkington," said the man, presenting a huge

pink hand to be shaken. "Given that this is our first acquaintance, you may have your single allotted guess as to what N. C. stands for and then you must leave me in peace. I have refused to tell anyone for the past forty-seven years and I shall not begin with you."

"Nebuchadnezzar Cuthbert," said Emma without missing a beat.

"Good for you," said Pilkington, breaking into a delighted smile. "Wrong, of course, but very witty. I can't tell you how weary I grow of all the Ned and Hats and Curts and Charleses. It was almost a relief last week when one of my wife's odious relatives suggested Nut Cutlet. Nebuchadnezzar Cuthbert, indeed. Is two open, Karen?"

"Yes, Mr. Pilkington," said the receptionist brightly. Like the people downstairs, she looked like something from the pages of Town and Country.

"Shall we go in here, Miss Passant?" said Pilkington, leading the way to the second of several small, bare rooms off a side corridor. Each room was big enough for only two chairs and a small countertop under the window.

"My favorite viewing room," said Pilkington, closing the door. "It brings me luck. In this very spot I daresay I've seen more sets of wooden false teeth purported to have resided in the mouth of George Washington than has any other living individual. Now, what do you have for me today?"

"Just a question, I'm afraid."

"Be not afraid, Miss Passant. All knowledge begins with questions."

"It's about a gold object. Something very unusual. You probably will never have heard of anything like it."

"Ha!" declared the big man, clasping his hands beneath his chins theatrically. "How luscious to think that there is something new under the sun. Or at least something old that these tired eyes haven't seen. You are doubtlessly wrong, of course. I am a veritable museum of esoterica. I have spent my life in the auction game, identifying bits of

treasure and pieces of trash. I am the one to whom the
direct all of the inquiries that do not fit into any neat cat
egory. What will happen to the silver-mounted coconut
and the ivory whist counters when I am gone? I wonder
And all those wooden teeth? Now tell me about your ob
ject.''

"It was found in the Caribbean, and I believe that it'
from the Spanish conquistadors. A gold ornament in the
shape of a dragon. Very intricate and beautiful workman
ship. It hangs from a long gold chain, also of great crafts
manship, and makes a whistling sound if you blow through
it.''

Pilkington was already shaking his head.

"You see?" he said. "Here, you have me all primed
for something unique, and what do you deliver? Yester
day's newspaper.''

"You mean you've seen it?" Emma gasped. "You've
seen the dragon?''

"I've seen several, actually. Not that they aren't quite
rare, mind you, but then the unusual is my call-and-trade
What you are describing is probably a badge of office.''

"A badge of office," repeated Emma. "What exactly i
that?''

"Do you know how generals and admirals nowadays
have stars on their collars and scrambled eggs on their
hats?" said Pilkington, squeezing himself gingerly into
one of the cubicle's little chairs and adopting a professoria
tone.

"Yes?''

"Well, this is the same thing. The custom of carrying a
whistle-and-chain insignia by naval commanders was prev
alent in several countries to signify their rank and impor
tance. Early in the sixteenth century Sir Edward Howard
threw his overboard to avoid its capture by the French
The one you have described was probably made to orde
in China in the late-seventeenth or early-eighteenth century
with gold from Latin America. Several such badges of of

ice have passed through these rooms, each with gold chains comprising thousands of patterned and faceted inks. The serrated dorsal fins of the golden creature are often hinged and served as toothpicks. The tapering bodies end in an ear probe—quite basic were our ancestors, or at east the Chinese gave them the opportunity to be. It is also quite a useful whistle, which indeed was its ceremonial purpose.''

"I have reason to believe that something just like what you've described was stolen from my family," said Emma. 'Has anyone approached you with one to sell recently?''

Pilkington peered, owl-like, over the rims of his glasses. "Stolen, you say? When did this occur?"

"I'm not sure exactly. Probably within the last month."

"Whew," he said, theatrically wiping imaginary sweat from his brow. "Thank goodness, we are in the clear. The one we just sold was consigned back in July, though the auction didn't take place until three weeks ago."

"You sold a dragon like my grandfather's three weeks ago?"

"I don't know what your grandfather had, but ours was very handsome. Would you like to see a picture?"

"I've already taken up a great deal of your time, but yes, I would, very much."

"Time is something I have a surplus of these days. Not many people come to see me anymore. Value is growing ever more standardized. Soon anything that does not fit into six or seven easily identifiable categories will be banished from the auction rooms forever, along with yours truly. Wait here a moment. I'll be right back."

Pilkington rose laboriously from his seat and exited, leaving Emma in a state of near shock. A second dragon appearing on the market within days of Pépé's death was as improbable a coincidence as Big Ed Garalachek showing up at her hotel in San Marcos. This had to be the same dragon, which would mean that it couldn't have been in the secret compartment in the model of the *Kaito Spirit*.

But then why had the model been stolen? Or was it no
stolen at all? Before Emma could figure out what to mak
of any of this, N. C. Pilkington had returned with tw
auction catalogs under his arm.

"Here we are," he said, opening one of the catalogs t
a full-page picture.

Emma took the book and stared at the glossy color im
age. It was a gold dragon on a long chain, just as Berna
Zuberan had described, though what Emma had envisione
was much different from what she saw in front of her. Thi
dragon looked smaller, somehow, yet more real than sh
had imagined, more like a fisherman's bait than a monster
Its beauty came from its workmanship rather than its sub
ject, yet the image was still powerful enough to send chill
down Emma's spine.

"How does it compare with yours?" said Pilkington.

"I don't know," said Emma. "I've never seen ours."

"Then you will have a hard time finding it, I shoul
think."

"How much did this sell for?"

"Fifty-five thousand dollars, not including our commis
sion."

Emma felt strangely disappointed. Zuberan had specu
lated that the dragon could be worth a fortune. Fifty-fiv
thousand dollars was a lot of money, but hardly a fortune
Was it the current price for two men's lives?

"That's all?" asked Emma.

"Well," sniffed Pilkington, "considering the fact tha
the bullion value of the thing is in the neighborhood o
eight thousand dollars, I don't think it made too shabby
premium. There aren't many collectors of seventeenth
century badges of office ready to battle it out at auctio
these days, you know. The last such badge we had on th
block here carried an estimate of seventy-five to a hundre
thousand and was passed. Even with all the hoopla abou
lost treasure, frankly I was relieved this piece sold at all.'

"Lost treasure? What treasure?"

"Oh, it's all speculation really. I probably shouldn't have allowed it into the catalog at all."

"What are you talking about?"

"I'm talking about the notion that this badge of office might have belonged to the admiral-general who commanded the ill-fated Spanish plate fleet of 1690. Nine galleons of this fleet went down somewhere near Puerto Rico in a hurricane in that year. Each ship was carrying a huge cargo of treasure from the New World back to Spain—thousands of bars of silver, hundreds of pounds of gold. The admiral's flagship, the *Santa Maria de Espinal*, was bringing up the rear, as was customary with Spanish flotillas. He presumably would have been wearing an impressive gold chain and badge of office."

"What would such a treasure be worth?"

"Oh, hundreds of millions of dollars, no doubt. Of course, even if our dragon did belong to the commander of the *Santa Maria de Espinal*, it would not be much help in locating the lost treasure ships unless you knew where it had been found. But being a commercial-minded soul, God help me, I figured it wouldn't hurt the sale to present this theory in the catalog as an amusing anecdote. It did provide a bit of publicity, though no one really took it seriously."

Emma was almost afraid to breathe. What if there really was a treasure? Bernal Zuberan had said that Pépé had made a map to the spot where they had found the dragon. Could that be what all this was about? The map to a whole fleet of sunken ships filled with gold? Or was it just her idiot imagination running amok again? Pictures of her on a treasure chest doing high kicks for pirates sprang into her mind. Yo-ho-ho and a bottle of rum.

Emma closed the catalog and looked at the date on the cover. The auction had taken place a full week before Jacques Passant's death. Perhaps she had just been wrong about the sequence of events. Maybe Pépé had put the dragon up for sale himself this past July, and by so doing

had set into motion a chain of events that had led
his—and Henri-Pierre's—death.

"Who consigned this piece?" Emma asked in a qui
voice, bracing herself to hear her grandfather's nam
"Whom did it belong to?"

"Ordinarily I couldn't tell you, you know," said Pil
ington. "Client confidentiality and all that. But in this cas
the provenance is a matter of public record. It was part
the collection of the last Esmond Dauber."

"Esmond Dauber?" said Emma, startled. "Who w
he?"

"Ah, Esmond," said Pilkington with a deep sig
"There won't be another like Esmond very soon—at lea
not another with so much money. He was a wonderful o
coot. Collected functional gold objects. Letter opener
Nutmeg graters. Thimbles. Anything, really, as long as
was gold, had some functional purpose and was beautifu
He bought many of his things here, I'm happy to sa
though he would go to the ends of the earth for an inte
esting piece. You'd be amazed at the things that peop
have made out of gold over the centuries."

"I don't understand," said Emma. "Did he know abo
this theory of a treasure?"

"Oh, yes. But couldn't care less. To him the thing w
just a useful thing made of gold. As I said, when you blo
through it, you really do get a very nice whistle."

"When did this Esmond Dauber die?"

"About a year ago. His delightful widow gracious
consigned the entire collection to us. The jewelry depar
ment got much of it. The table items and gold flatware a
going through our silver department—a bit in the prese
sale, though most will have to wait until May. If you'
around next month, however, you will be able to bid
Esmond's snuff boxes. They are the real prizes of the co
lection as far as I'm concerned, and I shall be wielding th
hammer."

With obvious pride Pilkington handed Emma the oth

atalog he was holding. Emma opened it to a page with a hotograph of a sober-looking man in a three-piece suit dentified in the caption as Esmond Dauber. On the adjaent page was a picture of a woman with the shoulders of fullback and the face of a hatchet. Beneath this were a ew paragraphs under the headline HOMAGE TO A COLLEC-OR, signed *Henriette Tawson Dauber, New York City.*

"How long was the dragon in Mr. Dauber's collecion?" asked Emma, leafing through the pictures of gold oxes and of the monarchs and military heroes for whom hey had been made. Nothing seemed to make sense anyore.

"I really have no idea."

"I'd like to talk with his widow, this Henriette Dauber. s it possible to get her address?"

"I'm sorry," said Pilkington, opening the door of the iewing room to signify that their meeting was at an end. That kind of information we really cannot give out."

"You've been very kind," said Emma, following him ut into the reception area. "This was very informative."

"We try to be of help. I shall keep my eyes open and lert you if another dragon badge should appear. Obviusly this couldn't have been the one that was stolen from ou. Where may I reach you?"

Emma gave N. C. Pilkington Charlemagne's number in an Francisco and thanked him again. Then she took the levator back downstairs to the lobby, where a guard dicted her to a bank of telephones. It was time to bring in e professionals.

"Poteet," answered the familiar short, fat, bald voice hen Emma finally reached the proper extension at the an Francisco Police Department.

"It's Emma Passant, Detective Poteet. I took your adice and went on a trip."

"Oh?"

Emma launched into a summary of what she had learned n San Marcos: about the golden dragon; how it had been

smuggled off the island in a secret compartment of th
Kaito Spirit—the very model that had disappeared off he
grandfather's bedroom dresser; how a suspiciously simila
dragon had come up for sale at Sotheby's barely a wee
before Jacques Passant's murder; how Pilkington had pos
sibly traced the artifact to a sunken treasure fleet wor
millions; how Jacques Passant had once made a map 1
what might be the very spot where it was located.

Poteet did not say a word throughout her entire stor
He waited a full five seconds after she had finished befor
he finally spoke.

"That's very interestin', Miz Passant."

"It's more than just interesting, I think," said Emm
"It provides a motive for Pépé's murder—a reason why
was not just a random mugging."

"Oh? And what's that?"

"Didn't you hear what I said about the flagship of th
Spanish treasure fleet of 1690?"

"I heard. I just don't see the relevance."

"The relevance is the map my grandfather made to th
treasure."

"The map your grandpa made was to where the gol
dragon thing and one little coin was found, if I heard yc
correctly. There's no proof there was ever any treasure.'

"My grandfather told me he couldn't go back to Sa
Marcos because he had stolen the greatest treasure of th
sea. A map could have been what was in the secret con
partment of the model boat. That would explain why
was stolen. Why he was killed. A map to such a treasu
would be worth killing for."

"Then why didn't your grandpa go back to San Marco
and get it? Thirty years is a mighty long time to tarry whe
you've got a sunken treasure waitin' for you."

"Maybe he was afraid of Peguero's men," sputtere
Emma, amazed that Poteet could be so matter-of-fact
light of what she had learned. "Peguero was the dictato

They must have believed that the treasure was theirs. That Pépé had stolen it from them.''

"You have evidence that such a map is still in existence, Miz Passant?" said Poteet in his quiet drawl. He seemed strangely uninterested, remote.

"No."

"Lots of things disappear over the course of time on their own, you know."

"Then what was in the model boat? Why else was it stolen?"

"Can you prove now there was something in the model boat?"

"No."

"Can you prove that it was in fact stolen?"

"No."

"Have you learned anything that would tie your grandfather to Mr. Caraignac?"

"No, but—"

"Then you don't got nothin' new, do you, Miz Passant?"

"What about the man who was following me?" said Emma angrily.

"What man was this?"

Emma recounted the appearance of Big Ed Garalachek in San Marcos, and how he was not who he claimed to be. In her excitement about the treasure she had almost forgotten about him.

"He doesn't sound like someone to worry about," said Poteet when she had finished.

"I'm glad you think so!" exclaimed Emma. What was it that Zubcran had called the police? Bunglers and fools.

"We'd check him out if it would make you feel better; only there doesn't seem much to go on."

"He gave me a telephone number," said Emma, digging into her purse for Big Ed's card. "Maybe you can track him through that."

Emma read the phone number.

"Got it," said the policeman. "Anything else I can d
for you, Miz Passant?"

"How is your investigation going? Have you learne
anything new?"

"We're working on a few things."

"Anything interesting?"

"As I say, we're working on a few things. Now, i
there's nothin' else, I hope you'll excuse me. I've got
lot to do today."

Emma hung up the receiver, feeling as if she had ju:
had a conversation with a wall. She had expected that th
detective might bawl her out for continuing to pok
around, but it had never occurred to her that he wouldn
take what she had learned seriously. Obviously he ju:
didn't care anymore. Jacques Passant was yesterday's mur
der; Poteet had other crimes to attend to, easier ones t
solve.

Emma wasn't going to give up, however.

She pulled out the Manhattan white pages from unde
the counter and looked through the listings for Daube
Perhaps the wife of Esmond Dauber would be able to te
her something. From the catalog Emma knew that th
woman lived in the city.

No Henriette Tawson Dauber was listed in the phon
book, but Esmond Dauber still was. The phone numbe
was followed by an address on Central Park West. Emm
put a quarter in the phone and dialed.

"Yeah?" answered a gruff female voice.

"Hello," said Emma, taken a little aback. "I'd like t
speak with Henriette Tawson Dauber."

"That's my name. Who the hell are you?"

Just another loopy New Yorker, Emma told herself. Sh
had just been telling someone about how New York wa
full of nutcases. Who had it been? Henri-Pierre Caraigna
Emma remembered, swallowing hard.

"Mrs. Dauber, my name is Emma Passant. Mr. Pilkin;
ton at Sotheby's has been telling me about your late hu:

band's collection. I wonder if I might be able to speak to you about one of the items that sold recently.''

"All right," said the voice. "Come on over."

"You mean now?" said Emma.

"At my age, honey, it don't pay to put things off. I could go at any minute. By this time next week I could be forgotten by everyone but the IRS. I haven't any family, you know. Esmond wasn't interested in collecting children, except gold ones you could light cigarettes with.''

"I'm sorry."

"I'll pull out some chops. You're not one of those nouvelle people, are you? Lunch on a radish, dine on grass?''

"I can handle a chop."

"Good. I'm at the Malvern. Eighty-second Street and Central Park West."

"I'm afraid I'm not from the city, Mrs. Dauber. Could you tell me how to get there?"

"Sure," said Mrs. Dauber. "You go outside and holler, Taxi!' at the top of your lungs. Then you get in and I'll see you here soon."

The line went dead. Emma made her way back through the lobby and retrieved her coat, wondering if everyone in New York City was crazy.

The doorman was occupied with an elderly couple, but Emma didn't need his help to get a cab. There wasn't one in sight, anyway. At least not an unoccupied one—you could tell whether a cab had a fare or not by the TAXI sign on the roof. If it was lit, they were available. When they took a fare and started the meter, the light went out.

Emma looked down the block. There was a large hospital below Sotheby's. Several people were standing on curbs of various cross streets, obviously looking for cabs. Across the street, not looking in her direction, was a man who might also be looking for a cab. A man with a heart-shaped scar on his cheek.

Emma was surprised to see him again, but it wasn't so unlikely, she told herself. Maybe he had been at Christie's

because he was looking to buy his wife or girlfriend
present and had settled on something in silver instead o
something in lingerie. Sotheby's was also having a silver
sale, according to the schedule she had noticed in the
lobby. There was nothing sinister about comparison shop
ping, was there?

Still, after her experience with Big Ed, and Detective
Poteet's treating her as if she were crying wolf, Emma'
nerves were frayed to the point of unraveling. She didn'
want even to consider the notion that someone else might
be following her. She turned, crossed Seventy-second
Street and walked briskly up York Avenue. After a block
she glanced back over her shoulder. The man with the
heart-shaped scar was walking uptown, too, on the other
side of the street.

There was still no reason to panic. It was probably just
an innocent coincidence. It was only when Emma saw the
city bus going up York Avenue a block ahead of her, and
another one heading downtown on the opposite side of the
street, that she realized how frightened she was.

It was the classic setup of an illusion, and Emma seized
the opportunity. She increased her pace, narrowing the dis
tance between herself and the bus ahead, which was creep
ing slowly through the thick traffic. The man with the
heart-shaped scar walked faster as well, keeping up with
her on the other side of the street. Emma caught up with
the uptown bus at the same instant that the downtown bus
was passing it in the opposite direction.

With the buses between them, the man with the heart
shaped scar would expect her to continue walking in the
same direction she had been going, hidden behind the up
town bus. He continued walking uptown, running to keep
up with the bus, expecting to see her emerge when it pulled
farther ahead.

The instant the buses crossed, however, Emma sprinted
into the middle of York Avenue and reversed direction.
She ran downtown along the yellow center-line marker

concealed by the downtown bus for two blocks, then darted in front as it stopped at a light. By this time the man with the heart-shaped scar had followed the other bus two blocks uptown, putting four blocks between them.

Emma tore down Seventy-second Street as fast as her legs would carry her, not stopping until she reached First Avenue, where she was able to hail a cab.

"Where you want to go?" demanded the driver happily as she got into the pine-scented vehicle.

Somewhere safe, Emma wanted to say. Somewhere where people didn't change their names or conceal their motives. Somewhere where they didn't run away or get killed or have to look over their shoulder, worrying who might be following them.

"Eighty-second and Central Park West," she whispered, wondering if she would ever feel safe again.

SEVENTEEN

EMMA STEPPED OUT of the cab and craned her neck at the Malvern. The huge old apartment co-op with its forbidding turrets and three entrances stood directly across from Central Park, a few streets up from the Natural History Museum.

Taking a deep breath, she walked directly to what seemed to be the main entrance. A gray-uniformed doorman with white gloves directed her through the ornate brass-grille doorway into a lobby overflowing with marble, wood-paneling and fresh flowers. Inside, another uniformed man asked whom she wanted to see.

"Mrs. Dauber is expecting me," said Emma and gave her name, still shaken by her experience with the man with the heart-shaped scar outside of Sotheby's. The last thing she wanted to do right now was lunch with some crazy woman, but what choice did she have? Henriette Tawson Dauber could be the key to whether the golden dragon plucked from the sea and smuggled out of San Marcos decades ago was the same one that had been auctioned last month at Sotheby's.

The doorman picked up a telephone. A brief conversation ensued.

"Eighth floor," said the man, putting down the receiver. "Jimmy will take you up."

Feeling queasy—not at all ready for a heavy lunch—Emma walked across the lobby as directed to a surprisingly small elevator, where another pleasant uniformed man with white gloves closed the steel gate and turned the old-fashioned control wheel. The elevator buzzed and whirred its way slowly up to the eighth floor. Finally it stopped, and the attendant unfolded the steel gate and opened the door.

Emma was startled to find herself not in a hallway, but actually in an apartment—or rather, its vestibule entryway. It was a two-story area with a black-and-white stone floor and a crystal chandelier. She took a few steps into the room, looking for signs of life. Ahead to the left was a dining room dominated by a three-pedestal, thirty-foot-long table of polished mahogany, surrounded by dark carved chairs. To the right was a cavernous living room with more furniture that looked as if it belonged in a museum. Directly in front of her a winding staircase led to a second floor.

"Hello?" Emma called out, not knowing what to do. For a moment nothing happened. Then a door swung open at the far end of the dining room, and the woman Emma had seen pictured in the auction catalog stuck her head into the room.

"You the girl who called?" shouted Henriette Tawson Dauber. She looked even bigger than she had in the picture—and more hatchet-faced, though somehow kinder in person.

"Yes. Emma Passant."

"Got my hands full. Park your coat on a chair and come on and join me in the kitchen."

The door swung shut. Emma took off her coat and laid it tentatively across one of the armless chairs in the hallway. Then, bracing herself, she crossed the long dining room and pushed open the door behind which Henriette Dauber had disappeared.

The spacious kitchen Emma found herself in was as warm and informal as the rest of the apartment was cold and stuffy. In the huge fireplace set into a brick wall, a fire snapped and crackled. Herbs and flowers were hanging everywhere from the ceiling to dry, in between pots and pans suspended from iron racks. The cabinets were of blue-painted pine. Around a pine farmer's table were half a dozen mismatched wooden chairs. The table was set for two. Henriette Tawson Dauber was standing at the enormous double sink cranking a salad spinner.

She was a woman of substantial girth and high hair— the dyed-blond mass on top of her head resembled an oversized football. She wore an apricot-colored muumuu that fit her like a sack. Over one shoulder was a dish towel. Her expression was animated, bemused. Emma guessed she might be in her seventies.

"Thanks for seeing me like this, Mrs. Dauber," Emma said, feeling herself relax a bit in the cheerful, homey room.

"Call me Henny," said the woman, picking up a platter of enormous veal chops and tossing one on a grille built into the eight-burner gas stove. "Everybody does. How many chops you want?"

"One will be fine, thanks."

"Suit yourself." Henny shrugged, placing another two on the grille for herself.

"I didn't mean to put you to so much trouble."

"No trouble. I like company. Don't get too much anymore, not since Esmond croaked. The couples we used to hang out with don't want to be stuck with a third wheel, and all the single men my age are either out with twenty-year-olds or dead."

"Can I help with anything?"

"No, just sit yourself down at the table. I got everything under control. These chops'll be done in no time. There's some pickles in the icebox you could bring out if you want. You a pickle eater?"

"Not too much," said Emma, walking over and opening the refrigerator—a two-door affair with pictures of Yorkshire terriers attached to it with magnets shaped like little pieces of sushi. The pickles were swimming in a large glass bowl, which Emma took out and brought to the table.

"You should try these anyhow," said Henny Dauber, whisking up a salad dressing while keeping her eye on the stove. "I get 'em down on the Lower East Side. One bite and you can practically speak Yiddish. Go on. Taste one."

Emma plucked one out of the crowded brine, took a bite, then closed her eyes and waited for her face to unpucker.

"So what you think?" said Henny.

"Oy," said Emma. Henny chuckled with satisfaction.

"Where I grew up in Oklahoma, we didn't have no Jews. No Orientals or Indians, neither—except the kind that lived on reservations and ate Spam sandwiches on Wonderbread like I did. We all thought that pickles were things that grew in jars, can you believe it? Now I send out for tandoori chicken and battle the mobs in Chinatown on Sundays for dim sum. God, I love New York. There still ain't nothin' like a good old-fashioned American veal chop every once in a while, though. Sometimes you just have to go for comfort food, know what I mean?"

"Sure," said Emma.

"Go on, sit down. You want a potato, don't you? You could use some more meat on your bones."

"Like I could use an extra appendix."

"Hey, that's rich. Extra appendix. Spuds are in the side oven; they should be about done. Get a couple out for me, too."

As Henny Dauber tossed the salad, Emma collected their plates and took them over to the small built-in oven across the room that Henny had indicated. She extracted a potato for herself and two for her hostess, then brought them back to the table on a serving plate.

"What do you want to drink?" said Henny after a few moments of poking the veal chops with a pair of tongs, then turning them over.

"Water will be fine."

"How 'bout a beer?"

"All right," said Emma, feeling as if she was being tested. She had a feeling that this wasn't the time to order milk.

"Get one for me, too. They're right under where you found the pickles."

Emma walked back to the refrigerator and took out two cans of Budweiser. She brought one to Henriette Dauber, who popped the top and stared at her expectantly. Emma popped the top on her own and raised the can to drink.

"Ain't we gonna clink?"

The can was almost at Emma's lips. Emma lowered her arm.

"Clink?"

"You know. Toast, like."

"Sure," said Emma, walking over and tapping her can lightly against the older woman's.

"To sex, drugs, and rock and roll," said Henriette Dauber and took a healthy swig. Emma followed suit, keeping an eye on her hostess, not knowing what to expect from her next. What came was a deep sigh.

"Esmond was big on clinking," said Henriette wistfully, after wiping her lips with her sleeve. "With him it was usually champagne glasses. He was one stuffy old bird, let me tell you. I used to tease him, make him clink beer cans, try to keep him from taking himself too serious-like. Don't have nobody to clink with anymore."

An odd, unreadable sadness descended over her hatchet face for a moment, then she glanced at the stove and perked up again.

"I think the chops are about done. Bring your plate."

Emma took two from the table and brought them over.

Henny Dauber put chops and salad on each, and they sat down at the table. Emma followed her lead, picking up a steaming potato and juggling it between burning fingertips over to her plate, then cutting a small piece of meat and raising it to her lips,

"Jumpin' Jehoshaphat!" said Mrs. Dauber suddenly, putting down her fork the instant Emma had put hers into her mouth.

"What?" said Emma, caught with her mouth full of

veal. She had never heard anyone actually use that expression before and couldn't image what emergency it portended.

"I forgot the ketchup," declared Henny.

"I'll get it," said Emma, chewing, rising. "Where is it?"

"In the icebox. Thanks."

In a moment Emma returned with the bottle, which Henriette Dauber opened and drenched her meat with.

"Want some?" she said, offering the bottle.

"Sure," said Emma, wondering if this, too, was some kind of test. She poured a little pool next to her meat and dunked a morsel as if she had been doing it all her life. To her surprise it wasn't a bad combination.

"So why you want to know about Esmond's stuff?" asked Henny after polishing off a few enormous mouthfuls.

Emma hurried to finish chewing before answering.

"There was a golden dragon of his that was auctioned in the sale a few weeks ago," she said finally. "A kind of whistle. My grandfather had one just like it that was stolen, and I'm trying to help the police."

"Hey, that's the same thing that that Frenchie came here about," said Henriette, after taking a sip from her can of beer. "Popular little articles, these dragon things."

"A Frenchman?" exclaimed Emma and put down her fork. "A Frenchman came here asking about the dragon? When was this?"

"A few weeks ago."

"Who was he?"

"The fellow who bought it at the auction. Sat right there where you are and had steak and eggs with me—sometimes you need good old American comfort food, if you know what I mean. He wanted to know the 'pro-ven-ance' as he put it. Had some fancy name I can't remember."

"Henri-Pierre Caraignac," whispered Emma, her mind reeling. Henri-Pierre had had the dragon all along!

"Henry Caraignac," said Henny with her mouth full "That's it. You know him?"

"I met him once. But I didn't know him. I didn't know him at all."

"Too bad. Real nice fella. Easy on the eyes, if you know what I mean. Promised to come back and see me some-time."

"He won't."

"Yeah? Why not? I may not be much to look at, but I know what men like and I got plenty of it—my butcher supplies the best steak houses in town."

"I'm sorry, Mrs. Dauber...Henny. Henri-Pierre Caraignac is dead."

Henny stopped chewing and stared at Emma.

"You're kidding," she said after a moment.

"I wish I were. He was murdered last week in San Francisco."

Henriette Dauber finished chewing in silence, then cut herself another piece of meat and ate that, too. Then she put down her silverware and pushed herself away from the table.

"Jesus," she said angrily. "What a world we got here. Nice young man like that. It's a cryin' shame."

Neither of them spoke for a moment. There was nothing to say.

"Were you able to help him?" Emma asked finally.

The older woman didn't answer. She cut herself another small piece of meat and pushed it around the ketchup on her plate. Emma ate a few bites of salad in silence.

"I'm sorry," said Henny after a moment. "I don't like to hear about young people dying. Makes me kind of sick. I been off my feed a lot lately, what with this AIDS thing. My stockbroker died from it this past summer, he was only thirty-six. I visited him a few times in the hospital and it was depressing as all shit. But it wasn't like somebody murdered him intentionally. Did they catch the guy who did it? To Henry Caraignac?"

"No."

"Figures. It's enough to make you want to holler."

"Were you able to give Henri-Pierre the information he wanted?"

"Yeah, sure," grunted Henny. "Esmond liked paper almost as much as he liked gold. I got a dozen notebooks full of bills of sale, all cataloged. I let the Frenchman go through them and he found the one for this dragon thing right away."

"May I see it?"

"Sorry," said Henny, shaking her head. "Frenchie took it with him. I figured he'd bought the dragon, so he should have the bill. I didn't have no use for it anymore. He said *merci* and kissed my hand."

"Do you have a copy?"

Henriette Dauber stared at her plate and didn't answer.

"Please, Henny. It's very important. It may have had something to do with why he was killed."

"You figure someone knocked him off for this dragon thing?" asked the old woman, glancing up. "Same guy who stole your grandfather's, maybe? Some wacko collector or something?"

"I know it sounds unlikely…"

"Hell, collectors are damned strange people. Believe me, I know. Tell you what. I got some records upstairs you're welcome to check through if you want. Finish your lunch first. I'll clean up later. I seem to have lost my appetite."

"I'm done, too."

"No, you're not, you're just being polite. Don't worry, I'm okay. It's just the shock of hearing about that nice young man. Go on now and eat. You're a growing girl."

Emma cut up what remained on her chop, shoveled it into her mouth and washed everything down with beer.

Henny Dauber waited until Emma was through. Then she rose and led the way back through the dining room and up the hall stairs. At the top was a corridor lined with paintings and prints. Emma followed Henny past bedrooms and marble baths to a closed door with fancy brass hardware. Henny turned the handle and flipped on a light switch. The room was full of filing cabinets and trunks aside from a simple wooden table and several hard-backed chairs.

"Esmond kept every single bit of paper ever came his way," said Henny, looking around in disgust. "The old fool was scared to death he'd need to prove to the IRS one day where he bought that fifteen-cent washer in 1956. Fat lot of good it did him. I think he was the only millionaire in America never got audited."

Emma walked over to the nearest file cabinet. Each drawer was neatly marked with the year and a typed list of contents.

"You're welcome to poke around," said Henny. "Esmond got appraisals every few years on his stuff. He was always trying to keep track of how much he was worth for some reason I never understood. You might find a copy of the bill you're looking for in one of the appraisals."

"Are you sure it's all right?" said Emma.

"Sure," said Henny. "I ain't got no secrets. You just make yourself at home. I'm gonna go have me a lie-down for a while if you don't mind. Haven't been feeling myself lately. Maybe I'm getting old. Either that or I just need to get laid; I don't know. I'll be in that first bedroom at the top of the stairs if you need me."

"Thank you, Henny."

The old lady nodded and padded off. Emma began working her way through the cabinets. Half an hour later in a decades-old file, she found what she was looking for. Attached to an old appraisal was a Xerox copy of the original bill of sale dated thirty years ago for "one fine Spanish gold dragon and chain, circa 1700."

The buyer was Esmond Dauber. The purchase price was forty-five thousand dollars—just ten thousand less than it had brought three weeks ago, after more than thirty years f inflation. Gold dragons apparently weren't the best investments in the world. It was the seller's name, however, that was the real surprise.

Emma stared at the familiar signature with a mixture of surprise and dismay. She had followed this trail back dozens of years and across thousands of miles, looking for the one common thread, the thing that would unite Henri-Pierre Caraignac, Jacques Passant, and a golden dragon that had waited in the sand off San Marcos for nearly three hundred years. At last she had found it. The name at the bottom of the page, in bold block letters on the line marked "Agent for seller," was Charlemagne Moussy, Esquire.

"LAW OFFICES OF Charlemagne Moussy," said the cheerful nasal voice on the other end of the line.

"Hi, Jean. It's Emma Passant."

"Emma! How are you? What are you doing? Are you having a nice vacation? I want to hear all about everything, but my other line is ringing, so I'm going to put you on hold; but don't worry, I'll be right back and we can talk. Okay?"

"Fine," said Emma as telephone music filled the receiver. She rolled over on the bed, happy to be back in her room at the hotel.

Finding that Charlemagne had been involved with the original sale of the dragon was disconcerting, but at least things were finally beginning to make a little sense. As she waited for Jean to come back on the line, Emma took the moment to review mentally the events as she had reconstructed them.

After smuggling the dragon out of San Marcos three decades ago, Jacques Passant had apparently contracted Charlemagne to broker a sale—Emma vaguely remembered that the lawyer had once lived in New York City.

It would have made good sense for her grandfather to go to an attorney, Emma realized. Because of the San Maran laws regarding recovery of treasure and because it had

been smuggled into the United States, the ownership of the
dragon—and hence Pépé's right to sell—was murky.
Moreover, her grandfather probably didn't speak much English then, may have just changed his name to throw Peguero's agents off his trail, and had a desperately ill young
daughter—Emma's mother—to look after. Jacques Passan
would have needed someone to protect his interests. Who
better than a French-speaking lawyer like Charlemagne
Moussy, who obviously had contacts with collectors?

Charlemagne must have arranged an anonymous private
sale so the dragon would not have to appear on the open
market. It had then remained in Esmond Dauber's collection until Dauber's death. When the dragon came up for
auction at Sotheby's three weeks ago, it had been pur-
chased by Henri-Pierre Caraignac.

But why Henri-Pierre?

This was where Emma's knowledge of the facts broke
down and speculation took over. There was still no evidence to take to Poteet. The Frenchman might have bought
the dragon simply because he had an interest in seven-
teenth-century badges of office. Or perhaps he had been
bidding for someone else, some woman with gaudy taste
in jewelry. Unless, of course, Henri-Pierre's knowledge as
an antique dealer had led him to see something in the
dragon that no one else had seen. Had he attempted to
track down its original owner because he believed there
was a treasure, and that the dragon was the key to finding
it?

"Hi, Emma, I'm back," said the machine-gun nasal
voice of Jean Bean in Emma's ear. "So tell me all about
it. Did you have a good time? Did you meet anybody?
God, I wish I could go to the Caribbean; I once went to
Miami Beach, but I was with Mother and she got stung by
a Portuguese man-of-war our first day and we had to spend
practically the whole week in our room. Not that I wasn't
concerned, mind you, but I really would have liked to get
out just a little and see the sights and have some drinks.

and maybe meet someone nice—like that's too much to ask for? But you don't want to hear about my lousy trip, I want to hear about yours, so tell me all about it.''

"I will later, Jean, I promise. Only right now I have to talk to Charlemagne. Is he there?''

"No, and it's funny you should be calling for him, because I know he wanted to talk to you. He had some interesting news for you, he said. Isn't it funny how things happen like that sometime? You're thinking about somebody and suddenly they call, or don't call, in my case, at least when it comes to men—synchronicity, I think they call it—that kind of coincidence. Has anything like that ever happened to you?''

"All too often," said Emma. "Maybe you can help me, Jean. Do you know if Charlemagne met with a Frenchman in the past few weeks? Someone who hadn't been in before—a new client, maybe?''

"I don't think so," said Jean. "No, wait a minute, I remember. There *was* a man with a French accent who called up a few weeks ago. He asked for an appointment to discuss a problem with a mortgage, said he had been referred by an acquaintance—another Frenchman who had done business with Charlemagne some thirty years ago, a man who had raised a granddaughter by himself, and I said, 'Oh, you must mean Jacques Passant,' since I knew that your grandfather was Charlemagne's oldest client, and the man said yes, that was his friend—did he still live in that same delightful area? And I said, 'Yes, if you mean Potrero Hill,' though I don't know if 'delightful' is the word I would use, no offense, Emma. Then we scheduled a time and he said thank you, but he never showed up, which I thought was very strange, and so did Charlemagne, because the man had sounded so nice on the telephone, but what can you do? I thought maybe he would call back, but he never did. I didn't do anything wrong, did I?''

"No, Jean," said Emma, taking a deep breath. "You

didn't do anything wrong. What did the man say his name was?''

"Dubois. Jean Dubois."

It must have been Henri-Pierre, thought Emma. Dubois is as common a French name as Smith is in English.

But something was terribly wrong in all this. All Henri-Pierre had had was a bill of sale for the dragon listing Charlemagne's name as the agent for the seller. How then had he known about Jacques Passant? How had he known that he was a Frenchman who had raised a granddaughter alone?

"I really need to speak with Charlemagne, Jean," said Emma, feeling more confused than ever. "Could you have him call me as soon as he gets in?"

Perhaps the little lawyer would be able to shed some light on all this, Emma hoped. After all, he had been the one who had sold the dragon originally.

"Oh, that's what I've been meaning to tell you," said Jean brightly. "He's out of town on business, in New York City."

"New York!"

"Yes, isn't it wonderful? The Big Apple. Times Square. Broadway. He wanted you to call him there. He's staying at the Plaza Hotel. Would you like the number?"

EIGHTEEN

"THEN YOU ARE NOT really certain that this scarred-face man was indeed following you at all," declared Charlemagne Moussy, smoothing his tiny mustache with a manicured finger and handing his menu to the waiter.

"No," admitted Emma angrily, surrendering her own menu and waiting to explode until the waiter had departed. "It might be just another coincidence. Like the phony car salesman just happening to show up in San Marcos. Like Henri-Pierre Caraignac just happening to be the person who bought the dragon. Like you just happening to have been involved in this whole thing up to your neck and now just happening to be in New York."

"Please calm down," said Charlemagne, glancing around uncomfortably.

The other diners in the Plaza's Edwardian Room didn't seem to have noticed Emma's tirade—or, if they had noticed, didn't seem to care. It was as if the enormous restaurant with its soaring wooden ceiling, white-jacketed staff, and preposterous prices had been invented specifically for indiscreet admissions and intrigue. A significant number of patrons looked as if they might have pilfered military secrets at some point in their afternoons. Charlemagne had suggested dinner here when Emma had finally reached him on the phone that afternoon. Hearing about sunken treasure and men with scars apparently brought out the gourmet in him.

"What are you doing in New York, Charlemagne?" Emma demanded, not attempting to conceal her frustration. "Why didn't you tell me about the dragon? Is there anything else you forgot to mention?"

"One question at the same time, please," said the little lawyer, raising his hand. "You make it sound like I might have had some involvement in this tragedy of events that has befallen us. This hurts me very deeply, Emma. Have not you known me since you were just the tiny little child? Do you not remember that Jacques was my best friend?"

Emma took a sip of her margarita and didn't answer. She had ordered a drink only because Charlemagne had wanted to start with a martini, but now she was glad she had one.

Emma had never dined with Charlemagne alone before. She had been dragged along to his office by her grandfather and seen him at large social gatherings like weddings and funerals. She hadn't even known that he drank. What else did she not know about him?

"All right, Emma," said Charlemagne, stiffening in reaction to her silence. "To answer your questions, I did not tell you about the dragon whistle that I sold on Jacques's behalf because this happened many years ago, and it never occurred to me that such a transaction had anything to do with the price of fishes. If you had asked me, gladly would I have told you, but you did not, so neither did I."

"You said in your office," said Emma, "that Pépé was able to put the down payment on the house because you helped him sell a 'certain property.' That certain property was the dragon, wasn't it?"

"Yes."

"So why didn't you tell me about it then?"

"Because I am a lawyer," replied Charlemagne in a low, irritated hiss. "Because I am discreet. I do not go around telling everybody everything I know about anything that comes up in conversation. I do not hang myself with my big mouth. By my nature and my training I respond precisely to questions. If I went around volunteering information about things that I had not been asked, half of my clients would be in jail or more deeply in debt than they find themselves already."

"Wonderful, Charlemagne. Marvelous."

"Disapprove if you must," declared the lawyer, glancing at his watch. "But in our society people they are not required to incriminate themselves. Nor is it necessary for them to hire the blabbermouth lawyer to do it for them."

"All right," said Emma in disgust. "Have it your way. Just tell me about the dragon now. Tell me everything."

Charlemagne pursed his lips, straightened his bow tie, and took a sniff of the carnation in the buttonhole.

"There is not a great deal to tell," he pronounced in a calm voice. "I was a young lawyer just starting out when Jacques came to see me those many years ago. My practice—such as it was—was then in New York because this is where my family had emigrated. But I hated it here. The city that is so glorious when one has money is equally dismal when one is poor, and we had been very poor indeed. As a young lawyer of French origin I sought out the business of my former countrymen by writing a legal-advice column for one of the French-language newspapers that were then being published. It was from seeing this column that Jacques learned of me and came forward with his dragon whistle to sell."

"So you knew all about it," said Emma in an accusatory tone.

"I knew nothing about it," replied Charlemagne indignantly. "Jacques told me that his dragon whistle was the heirloom that had been in his family for generations."

"And you believed that?"

"It is not the business of lawyers to doubt their own clients. What if he had stolen the dragon whistle? If I had forced Jacques to tell me this, then I would not have been able to help him pursue his interests and sell it, would I? I am an officer of the court. I have a responsibility."

"But it was okay if you didn't know."

"What was I supposed to do, Emma?" erupted Charlemagne. "Cross-question him until he confessed that

Jacques Passant was not his real name and that he was in the country illegally?''

"Oh my God," said Emma. "Do you think he was?''

"Thank goodness that I did not ask," said Charlemagne with a visible I-told-you-so kind of satisfaction, "so this was not my concern. You see how we lawyers make the strange kind of sense? I knew all I had to know—that your grandfather was my client and that he needed my help, which I was happy to give him. Okay?''

Emma nodded.

"I didn't mean to imply that you were doing anything improper," she said in a conciliatory voice. "I just need to get to the bottom of all this, that's all.''

"Of course you do," said Charlemagne, glancing at his watch, apparently placated.

"Do you have to get somewhere?" said Emma.

"No, why?''

"You keep looking at your watch.''

Charlemagne looked at his watch again.

"Do I?''

"Yes. You just did it again.''

"It is the time change," said the lawyer with a shrug. "My clock, she says seven but the rest of me says four. My doctor wishes me to take a pill each night at the dinnertime, and I am confused. Is the dinnertime now, or is it later?''

"Later," said Emma. "How did you know Esmond Dauber?''

"Who?''

"The man you sold the dragon to. Don't tell me he read about you in the newspaper, too.''

"No, it was the other way around," said Charlemagne. "It was I who had read about him. In an article in the *New York Times*. I looked the collector of the gold objects up in the phone book and we were able to consummate a sale—at a very good price, I might add.''

"That's all there was to it?''

"What more is necessary? Sometime later Jacques came back to me and asked me to help him relocate to some nice city, far away from New York. I thought of San Francisco because my brother, Napoleon, then lived there. We flew out together to California and with Napoleon's help were able to buy the house you grew up in and now wish to sell—Jacques still had much of the money left from the sale of the dragon. In the process I found that I, too, liked San Francisco, and moved there myself, several years later. I reconnected with my friend Jacques, made your tiny acquaintance, and that, my dear Emma, is the whole story—locks, stocks and barrels."

"I wish you had said something before," said Emma. "It would have saved me a lot of time."

"Oh, yes," said Charlemagne, throwing up his hands. "There you are in my office having fled your home because you believed some crazed murderer has just been there to steal a model boat, and what do I say? 'Excuse me, Emma. I am sorry to interrupt your fear and panic, but how would you like to hear the story of how I sold a family heirloom for Jacques several days ago?' That would have been very supportive, yes?"

"I'm sorry, Charlemagne. I know you would never do anything to harm me."

The little lawyer nodded and finished the rest of his martini in a single gulp. Their conversation apparently had upset him. He usually was the soul of calmness, but tonight he was more nervous than she had ever seen him.

"It's just that I'm so sure the dragon must have something to do with all of this," Emma went on. "Did Pépé ever say anything to you about a treasure?"

"The word was all over his vocabulary," said the lawyer with a dismissive wave of his little pink hand. "But that does not mean anything. You know how obscure was the way Jacques spoke, how he never called a thing directly. Even me he referred to as 'the treasure of the civil court,' when it was not 'my friend with his hand in my

pocket.' Dear Jacques was always philosophizing abou
wealth and wisdom and things obscure. Who knows wha
he meant? Why do you ask?''

"Because I think there might have been a treasure map
in the model boat that was stolen."

"*Mon Dieu.* But how can this be?''

Emma briefly recounted Zuberan's story of how the
dragon had been found and about the Spanish plate flee
that had gone down in the hurricane in 1690.

Charlemagne listened intently, asking an occasiona
question, shaking his head in increasing bewilderment.

"I knew nothing of any of this," he said finally.

"The model boat had a secret compartment. That's how
Pépé smuggled in the dragon. Obviously the dragon wasn'
in there anymore. It would have been a great place to hide
a map."

"Perhaps you should tell this to the police."

"I did. I spoke to Detective Poteet this afternoon."

"And what did he say?''

"Nothing."

"So he was not convinced there was a map. Why are
you?''

"Look, Charlemagne, there must have been something
valuable in the model, or why else would Pépé have told
me about it in the will? 'That she may take her place at
the helm and turn the wheel on the legacy that I have kept
hidden from her.' You turned the wheel of the model and
the secret compartment opened. What else could have been
in there but the map?''

"Maybe he kept money in there, Emma," said Charlemagne gently. "Have you thought of this? Maybe that was
the legacy Jacques wished you to have. And if there was
a thief, perhaps he was just looking for money. That is
what thiefs seek to find, is it not?''

They both fell silent as the waiter approached with their
dinners. Emma was still full from lunch, but the Cobb
salad she had ordered looked wonderful. She confirmed

his with a taste as the waiter deposited Charlemagne's fish
n front of him and departed.

"Well," said Emma, sighing, "at least we know for
ure now that Henri-Pierre Caraignac wasn't killed just
ecause he had the bad luck to let me pick him up on the
erry. He bought the dragon and came to San Francisco
ecause of it. He must have been following me that day.
Do you know that Jean Bean practically gave him our
address when he called your office? He pretended to be a
otential client. A Mr. Dubois."

"Oh?" said Charlemagne, picking at his fish.

"Don't you remember? Jean said she told you. He never
arrived for his appointment."

"I don't recall. How do you know it was Caraignac?"

"Who else could it have been? He had a French accent."

"My dear girl," said Charlemagne in a kind voice,
"half of the people who call my office have French ac-
cents; I am a French lawyer. I think your imagination, she
is working overtime, yes?"

Emma started to say something but stopped. Charlemagne was right. She was doing it again. It was all just
peculation, fantasy. She felt like a fool.

"Have the police learned anything new?" Emma said
unhappily, nibbling at a piece of lettuce. "Detective Poteet
wouldn't tell me anything when I talked with him."

Charlemagne put down his fork.

"There has been a development, Emma," he said
gravely. "This is in fact the reason I have come to New
York, why I have needed to talk with you."

"What development? Why haven't you told me?"

"I have been wanting to tell you since I sat down, only
you have not allowed me to get the word in edgewise."

"Sorry. So what is it?"

"It is difficult. I am not sure how to say this to you."

"Please, Charlemagne. Just tell me. My nerves are to-
ally shot."

"The police, they have taken you very seriously, Emma," said Charlemagne in a quiet, sober voice. "Although their experience would suggest that the deaths of Jacques and Monsieur Caraignac were random and unrelated acts of violence, Monsieur Poteet was impressed enough with your arguments to keep the cases open, to focus on the common thread."

"The dragon was the common thread. Pépé sold it, Henri-Pierre bought it."

"Yes, but you have only just now discovered this. The police, they have known nothing about the dragon whistle. They have been concentrating on finding out who might benefit from both deaths, which is why it is so awkward that Henri-Pierre Caraignac has named you his sole heir."

"What?!" exclaimed Emma.

This time heads did turn in the room, faces full of amusement, annoyance, curiosity. They turned back to their companions just as quickly.

"Just after you left for San Marcos, the American lawyers for the Caraignac family in France produced the handwritten will of Henri-Pierre Caraignac, dated the day before he died," said Charlemagne. "It names you as his beneficiary."

"But I hardly knew the man," said Emma in shock. "We were total strangers."

"Apparently you make the good impression."

Emma shot the lawyer an angry look. He grinned sheepishly.

"Sorry. I make the little joke."

"Very little," said Emma. "Why didn't Detective Poteet say anything to me about this? I thought he was my friend."

"He is not your friend, Emma," declared Charlemagne. "He is the police. Detective Poteet has been investigating. He has been trying to learn why Monsieur Caraignac would have done such a thing."

"Why did he? What did his family say?"

"Nothing, unfortunately. They are in Paris, so there is no way we can force them to cooperate. They have referred all questions to their U.S. attorneys. But now these attorneys they make the stonewall. That is what I am doing here in New York. I have been meeting personally with Doulange Henrik Swales & Carner, attempting to extract the reasonable explanation that Detective Poteet has not been able to secure. All the lawyers would say, however, was that the Caraignac family would not contest the will, although there appears to be a significant estate involved. Detective Poteet knows this, too. He is very unhappy about it."

Emma struggled to absorb this shocking development. Charlemagne appeared to be equally troubled. They sat in silence for a few moments, neither touching the lovely meal set out before them.

"You are not still mad with me, are you?" asked Charlemagne finally with a lopsized grin.

"No, I'm not mad at you."

"You have not touched your salad."

"You haven't eaten your fish."

"Neither of us is hungry, I think," sighed the lawyer. "A pity at these prices. But we must not let our reunion go entirely to waste. We should put our troubles beside us, not give in to them, yes?"

Emma didn't answer.

"I know," said Charlemagne, pulling the napkin out from around his neck and depositing it on the table. "Maybe we go for a walk. What do you say?"

"I'm sorry, Charlemagne. I don't think I'm up to it."

"Come, Emma," he implored, catching the waiter's eye and motioning for the check. "A walk will do us both good. Go get your coat and meet me in the lobby. I'll take you over to Lincoln Center, show you the sights."

Emma didn't say anything. Charlemagne reached over and raised her chin with a gentle touch.

"It will be okay," he said softly. "I promise. You do

not want to sit alone in your room and be unhappy now
It is not good. All these mysteries will resolve themselve
soon. I am sure of it. There is nothing about which to
worry. Now get your coat. Please.''

Emma nodded. Perhaps he was right. It was only seven
thirty. She could hardly go to sleep this early, and she
hadn't come to New York to watch television. Maybe a
walk would be good for her.

Emma rose and walked slowly out of the room. When
she returned to the lobby five minutes later in her coat
Charlemagne was standing by the door in his double
breasted overcoat and fedora, checking his watch. When
he looked up, he saw her and held out his arm with a smile

They walked out the Fifty-ninth Street door. Pedestrians
hustled to and fro in the brisk night air, but the crowds
were thinner. Behind a stone wall across the street the trees
in Central Park twinkled with Christmas lights.

Emma took Charlemagne's arm, as much for warmth as
for comfort. She was still severely shaken by the revelation
that Henri-Pierre had left her his estate. Each time she tried
to think of some possible explanation, the facts ran away
from her; it was like chasing clouds.

Charlemagne led the way across the street to the Central
Park side. They walked slowly toward the next avenue.
not talking, her arm in his. There weren't many people on
this side of the street. Emma and Charlemagne had the
sidewalk almost all to themselves. As they waited to cross
Seventh Avenue, Emma glanced back over her shoulder.
A tall thin man with his hands in his pockets was directly
behind them, no more than thirty feet away.

"That's him!" Emma exclaimed.

"Who?" said Charlemagne, not turning to look.

"The man I told you about who was following me before. The man with the heart-shaped scar. Quick, let's cross
to the other side of the street.''

"No, I wish to have words with this man," said Charemagne, grabbing her wrist with his small, surprisingly strong hand.

"What are you doing?" said Emma, struggling to free herself. Didn't he understand? Didn't he see the danger?

"We shall make the inquiry about why this man is bothering you," declared Charlemagne. "We shall demand to know his business. At least this is one mystery we can arrive to the bottom of."

The man with the heart-shaped scar had seen her, helpless in Charlemagne's steely grip. He started to walk faster toward them, then broke into a run.

"Are you crazy, Charlemagne?" cried Emma. "Let me go!"

"Trust me, Emma," declared Charlemagne, raising his chin aggressively. "It is always better to have things out in the open in matters like these. There is probably some innocent explanation."

Emma stared at the lawyer in horror. Suddenly she understood why he had been so nervous tonight, why he had kept looking at his watch, why he had suggested a walk. Charlemagne was somehow behind everything! He had known about the dragon from the beginning, and she had kept him posted on everything that had happened since. Now he had set her up for his scar-faced accomplice. Suddenly Emma was terrified of the little man she had known her whole life.

But why? Emma asked herself, her heart frozen. Why would Charlemagne have killed Pépé? Was it the treasure? Had the lawyer stolen the model boat and the map? Had Henri-Pierre expected Charlemagne to share the treasure with him? Was that why Charlemagne had killed him, too?

Emma realized that she would never know any of the answers. Everything was happening too fast, but at the same time seemed as though it were in slow motion. The man with the heart-shaped scar was racing toward them, whipping open his coat. Suddenly there was a hard, black object in his hand. A gun.

Emma let out a scream so loud it surprised even her. At the same time she stomped down on Charlemagne's instep as hard as she could. The little lawyer cried out in pain and he released his grip on her wrists and collapsed to the pavement. The man with the heart-shaped scar was practically on top of them. Emma spun around and, with a dancer's grace she had forgotten she possessed, executed her highest kick, catching the man with the heart-shaped scar directly in the chin.

Suddenly half a dozen other men with drawn guns and walkie-talkies were leaping out of taxicabs and from behind the stone wall of Central Park. They pounced on her dazed assailant and on Charlemagne, who was writhing on the ground in pain.

Emma turned to run, not looking where she was going, desperate to escape. She had gotten only a few steps, however, when she collided with a rock-solid figure. A rock-solid figure wearing tooled leather boots and a cowboy hat. A rock-solid figure the size of a refrigerator.

"Big Ed!" exclaimed Emma, horrified.

"That's right, little lady," replied the phony Chevy salesman with a radiant smile. "Only it's Agent Big Ed when I'm not undercover. Federal Agent Edgar M. Garalachek of the joint DEA/FBI Task Force on Narcotics Related International Currency Manipulation, at your service."

NINETEEN

"YA GOTTA UNDERSTAND, Emma honey," said Big Ed mournfully, hat in hand. "We was getting ready to pick im up as a illegal alien, maybe try for a conspiracy harge. Who knew he'd decide to go after you just when we was closing in?"

"I can't believe you, Ed," snarled Emma. "I can't believe you did this."

They were waiting in a corridor outside the emergency room of Lenox Hill Hospital, where the man with the heart-shaped scar and Charlemagne had been taken. Agent Big Ed had tried to make the little lawyer comfortable on the ambulance ride up, while Emma's assailant had sat in stony silence surrounded by federal officers, his swollen jaw beginning to turn purple where it had taken her kick.

No amount of hand-holding and happy talk was going to placate Emma, however. Now that she had learned that it was Big Ed, not Charlemagne, who was behind tonight's fiasco, she was more than hurt and confused—she was furious.

"You was never in any real danger, Emma honey," said Big Ed again. "I promise. You wouldn't have wanted us to try to take him in a crowded hotel, would you?"

"Like nobody could have been shot on the street, even accidentally?" she replied angrily. "Like Charlemagne or I couldn't have run out in front of a bus? But that's not even the point. You had no right."

"Well, there, little lady, I might beg to differ. Your federal government got all kinds of rights when it comes to pursuing international criminals and combating illegal

drug traffic. That's what your Drug Enforcement Admir
istration is all about.''

"Bernal Zuberan is not a drug trafficker.''

"Is too.''

"Is not!''

"All right,'' grumbled Ed, "maybe he ain't actually th
man going down the street selling reefers to little kiddie:
but he's the one who launders the money and keeps a
them coke barons in business.''

"I don't believe that. Bernal Zuberan is in financial ser
vices.''

"For cryin' out loud, Emma. What do you think mone
laundering is?''

Emma folded her arms in front of her and didn't answer

"What do you want?' said Big Ed. "You want to se
our files on Zuberan?''

"Yes.''

"Then you'll have to come to Washington, D of C, wit
me, now, won't you? 'Cause I got nearly twenty thousan
pages on this man. Goes back decades. Whole filing cab
inets full of stuff.''

"Has he ever been convicted of anything?''

Big Ed waited to answer until a team of frenzied emer
gency-room doctors wheeled a man full of tubes past o
a gurney.

"That's not the point,'' he said.

"I thought people were supposed to be innocent unti
proven guilty in this country,'' she hissed. "But I gues
that doesn't apply to people you don't like.''

"What do you think this is all about, Emma?'' said Ec
shaking his head in frustration. "You think Washingto
dragged me away from my job—I normally supervise thre
hundred agents and coordinate all drug enforcement in th
entire Southwest, in case you was wondering—you thin
they go to all the trouble of setting up an entire task forc
to go after some fella they got mild suspicions about? Nc
ma'am. Bernal Zuberan is one bad, bad man. He is slic

nd smart and ruthless, which is why he's gotten away
with it until now. But we are one hundred percent abso-
utely certain beyond the shadow of a doubt that Bernie
Zuberan is moving hundreds of millions of dollars of drug
noney into legitimate accounts each year, and we aim to
ail him. With your help or without it.''

"You son of a bitch," said Emma, shaking her head.
'You suckered me all the way, didn't you?''

"Now, come on, Emma. If we weren't such good
friends, I'd swear you was trying to hurt my feelings. Hell,
. thought you'd be pleased we're goin' after Zuberan.''

"Pleased? Why would I be pleased?''

"You don't get this at all, do you?''

"What's to get?''

"Don't you see that Zuberan's the one who killed your
grandpa?''

"You're crazy," sputtered Emma in disbelief and
urned to leave.

"Look, honey," said Big Ed, reaching out for her arm.
'You gotta calm down. You gotta sit down here, let me
xplain things from the beginning.''

Emma reluctantly let him guide her over to a hard
wooden bench against the wall. It wasn't until she was
eated that Emma realized how tired she was, how upset.
For the first time since the events outside of Central Park,
er hands began to shake.

"Now that's better, ain't it?'' asked Ed, smiling his big,
lopey smile. A woman went by leading a child who was
olding a bloodstained handkerchief to his nose. Two
urses passed, chatting about trading shifts. The corridor
melled of rubbing alcohol and disinfectant.

"What makes you think that Bernal Zuberan had any-
hing to do with Pépé's death?'' said Emma finally.

"Because I don't believe in coincidence, that's why.''

"Don't believe in coincidence? I thought you were the
Synchronicity King!''

"Well, I was just sayin' all that synchronicity stuff to

fool you in San Marcos so you wouldn't get suspicious
Didn't do me much good neither. If I hadn't put your name
on the custom boys' list, I would still be down there, wait
ing for you to show up for dinner tonight, wouldn't I?''

"If you know something about my grandfather's mur
der, Ed, just tell me."

"Okay, okay," said Ed. "But it's not that simple. You
gotta see this in context. You gotta get the big picture. I
all started when your grandpa's body was found, and the
San Francisco police sent the fingerprints off to the FB
for identification—standard procedure with unknown mur
der victims. What came out of the computer was more than
three decades old and didn't match the name that SFPD
had gotten off some credit-card receipt by then. The credit
card company said the dead man was Jacques Passant. The
fingerprints said he was Etienne Lalou."

He stopped and studied Emma for some reaction.

"Go on," she said, giving him none.

"Now, you gotta understand, Emma," Big Ed contin
ued, "I been looking for old Etienne Lalou from the mo
ment I took this assignment. You remember how I told
you about all them files we got in Washington on Berna
Zuberan?"

"Yes?" said Emma.

"Well, on the very first page of the very first folder i
that name. Etienne Lalou. I told you Zuberan's got no
convictions. Fact is, the only time he ever spent more than
a few hours in jail, it was for gunrunning with this Etienne
Lalou fella, a/k/a your grandpa. Case was eventually
dropped for lack of evidence. Somebody bribed it to go
away."

"That was a long time ago," said Emma defensively
"My grandfather was a decent man."

"Hell, I know that. The old San Marcos police weren'
mental giants, but even they weren't fooled by Zuberan
Even as a kid he was involved in all kinds of illegal crap
According to the police records, Etienne Lalou was totally

unaware of what Zuberan had been doing with his boat. He was an innocent dupe.''

"But Zuberan told me…"

Emma stopped and bit her lip.

"Don't worry," said Big Ed in a gentle voice. "I know you went and saw Zuberan. Hell, when you booked a ticket to San Marcos, I nearly flipped my wig. We had you under surveillance from the minute you stepped onto that island, sometimes even by satellite."

"Oh, for God's sakes."

"Now, I don't know what that old snake Zuberan told you, Emma honey, but you can be dead certain it wasn't the truth, the whole truth, and nothin' but the truth. The man's a world-class liar. Why, he's got one of the biggest banks in New York City believing that a certain company in Colombia makes forty million dollars a year cash money selling papaya juice to tourists."

"Then my grandfather didn't do anything wrong?"

"Nothing that we know about. His only mistake was trusting this kid, this Bernal Zuberan. Besides smuggling goods on your grandpa's boat without his knowledge, Zuberan was running prostitutes, extorting money, helping merchants cook their books—you name it, if it was profitable and illegal, he did it. In fact, the San Marcos cops thought Zuberan ran Etienne Lalou off the island just to get his boat. They couldn't prove anything, though. What we didn't understand was why, if Zuberan had chased Etienne Lalou away, was he so eager to find him again? Ol' Bernie's had a mess of expensive lawyers and private investigators on Lalou's trail for years, even posted a big reward for any information. Which is why I wanted to talk to Etienne Lalou myself."

"Mr. Zuberan told me that he just wanted to see my grandfather again to thank him."

"And you believed that?" Ed laughed. "Let me tell you something, Emma honey. Bernie Zuberan is one hundred and eighty-five percent business. There's not a sentimental bone in his body. If he invested his cold hard cash to find Etienne Lalou, you can bet your Aunt Edna's girdle that there was gonna be some kind of monetary return to him at the end of the trail. Something big.''

Emma started to protest again, then stopped. The map. The treasure. If Zuberan had lied to her about who had been smuggling contraband on the *Kaito Spirit* thirty years ago and why he and her grandfather had been arrested, then what else had he lied to her about?

"See?" said Big Ed triumphantly. "You're beginning to see how all this fits together, aren't you? So, anyways, when those Etienne Lalou fingerprints appeared on a dead man in San Francisco after all this time, me and my boys got real interested. We wondered if maybe Zuberan had finally found Lalou after all these years. And killed him. Why he would do that, we had no idea, of course. Until you told Detective Poteet this afternoon about that dragon thing and the treasure ship it came from. And the map in the model boat that got stolen.''

"I don't really know there was a map in the model," stammered Emma. "I was just guessing."

"Well, we think you're right. We think you've hit right on the head Zuberan's motive for killing Etienne Lalou, alias Jacques Passant.''

"Can you prove it?"

"Now you're talking," said Ed with a big smile. "That's what we're trying to do here, see? Get the evidence we need to prove our theory. We've never been able to come up with a case against Zuberan for his money-laundering shenanigans—at least nothing that any jury could understand. But murder is different. Everybody understands murder—hell, there's one every few minutes on TV. That's why I arranged to meet you in Phoenix. I needed to find out more about the victim, needed to get a feel for who this Jacques Passant fella really was, make sure he didn't go and get himself killed on his own.''

"Wait a second," said Emma. "What do you mean, you

arranged to meet me in Phoenix? I thought you just happened to be there with Lionel when the dog I had booked for my act got sick.''

"Well, not exactly,'' said Ed with a sheepish smile. "Actually I was outside your rehearsal room, waiting for you to use the phone, like I knew you would have to, sooner or later. Do you know that that unpatriotic Mrs. Schneiderman wouldn't agree to let her stupid Saint Bernard take a dive until my boys paid her triple what you were gonna give her?''

"I suppose Lionel isn't even your real dog,'' Emma muttered, dismayed at how easily she had been tricked.

"Oh, he's mine all right. He likes to go undercover with me on assignments where there's no danger of anybody getting shot.''

"Where is he tonight?''

Ed flashed a stupid grin, but didn't say anything.

"If you wanted information about my grandfather, Ed, why couldn't you have just come to me honestly and asked?''

"Involving a citizen in a complex federal investigation is not something we do at the drop of a hat, Emma,'' said the big agent. "That's the easiest way to get your career nailed upon the front page of the *Washington Post*. Besides, why spook you if it turned out there was nothing to any of this? You had enough troubles. Hell, after we talked in Phoenix, I saw my dreams of a case against Zuberan melting away. It looked like the Frisco cops were right, that it was just a robbery. That's what they been telling us all along. Then this Henry-Pierre Caraignac fellow got himself killed and all the pieces began to come together. The way we figure it, Caraignac was Zuberan's hit man.''

"That's ridiculous,'' said Emma, laughing reflexively. "Mr. Zuberan never even heard of Henri-Pierre Caraignac.''

"Oh yeah? Sez who?''

"Says Mr. Zuberan. I mentioned Henri-Pierre when I was in San Marcos, and he didn't recognize the name."

"I know you think this man is your friend, Emma," said Big Ed, shaking his head. "I'm sorry to disappoint you, but it just proves what I was saying to you before, that Bernie Zuberan is a world-class liar. Fact is, he did, too, know Caraignac. After Caraignac's death we got a court order and went through the records of his antique store. Fact is, Caraignac had made three separate sales to Zuberan over the past two years, according to invoices we found. We're talking nearly a hundred thousand dollars' worth of merchandise here."

"That doesn't prove Mr. Zuberan knew Henri-Pierre," said Emma, trying to hide her surprise. "Mr. Zuberan collects antiques. His house is packed with them. He's probably bought things from half the dealers on the planet."

"I told you I don't believe in coincidence, Emma. Zuberan moves millions of dollars each month and uses all kinds of fronts to do it, some of them mighty creative. You think a little bit about the antiques business, you realize it's a money launderer's dream. You take your cash money from your illegal enterprises and you go and buy antiques and fancy furniture with it. Then you sell the stuff for big legitimate bucks on Madison Avenue. We figure that's the way it started between these two, changing cash money into antiques and back again. Then somebody realized what a perfect hit man Caraignac would make. He traveled a lot. He was licensed to carry a gun. And it turns out the man was already a trained killer."

"What do you mean?"

"According to the French military, Henri-Pierre Caraignac served in an elite commando unit from the time he was eighteen until he was twenty-five," said Big Ed soberly. "He personally killed two terrorists in separate hijacking incidents, and who knows how many others in operations that weren't made public? The way I figure, Zuberan sent Caraignac to get that treasure map. Remember, Caraignac was in San Francisco the night your grandpa was shot, and he must have taken his gun with him in his luggage because it wasn't found in his effects in New York.''

"If Henri-Pierre killed my grandfather," said Emma, "then why did he make me his beneficiary? You must know about that—you seem to know everything else.''

"Yeah, that's confusing.'' Ed nodded. "I thought poor Mr. Poteet was gonna have a stroke when we heard about the Frenchman's will. But we'll put it all together, sooner or later. My working theory is that Caraignac wasn't really a professional killer, just a guy who fell in with the wrong people, and that his conscience started bothering him about what he'd done.''

"Then why would he have done it in the first place?''

The big federal agent shrugged his gigantic shoulders.

"Maybe Zuberan threatened to expose him for money laundering if he didn't make the hit,'' he said. "Or maybe Caraignac hoped to find the map and keep it for himself. It doesn't really matter. Conscience is an unpredictable thing, and a man like Zuberan can't afford to have people with consciences running around who can tie him to a killing. Probably Zuberan's men surprised Caraignac in his hotel room, took away the gun he had used on your grandfather, and shot him with it. That would explain why the bullets that killed both men matched.''

Emma started to speak, then stopped.

She had been fighting the conclusion that Henri-Pierre had had something to do with Pépé's death for so long, she had almost forgotten why. Henri-Pierre's perfect face suddenly sprang into her mind's eye.

Once again Emma looked into his cool blue eyes and amused smile. This time, however, she looked behind the surface beauty and saw for the first time what had previously only registered in her unconscious, what the cocktail waitress at the Alhambra had talked about: the sadness, the infinite regret, the despair. It was the face of a man who had done something terribly wrong and suffered tremendously because of it.

"Which brings us to the fella who was following you," continued the big federal agent, rubbing his huge hands together with evident glee. "Our boy's name is Paco Quintana, and we've been watching him ever since he followed you onto that airplane in San Marcos."

"He was on the same plane with me?"

"In first class," said Big Ed. "These drug guys really know how to live, let me tell you, and Paco is Zuberan's top lieutenant, has worked for him since he was a kid. Up to now Zuberan's been too smart to give us the opportunity to nab any of his soldiers on U.S. soil. This time, though, we got Paco, and through him we're going to get Bernie Zuberan. Assault with a deadly weapon, attempted murder, resisting arrest...yes, sir, we gonna crack that boy open like a lobster."

"Why would Mr. Zuberan send this man after me?" said Emma, struggling to find some flaw. "If he had wanted to harm me he had plenty of opportunity on San Marcos. I was right there with him on his estate."

"Isn't it obvious? Zuberan still wants the treasure, see? Caraignac must not have found the treasure map when he killed your grandpa. Zuberan realized you didn't have it yet either, but figured that if he put some bee in your bonnet when you were down there and then had you followed, you would eventually lead him to it."

Emma took a deep breath. It all made a horrible kind of sense. Was the kindly man who had served her coffee and spoken so wistfully of his old friend really such a monster? A horrifying image of Zuberan patting Timoteo on the head, then handing him a syringe and a revolver, sprang into her imagination.

"Now you see why we been so concerned about your safety?" said Big Ed happily.

Before Emma could answer, Charlemagne Moussy emerged from one of the treatment rooms on crutches. His right foot was in a white cast that reached halfway to his knee. He brushed away help from the nurse beside him and hobbled directly to Emma.

"My foot, she is broken in three places," pronounced Charlemagne with great dignity.

"I am so sorry, Charlemagne," said Emma.

"No." The little lawyer sighed. "It is I who am the sorry one. I should know better at my age than to be the hero. I must have had a rock in my head."

"I'm the one with a rock in my head," said Emma. "I actually thought you had something to do with all of this. I feel terrible."

"Not as bad as me, I assure you."

"Can you ever forgive me?"

"Of course, *ma chérie*," said Charlemagne, bowing at the waist, wincing only slightly as he did so. Then he turned to Big Ed. "But you, *monsieur,* are another matter. You are a dangerous lunatic. What possible explanation can there be for such reckless behavior on the part of a government agency, leaping out with the drawn guns at innocent people? Are these our tax dollars at work?"

"Come on, Moussy," said Ed defensively. "Gimme a break. This was a legitimate and highly successful operation. We were just doing our job here, just protecting this girl."

"Protecting her!"

"That's right. Just trying to make sure she doesn't have to live her whole life in fear."

"It's a wonderment you did not shoot her in order to make her really safe," said Charlemagne, limping over to the bench. "I have to sit down. So much idiocy has made me tired. What time is it? I have forgotten to take my pill."

As the little lawyer eased himself down and examined his watch, the door to the next treatment room down suddenly opened. Emma, Charlemagne, and Big Ed all turned at the same time and watched the man with the heart-shaped scar being led out by four men who looked like

IBM salesmen, except for the badges suspended from their suit-coat pockets and the radio receivers embedded in their ears. In addition to a pair of handcuffs, Paco Quintana now wore a large white brace around his neck that held his jaw rigid with steel pins and made him look like something that Dr. Frankenstein had just assembled from parts.

"We got you this time, Paco boy," said Ed with satisfaction, walking over and staring the prisoner directly in the eye. "I know they Mirandized you and you ain't gonna say nothing until you get your expensive lawyer, but Bernie Zuberan ain't gonna be able to help you this time. You remember what I'm telling you, my friend. You gonna go away for a long time unless you cooperate."

The man known as Paco Quintana regarded Big Ed with apparent uninterest. From what she had seen of Zuberan's men on San Marcos, Emma was certain he would never tell Big Ed a thing. She was therefore surprised when he began to speak. His voice was soft, and faintly accented. He spoke directly to her.

"Greetings, Señorita Passant. I am sorry for any inconvenience and distress you have endured tonight. My attorney will not mind, I hope, that I will convey to you Señor Zuberan's regards. I feel Señor Zuberan would wish me to explain what happened."

"Don't you get cute with me, Paco," said Big Ed angrily. "Save any explaining till we get a stenographer here. We got you dead to rights, and you're not gonna start playing no inadmissible confession games with us now."

"Stop harassing this poor man," declared Charlemagne indignantly.

"What's it to you, Moussy?"

"I do not approve of the police brutality. At this very moment I would be offering this poor man my own legal services *pro bono* were it not for the fact that he has just tried to kill me."

"Señor Zuberan was only concerned for your safety, señorita," said Paco Quintana.

"I told you to shut up, Paco," said Ed.

"Let him finish or I'll break *your* foot, Ed," said Emma. The man with the heart-shaped scar smiled and bowed his head slightly. Slightly was apparently as far as it would go. His eyes filled with pain.

"Knowing that two men had been killed and that you were on the trail of their murderer," he said, "Señor Zuberan instructed me to follow you to New York. He wished me to keep an eye out for your safety. He told me that your grandfather and he were very close."

"More bullshit from the bullshitter," sneered Ed.

"Señor Zuberan told me to do whatever was necessary to protect you," continued Paco, ignoring the interruption. When this man seized you tonight by the park, I ran to your defense. Mr. Zuberan will be gratified to learn that you are able to defend yourself, señorita. You have broken my jaw."

"You expect us to believe that cockamamie story, Paco?" exclaimed Big Ed. "You was just here trying to protect her? What kind of morons do you think we are?"

"I refuse to answer on the grounds that it might tend to criminate me."

"That makes all three of us who were trying to protect her," muttered Charlemagne. "She's lucky she's still breathing."

"I don't think she's got much to be worried about," said Ed. "In the space of two seconds she breaks one man's foot and another man's jaw. You know, you're a pretty dangerous character, Emma honey. You ever think about a career in law enforcement?"

"No."

"Well, if you change your mind, just remember you got a friend with connections."

Emma walked over to the handcuffed man and looked directly into his large brown eyes. "Will you tell me something honestly, señor?"

"If I can."

"Was Henri-Pierre Caraignac working for Mr. Z
beran?"

"You expect him to tell you the truth?" Big I
laughed. "You really expect that?"

"Yes, I do," said Emma.

"I do not know this man you ask about, this Carai
nac," said the man with the heart-shaped scar. "Who
he?"

"The antiques dealer who was killed," said Emm
"Agent Garalachek here says that Bernal Zuberan boug
things from Mr. Caraignac in order to launder money a
then hired him as a hit man to kill my grandfather."

"It is true that Señor Zuberan buys antiques from ma
legitimate sources to furnish his home and for shrewd r
sale, but he does not hire killers."

"Why not?" barked Big Ed. "'Cause he's got you?'

"Because he succeeds by using his brain, not by r
sorting to violence."

"Oh, really. Then why were you carrying a gun tonig
and following this young lady?"

"You have asked me a question, señorita, and on r
honor I have told you the truth. I will say no more unti
speak with my attorney."

The man with the heart-shaped scar turned up his brok
chin with a defiant look. Big Ed motioned in disgust
the four agents standing guard, who led the prisoner awa

"Alors," said Charlemagne when they were gor
"That was very illuminating, Agent Garalachek. You w
perhaps for an encore describe for us exactly which pa
Mr. Zuberan played in the disappearance of Jimmy Hof
and the assassination of President Kennedy?"

"You think this is some kind of joke, Moussy?"

"That is exactly what it is!" exclaimed Charlemag
"Do not you see how obviously we all of us have be
chasing the wild gooses? You, Emma, with your trip
San Marcos. Agent Garalachek with his insane conspira
theories. Even Monsieur Zuberan and his paranoid co

n. All of this speculation about what is at the bottom
everything else has all been just foolishness.''

''Oh yeah?'' said Big Ed. ''Then what's been going on
re, according to you?''

''Our friend Jacques has been killed in an irrational
inner. We long for to find some explanation that will
ike the sense of everything, so his death is not mean-
gless. But, alas, it was meaningless. There is no map to
unken treasure, no great conspiracy, no unifying theory
everything. I am afraid the police have been right all
•ng in this, Emma. Jacques was the victim of a random
ling. No more. Monsieur Caraignac, too.''

''That's right, Moussy, go ahead,'' barked Big Ed.
Hide your head in the sandbox like a ostrich. You can
:tend all you want that this is all just accidents and co-
:idences, but that ain't going to make the truth out of it.
:t is, there's just one single solitary explanation for the
irders of Jacques Passant and Henri-Pierre Caraignac,
d his name is Bernie Zuberan. You know I'm right,
n't you, Emma honey? Tell him that all this didn't hap-
n for no reason at all.''

Emma gazed at the white hospital wall and didn't an-
er. Wherever the truth lay, she knew now that her grand-
her had not been a smuggler and that Henri-Pierre
sn't a hit man. She was equally certain, however, that
ther man had died a random, senseless death. There was
eason behind everything that had happened and Emma
ll had to find it. Clearly neither Ed Garalachek nor Char-
nagne Moussy nor Bernal Zuberan knew what it was.
at left only one place to look.

Emma stared at the stark white wall in front of her until
nd the hospital and all the people around her vanished
o a vast snowy landscape, the snow that her grandfather
d told her she must have imagined or seen in a movie
dreamed. Great stone houses soared out of the whiteness

to the sky on either side of her, and Emma could on
again feel the loving hand that held her tightly and ke
her safe.

TWENTY

WAS SNOWING real snow in Paris on the day before
ristmas.

It had snowed yesterday and the day before that. To-
y's snow was a thick, wet bombardment that swirled
zily with each gust of wind and covered everything it
ched. The wide, tree-lined boulevards and ancient roof-
s of Paris seemed to be nestled under a great white
nket, but the wintery scene gave Emma no comfort.

She was standing, shivering, in the snow outside the
at bronze door of Caraignac et Cie when the reception-
arrived. The Caraignac companies were involved in ev-
thing from precision valves and eyeglass frames to Ca-
ian woolen mills and Swiss chocolates. Its headquarters
re located on the Avenue de la Bourdonnais, a Parisian
et of meticulous beaux arts buildings so exclusive and
nd that they bore only address numbers, not signs iden-
ing the prestigious occupants.

t was a little before eight-thirty, even earlier than Emma
arrived the previous two mornings. This time Made-
iselle Filante, the receptionist, did not offer a sunny
on jour'' and invite Emma to come in and make herself
nfortable, as she had the first day. She would have
sed the door in Emma's face if Emma had let her.

'I have said to you before, mademoiselle,'' Mademoi-
le Filante declared as Emma followed her into the ele-
tly appointed reception room, all green marble and pol-
ed walnut. ''Monsieur Caraignac is a very busy man.''

'Did you tell him what I told you? Did you tell him
o I was?''

'I told him. He said he did not wish to see you.''

"Then I'll wait until he changes his mind," said Emm

"Monsieur Caraignac is not even in the country, a
matter of fact," said Mademoiselle Filante, taking off
coat and beret and running a perfectly manicured ha
through her short hair. "So it will make no sense for y
to wait."

"I'll wait anyway, thank you," Emma replied, rem
ing her own coat and taking her place on the canary-yell
sofa, as she had on the past two days.

It had taken Charlemagne a few days to find out tha
was Armand Caraignac, Henri-Pierre's father and a w
known French industrialist, who had forbidden anyone
the Caraignac family from discussing why his son h
made Emma his beneficiary. It had taken Charlemagne
other few days to persuade the Drug Enforcement Adm
istration and the San Francisco Police Department into
ting her leave the country. Now that she was at last
France, Emma was going to stay until she had spoken w
Armand Caraignac. Whether he wanted to or not.

For the next forty minutes Emma sat quietly as empl
ees of Caraignac et Cie arrived. Most were middle-a
men with well-tailored suits and the blank expressions
people who had worked too long for someone else. 7
few women employees all appeared to be secretarie
young and pretty and dressed as chicly as low budg
would permit, though all had the same subservient look
their eyes.

At nine o'clock exactly the door was opened by a m
whose face was different from all the other faces. He
small and elderly and wore a quiet gray overcoat and a
hat.

Emma had noticed the old man yesterday as he
leaving and only realized who he must be after it was
late. If she had needed any confirmation of the man's id
tity, Mademoiselle Filante provided it. The receptio
nodded and tilted her head almost imperceptibly tow

nma, then cast her eyes to the ground as the old man
alked past.

Emma was on her feet before he had gotten halfway to
e unmarked door behind the reception desk.

"I'm Emma Passant, Monsieur Caraignac," she said in
oud, firm voice. "You'll have to see me sooner or later.
I never go away. You'll never be rid of me."

The old man stopped and turned, making eye contact
th Emma for the first time. His face was long, deeply
ed, hard—the fact of a man who was used to being
eyed. His eyes were the same blue as Henri-Pierre's had
en. His nose was surprisingly long and thin, almost as
ag and thin as Emma's own.

The man stared at her with a shocked expression, then
oked away after only an instant and rushed through the
or. Emma took a step to follow, but the receptionist
ood and barred her way.

"You are not welcome here, mademoiselle. You must
ave immediately or I shall call the police."

"Go ahead and call them. Do the police arrest everyone
om Monsieur Caraignac refuses to see? Are they so
edient?"

"Please, mademoiselle. Monsieur is not a well man.
nnot you understand? Will you not respect his wishes?"

"No," said Emma. They glared at one another for sev-
l seconds. Then Emma sat down.

Mademoiselle Filante, obviously angry, returned to her
ies, casting a chilly glance at Emma from time to time,
t making no move to call the gendarmes. After half an
ar, as Emma was beginning to lose hope, the telephone
the receptionist's desk rang. The young woman picked
the receiver and listened, frowning. Then she placed
phone in its cradle and stood up at her desk.

"Monsieur Caraignac has agreed to see you, after all,
demoiselle Passant," she said in a stiff, formal voice.
lease come with me."

Stunned, wondering what had changed his mind, Emma

followed the receptionist through the door behind the de
down a short, plushly carpeted corridor. At the end of t
corridor was a short flight of stairs. At the top of this w
an ornate mahogany door. Mademoiselle Filante knock
once, then turned the bronze knob.

Inside was a large, elegantly appointed room with a hi,
ceiling. The furniture was much like what Emma had se
in Henri-Pierre's Madison Avenue shop—fancy Fren
shapes and elegant fabrics. The old man who Emma kn
was Armand Caraignac was sitting in a large armchair
a blazing fireplace. The expression on his face was that
a man who had just seen his own death. His eyes we
red, his face ashen.

"*Merci,* Annette," he said in a high, cracking voi
rising laboriously to his feet. "*C'est tout.*"

The receptionist nodded and left, closing the door h
hind her.

"I am Armand Caraignac, Miss Passant. Won't you
down?"

The old man's English was perfect, barely accent
much like Henri-Pierre's had been. He gestured to a lar;
comfortable-looking armchair opposite his by the firepla

Emma walked over to the chair and sat.

"Will you have a coffee with me?"

"No, thank you."

"I know I must cut down, but it is very good cof
and I am addicted. I can ring for tea if you would pre
that."

"No. All right. I'll have coffee. I'm addicted, too. I ta
it black, no sugar."

Armand Caraignac nodded. He picked up a hand-pain
porcelain cup and saucer from the little table next to h
and poured coffee from a matching coffeepot. When
had finished, he brought it over and placed it on the ti
fruitwood table next to Emma's chair. He poured a cup
himself, sat down and took a sip, stealing a glance at h
as he did so, then looking away.

Emma picked up her cup. It was so thin that she could see through the porcelain to the level of the coffee inside by the light of the blazing fire.

"I have a million questions, Mr. Caraignac," Emma said after a moment. "I don't know where to start. Surely you must have questions too. Like why your son made me his beneficiary. Why wouldn't you see me?"

"I will answer all of your questions, mademoiselle," the old man said with a sigh. "It was wrong for me not to see you. I have been afraid, *n'est-ce pas?* And now there is so little time to make things right. I am like the old cheese which is getting moldy. They must cut off the bad pieces—a skin lesion here, a gall bladder there. Soon there will be nothing left."

The old man stopped and rubbed his eyes. Emma said nothing. After a moment he continued.

"All my life I have thought of myself as a brave man, but with you I have been the vilest coward. I have turned my back to you, closed my eyes as if I could make you go away by sheer desire, selfishness, force of will. For this, for everything, I am more sorry than I can possibly say. You are the innocent victim in this whole terrible affair, the happy life you should have had destroyed by your own grandfather."

"My grandfather never did anything to harm me," exclaimed Emma angrily. "He was kind and good and never hurt anybody in his life."

"I was speaking of your other grandfather," said Armand Caraignac.

"What other grandfather?"

"*Moi.* Me. I am the villain. All the terrible things that have happened, they have all been my fault."

"But how can you be my grandfather? Unless..."

"That is correct, mademoiselle. My son, Henri-Pierre, was your father."

"What are you saying?," whispered Emma, as the whole world shifted. "I don't understand."

"I must tell you everything," said Armand Caraignac, his voice filled with infinite sadness. "It all started more than thirty years ago. When Henri-Pierre was a boy. I used to take him on vacations each year with me. We went all over the world and were very happy, father and son. And then I took him to an island in the Caribbean. An island called San Marcos."

"My God," whispered Emma as the final pieces of the puzzle began clicking into place. "You were the tourists."

"Yes, we were tourists." Caraignac nodded in agreement. "We chartered a boat for a few weeks to do some skin diving, a boat owned by a man named Etienne Lalou. Over the course of those two weeks, Henri-Pierre became very friendly with Lalou's young daughter, Marie. I had no idea of how friendly until six months later, when Henri-Pierre came to me in a terrible state. It seems that Marie had written to him that she was pregnant. Henri-Pierre felt it was his duty to go to San Marcos and marry her."

"But she was too young," said Emma, remembering Zuberan's description of Marie. "She must have been only fourteen or fifteen."

"Henri-Pierre himself was barely sixteen," said Caraignac. "It is like the children today. The babies having babies. It seems impossible, but of course it is not. It is merely nature. Henri-Pierre was a responsible boy and he had real feelings for Marie Lalou. He wanted to do the right thing. I, however, was wise to the ways of the world. I convinced my son that this girl was merely after our money, that there was no way to know that he was really the father, that marriage to her would ruin his life. Henri-Pierre finally listened to me, God help him. Not that he had much choice. I am a strong-willed person, Mademoiselle Passant, used to getting my way.

"I even intercepted Marie's subsequent letters to Henri-Pierre and returned them unopened to make it easier for him, to keep him isolated from his feelings, from hers. All was well for a while. The letters stopped. The girl seemed to have gone away. Then a letter came addressed to me, a letter from her father, Etienne Lalou. He told me that his daughter had died giving birth to Henri-Pierre's child. Lalou had named her Emma, after his mother. He wanted us to know."

"I had no idea," whispered Emma.

"I would have kept this news from my son as well," said Armand Caraignac. "But my then-wife, his mother, told him, even though I had forbidden her to interfere. Henri-Pierre was devastated. Whatever guilt he had felt before was magnified now, tenfold, but still I would not leave the situation alone. Now that there was no question of marriage, I realized that the child was my blood. I am a greedy man, and I was greedy to increase the Caraignac line. I decided that it would be best for us to have custody of the child."

"You mean me. I was the child."

Armand Caraignac rubbed his eyes again and nodded.

"We invited Lalou to come here to Paris with the baby. The poor man did not have to contact us and tell us of the birth. He was merely being decent, but when he arrived here he was rewarded not with the Caraignac gratitude and sympathy, but by a legal assault such as only one like myself could muster. Using the best lawyers money could buy, I seized the child and petitioned the French court that Etienne Lalou was unfit to raise her alone, as he had sought to do. I won, of course. I always win. The Caraignacs took custody of the child. Of you, Emma."

"How could you do it?" said Emma. "My grandfather had just lost his daughter. And then to lose me? He must have been heartbroken."

"Yes, he wrote me letters, pleading for your return, but I ignored him. You were a Caraignac, I told myself. You belonged with us. Though he was just a boy, Henri-Pierre was distraught by my actions, taking you away from your grandfather, but he loved you dearly, as I knew he would. He was overjoyed just to see you each day when he returned from school. I told people that you were my own daughter out of wedlock. The French are more sanguine about such things than Americans, and besides, I did not care what people thought. I did not want Henri-Pierre's youth to be cut short. We had the best of servants to take care of you and protect you, lest Etienne Lalou try to take you back. You lighted our lives with your laughter.''

"How long did this go on?" asked Emma, realizing why Zuberan's investigators weren't able to find the trail of Etienne Lalou in New York. He was in France.

"We had you for about two years. Then we went on a vacation in Switzerland, the four of us: I, Henri-Pierre, his mother (whom I divorced shortly thereafter), and you in the custody of a nanny, a woman who had not been with us very long and was not too bright. Somehow, when the rest of us were away from the hotel, a man came to this nanny and persuaded her to give you to him. He said that her grandfather had sent him to fetch her. This man was Etienne Lalou himself, of course. He then changed his name and with the child he disappeared off the face of the earth.''

"But I don't understand," said Emma. "I thought my grandfather had changed his name and run away because he had stolen a treasure.''

"He ran away because he had stolen you," said Armand Caraignac.

"But he told me…''

"What did he say?''

"He said, 'I have stolen the most precious treasure of the sea.'''

"Were those his words?''

"No," said Emma. "He was upset and spoke in French. He always spoke in French when he was upset. He said, *'J'ai pris le plus grand trésor de la mer'*—I have taken the most precious treasure of the sea.''

"Perhaps it was not *'J'ai pris le plus grand trésor de la mer'* that he said," said Armand Caraignac after a moment of thought. "Perhaps what he said was *'J'ai pris le plus grand trésor de ta mère'*—I have taken the most precious treasure *of your mother.*"

Emma fell into a stunned silence. It was exactly the kind of obscure, convoluted phrase Jacques Passant would have used. The most precious treasure of your mother. The treasure was she.

"I hired detectives," Caraignac went on. "But of course Lalou had left France and would not return to San Marcos. I did everything I could to get you back, but no trace of Etienne Lalou or his little girl was ever found. Until three weeks ago."

"What happened then?" said Emma, desperate to know everything.

"Back when we had gone diving on San Marcos, Marie Lalou had found a funny gold whistle and chain in the sand one day. Three weeks ago it came up for auction in New York City. More than thirty years had passed since he had last seen this artifact, but Henri-Pierre recognized it immediately. He bought it and through it he somehow managed to track down Etienne Lalou—who had changed his name to Jacques Passant. I know this because Henri-Pierre told me. He made me fly to San Francisco from Paris to meet him in his hotel room on the last day of his life."

"You were in San Francisco? You saw Henri-Pierre before he was killed?"

Caraignac nodded.

"It was a brutal journey for an old man. Even in first class, thirteen hours in the air is very difficult. But when Henri-Pierre told me that he had found Etienne Lalou, and that something terrible had happened, I knew I must come at once.

"You must understand, Emma. Henri-Pierre was a handsome, confident man on the outside, and because we live in a world of appearances, people assumed certain things about him. But he was not what he seemed. He had mourned the loss of Marie Lalou and their child his entire life. He suffered from grave personal problems and depression stemming from guilt. His whole life had been dominated by his having allowed me to make these decisions for him when he was so young, before his character had had a chance properly to form. Henri-Pierre had had terrible arguments with me, first for forcing him to abandon Marie, and then for going to court and wresting Emma away from her grandfather, who clearly loved her. But he was just a boy then, and my will prevailed.

"After Etienne Lalou came to Switzerland and stole you away, however, Henri-Pierre found the courage to break away from me. He went off and enlisted in the army. Unable to forgive himself for what had happened, he did his best to get himself killed, I believe, but instead was just decorated over and over again for bravery."

"What happened when you got to San Francisco?"

"I met Henri-Pierre in his hotel room. He told me how he had tracked down and met with Lalou—Jacques Passant."

"Henri-Pierre met with Pépé?" said Emma.

"This was his second chance, you see. His opportunity to put things right. Henri-Pierre called your grandfather and told him who he was and insisted that they meet. They did so in San Francisco's great park. There, Henri-Pierre begged to see you, pleaded that a place be made in your life for him again. Henri-Pierre said that he could now be the father you had never had. He could give you money and opportunities. He could love you.

"Your grandfather refused, however. His granddaughter knew nothing of anything that had happened, he said; she believed that her father had died in an automobile accident. It was better to leave things that way, he said. Henri-Pierre argued. He pleaded. He desperately wanted a proper reconciliation, and for this he needed your grandfather's cooperation. But Jacques Passant was adamant in his refusal.

"They had wandered deep into the park, where no one

was around to see them. Henri-Pierre took out the gun he
was licensed to carry. The horrible gun he took everywhere
with him, because he often carried large sums of money
and valuable art objects, and because my son never felt
safe, pursued as he was by his personal demons. He was
not in his right mind, he told me, and foolishly began to
threaten Jacques Passant. He felt that this was his last
chance to correct the terrible wrong that had happened so
many years before. As near as he could remember, he just
wanted to show Jacques Passant how serious he was, he
told me, but Lalou reached for the gun. They struggled.
The gun went off accidentally. Jacques Passant was dead.''

"Oh, dear God," said Emma. "Do you mean that my
grandfather was killed by my own father?"

"Instead of rectifying the old wrong that had dominated
his entire life, Henri-Pierre had perpetrated a worse one,"
said Armand Caraignac, his voice cracking. "In a daze,
his military training took over. He made it look like a
robbery and walked away. He was paralyzed, in shock. He
did not know what to do. He sat in his hotel room for
days, agonizing. He could not go back to New York and
resume his life as if nothing had happened. He would have
liked to turn himself in to the police, but this was impossible, too, for then you would discover who he was and
what he had done. He was consumed with guilt, yet he
longed to see you, the daughter whom he had loved. And
lost."

"So Henri-Pierre *was* following me when we met on
the Sausalito ferry."

"Yes." Armand Caraignac nodded. "A week had
passed since his crime, and his passion had given way to
an icy calmness. Henri-Pierre went to your house in a
rented car, hoping just to catch a glimpse of you. You
came out and he found himself following you down to the
ferry. He couldn't resist boarding the boat with you for a
closer look. When he had an opportunity to meet you, to
talk with you, he told me he jumped at the chance."

"I can't take this," whispered Emma, but was unable to stop Caraignac from continuing.

"Knowing that you would be out of town, he later retrieved his rented car and drove to your house. He let himself in somehow; he was very clever with locks. My son told me that he just wanted to see where you had lived, Emma, to touch the things that you had touched. In a bedroom he found a model of the *Kaito Spirit*. He could not think clearly. Fearing it could somehow be connected with him, frantic that you must never be allowed to find out what had happened, what he had done, he took it."

"Then there was no treasure concealed in it?"

"Unfortunately, there was."

Armand Caraignac rose and walked to an ornate ormolu-mounted Louis XV desk, opened a drawer and took out a white box about six inches square and a stack of letters. He walked slowly back and handed the letters to Emma.

"These are your mother's letters to my son," he said, sinking into his chair. "The ones I had marked 'Delivery Refused' and sent back so many years ago. Henri-Pierre discovered how to open the secret compartment in the model boat when he returned to his hotel. Inside he found these letters and read them for the first time. Letters to his sixteen-year-old self from the only woman he had ever loved, would ever love."

So *that* was the legacy Jacques Passant had talked about in his will—not any monetary treasure, but the letters from her mother to her father!

"As I told you," Armand Caraignac continued, "my son suffered gravely all his life. Now he suffered worse. He had heard how much you had loved your grandfather—heard it from your own lips. He had stolen you from him once, and now he had stolen your grandfather from you. When Henri-Pierre read in the letters of Marie Lalou's deep love for him, and her despair that he could ignore her in her hour of need, it was too much. The enormity of

is crime, the hopelessness of his position crashed down
n him.''

The old man fell silent for a moment. Emma wanted to
ell him to stop—she didn't want to hear anymore—but
ound she couldn't speak.

"How could my son live with such guilt?'' said Armand
Caraignac. "And who better to share it with than me—the
wretch who had counseled him so poorly when he needed
father's wisdom the most. Henri-Pierre called me in Paris
nd demanded that I drop what I was doing and fly to San
rancisco right away. I met him in his hotel room and he
old me the story I have just told you. Then, before my
ery eyes and before I could stop him, Henri-Pierre took
ut his pistol, put it to his head, and pulled the trigger.''

Emma let out an involuntary gasp.

"The walls were thick, the shot was not heard,'' Ar-
and Caraignac went on, his voice barely audible. "You
ee, Emma, there is justice in this world. I had been re-
ponsible for what had happened thirty years ago and now
 had come back to me, been laid at my doorstep. Now
e guilt was mine alone. I took my son's money and the
odel boat to make it look like a simpler crime—and the
un, of course. How can suicide be suspected if there is
o gun? I stole away back to France, hoping that you
ould never learn what had happened. But now you have
ound me. Have found everything. This, too, I took from
enri-Pierre's room. It belongs to you now.''

The old man opened the white box and took out a thick
olden chain at the end of which was a strange, yet fa-
iliar, creature. The dragon.

Emma turned away. She had been looking for the
ragon all this time, but now she didn't want it. She never
anted to see it again.

"I know you must hate me very much,'' said Armand
araignac sadly, "but it doesn't matter. I am a broken
an. My life is over.''

"How could he do it?" said Emma. "How could Henr
Pierre kill Pépé?"

"I wish I could make sense of this for you, but I hav
made nothing but trouble and misery. I, your other granc
father, am not entitled even to console you. I shall live m
remaining days with this terrible thing on my conscienc
The deaths of my son, your mother, your Pépé. All I ca
tell you is that Henri-Pierre loved you very much."

"He didn't love me," said Emma, feeling the hot tea
running down her cheeks, not remembering when they ha
started. "He was selfish and cowardly and cruel, and I ha
him."

"He did love you, Emma," said Armand Caraigna
with tears in his own eyes. "He did."

"No," said Emma. "I'll never believe it. There's noth
ing you can say that could ever convince me."

"If only you could have seen," said the old man, shak
ing his head, wiping his eyes, "the way he used to loo
at you, Emma, when you were a baby. You would know
You would understand."

"I don't want to know," said Emma, rising and pickin
up her coat. "He killed my grandfather."

"I will never forget," said Armand Caraignac as sh
walked to the door, almost to himself, "how he was wit
you that last day in Switzerland, the last time we woul
see you again until now. We had gone there to ski, but h
had walked you through the village first, showing you you
first snow."

"Snow?"

"Yes, a big storm had just come through and a recor
snow had fallen. It covered everything like a benevole
white blanket. That is how I shall always remember hin
walking you through the great mountains of snow."

Emma had stopped at the door. As Armand Caraignac
tired voice trailed off, the image that had haunted Emm
her entire life sprang once again into her mind. The thic
flurries, punctuated by tall black skeletons of trees. Th

reat stone houses all around her. The hand in hers, the
·ving hand.

Only this time, for the first time, Emma could see to
hom the hand had belonged. She could see the person's
·ce. It was a young and handsome face with blue eyes
·d soft brown hair. It was the face of Henri-Pierre Car-
gnac. It was the face of her father.

"Maybe I'll take that, after all," said Emma after a long
·oment, pointing to the dragon whistle which the old man
as still holding in his limp hand.

Armand Caraignac handed it to Emma.

"It is over now, *ma petite*," he whispered, struggling
his feet. "The darkness that has hung over all these lives
ended now. Please, listen to an old man who knows too
·ell that justice has been served. I beg you, do not let the
·d tragedies consume you. There was no evil here, only
·ople who made mistakes."

Emma nodded and walked to the mahogany door.

"If there is ever anything I can do for you…"

"I'll let you know," she said and let herself out without
·oking back.

Emma walked back down the long hall of Caraignac et
·e the way she had come, ignoring the curious stares and
·eathless whispers. She breezed past Mademoiselle Fi-
·nte at the reception desk and walked out into the street.

Soft snow was still falling over Paris. The scene all
·ound was pure whiteness, but now for the first time in
·r life, the snow didn't make Emma feel frightened and
·one. It was as if a missing piece had at last been snapped
·ck into place and she was whole again.

Emma wiped the remaining tears from her eyes. Armand
·araignac was right, she knew. There had been no evil
·re. Everything that had happened, however misguided,
·d happened because of love. It was time to look to the
·ture, not the past. It was time to be reborn.

Emma opened her tightly clutched hand. The ferocious
·lden dragon seemed to be smiling at her. She opened its

golden jaws, brought it to her lips and blew with all h
might. The resultant whistle was clean and loud and brok
the pure white air like the song of a lark.